summer
on the island

Also by Brenda Novak

KEEP ME WARM AT CHRISTMAS
WHEN I FOUND YOU
THE BOOKSTORE ON THE BEACH
A CALIFORNIA CHRISTMAS
ONE PERFECT SUMMER
CHRISTMAS IN SILVER SPRINGS
UNFORGETTABLE YOU
BEFORE WE WERE STRANGERS
RIGHT WHERE WE BELONG
UNTIL YOU LOVED ME
NO ONE BUT YOU
FINDING OUR FOREVER
THE SECRETS SHE KEPT
A WINTER WEDDING
THE SECRET SISTER
THIS HEART OF MINE
THE HEART OF CHRISTMAS
COME HOME TO ME
TAKE ME HOME FOR CHRISTMAS
HOME TO WHISKEY CREEK
WHEN SUMMER COMES

WHEN SNOW FALLS
WHEN LIGHTNING STRIKES
IN CLOSE
IN SECONDS
INSIDE
KILLER HEAT
BODY HEAT
WHITE HEAT
THE PERFECT MURDER
THE PERFECT LIAR
THE PERFECT COUPLE
WATCH ME
STOP ME
TRUST ME
DEAD RIGHT
DEAD GIVEAWAY
DEAD SILENCE
COLD FEET
TAKING THE HEAT
EVERY WAKING MOMENT

For a full list of Brenda's books,
visit www.brendanovak.com.

brenda novak

summer on the island

mira

mira™

ISBN-13: 978-0-7783-8637-7

Summer on the Island

For questions and comments about the quality of this book, please contact us at CustomerService@Harlequin.com.

Mira
22 Adelaide St. West, 41st Floor
Toronto, Ontario M5H 4E3, Canada
BookClubbish.com

Recycling programs
for this product may
not exist in your area.

Printed in U.S.A.

To Vickie Watts, a wonderful member of my online book group on Facebook and part of the reason that community is so warm, inclusive and special. I love interacting with you online, really enjoyed having the opportunity to meet you in person and hope to see you at another signing in the future. Thanks for all you do to support me and my work—and other bibliophiles, too.

summer on the island

1

Teach Island looked exactly the same as Marlow Madsen remembered it. Since the entire world had been disrupted by the pandemic, the comfort and familiarity of this place nearly brought tears to her eyes. Part of that was how strongly she associated it with her father. John "Tiller" Madsen, who'd gotten his nickname because of his love for sailing, had died a month ago. But the island had long been his escape from the rat race of Washington, DC, where he'd served as a United States senator for thirty years.

"I can't believe I'm back. *Finally,*" Marlow said as she rolled down the passenger window to let in some fresh air.

Part of the archipelago of forty-five hundred islands off the coast of Florida, Teach was only seven square miles. Marlow loved its homey, small-town atmosphere. She also loved its white sand beaches and its motley collection of bars, restaurants, bait-and-tackle stores and gift shops, most of which, at least in the older section where they were now, had kitschy decor. Because the island was named after Edward Teach, or Blackbeard, one of the most famous pirates to operate in this part of the world in the early eighteenth century, there was pirate stuff all over. A black skull-and-crossbones flag hung on a pole in front of the most popular bar, which was made to look like a colonial-era tavern and was named Queen Anne's Revenge after Blackbeard's ship.

In addition to the Blackbeard memorabilia, there was the regular sea-themed stuff—large anchors or ship's wheels stuck in the ground here and there, fishing nets draped from the eaves of stores and cafés, and lobsters, crabs and other ocean creatures painted on wooden or corrugated metal sides. Her parents had a house in Georgia, a true Southern mansion, as well as their condo in Virginia for when her father had to be in Washington. But this was where they'd always spent the summers.

Now that Tiller was gone, her mother was talking about selling the other residences and moving here permanently. Marlow hated the sense of loss that inspired the forever change, but since Seaclusion—her father's name for the beach house—had always been her favorite of their homes, she was also relieved that her mother planned to keep it. *This* was the property she hoped to inherit one day; she couldn't imagine it ever being out of the family. And after what so many people had experienced with the fires in California, where she'd been living since she graduated college, and all the hurricanes in recent years that had plagued Florida, she had reason to be grateful the house was still standing.

"Sounds like you've missed the place." Reese Cantwell, who'd been sent to pick up her and her two friends, had grown even taller since Marlow had seen him last. His hands and feet no longer looked disproportionate to the rest of his body. She remembered that his older brother, Walker, had also reminded her of a pup who hadn't quite grown into his large paws and wondered what Walker was doing these days.

"It's a welcome sight for all three of us," Aida Trahan piped up from the back. "Three months by the sea should change everything."

Claire Fernandez was also in the back seat, both of them buried beneath the luggage that wouldn't fit in the trunk. They'd met at LAX and flown into Miami together. "Here's hoping," she said. "Even if it doesn't, I'm looking forward to putting my toes in the water and my butt in the sand."

"You'll get plenty of opportunities for that here," Reese said.

Claire needed the peace and tranquility and a chance to heal. She'd lost her home in the fires that'd ravaged Malibu last August. To say nothing of the other dramas that'd plagued her this past year.

Marlow looked over at their driver. Apparently, since her father's death, Reese had been helping out around the estate, in addition to teaching tennis at the club. His mother, Rosemary, had been their housekeeper since well before he was born— since before Marlow was even born. Marlow was grateful for the many years of service and loyalty Rosemary had given the family, especially now that Tiller had died. It was wonderful to have someone she trusted watch out for her mother. Eileen had multiple sclerosis, which sometimes made it difficult for her to get around.

"Looks as casual as I was hoping it would be." Claire also lowered her window as Reese brought them to the far side of the island and closer to the house. Situated on the water, Seaclusion had its own private beach, as well as a three-bedroom guesthouse and a smaller apartment over the garage where Rosemary had lived before moving into the main house after Tiller died so she could be available if Eileen needed anything during the night.

"There are some upscale shops and restaurants where we're going, if you're in the mood for spending money," Marlow told them.

"When have I not been in the mood to shop?" Aida joked.

"You don't have access to Dutton's money anymore," Claire pointed out. "You need to be careful."

Claire had lost almost everything. She had reason to be cautious. Aida wasn't in the best situation, either, and yet she shrugged off the concern. "I'll be okay. I didn't walk away empty-handed, thanks to my *amazing* divorce attorney."

Marlow always felt uncomfortable when Dutton came up, and sometimes couldn't believe it wasn't more uncomfortable for *them*. The way Claire and Aida had met was remarkable, to say the least. It was even more remarkable that they'd managed to become friends. But Marlow twisted around and smiled as though she didn't feel the sudden tension so she could acknowledge Aida's compliment. Although Marlow was only thirty-four, she'd been a practicing attorney for ten years. She'd jumped ahead two grades when she was seven, which had enabled her to finish high school early and start college at sixteen. A knack for difficult negotiations had led her to a law degree and from there she'd gone into family law, something that had worked out well for her. Her practice had grown so fast she'd considered hiring another attorney to help with the caseload.

She probably would've done that, if not for the pandemic, which had shut down every aspect of her life except work, making her realize that becoming one of the best divorce attorneys in Los Angeles wasn't everything it was cracked up to be. No matter how much money she made, she didn't enjoy dealing with people who were so deeply upset, and the richer, more famous the client, the more acrimonious the divorce. She hoped she'd never have to wade through another one. If a marriage worked, it could be wonderful. Her parents had proved that. But after what she'd witnessed with other people since passing the bar, she was beginning to believe Tiller and Eileen were the exception.

"All I did was make Dutton play fair," Marlow said. "But at least you have some money you can use to get by while you decide what to do from here."

"I liked being a trophy wife," Aida grumbled. "I'm not sure I'm cut out for anything else."

Like so many in LA, she'd been an aspiring actress at one time, but her career had never taken off. After she'd married Dutton, she'd spent more time at the tennis club, where she and Marlow had met, than trying out for any auditions.

"Don't say that," Marlow told her. "You can do a lot more than look pretty."

Claire remained conspicuously quiet. She'd been subdued since they left, so subdued that Marlow was beginning to wonder if something was wrong.

"We'll see." Aida shrugged off the compliment as readily as she had the warning. "But before I have to make the really hard decisions, I deserve a break. So where's the expensive part of the island again?"

Reese chuckled. "We're almost there."

"We'll be able to play tennis, too," Marlow told her. "The club's only a mile from the house. And Reese is our resident pro."

"No way! You play tennis?" Aida's voice revealed her enthusiasm.

"Every day," he replied.

"Can he beat you?" Aida asked Marlow.

"He was just a kid the last time we played, and he could take me about half the time even then. I doubt he'll have any problem now."

"I can see why you talked us out of renting a car," Claire said, finally entering the conversation. "Considering the size of this place…"

"Like I told you before," Marlow said, "most people walk or ride a bike."

"You only need a car if you're going off island," Reese chimed in. He was driving them in Eileen's Tesla.

Marlow was anxious to ask how her mother was doing but decided to hold off. If she questioned him while her friends were in the car, she'd probably get the standard "Fine." But she wasn't looking for a perfunctory answer. She wanted the truth. What he'd seen and heard recently. He was the one who'd been here.

Marlow hadn't been able to visit, not even when her father died. Thanks to the pandemic, they hadn't been able to give him the funeral he deserved, either.

Reese glanced into the rearview mirror. "Are the three of you staying all summer?"

Marlow suspected he was hoping Aida, in particular, would be on the island for a while. Although Aida was thirty-six, fourteen years older than he was, she was a delicate blonde with big blue eyes. The way she dressed and accessorized, she turned heads, especially male heads, wherever she went.

"We are," Aida said, and the subtle hint of flirtation in her voice told Marlow that she'd picked up on Reese's interest.

"We have some big decisions to make in the coming months," Marlow said, hoping to give Reese a hint that this wasn't the opportunity he might think it was. Aida was on the rebound. She needed to put her life back together, not risk her heart on a summer fling.

"What kind of decisions?" he asked, naturally curious.

Claire answered for her. "Like what we're going to do from here on. We're all starting over."

Reese's eyebrows shot up as he looked at Marlow. "Meaning...what? You won't be returning to LA?"

"I'm not sure," she said. "I sold my condo and closed my practice before I left, just in case."

His jaw dropped. "Really? But your mom said you're one of the most highly sought-after attorneys in Los Angeles."

No doubt her mother talked about her all the time. She'd heard a few things about Reese's family, too, including the fact that he hadn't finished school because he'd let partying come between him and a degree. But Marlow didn't know Reese that well. She'd spent more time with his much older brother, Walker, when they were growing up. "It's not that it wasn't working out. It *was*. I'm just...done with divorce."

He turned down the rap music he'd had playing since they got in. "Have you told your mother?"

"Not yet. I was afraid she'd try to talk me out of it. I know it's sort of crazy to walk away from what I had going. Not many lawyers would do that. But after being quarantined for so long, working with people who almost always behaved their worst, I'm finished suffering through other people's emotional turmoil."

"Can't say as I blame you," Aida agreed. "I feel so bad about how Dutton treated you."

Aida's ex hadn't just called Marlow names. He'd gotten her cell phone number from Aida, claiming he wanted to negotiate directly, and then proceeded to threaten her on more than one occasion. "We can all be glad Dutton's out of our lives."

"Amen," Aida said, but again Claire said nothing.

They reached the gap in the shrubbery that signaled the beginning of her parents' drive, and Reese turned into Seaclusion.

"Look at this!" Aida exclaimed. "It's a whole compound."

Reese parked in the detached four-car garage. "Welcome home," he said with a grin.

Marlow had her carry-on with her, but when she went to the trunk to get the rest of her luggage, Reese insisted he'd bring it in.

She thanked him, put her bag down and, eager to see her mother, hurried to the house.

Rosemary was waiting on the stoop, where her mother would normally be. "It's good to see you, Marlow."

"Thanks, Rosemary. It's good to see you, too. Is Mom okay?"

At fifty-five, Rosemary was five years younger than Eileen and tall and thin, like her two sons. They'd gotten their good looks from her—didn't resemble their father at all, who wasn't around anymore. Marlow could recall him showing up at the Atlanta house drunk and bellowing for Rosemary to "get her ass home." It wasn't any surprise to Marlow that the relationship hadn't lasted. He'd abandoned the family when Reese was four or five.

"She's fine. A little tired." Although Rosemary smiled, she seemed anxious and uptight herself. Was it because of Eileen? Was she worse off than Marlow had been told?

"Is it anything to be concerned about?" Marlow pressed.

"No. She was so excited to see you that she couldn't sleep last night. That's all. She's in her room resting if you want to go in."

Anxious to reassure herself that nothing more serious was going on, Marlow introduced Aida and Claire to Rosemary, and while Rosemary led them to the guesthouse, where Reese was taking the luggage, Marlow went inside. "Mom?" she called as she moved through the living room.

"In here!" her mother called back.

Marlow's stomach knotted as she reached the master bedroom and swung the door open wider. It was a beautiful day outside, not a cloud in the sky, yet the shades were drawn, making it dark and cool.

As soon as she reached the bed, she bent to kiss her mother's paper-thin cheek. "I'm so glad to see you again."

Eileen's hands clutched her wrists. "Let me look at you. It's been too long."

"Who could've guessed a pandemic would come between us? That wasn't something I even considered when I went so far from home."

Once her eyes adjusted to the light, Marlow could see that the room hadn't changed. Her father's watch glimmered on the dresser, his slippers waited under the side chair and his clothes hung neatly in the closet as though he might walk through the door at any moment. Her mother hadn't done anything with his personal property. That meant Marlow would have to deal with it, but she was actually grateful Eileen had waited. Touching his belongings was their only remaining connection to him, their only chance to say goodbye, and now they could do that together.

"Are you hungry?" her mother asked. "Rosemary made tea for you and your friends."

Marlow sat on the edge of the bed. Eileen had thick dark hair and bottle green eyes—both of which Marlow had inherited—and looked good despite being so ill. But she was pale today and had lost significant weight. "That sounds wonderful," Marlow said.

"I thought your friends might enjoy it. And I know how much you like clotted cream. When we were in London with your father several years ago, that was all you wanted to eat."

The twinkle in Eileen's eyes made Marlow feel slightly encouraged, until her mother winced as she adjusted her position. Eileen had to be feeling terrible, or she'd be up and around and asking to meet Aida and Claire.

"Are you having another attack?" Marlow asked. Her mother's disease came in waves, or what they called "attacks." Sometimes she grew worse for no clear reason—she didn't do or eat anything different—and then she improved just as mysteriously. Although the steady decrease in her functionality attested to the fact that each attack took a little more from her...

"I must be. But don't worry about me. It's...more of the same. How was your flight?"

The lump that swelled in Marlow's throat made it difficult to swallow. She'd already lost her beloved father. Was she going to lose her mother this year, too? The probability of Eileen's dying had hung over their heads ever since she was diagnosed twenty-six years ago, so it'd come as a total shock that Tiller had died first. He'd never been sick a day in his life—until he got shingles. Then he'd spent five weeks in bed and simply didn't wake up one morning. According to the autopsy, a blood clot had formed and traveled to his lungs.

"The flight was crowded and miserable," she answered. "But aren't all flights that way?"

"You should've come first class."

Marlow thought about her decision to sell her place and close her practice but decided not to mention it until later. Eileen's father had been a steel baron; she'd married into money, as well. She'd never known what it was like to struggle. Marlow hadn't, either, but she was out in the world and much more cognizant of the difficulties faced by those who didn't have quite as much. "I didn't want to ask Aida and Claire to spend the extra money. You know what happened to Claire."

"Yes. The poor thing. I'm so glad she had insurance to cover the rebuild. The fires in California have been *awful*. I've seen them on the news." Eileen lifted her head to look toward the door. "Where are your friends?"

"Rosemary's helping them get settled in the guesthouse."

"I can't wait to meet them."

"They're grateful to you for letting them come home with me. But with the way you're feeling, maybe I should've come alone—"

"No, no," she broke in. "They both needed a place to recoup, as you said. And having them here won't hurt me. New friends might help fill the terrible void I've felt since Tiller..." Her voice cracked.

Marlow squeezed her hand, wondering if it was the emotional toll of losing Tiller that'd gotten the best of Eileen, rather than MS. "I miss him, too," she whispered.

Her mother brought Marlow's hand to her cheek. "It'll be good to have you here for practical reasons, too. I think there's something that has to be done with the estate."

"What's that?" Marlow asked in surprise.

"I don't know. Samuel Lefebvre's been calling me, trying to get me to come meet with him, but I told him you're the one to talk to. I can't face it."

Sam was her father's attorney and had been since Marlow could remember. He'd written her a character reference when she applied to Stanford, since he'd graduated from there himself, which was how she'd landed on the opposite coast. "I can handle it. It shouldn't be hard. Most, if not all, of Dad's estate will pass directly to you. Maybe he left me a few trinkets."

"I'm sure he did. But Sam acts as though there's business at hand, so he must need something."

"You know Sam. He's fastidious, always in a hurry to wrap things up. It won't be a problem."

A ghost of her mother's former smile curved her lips. "You're so capable. You've always been capable—just like your father."

Marlow heard Rosemary come into the house with Aida and Claire. "Should I wait to introduce my friends to you until after we eat?"

"Maybe that would be best," Eileen said. "It'll give me the chance to rest a bit longer."

"Of course. There's no rush."

"I can't wait to spend more time with you. It's comforting to know we have the whole summer."

"It is." Marlow hugged her mother, breathing in the welcome scent of her perfume before going out to join Aida and Claire in the dining room, where Rosemary had put a tea caddy filled with small sandwiches, crackers with herb spread, homemade scones and chocolate-covered strawberries. The clotted cream was in small dishes at the side of each plate.

"Looks delicious. I don't think anyone in the UK could do it better."

"Then I did it right," Rosemary joked.

When Marlow sat down, she halfway expected Reese to join them, since she knew he was on the property, but he didn't come in. As generously as her family had treated Rosemary and her boys, there'd always been a distinction between the family and the help. Marlow supposed that, in many situations like this, it

19

was inevitable: there was a natural hierarchy when it came to employment.

"Reese has gotten so tall," she remarked to Rosemary, helping herself to a cucumber-and-cream-cheese sandwich.

"He's a handsome man," Aida said.

Marlow shot her friend a warning look but didn't dare say anything in front of Reese's mother, who seemed to take the compliment at face value. "He's six-four, as tall as his brother now," she said proudly.

"What's Walker been doing these days?" Marlow asked.

Rosemary used a towel to hold the hot teapot with both hands. "He's living here on the island now."

Marlow paused, her sandwich halfway to her mouth. "He left Atlanta to come here permanently? When?"

"As soon as he heard about COVID. Poor guy's always felt he needs to be there for me and Reese," she said with an affectionate chuckle. "I guess it's no wonder since, growing up, he had to be the man of the house."

Eileen hadn't mentioned that Walker had moved to Teach, but at thirty-six, he probably didn't come to the house much. "What part of the island does he live on?" Marlow asked. "He's not staying above the garage, is he?"

"No, Reese is there now. Walker bought the cottage down by the cove. It's not very big, but the setting is magnificent. I've never seen prettier sunsets than the ones I see from his front porch."

Marlow liked the cove, too. The beach there was small and completely cut off from the other beaches, so it was often overlooked by tourists, which made it feel almost as private as the beach her family owned. "What does he do for a living?"

"He's the chief of police."

Marlow sat taller. "The *chief* of police?"

Rosemary shrugged off her surprise. "It sounds loftier than it is. There are only two other officers on the force."

"But…how'd that happen? Last I heard, he was a street cop in Atlanta." She remembered someone telling her that a friend had talked him into going into the academy. That had been a while ago—probably a decade—but Walker's ascent still seemed quick.

"This is your oldest son?" Claire interrupted.

"It is," Rosemary replied before answering Marlow. "He didn't want to be separated from me or his brother during the pandemic, so he kept checking for jobs on the island—and he found one."

"The chief of police quit or was fired or something?" Claire asked.

"No, Walker got on as a regular officer first," Rosemary clarified. "But when the chief retired, he took over."

"Do you have a daughter-in-law, too?" Aida asked. "Or any grandbabies?"

"Not yet," Rosemary replied. "I bug Walker about finding a wife all the time, but he just laughs it off and tells me you can't hurry love."

"Maybe Reese will be the one to give you grandbabies," Aida said.

"He's got some growing up to do first," Rosemary said and headed into the kitchen.

Marlow and Claire both gave Aida a pointed stare.

"*What?*" she said, lifting her well-manicured hands as though she'd done nothing wrong. "He's twenty-two. It's not as though he's underage."

Rosemary reappeared before they could say anything further. "Walker's here," she announced. "I needed a few things for the soup I'm making for dinner tonight, and he said he'd grab them for me."

A knock sounded on the door. After Rosemary opened it, Marlow could hear Walker say, "Here you go. You'll find some of those dark chocolate–covered almonds you like in the bag, too."

Marlow could see a slice of Rosemary as she accepted the sack he handed her. "Thank you."

"No problem. I'll see you later."

"Walker?" his mother said, calling him back. "Marlow's home if you'd like to come in and say hello."

There was a slight pause, which indicated he wasn't thrilled with the idea. Marlow could understand why. They hadn't exactly been close, at least not during their teenage years. But he eventually said, "Fine. But just for a minute. I have to get back to work."

2

Walker had filled out since she'd last seen him. Marlow remembered him as tall and skinny, like his younger brother, but with a little more acne and a lot more attitude. He was still lean, but he looked far more powerful these days, especially through the arms and shoulders. The acne was gone—a shadow of dark razor stubble had replaced that—but she couldn't yet tell how much his attitude had improved. It was odd to see him in a police uniform.

His light eyes, more the color of ice than the cornflower blue of Aida's, circled the faces at the table as he nodded. "Nice to see you again," he said to Marlow, but he hung back instead of coming very far into the room, and he sounded more polite than sincere.

Marlow already knew he didn't like her. He'd made several attempts to get something going between them when they were teenagers, but she hadn't been interested. Back then, he'd had a chip on his shoulder a mile wide. She wasn't sure why, but he'd tried to kiss her several times, and the last time she'd refused, he'd accused her of thinking she was too good for him. After that he would scarcely even look at her.

"It's nice to see you, too," Marlow said as if those previous run-ins had never occurred and motioned to her friends. "This is Aida Trahan and Claire Fernandez. They're planning to spend the summer here with me."

"Great place to hang out for a few months," he said to them. "I hope you enjoy the island."

Duty done, he was already stepping back when Marlow remembered her manners. "We've got plenty of food here. Would you like to sit down and have a cup of tea?"

"No, thanks." He was eager to go. That was clear. He hadn't wanted to come in to begin with. But Aida wasn't about to let such a good-looking guy escape that easily.

"Are you sure?" She jumped up and pulled out the chair next to her own. "It's all delicious."

When he checked his watch, Marlow could tell he was planning to give them an excuse. "I would if I could—" he started, but was interrupted when Eileen came into the room.

"Walker!" She beamed at him. "I thought I heard your voice. I haven't seen you in months. What have you been up to?"

His first genuine smile appeared. "Oh, you know me. Just causing trouble."

"Can you believe Marlow's home? I'm so happy to have her back. And she's brought friends! Won't you join us for a few minutes?"

The sudden change in his body language signaled he wouldn't refuse Eileen the way he'd refused them. He seemed to have a soft spot for her. "All right. I guess I have a minute or two." He helped Eileen, who was a little less steady on her feet than usual, to a chair before taking the one Aida had pulled out for him.

"Welcome to Seaclusion," Eileen said to Claire and Aida when Marlow introduced them. "I hope you'll make yourselves right at home."

Claire leaned back as Rosemary came around to top up her tea. "Thank you. This is going to be a fabulous reprieve."

"Claire's house burned down in the Malibu fire last August," Aida confided to Walker.

The size of Walker's hand made his teacup look small by comparison. "I'm really sorry to hear that. California's fires seem to be getting worse."

"Yes, which is why we might not stay there much longer," Aida said ruefully.

"Don't tell me you lost your house, too," he said.

"No. I lost my marriage."

"Divorce is also hard," Eileen said.

"At least I had a good attorney," Aida joked.

Eileen covered Marlow's hand with her own. "Marlow handled the divorce," she explained proudly.

Walker's eyes flicked in Marlow's direction, but he glanced away almost immediately. "If I ever get married and it doesn't go well, I'll know who to call," he said as he lifted his cup.

Marlow got the feeling she'd be the last person he'd call for any reason. He still held the past against her. He'd probably been going through a lot when she rejected him. As an adult, she understood that his life hadn't been easy and wished she'd been kinder. Maybe he was right about her—she'd been rich and spoiled and immature, and he'd been the housekeeper's son. That type of bias wasn't easy to admit, but it was probably the truth.

"You said 'we,'" Rosemary said to Aida. "But Marlow has no plans to leave California, does she?"

Marlow had been hoping no one had picked up on that. "Actually, I've closed down my practice," Marlow told her. She'd planned to wait before going into this, but since the subject had come up...

"You...what?" Eileen said.

"My job wasn't working for me," she explained.

Eileen set her cup on its saucer with a clink. "What do you mean? You had more cases than you knew what to do with."

"That's the problem," she said. "It was a constant onslaught of negativity. 'She said this… He did that…' Some of my clients would tear their own kids to shreds if it meant getting a bigger piece of the asset pie. I couldn't take it anymore."

Aida cupped a hand around her mouth as though she was sharing a secret with Walker. "My ex was partially to blame. He got so ugly with Marlow."

"Because I was making him give you what you deserved."

"You didn't tell me about this," Eileen said, clearly alarmed.

"There was no reason to upset you. Dutton—or Dumbo, as I call him—didn't end up doing anything."

Her mother didn't seem comforted. "But he *could* have."

"Did you get a restraining order against him?" Walker asked.

As a police officer, he would immediately wonder if she'd gone to the authorities. "I tried. The judge wouldn't grant it, but I took other precautions."

"What other precautions?" Walker held her gaze for the first time since he'd arrived, and she couldn't help thinking she'd never seen such striking eyes. He'd always had them, of course. But they were somehow different these days. Wiser. More tempered. More mature. And more skeptical.

"I put a camera at both doors that I could monitor on my phone. And I was careful never to leave my office on my own."

"How long ago was this?" he asked.

She looked to Aida to confirm her memory. "We settled… what? Two months ago?"

"Three," Aida said. "The divorce is final."

The fact that Dutton was no longer a threat seemed to satisfy Walker. "I'm glad it didn't come to anything," he said and popped a sandwich into his mouth before downing the rest of his tea. "I'd better go. I have a lot to do today."

"You should come by more often," Eileen said. "You know I'll feed you."

"I'll do that," he said with a chuckle, but Marlow was willing to bet he wouldn't be back while she was there.

He told her friends it was good to meet them and left, but he and his mother—Rosemary was walking him out—hadn't been gone more than a few seconds when Eileen got up and started for the kitchen.

"Where are you going?" Marlow asked, since her mother seemed to be in a hurry.

"To wrap up some leftovers I can send home with him. Walker loves chocolate-covered strawberries."

"How do you know?"

"His mother told me."

Eileen had to catch her balance by grabbing the door frame, so Marlow shot up. "Let me do it," she said, but by the time she took over, Rosemary had already come back in alone.

"Oh, is he gone?" Eileen asked, disappointed. "I was going to send some of the sandwiches, scones and strawberries home with him."

"How nice," Rosemary said. "I'll ask him to swing by again later."

After finishing their tea and helping to clean up, Marlow, Aida and Claire thanked Eileen and Rosemary and walked over to the guesthouse to change. They couldn't wait to get out of their sticky clothes and into their swimsuits so they could hit the beach.

"Why haven't you ever mentioned Walker or Reese?" Aida asked as they crossed the yard.

Marlow glanced toward the apartment over the garage, where she'd learned Reese was staying, but she didn't see any movement. "Why would I?"

"You're kidding, right?" she said. "Two men who look as good as they do?"

"I grew up with them," Marlow said as if they were more like family. But she didn't feel remotely sisterly toward them. Especially Walker...

"I hope we run into them again, don't you?" Aida joked and nudged Claire to try to get her into the spirit.

Although Claire had hardly said a word since they left California, she spoke up now. "I wish I could move on as easily as you have."

Aida pulled them both to a stop. "What does that mean?"

When Claire didn't answer, just stared at the ground, Aida said, "Don't tell me you're still stuck on my asshole ex-husband."

A guilty expression flitted across Claire's face as she glanced up. "He's been calling me," she admitted.

Marlow almost couldn't believe her ears. *"Dutton?"*

"No way!" Aida cried. "Tell me that's not who you mean." But they both knew it was. Claire was the reason for Aida's divorce; she was the "other woman."

"Why didn't you say something?" Aida demanded without waiting for Claire's confirmation.

Claire's shoulders slumped. "Because I was secretly glad. I've lost everything this year—my house, my yoga studio thanks to COVID, and the exciting new relationship I thought I was starting. I know it's terrible of me, but... I'm still in love with him."

Aida gasped. "After all the lies he told you? After all the lies he told *both* of us?"

Claire looked downright miserable. She didn't answer, but her silence made the truth clear.

Now Marlow understood what had been going on with Claire, why she'd been so reserved on the flight and in the car. "Aida," she said softly, hoping to temper her response, but Aida wasn't listening—not to her.

Her gaze was riveted on Claire. "He threatened to destroy Marlow's reputation and her practice!" she said.

"I hate what he did," Claire responded. "But...he was angry and...and hurt. And he didn't act on it. He's told me he's sorry."

No wonder Dutton had stopped bothering her, Marlow thought. He was trying to get back with one of the women he'd lost—the one he'd been cheating with until Claire found out he was married and showed up on Aida's doorstep to tell her what had been going on. "Claire, I don't trust him."

"But...you should hear how terrible he feels."

"I don't believe he feels terrible, or that he's remotely sorry," Marlow said. "I believe he's placated because he thinks he can get you back."

"Besides, it doesn't matter if he didn't act on his threats," Aida chimed in. "He still said those things. He frightened her—after he abused our love and our trust."

Claire winced. "I know, but—"

"If he'll cheat on me, he'll cheat on you," Aida broke in.

"You can't be sure of that," Claire said, a slight wobble in her voice.

The last thing Marlow wanted was an argument erupting between them, especially on their first day here. Putting an arm around Claire's shoulders, she gave her a reassuring squeeze to help offset what she felt compelled to say. "He's not a good person, honey."

"People always act their worst when they're going through a divorce. You've said that a million times."

The pain Marlow had witnessed—heartbreak just like this— was why she refused to get involved with anyone. Love made people too vulnerable. "That's when someone's true character is revealed."

"You've never lived with him," Aida concurred. "Take it from someone who *has*—for ten years. He's too narcissistic to truly love anyone."

Claire began to blink more rapidly. "What if he's changed?"

"Oh, my God!" Aida cried. "He hasn't! It's an act. You have to get over him."

"And you will," Marlow added, more gently. "With time."

Claire didn't respond to her encouragement. She looked out

from under her bangs at Aida. "What about you? Are *you* over him?"

That Claire hadn't become combative despite their shocked and unhappy reaction—that she was so vulnerable and confused and hurt—took the fight out of Aida. "I don't know," she said. "All I know is that I can't go back to him, even if I'm not. So what does it matter?"

With a sniff, Claire wiped her nose and started toward the guesthouse again. "If you can do it, maybe I can, too."

Aida also put an arm around Claire so they were all three walking as one unit. "That's what we're here for. We're going to hit the reset button, remember?"

Claire attempted to smile through her tears. "I remember."

3

When Claire's phone vibrated under the towel protecting it from the sun, she told herself to ignore the call. She'd come to Teach Island for an escape, and she was going to take full advantage—forget the world she'd left behind and gain a healthier perspective so she could return to California stronger and in better control of her life.

But the fact that it was probably Dutton made her pull the phone out and lift her sunglasses for a peek.

Sure enough.

A quick glance at the ocean showed Marlow and Aida deep in conversation, standing in the waves that lapped gently at the beach. They were probably talking about her, and the bombshell she'd dropped a couple of hours ago. No doubt they were wondering how she could continue a relationship with Dutton. Sometimes she wondered that herself. But she hadn't been able to turn him away, couldn't just move on as Aida seemed to have done. Dutton was different from the other men she'd dated. Never before had she been with someone who seemed so capable of navigating the bumps of life. He stood up and took charge, and for someone who'd dated men who weren't willing to be responsible for anything, even making future plans, that was a strong aphrodisiac. He was always willing to go to the work of having a good time, too, no matter how much planning it took, and he was interested in so many things, which made him fun to be with.

Fortunately, this call had come while she was alone—or essentially alone. Otherwise, she couldn't have answered.

Tilting her wide-brimmed floppy hat to shield part of her face, she turned away from the water as she raised the phone to her ear. She'd never dreamed she'd ever get involved with a married man. She'd always considered herself a good judge of character and a person of strong character herself. But with Dutton, she hadn't seen it coming.

A little over a year ago, when she'd bumped into him while closing up her yoga studio as he was heading to the hair salon next door, there'd been an immediate spark. He'd teased her about how she had to struggle to get the darn door to lock properly and had offered a little elbow grease to get it to latch, and then he'd returned the next day to say he hadn't been able to quit thinking about her.

The relationship had progressed quickly from there—until, almost six months later, Tori Valens, the hairdresser next door, finally came forward to tell her he was married.

"Hello?" she said now.

"Hey, babe." His voice, as deep and rich as that of any radio host, sent a jolt of pure longing through her. This was the person who'd supported her—emotionally and financially—during the loss of her house and her business, when the state's shutdown lasted for months and months and she could no longer pay the rent on her studio. When she was so distraught she could barely climb out of bed in the morning, he was there to help her cope with the bitter disappointment of seeing her dreams come crashing down, especially after her house was destroyed in one of the biggest wildfires in California. He'd moved her into his apartment, given her security and financial support, and helped her wade through all the red tape of dealing with the insurance company, getting bids for the rebuild and choosing the contractor.

He'd lied so convincingly through all of that time, created a whole world for her that didn't actually exist. She'd never even suspected that the apartment he'd rented was just for show. The job he claimed to have as a pharmaceutical rep, the one that demanded he travel—his excuse for being gone so much—was nothing like his practice as a pediatric surgeon. And he'd told her his parents and his sister lived out of town, which was why she never got to meet any of his family.

He'd had an answer for everything. And she'd believed every word.

"What are you doing?" she asked.

"Missing you," he said.

She was missing him, too. But she didn't say so. She was trying to hang on to her principles, and what she knew would be best for her in the long run.

"How was the trip to Florida?"

"I'm not a big fan of flying, but it was okay as flights go, I guess."

"I told you—you have a greater chance of dying in a car crash than a plane crash."

"If only I could convince my subconscious of that. I almost had an anxiety attack when they closed the door."

"You should've taken a Valium."

"I don't have any."

"I would've prescribed some for you. All you had to do was say the word."

He saw nothing wrong with writing a prescription. His willingness to bend the rules was a problem. She saw it as the red flag that it was. So why didn't his lack of integrity stop her from caring about him? From wanting to be with him? "I made it safely," she said simply. "So it's a moot point."

"You still have the return flight. Do you want me to send you something?"

She couldn't argue with him. Not right now. Putting him off would be easier. "We'll talk about that when I'm closer to leaving the island."

"Don't tell me you're staying all summer," he said.

She straightened in surprise. She'd never indicated otherwise. "That's always been the plan."

"I can't go three months without seeing you."

She was afraid she couldn't last that long, either—not if she didn't manage to somehow strengthen her resolve.

"By then Marlow will have poisoned you against me," he said. "She and Aida have nothing good to say about me."

"They're looking forward, not back." Loyalty demanded she not tell him certain things. He was as angry with them as they were with him. He freely admitted that he'd been wrong to cheat, but he justified his behavior toward Aida by saying she'd never had to work a day since she married him, that for ten years he'd provided her with a fabulous life where all she had to do was get her nails done and sit by the pool, and yet they'd "taken him to the cleaners" in the divorce.

"I wish you'd come to me instead of Aida when Tori told you."

So he could…what? Lie some more? Hide his income so Aida wouldn't get her fair share?

Claire hated to assume the worst, but she had only his track record to go by. "Let's not talk about that," she said. They'd been over it before. When he called her out of the blue after the divorce had been finalized, he'd been careful not to fault her for telling Aida. But she'd noticed more and more blame creeping into their conversations in the weeks since, and she wasn't going to let him make her the villain for telling his wife. Aida had the right to know. *She'd* want to know if she were in Aida's shoes.

"I'm sorry," he said. "It's just that they screwed me so bad."

"I've told you how I feel about the situation."

"You believe what happened was my fault. But there are two sides to every story, Claire. Aida wasn't a perfect wife any more than I was a perfect husband."

She'd already heard all about that, of course. He'd told her that Aida lived her life barely scratching the surface of it, that after the decade they'd been together, he'd grown bored, listless. He craved someone to speak to at the end of the day who was interested in deeper conversation. And as much as Claire hated to admit it, she could sort of understand why Dutton wouldn't be satisfied—not if he was looking for a critical thinker who could see the many shades of gray in life.

Afraid to face the ocean again for fear Aida or Marlow, or both of them, had seen her talking on the phone and would guess it was Dutton, she kept her head turned away. "Look, I'd better go. I can't talk right now."

"Come back to California," he said. "What we had… You don't want to throw that away, Claire, not when we can finally be together on the up-and-up. It's a once-in-a-lifetime chance at happiness."

She squeezed her eyes closed as desire warred with loyalty, friendship, duty—and common sense. "I'm going to stay here for the summer, Dutton. If…if I still feel the same way about you when I get home, maybe…maybe something will change. But I need time to decide if I can forgive you and trust you enough to get back into a relationship."

Silence. She could feel the negative energy coming through the phone. "I'm scared," he admitted at length. "I can't imagine you'll come back to me after spending three months with my ex-wife. I mean…this isn't how it normally works. You two are supposed to hate each other, and I can't figure out why you don't."

Claire understood how unlikely their friendship was. Part of it was being in the same terrible situation. That was what had drawn them together in the first place, and supporting each other had made the past six months easier to survive. The other part was simply... Aida. Maybe she wasn't the deepest person Claire had ever met, but she was kind and optimistic and sweet. Not many wives would be able to see, almost immediately, that Claire wasn't to blame. From the very beginning, Aida had offered understanding instead of recrimination, which was remarkable. "It's unusual, but..."

"But..." he echoed.

She hated herself for hesitating. It had to be jealousy that made it difficult for her to praise Aida's many fine qualities, because doing so would've been easy and automatic if she were talking to anyone else. "She's special," she forced herself to admit.

He should know. He'd married her for a reason. There were moments when Claire wondered if he was only coming back to her because Aida had refused to reconcile. Before everything turned completely acrimonious during the divorce, Aida had indicated that there'd been a few weeks when he'd tried to win *her* back.

Later, he'd told Claire that it was because he'd already invested ten years in the marriage and didn't want to see it all go down the drain. But she suspected it had more to do with losing half his net worth.

Or was she being too hard on him? Relationships were complicated. Maybe he'd been sincere in trying to reconcile, because some part of him had truly loved Aida. But that was as difficult for her to contemplate as the opposite.

"You're right. I don't want to talk about her," he said. "What happened...it's over and done with. We need to move on. But I can't move on without you."

The doubts that crowded into Claire's mind made her feel as though her head might explode. Did he really love her? That was the million-dollar question. Or was he just trying to save what he could? Aida claimed he had to have a woman in his life at all times, feared being alone. Claire didn't want to fall for his lies *twice*. But he could get almost any woman he wanted. He didn't have to pick her. And she couldn't help remembering how wonderful things had been between them before she'd learned the truth. "We'll see. As I said, I'm going to spend the summer here on Teach and try to get my thoughts together. I'll let you know where I'm at once I'm home."

"It sounds like you're not even planning on talking to me while you're there."

"I think that would be best." How else could she get her heart and her mind in alliance? Just the sound of his voice made her start to question herself all over again.

"Isn't there anything I can do to convince you that what we had was real? That I wouldn't have cheated with anyone else? The day you walked out of your studio... I don't know how to describe it. It sounds corny, but I was just...struck."

She'd had the same reaction to him. She'd been so excited when he'd come back the next day, and everything had moved so fast from there. He'd told her later that he couldn't reveal he was married, that he was terrified he'd lose her, so one lie had led to another, which had led to another, and pretty soon he was living a life that wasn't even close to reality. But as wrong as it was to do what he did, she could understand how it could happen—because she'd been there. She'd experienced the power of their attraction, how instantly they'd connected, how his touch had set her skin racing with anticipation and excitement, how fulfilling their conversations had been and how often they'd talked until deep into the night. Those first love-drunk weeks together were unlike anything she'd ever known, which was why she felt so lost now.

Shit. What was she going to do?

"Claire?"

"What?"

"I know you felt the same way about me."

"I hate that I loved you and trusted you so much," she said.

"I've never felt the kind of pain I've experienced since I found out about Aida."

"The pain can go away if you'll let it. I'm right here, and I still want you. All you have to do is forgive me."

"And trust again," she added. That was the part she wasn't sure she could do.

"I'll earn your trust day by day. You'll see."

How? If she got back with him, she'd not only ruin her friendships with Aida and Marlow, she'd spend the next few days, weeks, *years* wondering if he was paying for an apartment for some other woman when he claimed to be called in to the hospital or working late.

"Just say you'll think about it," he said.

That was easy enough to promise, since getting back with him was all she *could* think about. "Okay."

After they disconnected, she slid her phone back under her towel and stared out at the sea. Fortunately, Aida and Marlow didn't seem to be paying her any attention. They'd started walking along the shoreline and had their backs to her as they approached a small jetty, where Marlow's family had a slip for their catamaran. What were they talking about?

Marlow was one of the smartest women Claire had ever known. She would definitely advise Claire not to allow Dutton back into her life. But Marlow was so cynical about men that she hadn't ever let a relationship get serious.

Claire wasn't convinced she was willing to pay that steep a price to keep her heart safe.

4

The warm, wet sand molded to Aida's bare feet, leaving perfect footprints as she walked beside Marlow until they reached the jetty. There, she wrapped the long red scarf she was wearing over her swimsuit around her head and tossed the tail over one shoulder as she turned to look back at the house. "It's so beautiful here," she said.

Marlow was wearing nothing except a pair of sunglasses and a bikini, the small triangles of white fabric creating a beautiful contrast with her golden skin, which tanned without any effort. She hadn't bothered with a hat or scarf, hadn't even put on sunblock because she was allergic to some of the chemicals in the various lotions. She said she'd pull on a T-shirt when she started to burn. "I've always loved coming to Teach, especially as a child," she said, facing the same direction. "It was the only time my father was really present. He was so busy when we were in Virginia. Even at home, in Georgia, he had people coming to the house all the time. But here it was different. He was able to leave his work behind and truly relax—be a father."

"I'm sorry you lost him." Aida had known Marlow for years. They'd met at the Toluca Lake Tennis and Fitness Club in Burbank when Marlow first moved to California—which wasn't too long after Aida had moved there herself—and had played tennis together ever since. But she'd never met Marlow's family.

"So am I. He was intelligent and kind, always fair—and honest. That's what I loved most about him. You could rely on what he said."

"Sounds like he would've made a good judge."

"That was a possibility for a while, until he decided to go into politics."

"Did your mother ever want a career of her own?"

"I think she was happy to be a politician's wife and a mother, which is a good thing, since her health would've made it difficult to do much more."

"How long ago was she diagnosed?"

"It's been twenty-six years. I was only eight at the time."

"That must've been a bad day."

Marlow slid her aviator-style Ray-Bans higher on the bridge of her nose. "It was."

"You've been really worried about her since your father died. Now that you've seen her, how do you think she's doing?" Eileen had seemed a little frail and not as mobile as other women her age, but she was still beautiful. To Aida, she looked exactly like her daughter.

"Okay, I guess. She has good days and bad days. Today was a bad day, but I've seen worse."

Aida gazed up at the house, which had been built on short pilings to protect it against hurricanes and had a whole wall of windows that faced the ocean, with expansive wooden decks on both levels and a spiral staircase descending from the top deck all the way to the sand. Ceiling fans turned slowly in the afternoon heat above the brightly colored cushions of the patio furniture. On the lower deck, there was a bar at one end. Aida had had money after marrying Dutton. Like his father before him, who was also a doctor, he made a good living. But nothing like this. This was a whole other level of wealthy. Even the guesthouse—painted white to match the main house and detached garage—had a stunning view, although it sat back a little farther amid the palm trees and other exotic flowering plants Aida wasn't familiar with. "Have your parents always had money?" she asked. "Or is all this the result of your father's time in the Senate?"

"Believe it or not, legislators don't make that much. Both my parents inherited quite a bit. My father was an attorney before he got involved in politics. He did pretty well for himself, too."

"Obviously." Aida peered up and down the exclusive beach. "I can't even imagine what it would be like growing up the way you did." As the daughter of an oil rig operator in North Dakota, she'd been in a much lower socioeconomic class. Her mother, Dottie, ran a day care out of the house to help cover the bills—something she did to this day—and now that Jim, her father, was too old for the oil fields, he worked as an auto mechanic. Her childhood home, where her parents had lived for almost forty years, wasn't even as big as the guesthouse here at Seaclusion.

A gold bracelet jangled around Marlow's thin wrist as she pulled her long dark hair off her neck, twisting it into a knot before letting it fall around her shoulders again. "Nothing about my childhood was normal. We had a housekeeper, a gardener, a driver—and three residences that we moved between. We were invited to important events, like presidential inaugurations. I enjoyed feeling as though I was somebody because of my father. I'm guessing any kid would. But...it could get lonely."

"Because you were an only child?"

"The only child of a woman who was often ill and a father who was extremely busy." She moved the string on her bikini top to check for color before moving it back again. "Plus, I skipped a couple of grades when I was seven, so my school years weren't quite the same as other kids'."

"You've never mentioned that before. Was it that the older kids wouldn't accept you or what?"

"They didn't treat me *badly*," she said. "I just never fit in. So I sort of withdrew, became aloof, as my father would say. Fitting in was easier as I got older, of course. But even my college experience was different, since I had to have a chaperone for the first two years."

"That would suck," Aida said. "I think you know I didn't get my degree, but I attended for a year, and that year wouldn't have been the same if I'd been only sixteen."

Marlow chuckled at Aida's expression. "I'm guessing a lot of alcohol was involved."

"Too much." She adjusted her scarf again. "So how long did it take you to get through college and law school? Did you do that faster than most other people, too?"

"It took six years."

"Instead of the standard seven."

"Yeah. But then I took a year off to travel and prepare for the bar."

Aida had never felt particularly smart. While Marlow had received attention for her brains, Aida had received attention for her looks. When she was a child, her mother had been obsessed with putting her in one beauty pageant after another. But once her two younger brothers came along, her parents couldn't afford the expensive dresses and the travel anymore. By then she'd had enough trophies to cover her entire dresser and then some—she'd won almost every contest she entered—but she didn't mind quitting the pageants. There'd been a lot of pressure to pose a certain way, walk a certain way, smile a certain way and not mess up on her talent, which was usually tap dancing. And although she'd never really applied herself in school, she'd always been well-liked and popular. That, along with the many compliments she'd always garnered, had made her feel destined to become a movie star. So it had come as a huge disappointment when she relocated to Hollywood but couldn't seem to land anything other than bit parts and commercials.

Maybe she would've succeeded eventually. But then Dutton came along, and he'd seemed like the perfect Prince Charming. Not only was he clever and sure to be successful, he was handsome and fit, with a great personality. He wasn't funny, exactly, but he had a dry quip or a one-liner for almost anything that often made her chuckle.

Never would she have guessed the fairy tale she'd been living with him would come to such a terrible end.

"Don't think about him," Marlow admonished.

Apparently what was going through Aida's mind was reflected on her face. She managed a smile but couldn't help glancing down the beach at Claire, who was lying on a towel with her hat covering her eyes, seemingly asleep. "It's hard not to."

Marlow's eyes wandered to Claire, too. "Does it upset you that he's been in touch with her again?"

"I'm trying not to let it bother me. I love Claire. Our friendship has been the one silver lining to this past year. I don't want Dutton to come between us. But..."

Marlow tilted her head to look more directly into Aida's face. "I hope Dutton isn't still calling you, too."

She grimaced. "No. He'd never be that stupid. He knows we're here together, that we'd find out he was two-timing us again."

"Not many men would attempt what he did, let alone get away with it for months and months." Marlow bent to pick up a shell, which she tossed back into the sea. "I've been curious—did you ever talk to his hairstylist?"

"Tori Valens?"

"Yeah, that was her name. I'd love to know why she finally came forward. She worked right next door to Claire and must've seen them together long before she blew the whistle."

"I wondered about that myself. She was his stylist, not mine—

we'd never met—so I tried to chalk it up to that and the fact that losing Dutton as a client would cost her at a time when her business was already suffering because of COVID. But after a couple of glasses of wine one evening, I looked her up on Instagram and DM'd to thank her for being willing to step forward at all."

"Did she respond?"

"I'd given her my number, so she called me the next day. She said she saw Dutton at the yoga studio a couple of times right after he met Claire, but he told her he was signing me up for yoga lessons and was thinking of taking them, too. Then both businesses had to close in the shutdown, so she didn't see either of them anymore. She might never have caught on, except an employee at the salon, one who stayed in touch with Claire, told her that Claire was involved with someone named Dutton and asked if it could be the same Dutton that Tori had as a client."

"I can see why she might ask. It's an unusual name."

"Exactly. She didn't think there could be two Duttons in her small circle of acquaintances. And sure enough…it was him."

Marlow adjusted her bracelet to bring the clasp around. "I wonder how long he would've tried to continue living a double life."

"So do I. He was working longer and longer hours. He was so distracted, so different toward the end. But I really thought it was the pandemic. I never dreamed he was pretending to be single, buying another woman gifts and trips, and putting her up in an apartment."

"That's bold," Marlow agreed.

"You know what hurts the most?"

Marlow caught and held her gaze. "What?"

"That I wasn't enough. That the love he felt for me could disappear so easily. Once someone who's supposed to love you forever abandons you, it's hard to explain what it does to your self-esteem, how you start to doubt whether you're even worthy of love."

"Don't say that! You're so beautiful and have so much to offer."

That was just it. Everyone mentioned her beauty. But what else did she have to offer? Maybe Marlow didn't get more specific because there wasn't anything else to say.

"Believe me, I've seen what it does," Marlow continued, oblivious to the fact that her comment had actually hurt more than it had helped because it triggered Aida's most troublesome insecurity. "Not only to you but to all my other clients who've had an unfaithful partner."

Aida dug a hole in the sand with her toes. "I almost wish he'd been a serial cheater instead of…instead of this. Then I could assume he'd done it for the excitement. Or the adrenaline rush of being so daring. Or to stave off the fear of getting old and undesirable."

"Not that any of that is justifiable," Marlow said wryly.

"No, of course not. But this…this is a far greater betrayal."

"What he did says much more about him than it does about you."

Aida heard the sympathy in Marlow's voice as she gazed down the beach again at Claire. She and the woman with whom her husband had an affair were so different—almost exact opposites. She was the blonde who loved high heels and fake eyelashes, had straight white teeth, big blue eyes and breast implants. Claire was the dark-haired, dark-eyed earthy girl who wore little or no makeup, dressed in yoga pants most of the time and demanded that everything be natural and organic. Aida knew Claire wasn't any prettier than she was. But Claire had a creamy complexion and a wide, easy smile. Her beauty was more wholesome, natural.

Apparently, that had appealed to Dutton.

"Earlier, when the three of us were walking to the guesthouse, I said he was too much of a narcissist to love anyone," she said to Marlow. "But what really bothers me is that he might truly be in love with *her*."

"It just seems that way because he's trying to salvage some semblance of the life he had prior to the divorce. He doesn't want to wind up alone."

Aida couldn't buy it. The fact that Dutton was in touch with Claire again meant he hadn't given up on her the way he'd given up on their marriage, and that terrified Aida. Would he and Claire end up together?

If so, she'd lose her friend as well as the man who'd promised her forever.

Walker sighed as he looked down at the new text on his phone. His mother wanted him to go back to Seaclusion. Eileen had some food to give him—those chocolate-covered strawberries and little sandwiches he'd had earlier—but he wasn't keen to return. Just being around Marlow made him feel the way he'd felt while they were growing up—like a second-class citizen.

He wished he could say he no longer found her attractive. That would make things a lot easier. But when he'd walked into the house and seen her sitting at the table earlier, he'd had to admit that she'd only gotten prettier. It wasn't just her appearance he liked, anyway. She was so damn smart. While some guys would've been intimidated by her intelligence, he found it incredibly sexy. It was her complete and utter indifference to him that got under his skin. He'd never had trouble getting a woman's attention—except hers. And that only made him want her more.

At least, that was how she'd affected him back then. He wasn't going to allow her to affect him that way now. Maybe his ego would tempt him to try again, to see if he could finally convince her to want him in return, but he wasn't going to fall for that. His ego could only get him in trouble if he let it.

Can't Reese bring them by? he texted back. He'd just gotten

home from work and was looking forward to taking a dip in the ocean before having dinner and a glass of wine while sitting on the beach, watching the sunset.

Reese isn't around. He must've gone over to a friend's.

What about tomorrow morning?

If you want these strawberries, you need to eat them tonight. They won't be good tomorrow.

He glanced at his SUV. He was standing on his front porch, hadn't even gone inside yet. He could easily drive a couple of miles, grab the food and make his mother and Eileen happy. And why not? Why let Marlow have any influence over what he did?

Okay. I'll be right there.

He told himself he'd be quick and probably wouldn't see Marlow, anyway. So, *of course*, she and her friends were coming up from the beach, crossing the lawn to the guesthouse, when he pulled in.

To make matters worse, she wasn't wearing anything except a tiny white bikini.

His mouth went dry the second he saw her, bringing back all the longing he'd felt, and he was tempted to back out again. There was something about her, and he couldn't seem to outgrow the way it made him feel.

But leaving wasn't really an option. She'd already spotted him. So had her much friendlier companions. As all three women stopped and waited for him to get out, he muttered an expletive under his breath and opened the door.

"Hey!" the one named Aida called as he started toward them. "Welcome back."

He managed a smile. "Thanks."

"Don't tell me you're still working," Marlow's other friend, Claire, said.

He hadn't had time to change out of his uniform. "No, just got off. My mother texted me to swing by and pick up some leftovers from earlier. I guess you ladies didn't do your part, so I have to take up the slack." He kept his focus on Claire, who'd spoken to him last, while pretending he wasn't supremely conscious of Marlow standing next to him, almost naked.

God, she was beautiful.

"It's nice of you to do us such a big favor," Aida teased.

"Have you had dinner yet?" Claire asked.

"Not yet. I—"

"Great," she broke in before he could finish. "Because we were talking about building a fire in the pit on the beach and roasting some hot dogs and marshmallows. Maybe you'd like to join us."

"You should," Aida agreed. "You can't eat all those strawberries on an empty stomach."

As arrogant as Marlow had always been, her friends seemed much more open to his companionship, but he knew better than to get involved. Assuming a pained expression, as though he regretted refusing, he said, "I was planning to throw a steak on the grill back home."

Aida's bottom lip jutted out in a flirty pout. "You'd rather eat alone?"

"Maybe he's not planning to be alone," Marlow said, speaking for the first time.

Walker couldn't tell if she was fishing to see whether he was currently seeing someone, offering him an easy out because she didn't want him to accept the invitation or simply stating that they shouldn't assume too much. "Maybe next time," he said, ignoring the comment. "I appreciate the offer, but I'll just grab the strawberries and get out of your way."

"We're going to hold you to that," Aida said.

"I'm looking forward to it," he told her with a nod and continued to the house.

He could feel their eyes on his back as he went inside, but when he came out again, he figured they were in the guesthouse, getting ready for their bonfire on the beach, because he didn't see them. He was relieved about that; he'd purposely chatted with his mother and Eileen for fifteen minutes to give Marlow and her friends time, hoping he'd be able to leave without running into them again. But his brother was now leaning against his police SUV, waiting for him.

"I thought you were gone," Walker said.

"I was," Reese responded. "Had to run to the store."

"For what?" Walker asked curiously.

Reese grinned. "Nothing."

Walker swiped the small brown sack he was holding.

"Hey," Reese complained and grabbed his arm, but Walker resisted his attempts to take it back while he peeked inside.

"Condoms?" he said in surprise. "Why would you want to keep that from me? I'm the one who's been on your ass to always use one."

Reese yanked the bag from him. "Because it's none of your business," he mumbled, but it wasn't too hard to put the puzzle pieces together.

"Wait a second. You got these because—" Walker glanced over his shoulder to make sure they were still alone but lowered his voice anyway "—because of the women who are staying here?"

"Have you seen them?" he responded. "They're freaking gorgeous!"

"They're at least ten years older than you," Walker said, pointing out the obvious.

"What's that to me?" Reese asked. "Age is just a number."

"No, it's not," he said. "You start messing with them, it

49

could threaten your place here. It might even cause problems for Mom."

Reese checked the yard before saying, in a low whisper, "The blonde wants me, dude. I could tell almost immediately. So... is there any way I could borrow fifty bucks until I get paid? I'd like to take her to dinner or something."

"I'm not going to loan you any more money," Walker said. "Especially for that."

His brother scowled. "Come on, man. It's just fifty bucks."

"You have to learn not to blow your whole paycheck. You won't do that if I keep bailing you out."

"You're not my father," he said, "even though you've always tried to act like you are."

"I'm about the only father you've ever had. And I'm not giving you any more money. But I will offer a piece of advice—stay away from Marlow and her friends."

"Yeah, yeah. I knew you'd say that. That's why I wasn't going to tell you."

"Reese—"

"I've got to go," his brother said, skirting around him. "They invited me to a bonfire tonight, and since I'm now prepared—" he lifted the sack with the condoms "—I need to shower up."

"Hey!" Walker called after him.

He stopped and turned.

"You're not going to listen to me, are you?"

"I don't know," he said. "We'll see how it goes."

Walker sighed as he watched his little brother climb the stairs to his apartment.

Reese looked back before going inside. "Whatever happens, I'm going to have a much better time than you are tonight."

"It's all fun and games until someone gets hurt," Walker muttered and climbed into his SUV.

5

It was too hot near the fire, so Marlow pulled her chair to the much cooler perimeter, where the bright flames gave way to the softer light of the fading sunset. Claire and Aida were joking and talking to Reese as he roasted yet another hot dog. But Marlow was too annoyed to get into the revelry.

She hated the way his brother had acted when they'd run into him on their walk back from the beach earlier. She hated the way he'd acted when he'd had a cup of tea with them shortly after they arrived, too. Talk about holding a grudge! She'd been a teenager when they'd had the encounters that formed his opinion of her, but he seemed to be holding fast to that opinion even though she'd grown up since then and they hadn't interacted much in the past ten years.

Surely he had to wonder if she'd changed.

Or maybe he didn't care. She hadn't handled his interest as kindly as she could have back then. She'd acted a little stuck-up. But it hadn't been *all* her. He'd once called her a rich bitch under his breath when she passed him, and she didn't hold that against him.

Probably because she'd deserved it. That was the year she'd

turned eighteen. They were at the Georgia house for Christmas, and she'd been especially brutal to him. She still felt bad about that and wished he'd give her the chance to start over, so it wouldn't have to be so stilted and awkward every time they bumped into each other. The island was only seven square miles. As the chief of police, he'd be roving around Teach all summer. And with his mother working at the house, his brother living on the property and her own mother so keen to include him whenever possible, Marlow was bound to encounter him again and again, even if he did his best to stay away.

Claire brought the new bottle of wine they'd just opened over to Marlow and refilled her plastic flute. "Hey, is something wrong? You've been quiet since we came out here."

Because she wasn't interested in flirting with Reese. "The wine's making me mellow. That's all."

Claire peered up at the sky. "Wow! Look at that."

As darkness fell, the stars were beginning to appear. "I never notice the sky when I'm in LA. The sunsets here are pretty incredible, too."

"This is so nice, Marlow. Thanks for inviting us."

"I'm glad you could come."

It was difficult to tell in the gathering dusk, but Marlow thought she read a sheepish expression on Claire's face. "Even after what I told you earlier—about Dutton?"

"Especially after what you told me earlier about Dutton." She took a sip of the extra dry merlot they'd brought from the house with all their other supplies. "Being away for three months might give you the space you need to decide what you really want for your future."

"I hope I make the right decision." She dropped down in the sand. "I saw you talking to Aida when we were on the beach earlier. Was she...very upset?"

"No. She's handling the news surprisingly well."

"I'm glad. The last thing I want is to hurt her."

Marlow had known Aida much longer than Claire. She hadn't met Claire until Aida had introduced them, and that was after Aida had learned about the affair. But Marlow had liked Claire from the start. She was down-to-earth, inherently kind, easy to be around. "I think she understands that you're a victim in this situation, too."

Claire pushed the bottle into the sand beside her so it wouldn't fall over. "How do you manage to keep your life on such an even keel?"

Marlow hadn't had any serious romantic relationships. That was how. She'd been so driven in her career, so determined to get her degree, open her practice and build a name for herself. She'd devoted all her focus and energy to those things.

Then the pandemic hit, and she'd been cut off from almost all other activities. That was when she'd realized just how tenuous human existence was. There had to be more to living than professional success. People said that all the time, of course, and she agreed. It made sense. But she'd been Icarus, flying too close to the sun—was never truly committed to achieving the proper balance until the past year, which was why she was pulling away from work to devote more of herself to her friends and family. Inviting Claire and Aida to the island to spend the summer with her had been part of that effort.

"I haven't gone through what you have. Losing your house would be catastrophic. But losing your business, too? And finding out the man you're dating is already married? You're holding up well, considering."

Claire grinned at her response. "When you put it like that, I guess I'm lucky I'm still functioning at all."

"Exactly. Things will get easier, though. Don't worry."

"They already have, in a way. At least my house has been rebuilt. Being homeless was...hard to describe. It felt like my whole life had been turned upside down, and it was Dutton who helped me catch my balance and put everything right again."

"Or he took advantage of the terrible situation to get away with stuff he wouldn't have been able to otherwise. Just because he helped you through a difficult period doesn't mean he's the hero of this story."

"It feels that way sometimes."

"Until you look at it from a different perspective."

"I wish I had your perspective more often."

"Fortunately, I'm here to remind you," Marlow said with a grin.

Claire smiled back at her. "Your year hasn't been easy, either. You just seem to handle rough waters better than the rest of us."

"Losing my father has been tough. And I'm worried about my mother. But I've been worried about her most of my life, so that's nothing new. And the pandemic was actually good for my business. I can't complain there."

"It's caused so many people to turn to alcohol," Claire commented.

"That's true. And alcohol and financial stress are two things that'll break up a marriage quicker than anything else."

"Alcohol, financial stress and *infidelity*. I hate what Aida's been through. And I hate being the cause."

"*Dutton* is the cause," Marlow clarified.

"If only I'd realized he was lying to me sooner, before I fell so deeply in love."

"You never doubted him?"

"Not once. He seemed totally straightforward and legit."

"A good con man always does." Marlow leaned back and looked up at the house that meant so much to her. Her mother had gone to bed early, and Rosemary had mentioned she planned to spend the evening with a book. Knowing they were there, as always, helped. But it was strange to think her father would never return to this place.

Aida and Reese put down their wineglasses and started to-

ward the water. "We're going for a swim. You guys interested?"
Aida called as they passed.

"I'm too comfortable," Marlow said.

Claire dusted the sand off her hands before pouring herself
another glass of wine. "I'm good, too," she said, even though
the two of them could no longer hear her.

Aida and Reese plunged into the sea, their laughter carrying
over the tumbling waves.

"Aida's going to sleep with your housekeeper's son," Claire
said, her voice low. "You know that, right?"

"Maybe she needs to reassure herself that she's still got it."
Marlow grimaced. "I just wish she'd choose someone else."

"It won't cause any problems between you and Rosemary,
will it?"

"Reese is twenty-two, not sixteen. Still, I'm hoping Rosemary doesn't find out."

"What about Walker? What do you think he'll have to say
about one of your friends hooking up with his little brother?"

Marlow was embarrassed imagining what Walker might make
of that. "I hope he doesn't find out, either."

Claire finished her wine, set the glass aside and hugged her
knees to her chest. "I noticed that he avoids looking at you when
he's around. Is there a reason? Or am I reading into it?"

This comment surprised Marlow. Aida would never have noticed. But Claire was more thoughtful, more observant. "We
have a bit of…history," she admitted.

"And you haven't mentioned that? You've been holding back
when you're so intimately familiar with *our* dirty laundry?" she
teased.

"There's nothing to talk about. Not really."

"What happened between you two? And when?"

Marlow was feeling a slight buzz. She'd had too much wine
but didn't put her glass down because she enjoyed finally being
able to relax. "We had several…encounters."

"That sounds interesting. What kind of encounters?"

"He had a thing for me when we were growing up. The first time he tried to kiss me, I was fourteen and he was sixteen."

"And you weren't interested?" she said in surprise.

"Not in the least."

"Is something wrong with him? Because he's gorgeous."

"There's nothing wrong with him. I just…took him for granted."

"Where were you when he tried to kiss you?"

"In Georgia. It was after a school dance."

"Rosemary's been with your family that long?"

"Even longer. She started working for my parents before I was born."

"So… Walker and his family would come to the island with you every summer?"

She nodded. "They'd stay in the apartment over the garage."

"What about Walker's father? Did he come, too?"

"No. He was part of the family then, but he had a job in Georgia and couldn't come to Teach. Rosemary and Walker—and then Reese, after he arrived—used to go home every weekend to see him instead."

"Who watched her kids while she worked?"

"She just kept them with her."

"How nice of your parents to allow that."

"They didn't mind."

"So where is Reese and Walker's father now?"

"I have no idea. He left when Reese was four or five. I once heard my father say he skipped out on paying his child support, too, so I get the impression he doesn't have a relationship with his boys."

"How sad."

"Yeah. I wish I'd had more empathy for Walker when we were young. He'd been around since I could remember, so he wasn't anything special to me. I had big hopes and dreams, and I didn't want any boy, least of all Walker, to get in my way."

"Maybe you weren't ready when he made that move."

"Yeah, well, he made plenty of other moves, both before and after I went to college. He was *too* devoted to me." Marlow closed her eyes for a moment. "I remember having a bonfire like this for my fifteenth birthday. My father was away, and my mother was trying not to hover, which wasn't easy for her, especially since she'd tried talking me out of having the party. A storm was on the way, so the sea was rough. But I promised her we wouldn't get in the water."

"Oh, no. I can guess where this is going."

"And you'd be right. A kid named Brandon Warner sneaked over some beer. We were drinking and starting to act stupid when someone dared me to go into the ocean."

"Was Walker there?"

"At the time, I assumed he was in their apartment. My mother made me invite him, but the way I did it let him know I didn't really want him around, so he didn't come."

"Did he know the other kids? Were they from the island or what?"

"He knew the ones my parents had flown in to celebrate with me. He went to the same private school I did."

"His mother could afford that?"

"My parents picked up the tab. They've always done extra things like that. I think it's part of the reason Rosemary has stuck with us for so long."

"Did you and Walker hang out with the same people at school?"

"Not really. I hung out with the rich kids, and he hung out with the kids who lived near him and went to the public school."

"Got it. So what happened when you went into the ocean that night?"

"I said I wasn't scared, that I'd swim out to the rock. And I did. But just before I reached it, I got caught in a riptide that dragged me under and threw me against it. I hit my head so hard I got disoriented and almost drowned." She took the last sip of her wine. "Walker saved me."

"He did?"

"Yep. The next thing I knew, he was there in the water with me. He towed me back to shore and dragged me out onto the beach. I'll never forget looking up and seeing the scared expression on his face as he knelt over me. Then I started throwing up beer and seawater."

Claire's eyes went wide. "Walker saved your life?"

"Who knows? Maybe I would've been able to get out on my own eventually. But we never had to find out because he risked his life to go in after me." Marlow hadn't thought of that incident for years; she'd purposely shoved it into the back of her mind. "The worst part is that I didn't even thank him. I was embarrassed that this had happened in front of people I was trying to impress and pretended I hadn't needed him to do what he did."

"That doesn't sound like you."

"What can I say? I was a little bitch when I was growing up." Walker had been right about that…

"You were dealing with your own issues. Being two years younger than all your classmates couldn't have been easy. Having a father who was a US senator probably put a lot of pressure on you, too."

Leave it to Claire to put the best possible spin on it. "Doesn't matter. I shouldn't have acted that way."

"You were just a kid. Don't be too hard on yourself."

Now that Marlow had opened that compartment in her brain, so many other memories began tumbling out—like the time Walker had been asked to drive her to the airport when she was going back to college after Christmas. Before she got out of the car, he told her he hated her but pulled her back to try to kiss her anyway. She'd told him she hated him, too, and shoved him away. "I don't even know how he realized I was in the water that night at the party."

"He must've been watching you—or watching over you."

The subtle change in the way Claire finished that statement made her feel even worse.

"Did he stay in touch after you got your law degree and opened your practice?"

"No. But he was always around for part of the summer or holidays when I came home. With time, I think he just...started to hate me for real."

"You don't believe he hates you now..."

"I do."

"Have you ever tried to talk to him about the past?"

"No. I'm sure he doesn't want to remember those days any more than I do."

"It's hard to move on if you don't address the problem. Get it out in the open. Maybe if you told him you regret not being kinder, and you're sorry if you hurt him, he'll forgive you, and you two could be friends."

Marlow bit her lip as she considered Claire's response. That would mean confronting the past. Bringing up an awkward topic. The way he treated her these days, she couldn't imagine he'd have any interest in doing that.

Or...was she just making excuses for not doing the right thing? She'd always been too proud for her own good.

"I *do* owe him an apology," she admitted, finally acknowledging the truth.

Claire nudged her with an elbow. "Then give him one."

6

Claire and Aida were asleep by the time Marlow worked up the nerve to get her bike out of the garage and pedal to the cove. She and Claire had wound up going swimming with Aida and Reese, after all. They'd talked, laughed and drank until eleven, but then Marlow had told them she was tired, and they all walked back to the guesthouse together.

She'd been a little nervous when they were saying goodbye to Reese that Aida would suggest staying out later with him, but she hadn't. She'd had so much wine she'd grown maudlin and teary over her divorce, and that had changed the dynamic. Marlow didn't know what would happen as the summer progressed, but she wasn't going to have to worry about Aida sleeping with Rosemary's youngest son tonight.

Once Aida and Claire had gone to bed, she'd tried to sleep, too, telling herself she'd apologize to Walker when she saw him next. But she had no idea who would be around then. And the memory of him risking his life to pull her out of the ocean, as well as the hurt on his face that day at the airport, as though he'd known better than to try to kiss her again but simply couldn't help himself, kept cycling through her brain. Since she couldn't stop thinking about him, she'd finally gotten up, pulled on some shorts and a T-shirt, and quietly slipped outside.

She might as well apologize now and get it over with. Maybe he wouldn't care, but at least she would've done all she could to right her wrongs where he was concerned.

She hadn't been to the cove since high school. She'd driven past the turnoff that led to it, but she'd had no reason to go any closer.

The dirt road that jutted off from the main road always used to wash out during hurricane season. The house down on the beach used to flood, too. Hurricane season started in June, so it was just getting underway. Fortunately, there hadn't been any major storms yet.

As she left the streetlights behind, along with the pavement, she had to use the flashlight on her phone to light the ground ahead of her, which made it hard to hold on. But she didn't have much farther to go.

It was nearly midnight—too late to show up at someone's house unannounced. But she hoped Walker would understand when he heard what she had to say. She also hoped the dark and the quiet would provide enough privacy to make the conversation a bit easier.

Or maybe he was already asleep. When she thought of that, and how nervous she was, she was tempted to turn around. But she'd already made the effort to come out here, so she decided to keep going.

Her arms acted like shock absorbers on the handlebars as she rolled over rocks and through ruts. The beam of the flashlight on her phone bounced around, too, but there was a full moon that hung low in the sky, giving her just enough secondary light that she knew she could make it.

Once she saw Walker's house, she knew it wasn't likely to get flooded again. It'd been repaired, painted and lifted on stilts.

And the improvements looked so new she assumed he was the one who'd made them.

"Here we go," she muttered as she got off her bike. She could no longer pedal on the gravel he'd used as part of his landscaping.

She would normally have paused to admire the setting—the fat moon above the water, the soft sand sloping down to meet the fingerlike waves of what appeared to be a calm sea, the palm trees that made his house seem remote. As Rosemary had said, it was particularly pretty here. But now that she'd arrived, she found her errand even more daunting than she'd expected.

The lights in the house were on, and once she leaned her bike against the closest piling and crept up the stairs to the door, she could hear the TV.

For a second, she was reminded of the flippant remark she'd made earlier suggesting he might not be spending the evening alone. Did he have company?

Rosemary had said he wasn't married. That didn't mean he couldn't be in a relationship, however. And if he *did* have a woman over, Marlow's appearance at his house in the middle of the night would be even weirder.

Attempting to check things out before she made him aware of her presence, she peered through the front window and saw him right there in the living room, watching TV while lifting weights. He didn't have anything on except a pair of cut-off sweatpants that hung low on his lean hips, but he seemed to be alone.

He looked good, she thought grudgingly. *Too* good.

Again, she almost left. Walker didn't need her friendship—not anymore. This was a case of too little, too late.

But somehow, it was important to her to make sure he knew she wasn't the person she'd been. She'd often considered apologizing to him, if the opportunity ever presented itself, not only so he might forgive her but so that she might be able to forgive herself. Why not follow through and get it over with?

Drawing a deep breath, she lifted her hand and knocked on the front door.

He continued doing arm curls, didn't react. He hadn't heard her, so she knocked louder.

When he dropped the weights, she felt the vibration through the floor and curved her fingernails into her palms as the door swung open.

"You." Visibly taken aback to find her on his doorstep without any prior warning and in the middle of the night, he wiped the sweat that was dripping off a few of the curly locks that fell across his forehead. "What's wrong?" he asked. "Is your mother okay? Is *my* mother okay?"

Of course he'd jump to the conclusion that there must be an emergency. Since when had she ever sought him out? "They're fine. I..."

The words jammed in her throat. What had made her think this was a good idea? Her conscience had put her up to it—her conscience and Claire. But now she was here and he was standing so close, she couldn't seem to focus on anything except his chest, muscled and slick with perspiration. He seemed so much taller than ever before, which was sort of intimidating, and he smelled earthy and warm with just a hint of cedar.

"Are you going to finish that statement?" he asked.

She cleared her throat. She was an attorney; she was never at a loss for words. But she didn't know how to get this conversation started. After so long, apologizing to him seemed random and out of the blue—like the stupidest idea ever. "Never mind. I shouldn't have come. I'm sorry for interrupting your evening."

Whipping around, she grabbed the railing so she wouldn't fall as she hurried down the stairs.

"Marlow!"

She was on the third step when she turned.

"You're not here to complain about Reese, are you? I told him to stay away from you and your friends, but..."

He'd told his brother to stay away? Why? "But…" she prompted, her curiosity piqued.

He shrugged. "I didn't get the impression he was going to listen to me."

"Why did you tell him to stay away?"

He blinked in surprise. "Because I knew you wouldn't like it. He's no different than me, right? He's the housekeeper's son."

He still thought she considered herself too good for them both. That should've given her the intro she needed to tell him how wrong she'd been when they were younger and how sorry she was. But everything she read in his body language indicated that, even if she said the words, it wouldn't make any difference. "So you've already made up your mind about me, and no matter what I say, you're not going to change it."

"Excuse me?"

"Is it going to be this terrible every time we see each other?" she asked.

"Terrible?" he echoed.

"I feel this…overwhelming negative energy coming from you."

He scowled. "Because I don't worship at your feet anymore?"

"I don't expect you to worship at my feet," she said. "But I was hoping we could—I don't know—bury the hatchet. Maybe… try to be friends."

"I've been nothing but polite," he insisted.

He'd purposely ignored her offer of friendship—another sign he wasn't interested. "I'm not saying you haven't. This is something else. I can tell how much you don't like me, and—"

"I never said that," he broke in.

Her mind flashed to their encounter at the airport, the one that'd ended so badly. "Actually, you did. You said you hated me."

"That was a long time ago."

"So?"

"I don't care anymore. And for the record, you said you hated me, too." He stepped out to look around. "Where's your mother's car or whatever you drove over here?"

I don't care anymore. She wasn't sure why those words hit her so hard, but it was all she could do not to flinch. "I didn't drive," she said numbly. "I rode a bike."

"You *what?*"

She gripped the railing a little tighter. "It's only a couple of miles."

"It's dark," he pointed out as though she must be an idiot.

"There were streetlights until I hit the turnoff. And I had my phone."

"Your phone's not going to be any help if you get hit and killed by a car."

"I'm not going to get hit. God, forget I came!" She finished descending the stairs, more eager than ever to escape. Tough divorce attorney Marlow Madsen was on the verge of tears, but she didn't want him to know that.

The wooden steps creaked as he followed her down. "Wait. Let me give you a ride."

"No, that's okay. There's no need," she insisted, so he'd go back inside, and was slightly relieved that she sounded somewhat normal, despite the tightening of her throat.

He took her bike away before she could get on it. "Have you been drinking?"

Shocked, she stepped back. "I had a couple glasses of wine earlier, but I'm not drunk, if that's what you're asking."

"I hope not. Because it's against the law to bike while under the influence. You know that, right?"

She felt her jaw sag. "Are you kidding me?"

"Not at all. What if you veered into the street? You could cause an accident."

"Are you looking for a reason to *arrest* me?"

"Only if I have to."

She got the impression he'd like to do exactly that. Apparently, he hated her even more than she'd thought. "You're serious!"

"It's nothing personal," he said. "I'm the chief of police on this island. The safety of its citizens is my responsibility."

True, but she suspected he wouldn't be making a big deal out of this if she was anyone else.

"That includes *your* safety," he continued. "I can't allow you to ride home in the dark, especially if you've been drinking."

"Don't let the power go to your head," she said. "I'm completely sober."

"This isn't about power. I owe it to your mother to make sure you're safe."

"No, you don't. Give me my bike." She tried to wrest it away from him, but he lifted it over his head, out of reach, before setting it behind him.

Angry, embarrassed and ashamed that she'd given someone her mother loved so much a reason to be treating her this way, she began to blink faster. "There's almost no traffic this time of night," she argued.

"All it takes is one car. But there's no reason to be upset." He put out his hand as though he was soothing a frightened or dangerous animal. "Just stay put until I get my keys, and I'll take you home. Okay?"

He was waiting for her to agree. "Okay," she said. But as soon as he went back up the stairs and into the house, she grabbed her bike, jumped on it and took off.

So much for attempting to apologize. He'd made it clear that he didn't want her apology. He didn't want *anything* from her. She should've known it would be a mistake to come here. The day he'd told her he hated her—and meant it—something had snapped inside him.

She'd seen the change in his eyes.

★ ★ ★

By the time Walker had thrown on a shirt, shoved his feet into a pair of flip-flops and jumped inside his SUV, Marlow was out of sight. But he caught up with her easily enough. She was still trying to power through the soft dirt and rocks to get back to the road.

He didn't try to stop her, though. His only goal was to make sure she got home safely.

"Just keep pedaling," he said, even though she couldn't hear him, as he rolled slowly along behind her. "And whatever you do, don't fall."

When she twisted around to look at him as though he was making her nervous, he slowed even more, giving her plenty of space. As long as he could see she was safe, he didn't plan on forcing her to get into his truck. Why would he? Marlow Madsen had always been his kryptonite. The less contact he had with her, the better.

As soon as they reached the main road, he flipped on his hazards. Although he planned to creep along behind her for the whole two miles, if that was how she wanted it, another few feet later she got a flat.

"No way," he said as he leaned up over the dash to see what was going on.

Marlow ducked her head to peer at her back tire, but she kept pedaling—or trying to.

Coming up beside her, he lowered the passenger window. "Do you mind if we make this easy?"

The bike wobbled so much she had to get off. But she didn't turn to him for help. She began pushing it instead.

"Marlow!" he yelled.

She looked over at him.

"I don't want to spend the rest of the night doing this. Do you?"

"You don't have to be here," she said. "Go back to your place. I can manage."

"I'm not leaving until I know you're home safe. There's not much crime on the island, but shit can happen anywhere. Can you imagine how your mother would feel if someone were to find your dead body on the side of the road in the morning?" Just mentioning the possibility brought the death of her father to mind. Walker had always respected Tiller Madsen, wanted to be like him instead of his own deadbeat father. Although Tiller had been too preoccupied with his work and his own family to give Walker much attention, he had paid for his education and been kind whenever he did notice him.

Walker felt he should probably say something to Marlow about her recent loss. But he didn't know how to broach the subject, not while keeping her at an emotional distance.

"My *dead body*?" Still pushing her bike, she gave him a dirty look. "That's gruesome."

"It could happen. Why risk it? Let me throw your bike in the back and drive you the rest of the way. We can be at Seaclusion in a couple of minutes."

Ignoring him, she plodded on.

"Quit being so damn stubborn!" he said. "This isn't even making sense."

He must've gotten through to her at last, because she finally gave up and stood in place while he got out and came around. "Thank you," he muttered as he took the bike.

He paused to check that the passenger door wasn't locked, so she could get in while he loaded the bike.

Once he'd finished with that and climbed in beside her, he turned off his hazards and veered back onto the road. "You must've picked up a nail," he said. "I've done so much remodeling in the past six months it doesn't surprise me. But Reese can change that tire for you tomorrow."

No response.

He glanced over at her. "Now we're not even speaking?"

"What do you want me to say?" she asked.

"My mother and brother live on your family's property. On top of that, this is a small island. We're bound to be thrown together now and then—at least until you leave at the end of summer."

"I bet you're already counting the days," she grumbled.

He didn't comment on that. He *was* sort of counting the days. He had three months ahead of him—three months to prove to himself, if no one else, that his lifelong obsession with Marlow no longer held sway over him. She'd extended an olive branch, which was kind enough on the face of it. But the fact that she was being nice only made her more dangerous.

Given his weakness for her, something he'd had since he could remember, he couldn't risk associating with her in any way. That might well tempt him back into the quicksand from which he'd finally escaped. "I'm saying there's no reason we can't be polite to each other while you're here."

"You want me to keep my distance—so there's no real friendship between us—but to be polite when we do happen to meet. Is that it?"

When he looked over at her again, he saw the tears glistening in her eyelashes and purposely strengthened himself against them. Whatever she was feeling, she'd get over it. He didn't have the power to hurt her; she'd never cared enough about him. "That sounds reasonable to me."

She nibbled at her bottom lip while he turned into the drive at Seaclusion and put his truck in Park.

"What do you say?" he asked before getting out. "For the sake of our mothers, can we be civil to each other?"

He saw her throat work as she swallowed. Then her chest lifted, and she turned toward him with a determined yet wobbly smile. "Of course," she said brightly—too brightly. "I realize my comeuppance is long overdue. So you've had the chance to hit me back, which I hope felt great, and now I'll stay away and respect your wishes."

"I would never hit you, so maybe you could choose a different metaphor. But thank you. I just want to be left alone."

"Understood. You're not interested in an apology, so I won't attempt to burden you with one. I'd still like to thank you for... for saving my life that night I almost drowned, though. I pretended it was nothing at the time, but... I was in serious trouble."

With that, she got out and waited patiently for him to unload her bike. "Thanks for the ride," she said softly, careful not to brush his hand as she took the handlebars.

"Good night," he said and let his breath seep out in a long sigh as he watched her put the bike in the garage and go into the guesthouse. He wanted to believe he'd put up a valiant defense against what she did to him—what she had always done to him. But as he got back into his truck, he knew she would haunt him for the rest of the night.

He was afraid she might just haunt him for the rest of the summer.

7

Rosemary felt slightly nauseous as she rearranged the pantry. She'd been a nervous wreck, waiting for the other shoe to drop ever since Tiller died. And now that Marlow was home, her apprehension had only grown worse.

"What's going on with you?" Reese demanded, frowning when she accidentally dropped a brand-new bag of flour, causing it to burst open on the floor.

She motioned for him to keep his voice down as she hurried to clean up the mess. Eileen had had a hard night. Rosemary had heard her weeping in her bedroom—the poor woman would probably never get over the loss of her husband—and now that she seemed to be sleeping soundly, Rosemary didn't want her to be disturbed. "Shh. Nothing's wrong," she whispered. "It was just an accident."

Reese got up from the kitchen table to help. "You've been acting strange lately."

A cold finger of dread ran down Rosemary's back, but she kept her gaze riveted on the mess so her son wouldn't see the anxiety that was eating her up inside. "Because everything's different now."

"Different *how?*"

"Tiller's gone. He was always so healthy. I never dreamed he'd die at sixty-one."

"Yeah, it's sad. He was too young to die. But…it shouldn't really affect you."

Tiller's death had more far-reaching implications than Reese realized. "You're kidding, right? He was the one who paid my salary from the very beginning. He was a kind, stabilizing influence for you boys, a good role model when…when I couldn't count on your father. He made sure we had what we needed, helped send you and Walker to a private school and then college, decided where we'd all live and when we'd go wherever we were going. Eileen and Marlow aren't the only ones who've suffered a loss. He was…he was the anchor to *our* lives, as well."

"I get that. I'm grateful to him, too. But it's not as if you have to worry about losing your job because he passed. Mrs. Madsen relies on you more than ever."

"It's a change, that's all I mean," she muttered. "I've never liked change." Especially not *this* change—because of the risk it brought.

Reese held the dustbin while she swept up the flour. "Mrs. Madsen is treating you okay, though, isn't she?" he asked when what he'd said so far didn't seem to offer enough comfort.

"Of course." Eileen had always been good to her. Although she could be persnickety and impatient, and she was definitely spoiled—she'd had money all her life—she was also very kind and generous.

"Then…is it Dad?"

"Of course not. What would make you ask about your father?"

He put up his free hand to indicate she should hold on a second. "Before you go too far down that road, I know he's contacting you again. I saw a text come in on your phone the other day."

She wished he hadn't seen that. She wasn't ready to tell him or Walker about Rudy, even though Rudy had been back in contact with her for over a year. She'd tried to convince him to leave her alone, but he claimed she was the only woman he'd ever truly loved, and that he was bound and determined to be the kind of man she needed.

And she wanted to believe him. The chance to have a complete family, the kind of family she'd always dreamed of, suddenly seemed like a possibility again. And that made it difficult, even at this late date, not to succumb to his entreaties.

"He's been sober for five years now," she said, giving Reese the rationale she'd been using.

Her son cast her a skeptical look. "So he says."

"He's different these days, Reese. Really." Or maybe she just wanted to believe that because she was lonelier than ever. With Tiller gone, and so suddenly, it felt as though her life had come to a screeching halt right along with Eileen's. There'd be no more traipsing back and forth to Washington, DC, or Atlanta. Eileen planned to put those properties up for sale. No more entertaining important dignitaries and other politicians. No more campaign advisers scurrying through the house. No more media companies shoving the furniture to one side so they could shoot ads whenever Tiller came up for reelection. He'd been the focus of so much energy and excitement.

With him gone and Eileen spending most every day in bed, there was far less for Rosemary to do. Besides that, Walker and Reese were adults now and didn't require nearly as much time and effort. She had a gaping hole in her life, and she was beginning to believe Rudy might be able to fill it.

"You can forgive him for taking off on you?" Reese said. "For sticking you with all the work and expense of raising two kids who also belonged to him?"

She still harbored some resentment, but she was trying to work through it. "I don't know," she admitted.

"Well, maybe you can forgive him, but I can't."

Rosemary got the mop so she could finish cleaning the floor while Reese went back to his breakfast. "He'd like a relationship with you," she found herself saying. He talked a great deal about Walker and Reese and how sorry he was for missing out on the majority of their lives.

Reese shook his head. "No way. And I doubt Walker will be open to having a relationship with him, either."

She sighed. She couldn't blame them. They'd seen Rudy at his worst, would probably never be able to forget the screaming matches, the objects he'd thrown around the house and the holes he'd punched in the walls. She still had a scar on her temple from when he accidentally knocked her against a brick wall while he was in one of his drunken tirades.

Tired of all the fighting, Walker had gotten involved and tried to get him to settle down. That had been their last big fight, the one that'd caused her to kick Rudy out, and when she wouldn't let him back in the house, he'd abandoned them entirely.

She paused to finger the scar, and Reese pointed his fork at her while he chewed. "There you go," he said. "Remember that."

"Rosemary, I heard a thump. Is everything okay?" Eileen came shuffling into the kitchen in her robe and slippers but stopped when she saw Reese at the table. "Oh! I didn't realize we had company."

Because Rosemary got up so much earlier than Eileen, she made breakfast for her son once in a while. It was their only chance for a private visit. He left for work by the time Eileen woke, so Rosemary assumed her employer wouldn't mind.

Still, she felt slightly self-conscious about inviting someone into Eileen's house without her express permission. After so long, the line between friend and employee could get blurred, but she knew if she took advantage of Eileen's kindness, she could find herself without a job. "I've made an egg scramble. Would you like to eat now or wait until later?"

"Look at me," Eileen said, too flustered to answer the question. "I'm not even dressed."

That was her way of letting Rosemary know she didn't appreciate Reese seeing her before she'd showered and gotten "presentable." The tension inside Rosemary tightened. Fortunately, Reese got the hint. He jumped up and brought his plate to the sink as he said, "You look beautiful to me."

"I look like an old hag," she insisted.

"You couldn't look like a hag if you tried." Reese dropped a kiss on Rosemary's cheek. "I'm going to be late if I don't go. I hope you both have a great day," he said on his way out.

Once the door closed behind him, Rosemary could breathe easier. "Would you like me to bring your breakfast into the dining room?" she asked Eileen.

"No. I'll wait," she replied. "I just had to see what caused that loud noise. I was afraid something terrible had happened to you."

Rosemary gave her a reassuring smile. She was used to placating her employer. As time went by, especially since Tiller's death, Eileen grew more and more sensitive to anything out of the ordinary. "No, of course not. I just dropped something."

Eileen crossed to the window, presumably watching Reese climb into his truck. "How often does Reese come for breakfast?"

Rosemary busied herself cleaning the dishes. "Two or three times a week," she admitted and couldn't help adding, by way of justification, "It's our only chance to catch up. I hope you don't mind." She was afraid to glance up for fear the expression on Eileen's face would show she *did* mind. But surely when Eileen asked her to move into the main house, she'd understood there would be times when Rosemary would have her sons over. She'd been careful to keep it to a minimum and not let it interrupt Eileen's routine.

"I didn't know that."

"He's only here for thirty minutes or so."

Silence. Then, "It's nice that you make breakfast for him. Now that I know he's here so often, I'll be careful to get dressed before I walk into the kitchen."

Rosemary could hear the tacit disapproval in that comment. "I should've told you," Rosemary said. "I didn't think it was a big deal, or I would have."

Eileen turned away from the window. "I guess I'll go back to bed. I didn't sleep well last night."

"I hope you'll be able to rest," Rosemary said. "Before you go, I'm planning to run to the market this morning. Do you need anything?"

"I don't. You might check with Marlow and her friends."

"I'll do that," she promised, but once Eileen had made her way slowly down the hall to her bedroom, she didn't grab the keys. She sank into the closest chair and wrapped her arms around herself in an attempt to calm her nerves.

Everything felt so tenuous right now.

Tiller had died, but she couldn't be sure the secret they shared had died with him.

From where she was walking on the beach, Aida heard Reese's truck when he started the engine, caught sight of the tailgate as he rolled through the opening in the ivy-covered fence, and was slightly relieved to know he wouldn't be around today.

He was as engaging as he was gorgeous, but she wasn't in the mood for pleasant conversation, and she doubted he'd want to hear anything more about her divorce. She'd probably said too much last night. The fighting with Dutton was over. They'd split their finances and their belongings, and he'd moved out of the house. But the shock, resentment and loss lingered. Sometimes she still asked herself—how had it come to this? Was she really single again?

She tightened the sarong she was wearing around her hips as

she turned to face the sea. She could get over Dutton while she was here, couldn't she?

After what she'd learned last night, she wasn't so sure. As beautiful and relaxed as it was on the island, and as lucky as she was to have a friend who was willing to share this place with her, she'd made the mistake of asking Marlow to invite Claire. Her parents had thought she was crazy for taking "the other woman" with her, and now she was wondering if they were right. In the beginning, she and Claire had both been so hurt and upset by what Dutton had done that they'd banded together to hold him accountable. Although their friendship may have seemed unlikely to some, Aida had been grateful for Claire's honesty and integrity. And because they were both caught in the middle of the same nightmare, they felt less alone, less powerless.

They'd spent so many nights comparing notes and complaining about how badly they'd been wronged she felt she knew Claire as well as she knew anyone. She simply couldn't have gotten through the past six months without her. And yet…now that she'd come out on the other side, the situation seemed to be changing. Instead of moving on, as Aida was attempting to do, Claire was possibly going to wind up with Dutton.

Her phone buzzed in her hand. She'd tried calling her mother a few minutes ago. This was Dottie getting back to her.

"Hello?"

"Sorry I missed your call, honey. Did you make it to Florida safely?"

"We did. Got in yesterday."

"And? What's it like there?"

"It's gorgeous. Tropical, warm, quiet."

"How's Marlow's mother?"

"About the same as usual, from what I can tell. Losing her husband has been hard on her, though."

"I bet."

Aida wanted to say something about the latest development

77

with Claire, but she was afraid to hear her mother's response. Dottie wasn't the type to say "I told you so," but she *had* told Aida so, which made finding herself in this position, especially only a day after arriving on the island, a little embarrassing. She'd thought she could be the exception to the rule. That she could blame Dutton for the affair and not the woman he'd cheated with. Claire hadn't even known Dutton had a wife. It wouldn't be fair to hate her.

That was what Aida's brain told her. Her heart had been okay with it, too—until Claire had admitted that she was still talking to Dutton.

Aida had believed she was over her ex, at least in some ways, but the jealousy that'd reared up last night made her feel she was losing something she should be hanging on to. She didn't want to see Claire with the man *she'd* married. When she looked at him through other people's eyes, most people's eyes, she still saw the dashing pediatric surgeon who seemed to have it all.

"Anything wrong?" her mother asked.

Aida curled her fingernails into her palms. "No. Why?"

"I don't know. I guess I thought you'd be more excited. You're kind of...subdued."

"I'm tired, that's all. We were up late last night."

"Doing what?"

Aida could hear the day care kids squealing in the background and wondered if her mother would ever be able to retire. "We had a bonfire."

"How fun!"

"It was. There's a...a man here who's staying on the property."

"Rachel, get down," she heard her mother say to one of the children. "That sounds promising," she said, speaking into the phone again. "Who is he?"

"The housekeeper's son." She purposely didn't mention that Reese was fourteen years younger than she was. She knew her mother would immediately caution her not to get involved in a relationship that had so little chance of working out. "Marlow's mother has had the same housekeeper for years. Her name's Rosemary, and Marlow was sort of raised with Rosemary's two sons."

"Marlow's mother has a housekeeper? Wouldn't that be nice," she said with a loud sigh.

"I wish you could afford one, too." Her parents had always worked so hard.

"You and me both," Dottie said with a laugh. "So this housekeeper *and* her sons live on the property?"

"Rosemary lives in the main house with Eileen. Reese is the resident tennis pro here on the island. He works at the club nearby and is staying in the apartment over the garage. But I get the impression he's only here temporarily." He still had a year of school to finish, if he ever decided to go back, but she didn't volunteer that.

"It's hard to believe a beach house could be that big."

"You should see it." She told Dottie about the layout of the guesthouse—how they each had their own bathroom.

"You're living in the lap of luxury. You're going to have a great summer." There was some screaming and then crying in the background. "Oh, boy. Looks like Marshall pushed Maisey off a chair. I'd better go."

"Okay. I'll call you later, then."

"Have a great time, honey."

"Mom?" she said, catching Dottie before she could hang up.

"What?"

Aida gripped her phone tighter. "I did the right thing divorcing Dutton, didn't I?"

There was a long pause. Then her mother said, "You're having second thoughts?"

"It's just that... I had it all. For a while. And now... I don't even know what to do with my life."

"Oh, honey."

Tears pricked the backs of Aida's eyes. "Did I ruin my best chance at happiness?"

"I don't know what to say," her mother said. "We always loved Dutton, never dreamed he'd do what he did. But you couldn't continue in the marriage, could you?"

She felt sick as she considered how unyielding she'd been the past six months. She'd been so hurt, so angry and so determined not to let him get away with what he'd done. Had she been too rash? Too inflexible and unforgiving? "I don't know. Maybe I shouldn't have been so hard on him. Maybe I should've tried to keep the marriage intact. People make mistakes."

"Your trust was shattered, Aida. It would be hard to go on after that. I... I think you did the right thing."

Was she just saying that because it was too late for Aida to change her decision? "Of course I did." She attempted a laugh, but it was futile. She couldn't laugh when it felt like someone was twisting a knife in her chest. "What do you have without trust?"

"Exactly," her mother agreed, as though divorce had been the only answer. But Aida remembered a time when she was pretty sure her father had strayed. There'd been crying and muted fights after she and her brothers were in bed, and her mother had taken them to visit Grandma Leanne for a couple of weeks. Somehow her parents had gotten through that period, however, and managed to stay together.

Her mother wasn't aware she knew. Bringing it up would be embarrassing for Dottie, humiliating, and it wouldn't cast her father in a very favorable light. So she didn't dare. "I love you," Aida said.

"I love you, too," her mother said.

As Aida hung up, she felt as shell-shocked and uncertain as she had the day she first found Claire on her doorstep. Dropping her head back to look up at the sky, she was fighting to keep her tears at bay when her phone buzzed again.

With a sniff, she drew a deep breath and looked down.

Reese had texted her: Why don't you, Marlow and Claire come to the club today?

8

They were having breakfast in the main house—an egg souf-
flé, fried potatoes and some sausage links Rosemary had left in
the oven for them—when Claire's phone signaled a text. Marlow noticed how quickly Aida looked up at the sound, and that
Claire silenced her ringer right away.

"Just my neighbor, assuring me she'll water my plants and get
my mail while I'm gone," she said.

That Claire had volunteered that information made it ring
false. Marlow suspected it was Dutton who'd texted her but
wasn't about to press the issue. If it was, she didn't want Aida
to know. Aida was already struggling with the fact that Dutton
was still in the picture when she'd thought she and Claire were
through with him for good, that they'd support each other in
moving on and leaving him behind. What she'd learned yesterday had to be stirring up a maelstrom of emotions, including
the worst of Aida's doubts and fears. But Marlow could understand Claire's position, too. It was hard not to love someone if
you already did.

With a frown, she finished buttering the toast she'd made to
go with her meal. Of the three of them, she'd slept the latest.

Her friends had been able to tell something was wrong with her the moment they saw her, so she'd told them she'd had trouble sleeping. She wasn't eager to explain what'd happened when she attempted to apologize to Walker. The whole thing was better off forgotten.

She supposed she *and* Claire had their secrets this morning.

"Reese texted me a couple of hours ago," Aida announced. "He wants us to come to the club and play tennis this afternoon."

Claire set her glass of fresh-squeezed orange juice next to her plate. "I've only played a handful of times," she responded.

"But you're athletic."

"I'm good at yoga," she said with a laugh. "That doesn't make me good at tennis."

"We'll need four for doubles," Aida pointed out.

In her current frame of mind, Marlow wasn't interested in doing much of anything. But, fortunately, a cold shower had helped cut the mental fog she'd found herself in after tossing and turning most of the night, going over her many past experiences with Walker and how terribly she'd behaved. She supposed getting out on the court would be preferable to moping around all day. "Reese can take you as his partner," she said. "It'll even up the teams, since I'm sure he's a lot better than Aida or me."

"If he's a pro, he might get frustrated with having me as a partner," Claire said.

"He might be a pro, but he's also a coach," Aida reminded her. "He's used to teaching people how to play."

"Not in one hour!" she quipped.

"Reese won't mind," Rosemary interjected, walking into the room from the kitchen.

Marlow hadn't realized she was back from grocery shopping. But there was a door, as well as a large pantry, off the kitchen to make it easy to unload and store supplies, so Rosemary must not have come through the house.

"How's breakfast?" Rosemary was carrying a peach tart she

placed in the middle of the table along with a pie server. "You must not have seen this."

"We did see it," Aida said. "It was sitting on the counter, but we weren't sure it was for us."

"Of course it's for you! I make quite a few of these each summer. Marlow's mother loves nothing more than a good Georgia peach, so I put them in a lot of things."

"How's Mom doing this morning?" Marlow had peeked in on her when she first came in, but Eileen seemed to be sleeping, so she'd backed quietly away.

"I'm afraid she's still a bit under the weather. But if we're lucky, this attack won't last much longer."

"I can hear you talking about me, you know," Eileen joked, surprising them by making her way gingerly into the room. She had her hair combed and was wearing a touch of makeup, but the dark circles under her eyes had never been more exaggerated, and she'd put on a "housedress," which wasn't something she generally wore in front of company. That alone indicated she didn't plan on going out.

Marlow got up to help her to the table. "I was just wondering how you're feeling."

"I'm doing fine," her mother said. "Don't worry about me."

Those words offered little comfort. Eileen obviously wasn't fine. "Is there anything you'd like me to do for you today?" Marlow asked. "Aida and Claire and I were thinking about going over to the club. If you feel strong enough to go with us, you could sit under an umbrella with a cool, fruity drink and watch us play."

"I'd like that, but I don't think I can make it today."

"Maybe when you're feeling better, we can go for a drive. Claire and Aida would like to see more of the island as well as some of the other islands that are close by."

"That would be nice," Eileen said.

Rosemary hurried to bring Eileen a plate and scooped some

food onto it. But Eileen showed no interest. She didn't even pick up her fork. Marlow guessed she'd come to the table only to make an appearance and say hello.

"Can I get you a cup of coffee?" Rosemary asked her softly. "A little caffeine might give you some energy."

"No, thank you. Not right now." Eileen turned to Marlow. "Have you heard from Sam?"

Marlow swallowed the bite she'd just taken. "Dad's attorney? No, not yet."

"You should call him."

For some odd reason, Marlow happened to notice Rosemary standing with a hot pad in one hand and the coffeepot in the other, her forehead creased with worry. But before Marlow could ask if something was wrong, Rosemary realized she was being watched and hid the concern on her face beneath a professional-looking smile as she continued to move around the table, refilling cups.

"Okay. I'll get in touch." They hadn't even gone through her father's belongings, but Marlow figured she might as well plunge into the work required by her father's estate. It had to happen at some point.

Eileen made small talk with Aida and Claire as Rosemary served the tart. Aida told her about the family she had back in North Dakota, what her parents did for a living and that she had two younger brothers, both of whom worked in the oil field like their father had before he retired.

"Ricky is a well tester," she said proudly. "He makes almost a hundred thousand dollars a year, even though he only has a couple semesters of college."

"What does your other brother do?" Eileen asked.

"Dan's three years younger than Ricky, so he's just a roughneck trying to work his way up to drill operator. He'll make almost as much as Ricky when he does."

"I didn't realize the oil field paid that well," Marlow said.

"It's difficult work," Aida responded. "It can be dangerous, too. One of Ricky's friends lost his arm on a rig a couple of years ago."

Claire looked horrified. "How'd that happen?"

"He was on a sliding ladder that collapsed and caught his arm."

"How sad." Eileen took a small bite of the peach tart, which was the first thing Marlow had seen her eat. "What made you leave North Dakota?"

"I wanted to be an actress."

"So you moved to Hollywood? Are you interested in returning to acting now that…now that certain parts of your life have changed?"

Marlow nearly chuckled at the euphemism, but Aida didn't comment on it. She pursed her lips as she considered her response. "I don't think that's realistic. Not at this age."

"You say that as if you're over-the-hill," Eileen joked.

"In Hollywood, I am."

Eileen allowed Rosemary to pour her some coffee, after all. "So what will you do?"

Marlow had been wondering the same thing. Aida was good at tennis, but not quite good enough to give lessons, and that was all Marlow knew she could do, other than a little singing, dancing and acting.

"I love fashion. I'd like to open a boutique."

"That's a great idea!" Claire exclaimed.

Marlow liked it, too. But would Aida have enough with the settlement from her divorce?

She couldn't help glancing at Claire. If Claire got back with Dutton, and started enjoying the income Aida once had, it would spell the end of their friendship.

Marlow shoved those thoughts into the back of her mind while they discussed the kind of chic boutique they could see Aida owning—in Beverly Hills or somewhere like that.

"What about you?" Eileen turned her attention to Claire. "Were you born and raised in LA?"

"In Long Beach," Claire replied. "My mom had me when she was only sixteen, so I was raised by my grandmother."

"And your father?"

"He was only seventeen, so he was young, too. He's never been part of my life. My grandfather was, for a short time, but he had a stroke and passed away when I was ten."

"Her grandmother has since passed, too," Marlow murmured.

Finished eating, Claire set her utensils on her plate so Rosemary could take them away. "She would've been eighty this summer."

Eileen shifted positions to face Claire more directly. "If you don't mind my asking, where is your mother these days?"

"She lives in Santa Barbara with her husband and children."

"You have half siblings, then."

"Yes. Three little sisters—twelve, ten and seven."

"So your mother is doing well?"

"She is. Once she graduated from college, she met a great guy and they're happy together."

Marlow understood that Claire had to feel somewhat as she herself had always felt—different. Neither of them had a standard childhood. That made it difficult for Marlow not to be sympathetic when it came to Dutton. The only person Claire had ever been able to rely on, after her grandfather died, was her grandmother. It was the money she inherited from "Bea" that'd enabled her to set up her yoga studio and buy the house she'd lost in the fire. Fortunately, when she'd received word that she needed to evacuate, she'd managed to save most of her memorabilia.

Eileen took a sip of coffee. "Marlow told me you're a yoga instructor."

"I am. Or I was," she added with a grimace.

"If you'd like to work part-time while you're here, you might check with the club, see if they're interested in an instructor. They offer Pilates and spin classes. I bet they'd love to add yoga to the schedule."

"And Reese could put in a good word for you," Rosemary said. "So could Walker, for that matter. He spends a lot of time at the club, playing tennis with his brother."

Marlow nearly choked on her last bite. She planned to spend a lot of time at the club herself—to get plenty of exercise, forget about troubled marriages for a change and enjoy whiling away the hot days of summer. The last thing she wanted was to run into Walker whenever she went there.

"That's a good idea," Claire said. "I'll ask when we go this afternoon."

Marlow touched Rosemary's arm as she came around to collect the plates. "Thank you. Breakfast—especially that tart—was delicious."

"I like having a houseful of people," she said.

Company was likely a welcome distraction. No doubt it'd been quiet since Tiller died. Probably too quiet.

Marlow was just getting up when her phone went off. "It's Dad's attorney," she told her mother and walked outside so she'd be able to hear him above the voices of the others, who were thanking Rosemary and saying goodbye to Eileen. "Hello?"

"Marlow, it's Sam."

"Thanks for calling," she said. "My mother's been eager for us to touch base."

"Yes. I've been trying to reach her, but it's been almost impossible."

"She hasn't been feeling well."

"That's too bad. It's the MS?"

"Yes."

"Such a difficult disease," he said. "But what about you? How are you doing these days?"

Should she tell him she was going to quit practicing law after all the time and effort she'd put into becoming an attorney?

She decided not to bring it up. Who could say? Maybe she'd miss some aspect of her work and change her mind over the course of the summer. "I'm doing okay," she said. "And you?"

"Hanging in there. I feel terrible about your father."

Marlow had thought she'd cried all she could cry over her father's death, and yet Sam's sympathy evoked fresh emotion. "Thank you. It came as a shock. But…you must be calling about the reading of the will or something."

"Yes. I was hoping you and your mother could come to Georgia to meet with me so we could take care of some estate business."

Meet with him? She thought that only happened in the movies. "My mother hasn't been feeling well enough to travel."

She heard him sigh into the phone. "Well, if she can't make it, can you come on your own?"

"To sign something or…"

"We need to go over a few things. Your father has made some…unusual stipulations. I feel it would be best to speak to you in person."

Marlow couldn't imagine what that meant. Most everything could be handled via Zoom and DocuSign. But she'd never had anyone close to her die, especially someone who had wealth they'd be passing along. "Okay. Let's see…it's Friday. How about a week from today?"

"My niece's wedding is that day, so I've asked my staff to take Friday off and come in on Saturday instead. Will that work?"

"Sure. I'll make my flight arrangements and confirm with you once I know what time I'll be there."

"Sounds good. I look forward to seeing you next week."

"Thanks." He was about to disconnect, but Marlow felt so unsettled she couldn't help trying to catch him. "Sam?"

"What?"

"This isn't anything *too* out of the ordinary, is it?"

There was a slight hesitation before he answered. "We'll talk when you get here."

He hung up so fast she couldn't question him further. Why couldn't he have offered her some reassurance? *No, it's just routine... Nothing to worry about...*

He could easily have said something like that.

And yet he hadn't.

Tired of spending so much time in her bedroom, Eileen rested on the couch while Rosemary worked around her, dusting the living room. Rosemary was only five years her junior, but Eileen thought she looked fifteen years younger, at least. She was certainly a great deal more energetic and spry. Although most people would consider *her* to be the luckier one—she'd always had money, she'd been a senator's wife, she'd once been considered a great beauty—she'd give almost anything to be as healthy and able-bodied as her housekeeper.

Rosemary was attractive, too, like her sons. And she had a nice figure, as well as an engaging smile and a good heart. Eileen was lucky to have her, especially now that Tiller was gone.

"Are you okay?" A look of concern came over Rosemary's face when she caught sight of her.

Eileen quickly cleared her expression. "Yes. Thank you."

"It's great to have Marlow home, isn't it?"

Rosemary often talked about Marlow, especially when she was trying to cheer up Eileen. Eileen recognized the tactic for what it was, but she was happy to let the conversation move in that direction. "I've been looking forward to it for a long time."

"I like her friends."

"You know how Claire and Aida met, don't you?"

Rosemary removed the plants and books from one of the bookshelves that covered the far wall. "I'm afraid I don't."

Eileen shared almost everything with her housekeeper. Some

days Rosemary was the only person she had to talk to. Eileen thought for sure she'd told Rosemary what Marlow had relayed to her about Aida and Claire. But she'd been so consumed with grief and so ill that maybe she hadn't. "Aida's husband was having an affair with Claire."

Rosemary froze with the dusting spray in her hand. "You're kidding."

"No. He pretended to be single, never told her he was married. Can you believe that?"

"No. That's hard to believe."

"He lied about everything. His job, his family, his upbringing. He even rented an apartment so Claire could move in with him after the fire destroyed her house."

"How did they figure it out?"

"Someone told her."

"That must've broken her heart."

"It did. And then she went straight to Aida's house to tell her."

Rosemary slowly wiped the bookshelf she'd prepared. "This is why Aida's divorced."

"Yes. After ten years of marriage. Claire broke it off, too." Eileen shifted so that her left leg wouldn't ache quite so badly. "Serves him right, don't you think? He betrayed them both."

Rosemary replaced the books and plants before moving on to a different shelf. "Anyone can make a mistake, but that sounds... beyond a mistake."

"I don't buy that 'mistake' garbage. Either you love someone and you're committed to them, or you don't and you're not."

Rosemary didn't comment.

"Don't you think?" Eileen pressed.

"I think it's a tragedy. That's what I think. And that it's unusual Claire and Aida would wind up being such close friends."

Eileen took a sip of the lemonade Rosemary had left on the coffee table for her. "I was surprised by that, too. Claire didn't know Dutton was married. It wasn't her fault. But...can you imagine? Infidelity would've been the one thing I could never forgive. I let Tiller know that right from the beginning."

The spray sounded before Rosemary responded. "Tiller loved you very much."

"He was an honorable man." Eileen felt tears well up. "Sometimes I wonder how I'll ever go on without him."

Rosemary left her dusting to come over, perch on the edge of the couch and take her hand. "You're stronger than you know. You've seen a lot of things come and go over the years. You'll get through this, too."

Although Rosemary's words were kind, something about the way she said them gave Eileen the impression she was actually talking to herself.

9

Reese was even better at tennis than Marlow had expected, but it was impossible for even a great player to compensate for having a partner who couldn't hit the ball. After she and Aida won the first two games in only a few minutes, Claire said she needed to find Reese's boss so she could ask about teaching yoga classes at the club. She looked so relieved to be off the court that Marlow didn't have the heart to ask her to return.

Fortunately, Reese recognized a teenager named Grant who'd come to practice his serve and roped him into playing with them. Aida had Reese as her partner, and Marlow had Grant, which meant she lost the entire set. Reese dominated the game that much. But at least Grant knew how to play and the games were more competitive than when they'd been playing with Claire. Frustrated that she hadn't really found her stroke or any success so far, Marlow wanted to keep going, but Grant said he had plans with friends and had to leave.

Although Claire had returned from her errand and was sitting in the stands, watching them, Marlow didn't want to bring her back out. She assumed they'd have to quit—until Reese suggested they take a break and get a drink while he gave his next lesson. He said he'd be available at five, and he'd have another competent player by the time they came back.

Claire was so excited that the manager of the club was interested in hiring her that it was all she could talk about as they ate fish tacos and drank margaritas at the club's small café.

"I can't believe they don't already offer yoga," Aida said. "Yoga's so popular."

"Phil, the manager, said they used to, but the instructor moved to Orlando to get married."

"I'll sign up for one of your classes," Aida said.

Claire smiled at her support and generosity. "Thank you."

Marlow was relieved to see them still getting along so well, but she knew there had to be a lot going on under the surface.

Aida checked her watch as Claire gathered up the trash. "Reese should be done. You ready?"

Marlow grabbed her racquet. "Let's do it."

"Would you rather go home while we play for another hour or so?" Aida asked Claire as they started back.

"No," she said. "I like watching."

She veered into the stands with the small bag of chips she'd purchased at lunch as they walked onto the courts. That was when Marlow spotted Walker. He was standing next to his brother dressed in tennis shorts, a club T-shirt and tennis shoes.

And he was holding a racquet.

"Oh, no," she murmured under her breath.

"What is it?" Aida asked, but Marlow couldn't respond. The few steps they'd taken had brought Reese and Walker within hearing distance.

"Look who it is!" Reese gestured proudly toward them, but Walker obviously wasn't pleased. His brother must not have mentioned who he'd be playing.

"You got Walker to come over, huh?" Marlow said.

"Oh, yeah. He's great. But it wasn't easy to convince him to change his clothes and take the time off. He's a workaholic these days. I knew my only shot was to tell him I have two beautiful women who want to play, and we need him as a fourth. Fortunately, he's usually pretty good about helping me out when I get into these types of situations."

Walker sent his brother a withering look, but Reese laughed. "At least I wasn't lying about the beautiful part."

The hard set to Walker's jaw made Marlow wonder if he'd walk off. But, to his credit, he managed to overcome whatever he was feeling.

Aida treated him to a welcoming smile. "How should we arrange the teams?"

Marlow was grateful her friend had jumped right in, because she wasn't ready to address Walker directly.

Reese gave his brother a sheepish grimace—an apology for upsetting him. "Why don't you and Walker take on me and Marlow?" he said. "Marlow and I haven't played together yet."

Marlow wondered if Reese had arranged the teams this way because he knew Walker wouldn't want to play with her as a partner.

"Sounds good," she said and took the cover off her racquet.

While Walker and Aida rounded the net to the other side, Marlow thought she and Reese would easily win. She and Aida were evenly matched, but Walker hadn't had the hours of training his brother had. For some reason, her father had encouraged Reese to take tennis lessons. Marlow was pretty sure Tiller had paid for them. He'd paid for quite a lot when Reese was growing up, including braces, but he was generous that way.

After reaching deuce, she and Reese won the next two points on her serve to put away the first game. Marlow was relieved to have played so well. After her encounter with Walker last night, it was more important to her than it probably should've been to beat him. She could tell it bothered him, which made it even more enjoyable—so enjoyable she couldn't help shooting him a triumphant smile.

His eyes narrowed when he saw her gloating, and he began to play harder. He'd been hitting his most powerful shots to his brother. She could tell he thought it was impolite to slam the ball on a woman, but her cockiness goaded him enough that he included her on a few tough shots, all of which she missed. When she and Reese lost badly in the second game, Walker treated her to the same "take that" smile she'd given him.

As they played game after game, the battle waged on and they all grew more serious. Even Aida seemed to know there was a lot riding on this match. At three games each, Marlow finally realized that Walker probably could've been a pro player, too—if that was what he'd wanted.

Before they started the seventh game, Reese turned his back on their opponents as he said, "We can't let my brother win, or I'll never live it down."

"What are you muttering about over there?" Aida called out playfully. "Are you plotting against us? Sharing our weaknesses?"

"That's exactly what we're doing," Marlow called back with a laugh. But to Reese, she said, "I think I might've pulled the tiger's tail. Your brother has it in for me."

"He usually lets me look good, since I work here, but tonight he's out to win," he admitted. "I don't know what it is about you. For some reason, you seem to bring out the worst in him. You two have more sibling rivalry than we do."

"It's not sibling rivalry," she mumbled, but Aida was about to serve so Reese was already moving back into position, and she could tell he hadn't heard her. She was actually glad of that, because she wasn't sure how she would've answered had he asked her to clarify that statement.

The next game took the longest and proved to be her worst ever. They lost, but she and Reese won two after that, making it five to four in their favor. "This can't come down to a tie," she said to Reese. "We *have* to win the next one."

"Agreed," he said and, solely due to his skill, they did win and managed to avoid a stressful tiebreaker.

"That was fun," Marlow said, meeting Walker and Aida at the net.

"Yeah, an absolute blast," Walker said dryly.

Marlow had to laugh at his sarcasm. "You're not a sore loser, are you?"

He arched one eyebrow. "We're playing again. That's all I've got to say."

"Now?" she said.

"I can't." Reese bounced the ball and caught it again. "I have a student coming in ten minutes."

"Tomorrow, then," Aida said.

Reese drank some water from his Gatorade bottle. "I'm up for that," he said once he'd swallowed. "But Walker works all the time. I doubt he can make it. Right, bro?"

"I'm off tomorrow," Walker said.

Marlow got the impression he'd take the day off even if he was supposed to work; he was that eager for another crack at her.

Reese seemed to be as surprised as she was that he'd agreed. "Great," he said. "I have back-to-back lessons all morning, but I could play over lunch. Should we meet at noon?"

"Aren't you afraid you might lose again?" Marlow said to Walker, unable to resist needling him a little more.

"That's not going to happen. See you all tomorrow." He started to walk off the court, but Aida stopped him.

"Hey, we're having another bonfire tonight," she said.

Claire had come out of the bleachers to join them. "Your mother's making shish kebabs and corn on the cob," she added as she walked up. "And Reese will be there. Why don't you join us?"

"Yeah, why go home and eat alone?" Reese said. "Mom promised to make some of her garlic mashed potatoes, too. And I'm cutting up a watermelon. It's going to be a summer feast."

When Walker opened his mouth, Marlow was sure he'd refuse. Although they hadn't exactly made a pact last night, it was her understanding that they'd avoid each other whenever they could. So she was shocked when he said, "Sure. I'll come eat. I'll be over after I shower."

He shot her a glance that seemed to say he wasn't going to miss a great meal just because of her. But she didn't care if he came. She was the one who'd suggested they be friends.

"You don't mind that I invited Walker to join us tonight, do you?" Aida asked as they strode out to the car.

Marlow tossed her racquet in the trunk of her mother's Tesla and waited for her friends to do the same. "Of course not," she said, but she knew that she'd be far too conscious of his presence to relax and enjoy herself.

Why had he agreed to go to dinner at Seaclusion when he'd promised himself he'd stay away from Marlow?

Walker had no answer for that. He'd been asked while his competitive juices were flowing, and he hadn't wanted to feel as though he was going to miss out just because Marlow would be there, he supposed. It was a group thing—and the group included his mother and brother. He should join the fun.

Still, he'd hardly been able to look away from Marlow in that short tennis skirt—a clear sign of danger. That and the gloating smile she'd given him had made it difficult to make good decisions. *Damn it.* She had such a strange power over him. Even after all these years.

Like Samson and Delilah, he thought. But he wasn't going to let her get the better of him. He'd been down that road too many times before.

After he got out of the shower, he pulled on a pair of trunks, assuming they'd probably go swimming, and a T-shirt, before reclaiming his flip-flops from the living room. Then he went out and fired up his Harley. Two miles wasn't far to take the bike, but it beat driving his SUV, which reminded everyone that he was a cop.

When he arrived, the sound of the motor drew Claire and Aida out of the guesthouse before he could even put down the kickstand. Fortunately, Marlow wasn't with them.

"I love motorcycles," Aida said. "That looks like fun! Any chance you'd be willing to take me for a ride?"

He hadn't thought to bring an extra helmet. He so rarely needed one. But as small as the island was, he wouldn't be going very fast. He figured she could use a bicycle helmet. She went in search of one, which brought Marlow out of the guesthouse, too, but she didn't say anything to him. She just went to the garage and got the helmet.

Aida was wearing white shorts with a man's button-down shirt tied at the waist over a red bikini top. She was smaller than Claire and Marlow and pretty in a curvy, Dolly Parton sort of way. She seemed sweet. He realized he couldn't hold the fact that she was a friend of Marlow's against her.

The engine was too loud for conversation, so they didn't say much, but she tightened her arms around his waist whenever he accelerated. Imagining the thrill it gave her made him smile. He loved his bike. The raw power of it. The freedom it symbolized. He was never happier than when he was racing down the highway with the wind ripping at his clothes.

He drove Aida around the island for fifteen minutes before going back to do the same for Claire, who was wearing a sleeveless top with a pair of denim cutoffs. She clung to him even more tightly than Aida had and, shouting above the roar of the engine, made it clear she'd never been on a motorcycle before. According to what she said, her grandmother, who'd raised her, wouldn't allow it.

When they got back, he could tell Marlow wanted a ride, too, but she was too proud to ask for one—and he didn't offer. They'd set some boundaries last night; if he didn't want her to wreck his life again, he needed to be smart enough to honor them.

Turning off the engine, he pocketed the key and pretended he had to go inside to say hello to his mother so leaving her out wouldn't look like a purposeful slight.

But he knew that she knew it was.

Her eyes narrowed as he stalked past her. Her gaze felt like it would burn a hole right through him, but he refused to acknowledge the attention. She was in some kind of pool dress. Long, straight and black, it was made of soft T-shirt material and had a slit up to her knees on both sides with a sheer panel above her breasts, showing just a hint of cleavage.

He'd always thought she had good taste in clothes, that she had class, but, once again, he reminded himself to quit noticing. She'd never been interested in him. Apparently, it was going to take a sledgehammer to get that through his thick head.

His mother was excited to see him. "Hey, you," she said, hugging him tight. "When Reese said you were coming to dinner, I almost didn't believe him. You turn us down more often than not."

It was usually his work that kept him away. "I couldn't miss out on your garlic mashed potatoes."

"I'm glad I have something to keep you coming back," she joked. "Can you help me carry the food out to the deck?"

"I thought this was going to be a bonfire."

"Eileen is going to join us. She'll be more comfortable on the deck. Then you kids can go down to the beach, light your bonfire and dance the night away, if that's what you want to do."

He wasn't sure about dancing, but it was so hot out that swimming sounded good.

He carried dish after dish to the table. On his last trip, Eileen came out. "Walker, I thought I heard your voice," she said when she saw him. "How nice of you to join us. I'm so glad you could come."

Since Reese had commented on it some time ago, Walker had noticed that she consistently treated him better than she did his brother. He wondered why, but he supposed it was just that he was older and hadn't been a pain in the ass quite as recently. "Good to see you again, Mrs. Madsen. Can I help you to a chair?"

"Why not?" she said. "I couldn't get a better offer."

Her hand was cold on his arm even though it was probably eighty degrees out. He'd remarked on her cold hands before, and she'd told him it was part of her disease. She had poor circulation and was almost always chilled, which was why she loved the warm weather.

When Marlow and her friends came onto the deck, Marlow was careful to sit as far away from Walker as possible, and he didn't mind. As a matter of fact, he was happy with the arrangement—until Eileen complained about a draft and Marlow offered to switch places with her. Then Walker found himself seated right next to his nemesis. Not only could he see the pretty nude-colored polish on her fingernails, he could smell her perfume and feel the heat of her leg so close to his under the table.

"Tell us about your job, Walker," Claire said as they were passing the food around the table. "Is there much violent crime on the island?"

"Fortunately, not a lot. Not since I've been here, anyway. We've had some domestic disputes and some neighbors who've gotten into a rivalry over street parking and the like. And we have the occasional drunken brawls at various bars, especially in normal years, when we have a lot of tourists from January to April. But it's quiet most days."

"Weekends have to be the worst when the island is crowded," Aida said.

"They are," he agreed. "But we don't have a lot of tourists right now, and I've got my best man working tonight. He'll call me if anything comes up."

Marlow's hand accidentally brushed his as she passed him the shish kebabs, and she recoiled so fast she nearly dropped the platter. Fortunately, he managed to grab hold of it before it fell, select a skewer and pass them over to Aida.

"Being a cop must be hard," Claire said.

"You definitely see things you'd rather not see," he admitted, then turned the focus of the conversation on Claire so that he wouldn't be the center of attention all night. "What about you? What do you do?"

She told him she'd owned a yoga studio, which she'd had to close because of the pandemic, and how she'd love to start another one.

"Is that what you plan to do this fall?" Reese asked.

"Once I get back on my feet," she replied.

"Claire and I have both had a rough year," Aida volunteered. "I think I told you I just went through a divorce, and Claire lost her house to the Malibu fire last year."

"Yes..." Walker said as he ripped a piece of bell pepper off his skewer.

"Well, there's a little more to it. My husband was having an affair with Claire. That's how we met."

Walker held a forkful of potatoes in midair. "What did you say?"

The two women exchanged a glance and somehow managed to laugh before explaining the situation.

"Is this the dude who threatened Marlow?" he asked.

Marlow blinked as though she was startled he'd said her name. They were being so careful not to acknowledge each other, wouldn't even look at each other. "Yeah, that's Dutton," she muttered when all eyes turned her way.

Although Walker would never have said it out loud, he figured this Dutton should be glad he hadn't acted on those threats. Walker could dislike Marlow himself. She'd earned that. But anyone who hurt her had better watch out for him.

The fact that he still felt protective of her made him as mad as everything else to do with her. He tried telling himself it was only natural, considering how generous her family had been to his. If not for the senator paying for all the coaching Reese had as a boy, he wouldn't have a vocation as an adult. But Walker knew his devotion to Marlow went beyond that. He just couldn't help himself where she was concerned.

"It's hard to believe Dutton could keep that secret as long as he did," Reese said.

Aida rolled her eyes. "No kidding. Makes me feel pretty gullible."

"Me, too," Claire piped up.

Marlow pushed her plate back, even though she'd barely touched her food. "Enough about Dutton," she said as she sipped her second glass of wine. "We've come here to forget about him, remember?"

"You've already finished your meal?" Rosemary asked.

"I wasn't very hungry," she said, obviously distracted. "But what I had was wonderful."

"She's eager to hit the beach," Claire said.

"Why don't you kids go have your fun?" Rosemary said. "I'll do the dishes."

"I'll help you clean up," Marlow said.

Claire and Aida started to protest that they'd help, too, but Marlow insisted they couldn't all be in the kitchen at the same time, anyway. She told them she'd join them soon, and as they headed down to the beach, Walker had to wonder if she'd stayed behind so she could avoid him.

10

After he'd had a few beers, Walker was feeling almost bullet-proof. He wasn't going to worry about Marlow, he decided. He was having too much fun with her friends, drinking, talking and throwing a football around in the surf.

Once they started swimming, Reese had Claire get on his shoulders and Walker had Aida get on his, and they proceeded to do everything they could to knock each other into the waves. They were laughing so hard it was difficult to keep their footing, but that was part of the challenge.

He and Aida won the first fight; Reese and Claire won the next. They were in the middle of an intense tiebreaker when Marlow finally appeared.

She stopped at the fire, poured herself a glass of wine and sat in one of the chairs, watching as they pushed and shoved each other and staggered around in waves that were threatening to knock them down before their opponent could. Walker and Aida finally caused Reese and Claire to fall, claiming victory, but then Claire didn't want to play anymore, even though Reese was dying for another chance, so he called out to Marlow.

"Come be my partner!" he yelled as Claire flipped her wet

hair out of her face and headed back to the fire. "We can take them!"

Marlow seemed reluctant—until Walker said, "She won't come. She's too afraid to lose."

That brought her to her feet almost instantly. She put down her wine and pulled off her pool dress, revealing that smoking-hot white bikini she'd had on before. Then she marched down to the water, and Reese squatted so she could get onto his shoulders.

Walker knew almost instantly that he wasn't sober enough to withstand someone as determined as Marlow. She had it in for him, and she was going to win this battle even if it meant dunking her friend. They were all laughing—it was too awkward a contest not to laugh—but he could sense Marlow's steely purpose.

She ended up yanking Aida off his shoulders, since he refused to go down, and that was when Aida decided she'd had enough of the game, too.

"I don't think I'm cut out for shoulder wars," Aida said. "I'm going to have another glass of wine."

As she left the water, Walker grinned up at Marlow to make sure she understood she hadn't knocked *him* down. "Nice try."

"We won," Marlow said, arching her eyebrows as Reese set her down. "That's all that matters."

"You only half won," he told her and started up the beach. He was expecting his brother and Marlow to follow, but they didn't. When he glanced back, he saw Marlow slip her arm through Reese's as they began to wade through the surf toward the jetty.

"I'm exhausted, and I wasn't even doing the heavy lifting," Aida said with a laugh when he reached the fire.

"You hardly weigh anything. It was Reese who had the hard job," Walker joked, teasing Claire.

"Ouch!" she cried. "And I was just starting to like you."

He flashed her a grin as he offered her a beer from the cooler, which she accepted. Then he sat down to catch his breath, and after chatting with them for a few minutes, he noticed Marlow and Reese still arm in arm and deep in conversation near the catamaran.

What were they talking about? As he finished his beer, he told himself it was none of his business. He didn't care that she and his brother were getting friendly with each other. But it *did* occur to him that Reese was a couple of years older than he'd been when Marlow had come home last. Reese was a man now. Maybe she was attracted to him. Maybe, to Marlow, the age difference didn't matter.

The idea of them together made Walker feel sick. He wouldn't be forced to watch a summer romance blossom between them, would he? Here he was, biding his time like he'd planned, waiting for her to leave. He couldn't imagine how much harder it would be to get through the next three months if she had a fling with his brother. Jealousy would eat him alive.

"Walker, did you hear me?" Claire asked.

Clearing his throat, he pulled his gaze away from Reese and Marlow. "No. I'm sorry. I think I've had a little too much to drink. What'd you say?"

Claire was sitting close enough to squeeze his shoulder. "Don't worry," she murmured. "Marlow has no interest in Reese."

Embarrassed that she could tell what he was feeling—was he *that* transparent?—he manufactured a shrug he hoped came off as careless. "I'm not worried about that," he lied.

Marlow was so aware of Walker. *Too* aware. She couldn't avoid noticing how open and easy he was with her friends and how closed off and unyielding he was with her. It was far more comfortable just to stay away from him.

Claire and Aida were roasting marshmallows when she and Reese returned to the group, but Walker didn't seem interested in anything except the beer in his hand. There were more crushed cans near his chair than she would've expected. Even his brother noticed—and said something about it.

"Wow, bro. I've never seen you drink like this. What's going on?"

Walker held the can in front of his face as he considered the question. "Everyone deserves a break now and then," he said, but Marlow could tell he was upset about something, and he was trying to drink it away.

Reese got a skewer and shoved a marshmallow on the end.

Marlow grabbed a blanket and wrapped it around her shoulders before getting her own skewer. "You don't want any s'mores?" she said to Walker.

He met her gaze as he crumpled the can in his hand and tossed it on the pile with the others. "No, I'm good."

"Oh, you're missing out," Aida moaned as her marshmallow oozed all over her chocolate bar when she took her first bite. "It's *so* delicious!"

Marlow tried to forget about Walker so she could enjoy herself, but something had changed with him. Instead of ignoring her as usual, he watched every move she made. She told herself to focus on her marshmallow and the fire leaping around it, but she caught herself, time and again, staring back at him through the flames. He was easy to look at, especially since he was only wearing a pair of swim trunks. And he was studying her as though he'd never seen anything like her before, as though he was trying to figure out a puzzle that had him completely stumped—and frustrated.

"Your marshmallow's on fire!" Reese grabbed her hand so he could blow it out for her.

"Thanks." She chuckled at her carelessness, but as soon as she went back to roasting, her gaze shifted to Walker again.

He was *still* watching her. And he didn't look away once he knew he had her attention. Their eyes held for several long seconds before Reese grabbed her hand again.

"You can't stick it right in the fire. Haven't you ever done this before?"

She blew out the flames, but it was too burned to eat. "I'm not hungry anyway," she said. "I'm going swimming."

She had to get away, break what felt like an electrical current running between her and Walker. She was beginning to think strange thoughts—like that she'd been crazy not to want him.

Maybe *she* was the one who'd had too much to drink.

The others eventually joined her in the ocean—all except Walker. He was still in his chair by the fire when they got out and dried off.

They lounged in various chairs or sat in the sand with towels or blankets to keep warm while talking for another hour. Walker answered any direct questions but didn't volunteer much. And he didn't seem to be cold. He never covered up.

It was nearly midnight when Claire said, "I'm exhausted. I'm going to bed."

Aida shot a glance at Reese but, fortunately, seemed to think better of staying out any later with him. Since Walker was around, it would've been awkward. "Me, too."

"What about all this stuff?" Claire gestured at the supplies they'd brought out. "Should we take it in?"

Marlow shook her head. "We can do that in the morning."

Walker made a move to get up since everyone was leaving, but Reese pushed him back in his chair. "You're too drunk to drive home, buddy. You'll have to stay with me. So why don't you sit tight until I can put out this fire?"

"I wasn't planning to drive home. I can call whoever's on duty and have them swing by to grab me."

"There's no need to bother anyone else. You can stay with me."

"Okay." Walker cracked open another beer. "I'll take care of the fire. Just leave the door unlocked. I'll be up as soon as I finish this last one."

Reese covered a yawn. "Got it."

Everyone else said good-night and left the beach, and Marlow told herself she was glad the night was over. It was too difficult to be around Walker. She needed to remember not to invite him again, even if his mother and brother were there.

But once she went to bed, every time she closed her eyes, she saw Walker staring intently at her through the flames.

He didn't hate her, she realized.

Or maybe he *did* hate her. But she was pretty sure he still wanted her, if only to finally get the girl who'd always rejected him.

Walker pressed the cold can of beer against his forehead. All he could hear was the crackling and popping of the fire and the pounding of the waves not far away. Those soothing sounds were somehow making him feel better.

He shouldn't have come over tonight. He knew that now. He'd thought he could handle being around Marlow, had wanted to show her how easy it was to resist her now that they were both older.

But he'd made a grave miscalculation. He'd been prepared to have her ignore him; he hadn't been prepared for her to act so affectionate with his little brother.

In the morning, he needed to get up and head home—and then stay away. Maybe he'd even cancel their tennis match. Why put himself through the agony of being around her? Of wanting to touch her and have her touch him? There were plenty of other women out there.

Leaving his beer half-finished, he dumped what was left of the ice onto the fire, carried the cooler to the sea and filled it with water to douse the embers. So many people put out a beach fire with sand, but all that did was insulate the hot coals.

Once the fire was nothing but a thin stream of smoke curling toward the sky, he considered wading in the waves while finishing his last beer, but he'd already had too much to drink. Nothing seemed to deaden the emotions churning inside him, anyway. He'd just have a hangover to show for it in the morning.

"At least that'll give me an excuse to cancel tennis," he muttered and grabbed his T-shirt to take with him.

Once he started toward Reese's apartment, however, he came to an abrupt halt.

There was a figure standing where the grass gave way to the sand.

It was Marlow in her pool dress.

Why had she come back? Had she forgotten something? Was she checking that he'd put out the fire? Or…what?

"Fire's out," he said, just in case. "I made sure of it."

When she didn't answer, he moved closer. "Did you hear me? The fire's out."

"That's not why I'm here."

At this, his heart began to thud. "So…why are you here?"

"I want to be friends, Walker. Why can't we be friends?"

"We *are* friends," he insisted. "For all intents and purposes."

"I mean *real* friends. You know the difference."

He rubbed his forehead with his free hand. "I would never let anyone or anything harm you, Marlow—"

"There's more to friendship than that," she broke in. "You're the chief of police. It's your job to protect people."

She didn't understand the lengths he'd go to for her, even though he'd proved it when he saved her from drowning at her fifteenth birthday party, but he wasn't about to clarify. "You have enough friends. You don't need me. I don't think I'm capable of having that type of relationship with you, anyway."

"Because you can't forgive me?"

Because he still wanted her. But he wasn't going to say that, either. "We have too much history."

She stepped up to him, so close he could smell the shampoo in her freshly washed hair. "Even if our friendship includes this?"

When she rose up on tiptoe and pressed her lips to his, he dropped his T-shirt. He intended to set her away from him. But as he gripped her shoulders, her hands came up to touch his face, and her kiss was so gentle and sweet it completely disarmed him.

"What are you doing?" he asked in confusion after she pulled away.

"This is what you want, isn't it?"

He wished he could read what was going on in her mind. "What I want has never mattered before."

"I tried to apologize for that. You wouldn't let me."

She was still close enough that he could feel her breath on his lips. He was tempted to hold the back of her head and kiss her— really kiss her—but he resisted. Part of him didn't trust what was happening. He felt it had to be a trap, even if she didn't intend it as one. "This will only complicate things between us."

"Our relationship is already complicated," she said.

"I can't argue with that."

Her lips curved into a sexy half smile. "What do we have to lose? At least we'll have one hell of a summer."

He allowed himself to slide his hands down her arms. "I think we might be making a mistake."

Her tongue darted out to wet her lips. "And yet you're not walking away..."

"There are worse ways to crash and burn," he said and finally bent his head to kiss her.

For the first time, she didn't stop him. When her arms went around his neck and her mouth opened beneath his, he couldn't help thinking that she tasted every bit as good as he'd always known she would.

"I like the way you kiss," she said, taking a long breath.

He liked the way she kissed, too. But he was so afraid she'd change her mind about going any further that he went slowly at first, so slowly that she was the one who finally moved his hands to her breasts. Although he'd been able to tell she wasn't wearing a bra through the thin fabric of her dress, the soft mounds in his hands confirmed it.

"Are you really going through with this?" he asked, drawing back to look down into her face. He could feel her chest rising and falling; she was as breathless as he was.

"You don't trust me…"

"I have reason *not* to trust you." She'd messed with his head as far back as he could remember. Usually, she wouldn't have anything to do with him. That was when her answer where he was concerned was clear. But there were times when she was bored or lonely that she'd led him to believe she might have *some* interest. Otherwise, he wouldn't have kept trying.

Instead of speaking up to reassure him, she pulled her dress over her head and dropped it next to his shirt. "Does this answer your question?"

She was completely naked and every bit as beautiful as he'd imagined. He sucked his breath in through his teeth as he let his gaze move over her. "Holy shit," he said.

Her throat moved as she swallowed. She was acting cocky, brave, but he could tell she was nervous. "Now's your chance to reject me," she said. "Take your revenge."

Revenge? Or what he'd always wanted? Which was it going to be?

"I guess I don't want revenge that badly," he said and lowered his head to kiss her again.

As soon as he drew her up against him, he knew it didn't matter if this was a mistake.

He was going to do it regardless.

11

The palm trees and thick shrubbery shielded them from the house, the guesthouse and the apartment above the garage. But the darkness was so complete no one would've been able to see them, anyway. It was quiet, too, the only sounds the rush of the waves on the beach and the wind whispering through the fronds overhead.

The tranquility of the night directly opposed the intensity of what was happening on the grass, however. The sex between her and Walker had turned into more of a battle of wills than anything else. But she couldn't blame him. She was the one who'd instigated it, and set the tone.

First, she was on top. Then he was on top. Then he was pinning her hands above her head as he drove into her. Then she was nipping and sucking on his neck to cope with the tension winding tighter and tighter inside her. She couldn't seem to get enough of him. She could smell the sea in his hair, taste the salt on his warm skin and feel his lower body connecting with hers in a way that filled her completely. What they were doing promised satisfaction, and yet there was a strange hunger that remained.

She was fighting for more, a concession of some sort, and he seemed to be fighting for the same.

An emotional tug-of-war developed as the pleasure ratcheted up to dizzying heights. He seemed to be completely consumed with experiencing every inch of her at last, with making sure there was nothing she would deny him, a sensation that was erotic and exciting and all-consuming. So she was shocked when he stopped abruptly, right before she climaxed, and said, "I don't care about you."

She'd attempted to apologize for her past behavior. She sincerely regretted it. But if he wouldn't accept it, that was on him. "I don't care about you, either," she said stubbornly.

They were both leery of the other. She could see the skepticism in his face as he stared down at her, and she was convinced he could see the same in hers.

"Do you want to stop?" she challenged, steeling herself in case he pulled away.

He closed his eyes as though he was grappling with the decision.

"Walker?"

"No," he said, suddenly purposeful as he clenched one hand in her hair so she couldn't look away from him as he began to thrust with absolute focus. It was almost as if he was saying, "You see this is me, right?"

She knew exactly who it was. She also knew that he couldn't stop even if he wanted to. That was a small victory for her. But when the climax he gave her was so powerful she had to cry out, Walker's teeth flashed in a self-satisfied smile, and she knew he'd won in some way, too.

Pulling his face down to hers, she kissed him deeply as she urged him to roll over, allowing her to get back on top, at which point she rode him until he was on the brink of climax—as close to that pinnacle as she'd been herself a few minutes earlier—and then she stopped.

He glared up at her. "What?"

"Aren't you glad you stuck around?" she said and began to move more slowly, drawing out the pleasure as long as possible before smiling triumphantly when he quickly lifted her off him, up onto his stomach, as his body shuddered in release.

His hands had been gripping her thighs as she moved, communicating his need. Now that he was satiated, they fell away.

"I can't believe we just did that," he said when he'd recovered enough to speak. "Please tell me you're on the pill."

"I'm not," she admitted. "I haven't been with anyone in a long time. But you pulled me off in time."

"That was still careless. If the withdrawal method was reliable, no one would buy condoms."

"It'll be okay," she insisted. "I'm not likely to be ovulating right now."

"'Not likely' isn't all that reassuring."

She opened her mouth to respond, but before she could, they heard Reese's voice.

"Walker?"

"Shit," he muttered and set her aside, so he could grab his swimsuit and toss her dress to her.

"Stay here," he whispered and yanked on his trunks before striding toward the sound of his brother's voice.

As Marlow scrambled to get her dress over her head, she heard him say, "Reese? I thought you were going to bed."

"And I thought you were coming in. I was afraid you'd decided to go swimming, or you'd fallen into the fire or something."

"You sound like Mom. I'm not that drunk. And I'm familiar with these waters—I'd be unlikely to get hurt in them."

"I know that. I just...couldn't imagine what was taking so long."

"I was finishing my beer and putting out the fire, like I said. Let's go in and get some sleep."

After he guided Reese away, all Marlow could hear, besides the wind and the waves, was the sound of her own breathing. She felt slightly shaken, as though she'd been through a hurricane.

"Wow," she whispered. After promising herself she wouldn't so much as invite Walker back to the house, not if she could avoid it, she'd boldly approached him for sex. And he'd given it to her. She'd thought if she gave him what he'd always wanted, he'd *have* to forgive her, she supposed, and they'd finally be able to reach some sort of emotional equilibrium—something that had eluded them for years. But the result had done just the opposite. Being so intimate with Walker had been unlike anything she'd anticipated. Their history and lifelong connection had opened a whole new dimension.

Goosebumps rose on her arms as she got up. Not only had the temperature dropped, she'd worked up a sweat and no longer had Walker to keep her warm.

She picked up his flip-flops and his T-shirt, which were lying on the ground, discarded because he hadn't had the time to collect them. She figured it would be smartest to put them with the beer cans and other detritus from the bonfire. They'd be easy to find in the morning, and if someone else came upon them, it wouldn't seem strange that they were there.

She headed toward the water, the soft sand shifting comfortably beneath her bare feet, and put his flip-flops near the chair he'd been using. But she couldn't bring herself to do the same with his shirt.

Lifting the soft cotton to her nose, she inhaled deeply.

If he wondered where it had gone, he could ask her, she decided, and carried it back to the guesthouse, where she quietly let herself inside, slipped into her bedroom and shoved it under her mattress. She felt a little silly, like a man who keeps the panties of a woman he slept with as a trophy. But she wasn't willing to examine the implications too closely. The shirt had sentimental value to her. It was that simple. And she doubted he'd even miss it.

Sleep didn't come easily. All she could think about was Walker's mouth at her breast, his hand between her thighs, how eager he'd been to get inside her—and how much she'd liked it.

Maybe she'd regret what she'd done in the morning.

But she already knew she'd never forget it.

"Hey, are you ever going to wake up?"

At the sound of Aida's voice, Marlow lifted her head and squinted against the sunlight streaming into her bedroom. "What time is it?"

"Ten thirty. If you're going to shower and eat before we play tennis, you might want to get moving."

The memories from last night came flooding back to Marlow. She'd had raw, carnal sex with Walker. And she'd stolen his shirt.

"Marlow?"

She cleared her throat. "Right. Okay. I'll go have a shower."

"Great. Rosemary came by. She said there are bagels, cold cereal, oatmeal, coffee and fresh-squeezed juice for breakfast. She had to take your mother to pick up a refill on her meds. You sleep okay?"

For a second, Marlow feared that was a leading question. Had her friends realized she hadn't stayed in bed last night? She leaned up to get a better glimpse of Aida's face but decided it was only her guilty conscience that was making her feel she was busted. It was sort of ironic that she'd been afraid Aida would complicate things by hooking up with Reese when she'd hooked up with one of the Cantwell boys herself.

She wondered how Rosemary would feel about it if she ever found out...

"Did you hear me?" Aida asked.

"Oh, yeah. Sorry. I'm not quite with it yet."

"Wasn't last night fun? Reese and Walker are *really* nice."

Marlow pretended to be preoccupied with checking her phone. "So is their mother," she said in an attempt to shift the conversation to safer ground.

"Yeah. I like Rosemary, too. She takes such great care of your mom. You can tell she really loves her."

"They've been together, day in and day out, for years."

"That would form a strong bond."

It had also put Marlow in constant contact with Walker and Reese—more so Walker, since he was closer to her age. She'd left for college when Reese was just a little boy. No wonder her relationship with Walker was so complicated, she told herself. He'd been raised with her, but he wasn't any relation. He'd had a thing for her as far back as she could remember, yet she'd had no interest in him. And now they'd just had sex on the beach.

What was she doing?

"Claire and I are going to clean up the mess from last night while you shower," Aida said. "Meet us at the big house when you're ready."

Marlow threw off her bedding. "I'm happy to help. Just wait for me."

"It'll only take a few minutes. We've got it," she said and went out to the living room, where Marlow heard her ask if Claire was ready to go.

Slumping back onto her pillows, Marlow waited for her friends to leave the house.

After she heard the front door close and their voices begin to drift away, she pulled out Walker's T-shirt and smelled it again. It smelled wonderful to her; *he'd* smelled wonderful to her. But what was it going to be like playing tennis with him today?

Briefly, she considered canceling. But she knew he'd immediately guess why she wasn't there, and she didn't want to disappoint Aida. She was probably going to see a lot of Walker this summer, so she might as well get that awkward "first encounter after sex" over with.

Or…maybe *he* wouldn't show. Reese said he worked a lot.

After shoving his shirt back under her mattress, she rolled out of bed and headed to the shower.

When she was ready and walking over to the main house, she couldn't resist looking for Walker's motorcycle in the drive. But it was gone.

While they had breakfast, she half expected Aida to say there'd been a message from Reese indicating they'd lost their fourth player. But that didn't happen. Before she knew it, they were all piled in her father's Jeep, since Rosemary and her mother had taken the Tesla, and when she pulled into the lot at the club, she saw that Walker's motorcycle was already there.

"I can't wait to see who's going to win today," Claire said as they got their racquets.

"This is going to be great," Aida said.

Marlow eyed Walker's motorcycle out of the corner of her eye. "Yeah," she muttered. "It's going to be great."

Walker couldn't wait to see Marlow. Last night, after getting what he'd always wanted—not just the sex, but Marlow's interest and receptiveness—he was positive he'd finally be done with her, so there was no need to beg off tennis. Seeing her would be a nonissue for him; he'd feel nothing when he encountered her.

He'd left a little early, so he arrived before she and her friends did. Carrying the small bag that contained his racquet and some tennis balls, he breezed through the club and onto the courts to find his brother with a client.

While he waited for Reese to finish up, he kept checking his watch and the door, hoping Marlow and her friends wouldn't cancel. Beating her at tennis today would put an exclamation point on the end of all the pain, turmoil, angst and frustration she'd caused him over the years.

As soon as Reese said goodbye to his student, he strode over. "Hey, I'm out of water. Did you happen to bring any extra?"

"I didn't," Walker said. "I rode the bike, so I was traveling light. Planned to buy a bottle myself when I got here."

"Do you have a couple of bucks, then, so I can get one, too?"

Reese worked at the club at least five days a week, depending on his clients' needs. He knew he'd be out in the hot sun and would need plenty to drink. Why he wasn't prepared, Walker had no idea, but it didn't surprise him. It was just like his little brother to drive away from Seaclusion without enough water to sustain him for the day—and without thinking to grab the money to buy more.

Reese was too used to being sheltered and cared for. And because his lack of caution and concern never came back to bite him, he didn't learn. Walker had always been the responsible one; being the older brother, and trying to look out for their mother when their father was drunk and rampaging through the house, bellowing at the top of his lungs, had forced him to grow up fast. But he was in too good a mood to allow such a minor irritation to put a wrinkle in his day.

He took a few bucks from his bag, but as he straightened to hand the money over, Reese stepped back. "What's on your neck?"

Walker had seen the mark Marlow had left when he showered this morning. He'd worn a golf shirt hoping the collar would hide it. But, apparently, the love bite was still visible when he moved certain ways. "I tripped last night and—"

"And got a hickey?" his brother broke in.

He rubbed the spot as though it was a smudge that might come off. "It's not a hickey."

"Sure looks like one to me."

"Well, it's not," he insisted. "I was with *you* last night, remember?"

Obviously bemused, Reese knitted his eyebrows. He was trying to sort out what was going on, but then Aida, Claire and

Marlow walked onto the court. "Hey," they called out, and Reese let the subject go as he turned to face them.

"Glad you could make it," he said.

Claire lifted both hands as they converged. "Don't worry. I won't be playing. I'm only here to watch. I need a few lessons before I try to take on these guys again," she said, gesturing at the rest of them.

"If you come after I'm done on almost any weekday, I'll coach you for free," Reese said.

Walker could tell Aida didn't like the idea of Claire hanging out with Reese. The way Aida used any excuse to get close to Reese said she was too interested in him to be happy seeing the woman who'd had an affair with her ex-husband spending time with Reese for any reason.

"I think I'll stick to yoga," Claire said. "I doubt three months is long enough to learn tennis."

Smart girl, Walker thought. He'd been feigning interest in the conversation, biding his time. Now that it wouldn't seem too eager, he shifted his gaze directly to Marlow. This was the moment he'd been waiting for—when he'd look at her and be able to tell that his fascination with her was gone at last.

Except that it wasn't. The second their eyes met, every detail of last night whipped through his mind, and he realized he'd been a fool to think it would free him.

He didn't feel less; he felt more.

When she avoided his gaze as though she was slightly embarrassed, he frowned. No way would he allow his infatuation with Marlow Madsen to continue. He was done with her. He would exorcise her from his soul no matter what.

He spent the next hour trying to prove it on the court. He was playing so hard that, when they took a water break, his brother came up to him and murmured, "Bro, you're being a little aggressive with Marlow, don't you think? What's going on?"

"Nothing's going on," he said.

"Then don't be a dick and hit it to me once in a while, okay? I understand you've always had a thing for her. But stop pulling her ponytail."

"I don't know what you're talking about," he grumbled, but he understood all too well why Reese was shocked. Walker never treated a woman the way he was treating Marlow.

He tried not to be as rough on her the next set, but he was so angry that nothing had changed, that he couldn't get her out of his system, it wasn't easy to see her across the net and not slam the ball so she couldn't return it.

Get out of my head. Why can't I be as indifferent to you as I want to be?

When he went up for an overhead shot and absolutely smashed the ball, causing it to rocket to the other side like a missile, barely missing her, Marlow said she had to go to the bathroom and left the court.

Even Aida winced as Marlow walked away. "Are you mad at her or something?" she asked once her friend was gone.

"No, of course not," he replied and quickly excused himself, too. He didn't want to stand there and let them grill him about why he was being such a douchebag. He needed to calm down and get hold of himself. Treating Marlow badly wasn't making him like her any less. It was only making her hate him that much more.

Actually, maybe that was his true intent. If she hated him enough—more than she did now—she wouldn't want anything to do with him. She'd make it a point to stay away. *Then* maybe he could get over her.

He saw that Claire was in line to buy a coffee drink, so he veered away from the restrooms that were in the café and went to the ones that weren't used as often in the locker area. He was just about to walk in so he could splash some water on his face when Marlow emerged and nearly bumped into him.

Damn. She'd come to these bathrooms, too.

Her eyes narrowed the second she saw him. "You're a jerk," she said, her expression sullen.

He didn't bother to argue; he had no defense. "I know."

"What do you think you're doing out there? What are you trying to prove?"

He shook his head. "I wish I could tell you."

"I hate you," she muttered.

If only he could truly hate her, too. "I don't blame you," he said.

She seemed taken aback by his response. "That's all you've got to say?"

"What more do you want?" he asked.

Giving him a funny look, as though she couldn't decide how to interpret his response, she started to walk away.

He wanted her to leave. But he couldn't stand to see her go. So he caught her by the wrist and pulled her back, and the next thing he knew, they were kissing so deeply he had to use his shoulder to maneuver them into the bathroom she'd just vacated.

"This is the women's room," she mumbled against his lips, but she had her arms wound tightly around his neck, and she wasn't letting go.

He raised his head long enough to respond. "Is there anyone else in here?" He started to look for feet beneath the stalls, but she drew his mouth back to hers before he could thoroughly check.

"No," she replied.

"Good." He fumbled around behind him and managed to lock the door. Then everything he'd been feeling on the court began to manifest itself in an entirely different way. Within seconds, he'd removed her cute little tennis skirt and lifted her onto the sink.

"We can't do this in here," she gasped, but she was clinging to him and kissing him as though she was actually saying, "I *have* to have you now."

Another contradiction. She was full of them. But he was going to force himself to listen to her words. Even if having sex in a public restroom wasn't expressly illegal, he was the chief of police and could lose his job. "You're right." He drew a deep breath, fighting for control as he extricated himself from her arms.

He bent to pick up her skirt, but she didn't take it when he tried to hand it to her. "Oh, what the hell," she said and went for his shorts.

Walker hoped anyone who needed a bathroom went to the one off the café. "This is a first for me," he said and felt the most incredible sense of satisfaction as he gripped her ass for leverage and pressed inside her.

She groaned as she accepted him and dropped her head back to give him better access to her neck. "Me, too."

Playing tennis against Marlow hadn't done anything to relieve the tension inside him, but having sex with her was another matter entirely. Nothing else was quite as thrilling. He just wished they had more time. All he could do was take her hard and fast, and pull out before he came inside her.

After he withdrew, he said, "Come over tonight if you want to." Then he cleaned up and got the hell out of there.

As he strode quickly back to the court, the owner of the tennis club, Dave McGowen, waved at him from several feet away. "Hey, man," he called. "Good to see you."

Walker's heart was still pounding at the daring of what he'd done. Had he just ruined his life? Or had he gotten away with it? "Good to see you, too," he said and kept his head down from there on so he wouldn't be greeted by any other acquaintances.

As soon as he reached the court, where Reese, Claire and Aida were waiting for him and Marlow, he packed up his racquet.

"Where are you going?" Reese asked. "We were planning to play another set."

"And then we thought we'd have some lunch," Claire added.

"Sorry," he said. "Something's come up at work."

That was a lie. He hadn't even taken his phone with him to the bathroom. But he had to get away from Marlow as soon as possible, and he had to stay away from her. He'd just risked his job, a job he loved, for three minutes in a public restroom with her.

Being around her affected his brain and made him do irresponsible, reckless things.

With any luck, she, too, would realize that they were better off staying as far away from each other as possible this summer and wouldn't appear at his door tonight, despite the invitation he'd foolishly given her.

12

Marlow stared at herself in the mirror. She'd righted her clothes and tightened her ponytail, but her face was still red—and not from playing tennis.

What had she been thinking since she'd come home to Teach? What was she doing having crazy, out-of-control, hormone-fueled sex with Walker? Was this a reaction to her father's death? The worry she felt for her mother? The crisis in her professional life?

Maybe this was how she was trying to cope with it all—by acting like a randy teenager.

She'd grown up so fast. It could be that she was making up for her lost adolescence, because nothing about what she was doing made sense. Seconds before he kissed her, she'd told Walker she hated him. That wasn't true. Not even remotely. But he *had* been acting like a jerk, and it was easier to tell him she hated him than to admit he was making her feel terrible. She wasn't used to him treating her poorly. He'd always done everything he could to look out for her, make things easy, give her what she wanted.

In short, like her father, he'd spoiled her. So the way he'd accepted her words today, as though he fully believed them, as though he didn't expect any gratitude for his many kindnesses in the past, had made her feel like a jerk herself.

How had that led to sex in a public bathroom?

The door opened, and Marlow turned on the water as though she was about to wash her hands. An older woman, dressed entirely in Ralph Lauren, went into the far stall, and Marlow realized how narrowly they'd escaped being caught. It would've been terrible if that woman, or anyone else, had tried to get into the restroom just two or three minutes earlier.

So many people on the island knew her mother. She didn't want to embarrass Eileen. She didn't want to embarrass herself or Walker, either. Why had she been so aggressive? He'd tried to stop it before it went too far. She was the one who'd insisted they continue. For the life of her, she couldn't understand why. She'd been angry with him—until he'd kissed her. Then all of that anger had turned into red-hot desire.

She shut off the tap and went through the motions of drying her hands. She needed time to regain her equilibrium before returning to the tennis court. But she was taking too long. She had to get back out there before Claire or Aida came to check on her.

How would he treat her once they started playing again?

After this morning, she was afraid to find out.

But he was gone when she got back, and that bothered her almost as much as having him slam the ball at her. Reese said he'd been called in to work, but Marlow didn't believe it. The timing was too suspicious. He'd escaped the situation, pure and simple.

"I'm sorry for how Walker treated you," Aida said as they meandered out to the Jeep after having lunch with Reese. "He must have some sort of ego problem, huh?"

"What?" Marlow said.

"The way he kept smacking the ball at you, trying to prove how good he is," Aida clarified. "I was shocked."

Marlow couldn't explain what was going on when they'd

been playing, but Walker hadn't been trying to prove his supe- riority. "I think he was just…having a bad day," she mumbled.

Her friends hesitated before getting into the Jeep. "You're not mad at him?" Aida said. "Even Reese was embarrassed."

"I've played plenty of other games with Walker over the years," Marlow responded. "This is the first time I've ever seen him act like that."

"What kind of games?" Claire asked as they climbed in.

Marlow started the engine. "Sand volleyball. Flag football. That sort of thing. My father never had a son, which I think he really wanted. He loved putting together games on various holidays with the kids in the neighborhood. I always got to play. So did Walker. Reese was too young."

"And Walker wasn't overly competitive back then?" Claire asked.

Not with her. As a matter of fact, there were plenty of times when she was fairly certain he'd let her win. It was easy to tell; she'd seen how much better he played when he was with op- ponents he felt he could compete against without dominating. Chess was the only game where he always had to try his best, be- cause he didn't have a physical advantage. "No. Not like today."

"Reese said you and Walker have never really gotten along," Aida said.

Marlow didn't want to admit that was true, because it was more her fault than his. "Reese is making too big a deal out of it."

Aida switched stations on the radio as they pulled out of the lot onto the main road. "Did you see the hickey on his neck?" she asked with a conspiratorial grin. "I was tempted to tease him about it, but I couldn't predict how he'd react, given the mood he was in."

"I saw it, too," Claire said with a laugh. "It wasn't there last night, so it's *very* recent."

Marlow tightened her hands on the steering wheel and said nothing.

Claire's laugh turned into more of a giggle. "Maybe he didn't get enough sleep last night, and that's why he was such a bear today."

"Whoever he was with is lucky," Aida said. "He's gorgeous, isn't he? Even better-looking than his brother, although Reese is a lot sweeter."

That wasn't true. They didn't know how sweet Walker could be. That was all. But Marlow kept her mouth shut.

Claire held her hair back to keep it from whipping into her face as she leaned around the seat. "I asked his brother if he was seeing someone, and he said, 'Not to my knowledge.'"

"Does it matter if he is?" Marlow asked. "What he does is none of our business." She didn't like hearing them talk about Walker, especially with so much interest.

Aida, who was sitting in the passenger seat, looked over at her in surprise, and a glance in the rearview mirror showed an equally startled Claire.

"Sorry," Claire said.

"We didn't realize we were upsetting you," Aida added.

Marlow hadn't meant to sound so irritable. She put on her sunglasses. The sun was bright today, but she also needed a shield. "You weren't upsetting me. Sorry I snapped."

"So...are you interested in Walker yourself?" Aida asked.

"No. Of course not." Marlow spoke stridently, insistently. But when she breathed in, she could smell Walker's cologne on her clothes.

That right there called her a liar.

Claire stepped under the shade of a palm tree at the far end of the property, where she felt safe that the others couldn't see her. After losing to Marlow at chess, she'd said she was going to take a walk along the beach and enjoy the sunset while Aida played the next game. Marlow would probably win again; she was magnificent at chess.

Claire had left them on the main deck of the big house with Eileen, who looked on from a chaise nearby. Marlow's mother wasn't completely up and around, but the poor woman was obviously tired of spending the majority of her time in bed. She needed to be with people, was eager to interact with her daughter, even though she'd said she didn't feel up to playing chess herself. Claire felt sorry for her. It would be hard enough if you were sick some of the time; she couldn't imagine how terrible it would be if you were sick almost all of the time.

At Eileen's request, Rosemary had made a delicious Italian dinner. After she'd cleaned up the meal, she'd served a round of refreshing mixed drinks and then left. She didn't say where she was going. It was highly possible she just needed to get out, take a break. Claire couldn't help feeling some sympathy for the Madsens' housekeeper, too. Rosemary probably made good money, since she'd been with the family for so long, but she must find it difficult to be needed at all hours. It seemed she was forever at Eileen's beck and call, that she had little or no life of her own.

Did she ever resent it? What about Walker and Reese? Because Claire had never had household help—never had friends who'd been raised the way Marlow had been raised, either—the arrangement seemed unnatural to her. Didn't Walker and Reese get tired of seeing their mother serve Eileen and her family? Or were they so used to it they didn't think twice about it?

When Rosemary's boys were at the house, Claire watched them curiously, but she hadn't even seen them tonight. Neither Reese nor Walker had been at dinner. As far as she could tell, Reese had never come home from the club.

She took a photo of the sunset, which looked like it was melting into the sea. After all the worry and upset of the past year, it was soothing to gaze at such a beautiful sight. She loved being on the island, and yet she felt lonely at the same time. What was she going to do with her life after the summer?

Whenever that question came up, her thoughts naturally gravitated toward Dutton. She'd planned to build a future with him. But the bottom had fallen out of her life, and at times, it felt as though she was still in free fall.

She knew better than to contact him, but she was missing him so badly she couldn't resist sending him the picture she'd just taken on her cell. She was also a little concerned that she hadn't heard from him today. Had he given up on her and moved on? Was he already dating someone else?

Part of her believed he was capable of forgetting about her that easily. And if that was true, it would be safer for her if he *did* move on. But the thought of letting him go brought such abject misery she was ready to do almost anything to stop the pain.

It's incredible here, she wrote and sent that with the photo.

She waited ten minutes, then fifteen, but didn't get a response. She wished she hadn't reached out. Any contact with him made her feel disloyal to Aida. Yet she couldn't seem to stop herself. She was caught in a war between her heart and her conscience.

With a sigh, she started trudging back toward the house, but her phone buzzed before she'd gone halfway.

There he was.

A tsunami of relief swept over her—with equal parts guilt— as she glanced down at her phone.

I can't wait to see it.

She stopped in midstride. What did that mean? That's the view from the private beach at Seaclusion, she texted.

How rich do you have to be to name your house? 😃

She felt a scowl tug at her eyebrows. Don't change the subject. How will you see it?

I have a week off at the hospital. Starting next Saturday.

And?

I plan to spend the week with you.

Surely, he didn't mean that. Turning quickly so that she was no longer facing the house, she hurried back to the small area of privacy by the palm tree and hit the phone app.

"Hey, babe," he said when he picked up. "Can you believe it?"

She ignored the "babe" part. He didn't seem to get that they weren't currently in a relationship. "What's going on?" she asked without preamble.

"I just told you."

She closed her eyes for a second. "You're not coming to the island, are you?"

"I am," he replied with a smile in his voice. "I just bought my plane ticket."

Her hand flew to her chest. *"What?"*

"I was going to surprise you, but when you sent that picture, I couldn't resist giving you the good news."

Good news? "Dutton, you know I'm here with Aida!"

"Claire, Aida won't be any better off if we stay apart. Remaining lonely and miserable just because it'll offend her if we get together is stupid."

There was some logic to that. Or was it simply the best rationalization for doing what she really wanted? "You can't come here," she insisted. "There's no way."

"Of course I can. Aida will adjust. Or she won't. That'll be up to her."

"You might not care if it upsets her, but *I* do."

"You would never even have met Aida without me, Claire. So why is her friendship suddenly more important than us?"

"Because I *have* met her, and I care about her."

"More than me?" he pressed.

Claire didn't know how to answer that question, so she avoided it entirely. "You can't come here," she reiterated. "I don't know where you'd stay, anyway. It's a very small island."

"I'm sure they have houses for rent. And if they don't, I'll stay somewhere close by."

"But you have no idea how difficult it'll be for me—and for her—if you show up."

"I won't cause a problem," he said. "They won't even have to know I'm there. I just want to see you, to remind you of what we have before they poison you against me entirely. It's time we remembered just how amazing things can be between us," he said. Then he told her he had to figure out the rest of his plans and disconnected.

Claire battled an all-out panic attack as she lowered her phone. What was she going to do now?

Rosemary drove to Miami as quickly as she could without risking a ticket. She didn't want to explain to Eileen, her boys or anyone else why she'd left the island and traveled to the mainland, so she couldn't be gone for too long.

She checked the clock on her dashboard. She was going to be a little late, even though she was hurrying. She shouldn't have offered that round of drinks after dinner at Seaclusion before she took off, but she'd been so eager to make sure everyone was well taken care of and wouldn't miss her while she was gone that she'd probably done more than she needed to. Rudy wouldn't be happy about having to wait for her. But he wouldn't say anything. Not these days. A lot had changed since they'd been married.

When she came to the small house he rented along with two

other men, she didn't go to the door. She called him on her phone instead. "I'm here."

"I'll be right out."

A few seconds later he appeared, looking more handsome than he had any right to look, given everything he'd done to destroy his body over the years. Rudy's behavior hadn't only been hard on him, it'd been hard on her, too, and there were moments when she still resented it.

But deep down she loved him, and he claimed to have turned his life around. If that was true, she couldn't see how spending the rest of her days alone would serve any good purpose.

"Did you have trouble getting away from Eileen?" he asked as he got in.

"Not really. I can leave the house whenever I want to," she said.

"As long as she doesn't need you."

"Of course."

"Did you tell her where you were going?"

"It didn't come up." She'd done all she could to ensure that it wouldn't. She hadn't wanted to reveal where she was going, because she preferred Eileen not to know she was seeing Rudy again. Her employer would be concerned about "the dangers."

"Where are we going?" she asked.

His seat belt snapped as he latched it. "A little Greek restaurant in the courtyard at Mandolin."

"Where's that?" She hadn't spent much time in Miami. It had always been just a transfer city for her—the place they flew into and out of when traveling to the island.

"I've got the address on my phone." He started his navigation as she pulled away from the curb, and she began to follow the instructions.

"How are the boys?" he asked as she turned out of his neighborhood and onto a much busier street.

Neither Walker nor Reese would speak to him, so he had to

find out what was going on in their lives from her. Like Eileen, they'd be unhappy if they learned she was contemplating a reconciliation. But they didn't have the right to decide what was best for her. She could pursue what she thought would make her happy, just as they could. "They're doing fine."

"It's so hard for me to believe Walker's the chief of police." She stopped at a red light. "He loves his job."

"Reese seems to like his, too."

"Who wouldn't like being a tennis pro?"

"We have the old windbag to thank for that."

The "old windbag" was Tiller. "Don't talk about him like that, especially now that he's gone."

Rudy rolled his eyes. "I guess I don't feel as kindly toward him as you do. Without his interference, we might still be married."

Tiller hadn't interfered. He'd tried to help by offering to cover the cost of counseling and rehab. "He had nothing to do with it."

The light turned green, and she gave the Tesla some gas. Since she was allowed to use the vehicles at Seaclusion, she'd sold her Camry before leaving Georgia.

"I feel like they both did," he grumbled. "I won't dredge up those old complaints, though. Not tonight. We're going out for a nice evening."

"Thank you for the restraint," she said and hoped he wouldn't expect her to sleep with him after dinner. She wasn't going inside his house, not with his roommates living there. She wasn't ready to make that kind of commitment even if they had the privacy for it. While she wanted a relationship with him—she'd always cared about him or she wouldn't have put up with so much—she was being cautious. She couldn't allow herself to be suckered by someone she'd already deemed unreliable.

"So what's it like having Marlow and her friends on the island?" he asked as she followed his GPS.

She'd been keeping in daily contact with him, which was how he knew about Marlow and her friends. "I like it. It's fun to have more people around, more activity, especially now that Tiller's gone. It gets pretty quiet the days Eileen doesn't feel well."

"Sounds boring to me."

"For the most part, I like it," she said, feeling defensive. "When she's resting, I put in my ear buds while I cook or clean and don't have to worry about making conversation."

"When are you going to quit that job?"

She glanced over at him in surprise. "Well, unless I win the lottery, I guess I'll quit when I retire. Otherwise, how will I pay my bills?"

"I'll help you," he said. "I can take care of you now."

While he finally had a steady job maintaining the landscaping for county parks and roads, he wasn't making all that much. He could barely take care of himself, so she knew better than to rely on that.

"I've got a good salary, and I don't mind the work," she said. "Besides, Eileen needs me more than ever since Tiller died."

He didn't say anything about Eileen's poor health or her loss. Rosemary knew he didn't have much sympathy for the Madsens, who'd always had far more wealth, friends and respect than they'd ever had. He still blamed Tiller and Eileen for interfering in their marriage, but all the Madsens had done was try to support her through the worst of it. It was Rudy's own fault that they didn't admire him. They'd only been reacting to his poor behavior.

"I bet Walker's excited to have Marlow back," he said.

She got onto the freeway. "Why would he be excited?"

"Don't you remember how he felt about her? I've never seen a boy so lovesick."

"That was a long time ago, when they were young."

He shrugged. "Doesn't matter. Some things never change."

She supposed she could agree with that. Here she was meeting Rudy for dinner when she'd sworn to herself on multiple occasions that she'd never have anything more to do with him. "I guess love finds a way."

When he gave her that dazzling smile of his and reached over to take her hand, she knew she was already in trouble. "Exactly," he said.

13

The evening passed on leaden feet. Marlow couldn't help being distracted. It felt as though she could hear every tick of the clock, even though they were out on the deck playing chess and there was no clock.

"Wow!" Aida exclaimed. "Am I really going to beat you?"

Marlow forced her attention back to the board. She'd lost a bishop, a rook, both knights and several pawns—a lot more pieces than Aida had lost. "It's not looking good for me," she admitted.

She'd been too busy trying to make up her mind about whether she should go to Walker's tonight. They needed to talk, try to find some calm in the storm that raged around them whenever they were together.

Aida used her knight to take Marlow's last rook, which put her in an even worse position. She had to risk losing her bishop to save her queen. She was being forced into a defensive game. That wasn't how she usually played, but it served her right for not paying attention.

Claire had returned from her walk and was sitting at the table, sipping a glass of wine while looking through Pinterest, she said, for various ideas for Marlow's birthday, which was five days away. When she heard what Aida said, she sprang to her feet and came over to see for herself. "Wow! You're going to beat Marlow!"

Eileen got up to take a closer peek at the board, too. "Way to go," she said to Aida. "I can't remember the last time I beat her. I think she was twelve."

The game wasn't over yet. There was a chance Marlow could recover, but she didn't care enough about the win to fight for it. She just wanted everyone to go to bed so she wouldn't have to keep up the pretense of being engaged in what was going on around her.

"I'm tired." Eileen dropped a kiss on Marlow's cheek before telling her friends good-night.

"Let me walk you in," Marlow said and promised Aida she'd be right back to finish the game.

"It's so good to have you home," her mother said as Marlow took her arm and they went inside.

"It's good to be here, too," she said. What she didn't add was that she missed her father terribly, and the memories being on the island evoked made her feel his loss all the more poignantly.

"You don't miss your work?" Eileen asked. "You're really going to let it go?"

"I haven't made up my mind about that completely." She released her mother's arm so Eileen could precede her into the room. "It's early in the summer yet."

"I agree. It's never wise to make a snap decision, especially about something as important as your future."

"Whatever I decide, I won't do it impulsively," she promised and got her mother's nightgown for her and draped it across the bed. "Dinner tonight was delicious, wasn't it?"

"It was. Rosemary is such a good cook."

"Where is she tonight?"

"She didn't say."

Marlow was glad Rosemary felt free to come and go as she

pleased. With Tiller gone and no one else around to look after Eileen, Marlow had been concerned that her mother's house-keeper might be feeling trapped. "Does she go out very often?"

"More so lately. After being cooped up for so long, she's probably thrilled to have a chance to leave the house, especially now that you're here so she doesn't have to worry about me."

"I'm happy I can help. Do you need anything before I finish my game with Aida? We're going to the guesthouse to watch a movie in a few minutes."

"Not a thing."

"I'll keep my phone with me, just in case."

"Thank you." Her mother embraced her, and they wished each other a good night. Then Marlow returned to the deck and quickly lost the chess game, partially on purpose. She hoped the movie would be more successful at distracting her from what she'd done with Walker in the restroom at the club today.

Before they started the movie, Aida wanted to bake some chocolate chip cookies, and Claire, who'd gone into the ocean before dinner, decided to take a shower. Grateful that her friends would be occupied for a short time, Marlow went down to the beach so she could be alone.

As she walked in the wet sand, the warm waves occasionally rolling up to cover her feet, she wished she could turn around and see her father standing on the deck in a pool of light from the house, waving at her. It was hard to imagine that he'd never be there again. If only she'd spent more time with him while he was alive. But she'd never dreamed he'd pass away at such a young age.

She dropped her head back to gaze up at the stars that were beginning to come out. At least she had this place, where she could still feel close to him. She breathed deeply, taking in the salty air—and reached for him with her mind.

I miss you.

She was about to head back to the guesthouse when she saw the gumbo-limbo tree at the very edge of the property that she and Walker had discovered as children. A fast-growing tree that was common all over the island, it had red, peeling bark, so the locals jokingly referred to it as a "tourist tree." She was only eight—Walker was ten—when they found that this particular gumbo-limbo had a hole in the trunk. Pretending it was where Edward Teach had hidden some of his pirate booty, they started hiding cookies and small treasures in it. And as they grew older and quit playing together, she'd occasionally find other gifts he'd left her.

Walker had never admitted that he was the giver of these small, sweet items. But she knew it couldn't be anyone else. She remembered finding coins, a pack of gum, a pretty rock, some flowers. Nothing very expensive, of course. They reminded her of the gifts Boo Radley had left for Jem and Scout in *To Kill a Mockingbird*. Walker simply gave her what he had—anything he thought she might like.

Remembering that now made her feel so much worse about how she'd treated him in later years.

"Why couldn't I have been born an adult?" she muttered.

There was nothing inside the tree now. She felt silly even checking, but as unlikely as it was, she was halfway hoping there'd be a token of his forgiveness.

Then it occurred to her—maybe she should be the one to leave something for him.

She hurried to the big house, quietly let herself in so she wouldn't disturb her mother and went into her old bedroom, where she dug through the drawers of the dresser until she found what she was looking for. She doubted Walker would ever think to check the gumbo-limbo—not these days. He probably wouldn't want to find anything from her even if he did.

But for the sake of her own conscience, she had to close that gap.

★ ★ ★

Aida stared at the ceiling, unable to sleep. All she could think about was Claire and Dutton.

Although Claire hadn't mentioned it, Aida was certain Dutton was still calling and texting her, and that drove Aida crazy. She wished she was so far beyond the divorce that she no longer cared. But she did care; she couldn't help it. Just the thought that they might be getting back together had claws, and those claws seemed to be tearing her apart from the inside.

"She *knows* he's no good," she whispered to herself. "She'd be stupid to get involved with him again." But that didn't mean she wouldn't. Who could say no to Dutton, especially when he was being his most charming? When he smiled that captivating smile and made a woman feel as though she was the most important person in the room? And didn't most women want to marry someone as smart and successful as he was? Being the wife of a surgeon was something to be proud of.

She'd always been proud of it, anyway. No doubt she was mourning the loss of her previous status along with everything else. Being a divorcée wasn't the same.

"What does that say about me?" she mumbled, but decided not to even try to answer that question. It was more than she could handle right now. She was already wrestling with such a huge sense of loss. With the news that Dutton was trying to get Claire back, that loss suddenly felt fresh again.

Before, she'd felt cheated by Dutton. Now she felt cheated by Claire.

What was she going to do? How was she going to get through this?

Sitting up, she dropped her head in her hands and began rubbing her temples. She had to leave what Claire did up to Claire and continue to heal and move on. What happened between the two of them shouldn't matter to her.

And yet it did.

With a sigh, she got up and went out to the living room. They'd watched a movie before wandering off to their separate bedrooms. Maybe Claire had left her phone charging on the counter. Aida had seen it there earlier. She had no idea if it was locked and would require facial recognition or a passcode to get in, but she had to at least try to find out what was going on. What the two of them were saying to each other. If Claire was now lying to her the way Dutton once did.

And if there was none of that, if Claire had told him to leave her alone, maybe Aida could stop torturing herself.

She searched the room, but the phone was gone. Of course Claire would take it to bed with her.

She was on the way back to her own room when she noticed that Claire's door stood slightly ajar. Compelled in spite of her conscience, Aida pushed it wider, wondering if it would make a sound, but it didn't. She managed to push it far enough to see the shape of Claire's body in the bed.

She waited to see if her friend would lift her head and ask what she wanted, but that didn't happen. Aida could hear Claire's soft, steady breathing. She was sound asleep—and her phone was charging on the nightstand beside her.

Aida's heart began to thump against her breastbone as she stepped inside the room. She almost couldn't bear to see what she might find on Claire's phone; at the same time, she was obsessed with it.

When the wooden floor creaked under her feet, she froze, but Claire didn't even stir.

Holding her breath and moving as slowly as possible, Aida inched closer to the nightstand, where she carefully unplugged the phone.

A wave of guilt swept over her, and she put the phone back down only to pick it up again. She had to see what they were saying, had to know if she had anything to worry about. Was Dutton telling Claire the same things he'd once told her? That he couldn't live without her? That he'd make her happy? That he'd always be faithful?

The passcode prompt came up on the screen. But she didn't know Claire's passcode. She could try holding the phone up to Claire's face to see if it would unlock that way, but that might wake her.

Hot tears welled up as Aida punched in a few numbers, trying to guess the password. Nothing worked. She couldn't believe she was stooping so low. What was wrong with her? This wasn't the person she wanted to be. She and her friends were hoping to use this summer to improve themselves, not fall to new lows.

Dashing away her tears, she carefully plugged the phone back in and put it on the nightstand before creeping out of the room. But she couldn't leave the matter there. When she returned to her bed, she took her own phone from the charger and texted Dutton.

Please don't be that big an asshole.

It was three hours earlier in California, only ten thirty. She saw three dots, signifying that he was texting her back. But he must've decided not to send whatever he'd composed, because she never got a response from him.

Walker prowled around the house, waiting to see if Marlow would show up. He told himself he hoped she *wasn't* coming. She'd always been the worst possible thing for him. But the later it got, the more he began to listen for her car and get up to check the windows if he heard something.

Fortunately, he didn't have her number. He'd had it at one time, for practical reasons, but had deleted the contact, and he was now glad, because he probably would've called her.

He thought of his brother. Reese lived at Seaclusion and might have some idea of what Marlow and her friends were doing. Maybe they were all having another bonfire.

Just in case his brother was with Marlow, he texted instead of calling. What're you up to tonight, bro?

He didn't get an answer right away. It wasn't until after he'd watched another episode of *Forensic Files* that he felt his phone buzz.

Out with Alicia Pendergast. Why? What are you doing?

Reese wouldn't know about Marlow, not if he was out with one of the girls he dated.

Not much. Just wondering if you wanted to come over and have a drink.

It's almost one. Since when have you ever texted me to see if I want to come over in the middle of the night?

"Smart-ass," Walker muttered. You're up, aren't you?

I won't be for long. ☺

Fine. We'll do it another night. Have a great time. He was tempted to warn his brother to use one of the condoms he'd purchased but didn't have the audacity after two encounters within the past twenty-four hours where he'd resorted to the risky withdrawal method.

What if, by chance, he'd gotten Marlow pregnant?

He heard a noise outside and got up again to check, but it was just the wind or the usual house-settling noises, because no one was there.

Fairly certain Marlow wasn't coming, he pulled off his clothes so he could drop into bed and was just reaching over to set his phone on the charger when he received a text.

It wasn't from Marlow; it was from his mother.

You awake?

He sat up. I am. Why?

I have a flat and could use your help.

That was the last thing he'd expected her to say. He'd thought maybe there was a problem with Mrs. Madsen and she needed to be taken to the hospital. Where are you?

I'll send you a pin.

Impressed and relieved she knew how to do that, he got dressed while waiting to receive her location. But when he picked up his phone again, he was shocked to see she was half-way to Miami. What are you doing there? he wrote.

I went out.

In the middle of the night?

I had a date, okay?

"A *date*?" he said aloud. That was something he'd never heard his mother say before. With who?

I'm stranded on the side of the road, Walker. Can you please come help me?

Of course. I'm on my way. Just get in your car, lock your doors and don't open them for anyone until I get there.

As he scooped his keys off the kitchen counter, he glanced down at their text exchange again. "A date," he repeated.

Marlow's alarm went off so early it was still dark outside. She turned it off, hoping that Aida and Claire would do the same with theirs. But she knew she wasn't going to get that wish when she heard Claire call out from her bedroom, "Rise and shine! We have to hurry or we're going to miss it."

"Miss what?" Aida called back, sounding as groggy as Marlow felt.

"The sunrise!" Claire said. "Last night, you said you'd do yoga on the beach with me."

Why on earth had she agreed to that? Marlow wondered. Wasn't yoga at ten just as cathartic as yoga at six? She let her eyes slide closed, but Claire spoke again, this time from the doorway to her bedroom. "Are you coming?"

"Yes, of course," she mumbled. "I'm getting up to do yoga."

"Okay, I'll check on Aida."

"You do that," she said, but it wasn't until she smelled coffee and heard Aida moving around in the bathroom next to her bedroom—proof Claire had been successful in rousing her, too—that she was able to drag herself out of bed.

"I need to remember that I'm not a morning person," she grumbled and yawned her way through getting into her yoga pants, a sports bra and tank. When she'd stuffed her feet into her flip-flops, she shuffled into the kitchen to see Aida covering a yawn of her own.

"Why did we agree to this?" Marlow asked.

"We must've forgotten that we're on vacation," Aida replied.

Claire sent them a remonstrative look while pouring them

each a cup of coffee. "We're hitting reset on our lives. That isn't vacation. We have a lot of work to do."

"We're *that* far away from becoming our best selves?" Aida joked, and Marlow chuckled.

"Probably farther than we'd like to admit." Claire sounded annoyingly chipper, but Marlow didn't mind so much once she'd taken a few sips of coffee.

"You're going to love greeting the day like this," Claire promised them. "Actually, you're greeting the whole week. It's Sunday."

"Feels more like a Monday than a Sunday," Marlow muttered. But after finishing her coffee, she hurried to brush her teeth and put her hair in a ponytail while Claire and Aida did the same.

By the time Claire shepherded them down to the beach, Marlow's mood hadn't improved by a whole lot. Once she was there in the peaceful dawn, however, with the sandpipers picking through the silt of low tide, the frigate birds, which could stay aloft for months without ever landing, wheeling high overhead, and the fiddler crabs sticking their claws and eyeballs out of their burrows as if to see what was going on, she was glad she'd made the effort. She'd forgotten how beautiful Teach was at sunrise.

"What's most important is remaining mindful," Claire instructed. "So we'll start with ten minutes of meditation to help us quiet our minds and find our center."

Marlow's mind had been quiet while she was sleeping. But as they sat in the lotus position, eyes closed, and Claire gave them instructions to focus on their breathing, Marlow's thoughts automatically returned to her encounter with Walker on the beach and then in the bathroom of the club, and whether or not it would've helped to show up at his house last night to try to talk about it—all the things she'd been obsessing over before falling asleep.

Fortunately, she was able to forget Walker once they started doing the more challenging poses. She had to focus to have the strength. She was in the middle of a headstand, which Claire could hold forever, when she caught a glimpse of someone standing on the deck of the big house. She so desperately wanted it to be her father that she fell over, then jumped up and turned around to get a better look.

It wasn't Tiller, of course, but she was still surprised to see that Walker had been leaning on the railing in his uniform, drinking a cup of coffee and probably watching the sun come up—before she and her friends had spilled onto the beach, giving him something else to watch.

She didn't wave, and neither did he. As soon as he realized she'd noticed him, he straightened and went back inside.

14

Rosemary had stayed at Walker's overnight. After Walker had finally reached her on the side of the road last night, they learned the car didn't have a spare and the hole in her tire was on the sidewall, where he couldn't patch it. By the time they started home in his SUV, it was so late she was afraid she'd wake Eileen if she went in, and she didn't want to explain where she'd been, especially since she could just sleep at Walker's. He had to be at work early and could drop her off before Eileen ever got out of bed.

"Thanks for breakfast," Walker said as he rinsed out his coffee cup and put it in the dishwasher. "I'd better get going or roadside assistance will beat me to the car."

He'd seemed quiet, distracted, while they were eating, but neither of them had gotten much sleep. "I appreciate you rescuing me last night—and taking care of the car this morning." With luck, Eileen wouldn't even realize the Tesla was gone. Rarely did she go out front where the cars were parked.

"No problem."

He'd asked her who she was seeing last night and clearly hadn't been pleased when she wouldn't say. He had argued that she should tell him where she was going and who she was with whenever she went out with a man, especially one she'd met on the internet. It wasn't safe to do otherwise. He'd assumed the internet part—how else would she meet a man in Miami?—but she wasn't going to correct him. She'd insisted that what she did was her own business and she could take care of herself. The fact that she'd called him to come change the tire was evidence to the contrary, and he was quick to point that out, but she wasn't ready for the backlash she'd receive if she told him it was his father.

You know you can't trust him. That was what Walker would say. And it would be true, based on what they'd experienced in the past.

But she'd had such a good time with Rudy last night. He'd avoided alcohol, including the wine the waiter had offered them. He'd been funny and attentive, and he hadn't pressed her for sex, which made her feel as though that wasn't all he was after. She needed more time to decide what to do about him, didn't want to ruin the excitement she was feeling by having to fend off warnings from Walker and Reese, or Eileen, no matter how well-intentioned.

Her son took a blueberry muffin for the road. "What time does Reese have to be at the club this morning?"

"He typically doesn't work until noon on Sundays."

She knew why he was asking. Her youngest son hadn't come home last night. His truck hadn't been in the drive when they pulled in this morning; she assumed he'd stayed over at a date's place.

"I'm sure he'll be there when he's supposed to be," she added.

"I hope so."

Walker had to be thinking about last month, when Reese had pulled a no-show and nearly lost his job. He'd claimed he'd thought it was his day off.

"I'll start nudging him around ten thirty, see if I can reach him," she said.

Walker rolled his eyes. "You shouldn't have to nag him."

"I prefer to think of it as doing him a favor." She couldn't let him lose his job.

Walker chuckled and kissed her cheek. "The Tesla will be back soon."

"Thank you."

He walked out, but she chased him down before he could get in his SUV and pull out of the drive. "Walker?"

When he turned, she glanced around before lowering her voice. "Any woman would be lucky to have you."

"I'm not even going to ask why you felt the need to say that," he said and got behind the wheel.

She caught the door before he could close it. "You know why I said it. Let's not pretend."

"I don't want to talk about Marlow."

He'd never been willing to discuss her. He internalized everything, pretended he didn't feel it—not if it was painful. She'd assumed he'd gotten over Marlow, that the Madsens' daughter would be irrelevant to him by now, but after what Rudy had said in the car last night, and how Walker attempted to ignore Marlow whenever she was around, she was beginning to wonder. "Just let me say that Marlow's a nice person. I've always loved her, even though she acted pretty spoiled there for a few years. I think she was struggling with being too smart and not fitting in anywhere—and any child who'd been given everything they could ever want would probably behave like that."

"Mom, you don't have anything to worry about," he insisted. "Really."

"Let me finish," she said. "She seems to have grown out of it, but even if you're still attracted to her, it wouldn't be smart to act on those feelings." What she said probably made it sound as though she was trying to protect her job. She knew that was how he'd take it. But she was actually far more worried about protecting other things—bigger things. He didn't know they were already sitting on a powder keg, and the smallest spark could cause it to blow.

"Are you done?" he said. "Because it's getting late, and I have a lot to do."

"I'm done," she said, but her stomach knotted as she watched him drive off.

Rudy was right. Walker still cared about Marlow. And what he didn't know could definitely hurt him.

Aida felt better toward Claire after yoga—and guilty for trying to break into her phone in the middle of the night. For the most part when she was with Claire, she remembered all the reasons she liked her. Claire was quirky and sweet and demonstrative. They always had a great time together.

Claire wouldn't let her down. Trying to fully believe that, Aida slipped her arm through Claire's as they walked along the street, going from boutique to boutique in the shopping area Marlow had mentioned when they first arrived on the island. Obviously surprised by that move—probably because things had been so tense between them lately—Claire gave her an affectionate smile. There was relief in her face, but Aida thought she detected a hint of concern, too.

"We're okay, aren't we?" Aida asked. "The two of us?"

Claire nodded. "Of course."

Aida worried that she read even more concern in Claire's eyes at that point, but Marlow, who was up ahead, stopped and turned around to tell them that the next shop had amazing swimsuits, and the moment passed as they walked into the store and began to meander around.

"You don't think she'll go back to Dutton, do you?" Aida whispered to Marlow once Claire went into the tiny dressing room to try on a suit.

"No way," Marlow said. But no matter how hard Aida tried to accept that, the friendship she had with Claire just wasn't the same.

Marlow had dinner with Aida and Claire in town at a tiny seaside bistro where they ate crab salads outside before returning to Seaclusion. Then she left Aida and Claire to hang out on their own for the rest of the evening and went to the big house. She and her mother were planning to go through her father's things and begin that difficult sorting process.

"Are you really feeling up to this?" she asked Eileen. There was no huge rush. But since Tiller had belongings at all their various properties, it would be a big job. If they started right away, they could take it in bite-size pieces, so it wouldn't be too overwhelming.

"Physically, I'm feeling stronger today than I have in a week," her mother said. Her voice was flat as she added, "But I don't know that I'll ever be up to this."

Marlow took her hand as they stood facing Tiller's side of the large walk-in closet.

"Getting rid of his things feels like I'm betraying him in some way," Eileen confessed.

"You'll only be getting rid of the stuff that doesn't have sentimental value," Marlow said. "You can keep anything you love, but combining three households isn't going to be easy, so try to be selective."

"I can't do it." Her mother released her hand and walked out of the closet.

"Mom?" Marlow said, following.

Eileen frowned at the large dresser that took up one wall. "Or—what if we start here?"

Relieved that she hadn't given up entirely, Marlow let her breath seep out. "Okay."

Probably as a means of delaying the inevitable, Eileen picked up the photograph of their family she kept on the dresser. "I wish we'd taken a more recent picture."

"There are all kinds of photos of Dad, Mom," Marlow said as gently as possible. "Being in the public eye meant his life was well-documented."

Clearly not placated, Eileen hugged the picture to her chest. "That's not the same as having a recent family photo."

"I'm sorry." The photograph Eileen held was taken only three years ago at Christmas. As far as Marlow was concerned, that *was* recent. She'd finally said she was too old to be part of her parents' annual Christmas card; now she felt guilty for not continuing the tradition. "Maybe we should make a scrapbook together to commemorate his life. That's something you've always talked about doing." And it might be easier for Eileen to let go of his clothes, shoes, tools and other practical possessions if she had the most meaningful stuff in one place, carefully preserved.

"I started that already," she said, "but I'd love to have you help me while you're here."

"You bet."

Taking a deep, bolstering breath, Marlow pulled out one of her father's drawers—the one that contained his socks. She figured socks would be about the safest place to begin, but as soon as she tried to scoop them into a box, her mother broke down and asked her to stop.

A noise at the door caused Marlow to look up. Rosemary was standing there with a tray that held two slices of homemade apple pie. "I thought you two might like a piece of pie while you work."

Eileen was already crying, but when she saw what Rosemary held, the tears came faster. "Apple was his favorite," she said and threw her arms around Marlow.

"Oh, I'm... I'm sorry." Rosemary seemed rattled. Marlow could tell she'd only been trying to show support.

"It's fine," Marlow said. "We'll come out to the kitchen and have some pie later."

"Okay." Rosemary beat a quick retreat as Marlow attempted to console her mother.

"Maybe it's too soon to sort through his stuff," Marlow said. "We can do it next week or the week after."

"Yeah. I'm not ready," Eileen admitted.

They ended up moving to the dining room table, where they worked on the scrapbook that Eileen had started. It was a bittersweet few hours, immersed in memories of the man they'd both loved and admired.

When Eileen said she was ready for bed, Marlow helped her into the room and returned to clear the table, but Rosemary insisted she'd do it so Marlow could be with her friends.

"Thanks," Marlow said, but she didn't go to the guesthouse. She wandered around on the beach alone for probably another hour, even though it was starting to rain. She was soaked within minutes, but she still didn't go inside.

She'd managed to talk herself out of going to Walker's last night. But he was always on her mind, there in the background, no matter what else was going on, and the longer she went without seeing him, the harder it got to stay away, especially when she was feeling so vulnerable.

Unable to hold back any longer, she grabbed the bicycle from the garage and rode it over to the cove.

After going all day on almost no sleep, Walker had nodded off on the couch as soon as he finished dinner. When he heard the knock on his door, he glanced at the clock—it was nearly eleven—and his thoughts immediately turned to Marlow. Could this be her?

She hadn't shown up last night, so he wasn't expecting her. He actually hoped it wasn't her, because now he'd just have to send her away. He knew that wouldn't be easy—but it became virtually impossible once he opened the door. She was standing on the stoop wearing nothing but a pair of cutoffs, some flip-flops and a tank top, shivering and soaked to the skin.

She was also crying.

"What's wrong?" he asked, immediately concerned.

She opened her mouth to answer but couldn't get any words out.

He pulled her inside and went to grab a towel, which he wrapped around her shoulders. "Are you hurt? Did someone hurt you?"

"No," she managed to say.

She must've ridden her bike over again. She wouldn't be so wet otherwise. But he didn't say anything about that. "Is it Eileen?"

She shook her head, and he remembered that when he finally called his mother to tell her the Tesla was back in the garage and Reese had shown up for work on time—something she'd already known because he'd gotten busy and waited so long—she mentioned that Eileen and Marlow had been sorting through Tiller's belongings tonight.

"Is this about your father?" he guessed, softening his voice.

She pressed her lips together as though she was struggling to hold back her emotions, but fresh tears streamed down her face as she nodded.

She'd been an only child, and Tiller had worshipped her. Walker could only imagine what it would feel like to have a father like that—and then lose him. "He was a good man," he said. "I'm sorry he's gone."

Squeezing her eyes closed, she leaned into him, and when he didn't step back, she slid her arms around his waist and rested her cheek against his chest. "I miss him," she managed to say in a strangled voice, and he wrapped his arms around her. This woman wrecked every defense he put up, but he couldn't send her home like this.

"You're going to be okay," he murmured.

She snuggled even closer, seeking comfort and warmth, and he held her until she stopped shivering. Then he stepped back to suggest she go take a shower and get warmed up while he dug through his drawers to find her some dry clothes. Before he could speak, however, she pressed her lips to his.

Now was the time to set her away from him, before everything got out of control again. But this kiss was different from before. It was the personification of an apology.

"Marlow—" he started, but she spoke at the same time.

"Make love to me."

The jolt of testosterone that shot through him at her request nearly stole his breath. "I can't."

"Why not?" she murmured against his lips. "You already have."

They'd had sex. Making love was different. He was surprised she'd even frame her request that way. "It's not a risk we should take." He was trying to remember what Rosemary had said to him earlier. His mother had been through enough in her life. After all she'd sacrificed for him, he should try to respect her wishes. "What about my mom?"

She seemed slightly hurt that he'd even suggest it might cause a problem for Rosemary. "I would *never* let this affect your mother's job. I think you know that."

He did. He and Marlow had had their issues, but they'd always handled those issues themselves. "Still, our families are close, and this might—"

"It won't do anything," she broke in. "It's just for the summer. What could one summer hurt?"

Why was he still fighting when he wanted so badly to give in—and when it might even be smarter to do so? Maybe if he went this route, Marlow would become no different than the other women he dated. When he first started seeing someone, there was a lot of excitement. But after a while, he slowly began to realize he wasn't all that interested anymore.

The beginning of the end.

With any luck, this relationship would follow the same course. "Okay," he said and started stripping off her wet clothes.

15

The anger was gone. Without it, sex with Walker was an entirely different experience. He took his time. He was more thoughtful, more attuned to what her body was telling him, more deliberate in the way he touched and kissed her. Marlow had to admit that their first two encounters had been thrilling in their own right, if only because they'd been so impulsive and unexpected—a cataclysmic release of years of pent-up frustration. But her needs had changed. With the sadness she was feeling about her father, she craved gentleness, especially from Walker. He'd known her almost her whole life. He'd known Tiller, too. He understood her loss in a way no other man could.

Fortunately, he seemed to understand what she was looking for, because he was giving her exactly what she wanted.

Although he hadn't turned on the light when they stumbled into his bedroom, kissing and clinging to each other, there was enough moonlight slanting through the French doors overlooking the beach that she could see his expression whenever he lifted his head, and she was glad of that. She loved the intensity on his face, the evidence of how much he was enjoying himself. It gave her as much of a thrill as all the rest of it.

"You smell so good," she said, and it was true. She'd never met a man who smelled better, and the scent of him was all around her—on his sheets and pillows and his warm, naked body.

"Be careful," he warned. "I might start to think you like me."

She couldn't tell if he was serious. "And that would be terrible, why?"

He lifted his head from her breasts. "We wouldn't want to ruin years of tradition."

She closed her eyes as he moved lower—until he was between her legs. "Yeah, well, you're acting as if you like me, too."

"Don't let this fool you," he mumbled, but she couldn't imagine him doing what he did next to a woman he didn't like. He held her thighs apart as he settled his mouth on her, making her jump at that first thrilling contact.

"Walker—"

"Trust me," he murmured.

She tried to relax, but she'd never had a man use his tongue and his fingers quite the way Walker did. She could hardly breathe. Clenching her hands in his hair, she groaned as the pleasure grew so intense she was desperate for release—a release he wouldn't give her until he'd put on a condom and joined their bodies instead.

She could feel his gaze on her face as he pressed inside her. He'd changed positions because he wanted to watch her climax beneath him—she could tell—and she couldn't have withheld that even if she tried. He had her so close already that she felt her body convulse almost as soon as he began to thrust, at which point he stopped and gave her a lazy smile before taking her right back to the same pinnacle.

A knock woke Walker again. Only this time Marlow was sleeping beside him, so he had no idea who it could be.

He squinted at his alarm clock. It was almost midnight. They'd barely drifted off. No wonder he felt like hell.

"Hey, bro! You want to have a drink? I'm available tonight."

"Shit," he muttered when he recognized the voice yelling from outside.

Marlow stirred beside him. "Is that—"

"Reese, yeah," Walker said and jumped out of bed to put on some shorts.

She sat up and yanked the bedding with her as if she was afraid Reese was about to walk in on her. Walker began to worry about that, too, when he heard his brother yell his name again and realized he was coming down the hall. Walker hadn't locked the door after admitting Marlow; he hadn't even thought about it.

"Walker?" Reese called.

"Stay where you are," Walker said. "I'm coming."

Marlow darted into the bathroom, just in case, and that turned out to be a wise move, because Reese didn't seem to hear him. When he entered the room, Walker understood why. His brother was so drunk he could barely stand up.

"What are you doing, man?" Walker asked.

"You wanted to have a drink with me last night, but I was… otherwise engaged." He wiggled his eyebrows. "I thought we could do it tonight. You know…a little male bonding."

Walker wasn't sure how to react. His brother drank too much, but Reese had never shown up at his house completely shit-faced. Was something wrong? "In case you haven't noticed, I was in bed."

"It's early."

"Not for those of us who have to work in the morning."

Putting a hand to the wall to steady himself, Reese scowled. "Come on. You're the boss. The big cheese. The chief of *po-lice*," he said, overemphasizing the first syllable. "You can go in later if you want."

Conscious of Marlow cowering in the bathroom, probably terrified she was about to be discovered without her clothes, Walker wanted to get Reese out of the room as fast as possible.

But he had to be careful, or he'd alert Reese to the fact that he was trying to hide something.

Casually moving toward his brother, he guided him back down the hall. "Come on. I'll put on a pot of coffee. How did you get here, by the way?"

"My buddy dropped me off."

"Great. Then I won't have to arrest you for driving under the influence."

Reese shot him a sulky look. "You would, too."

"I would. I don't want to see you hurt yourself, and I don't want to see you hurt anyone else, either." He was relieved Reese hadn't driven. But if he'd been dropped off, he didn't have a vehicle and was probably expecting to stay the night. Walker couldn't say he was too happy about that.

Reese opened the refrigerator. "You got any beer?"

Walker knocked his hand away and closed it. "You've had enough."

"I don't want coffee. I'm not interested in sobering up. Getting this numb took some effort, and I plan to stay this way as long as possible."

Instead of finishing the coffee, Walker gestured at the stool across the island from him. "Why don't you sit down and tell me what's going on?"

"Nothing that hasn't been going on all our lives."

"What's that supposed to mean?"

"I heard from Dad today. Can you believe that? It's been what…over a year?"

Walker stiffened. "What'd he want?"

"Told me he loves me." Reese started to laugh, but there was no humor in his eyes, and Walker could identify with his disillusionment.

"He screwed up his life, and he screwed up ours, but that doesn't mean he doesn't love us," Walker said.

"Love isn't words, man. Love is…love is doing the hard stuff."

163

"Maybe he regrets screwing up so badly."

"A bit late for that, since I'm already fucked-up."

Walker didn't know what to say. It was a terrible time to have this conversation, but he completely understood what his brother was feeling and his need to get the pain off his chest. Walker had spent his life asking himself why their father didn't care more about them. He'd watched Tiller dote on Marlow, would've given anything for even half that much love. "We can't control what other people do," he said. "But we can control how we react to it."

"And how am I supposed to react? By pretending it doesn't bother me, like you do? By pretending I don't need anyone?"

"That's not what I've done." He'd *had* to suck it up. His mother needed him to.

"I wish I could be more like you," Reese said. "Then Mom would respect me, too. Instead, she looks at me and sees Dad."

Walker raised his hand. "Stop. That's not true."

"It is. When I look in the mirror, I see him, too." He grimaced as though he hated the sight. "That's the worst part."

"It doesn't have to be that way. You can be anything you want."

Ignoring Walker's last statement, Reese said, "Dad wanted me to put in a good word with Mom. He's hoping to get back with her."

Walker felt his jaw drop. "No…"

"Yes."

"What'd you tell him?"

"I told him to fuck off and hung up. He didn't call because he cares about me. It was all about Mom."

"She'd never go back to him. Not after what he put her through."

Reese raised his eyebrows.

"What?" Walker said.

"Sounded to me like he thinks he has a real shot. She must've said or done something to make him believe that. I know they've been in contact."

Walker's mind flashed back to the call he'd received from his mother, telling him she was stranded with a flat tire. "Where's Dad living now?"

"Miami. He only went to Texas for a short time, when he hooked up with that harpy who was as much of an alcoholic as he is."

"He's done with her? Already? That barely lasted two years."

"I'm surprised they lasted that long. Said he has a steady job and that I should come over and see him."

In Miami. Rudy was that close. Walker hid a wince. Now he knew why his mother wouldn't tell him who she'd been with last night. It wasn't some stranger. But Walker wasn't going to tell Reese, not when he was like this. "Look, it's late, and we're not going to solve anything tonight. Let me throw some sheets on the bed in the extra bedroom so you can get some sleep."

"No, I'd rather stay here."

"Why?"

Reese didn't answer the question. Maybe he didn't want to be segregated off in the other room alone. Regardless, he was still too caught up in his anger to think of anything else. "I swear, if that fucker comes anywhere near me, I'll break his jaw."

Walker decided to make him a bed on the couch. It'd be easier than trying to coax him into moving. But when he grabbed the extra blankets and pillow from the closet, he saw Marlow's wet clothes on the floor in the hall. Fortunately, Reese had been too preoccupied to notice and had stepped right over them, but just in case he came back this way, Walker shoved them to one side until he could do more.

"Did I ever tell you about the time Dad cut his hand by putting it through the window?" Reese said. "He was swinging at his own reflection. I was six, bro. I thought the world was coming to an end."

Walker understood what that was like. He'd seen his father fly into a rage plenty of times. Fortunately, he'd never struck anyone on purpose, but he'd broken lamps and plenty of other things. "I must've been at college. I don't remember it. But *he* was supposed to be gone by then, too."

"Oh, he didn't live with us anymore, but he kept coming back."

Walker hurried over to arrange the bedding on the couch. He didn't want to talk about this stuff tonight. He was too afraid Marlow would hear the conversation, and he didn't want her to learn what his childhood had been like. She had to know it wasn't as good as hers, but he was pretty sure she had no idea about the details. Rosemary had always done what she could to downplay Rudy's behavior. She found it embarrassing, and she didn't want the Madsens to decide she was more trouble than she was worth. Of course, there were times when she couldn't hide it, but he didn't think Marlow was ever privy to what was going on. "Here, come lie down. I'll turn on the TV, and we'll find a show to watch."

Reese made no move. He was so deep in his thoughts and his cups Walker doubted he'd even heard him.

"Come on," Walker insisted, helping his brother up. But before he could lead him to the couch, Reese started to talk about another bad memory, choking up before he could finish getting the words out.

"I hate him," he said when he could speak again. "I hate that bastard."

Walker pulled his little brother in for a hug. "You're going to be okay. You can't let him get to you. And you certainly can't head down the same road."

"There's no fixing me," he said, shaking his head. "All I can do is deaden the pain."

Walker pulled back and gripped his brother by the shirt.

"That's bullshit," he said, giving him what he hoped was a convincing shake. "Talking to someone might help."

Reese didn't commit, but he didn't refuse, either. He allowed Walker to help him over to the couch, then curled up like a child.

Walker covered him with a blanket and put on a movie. But he didn't know what he was going to do next. Marlow's clothes were still soaked. It would take some time to dry them. He couldn't let her ride a bicycle home this late, anyway. It wasn't safe.

"I'll be right back," he told Reese. "I've got to go to the bathroom."

Grabbing Marlow's clothes on the way, he hurried to his room. He figured he'd have to tell her that he'd take her home after Reese fell asleep.

But she was no longer in his bathroom or his bed. Although he still had her clothes, Marlow was gone.

"Really? *That's* what you chose from my drawers when you knew you'd be riding a bike?" Walker said, pulling up alongside her and yelling out the passenger window.

Marlow had heard his SUV coming up behind her. She'd borrowed a pair of his sweats, and they were so baggy, and she'd been in such a hurry, that she hadn't been able to keep the left pant leg out of the chain. It'd gotten stuck before she could even reach the road.

When he stopped beside her, she was trying to release it, but that wasn't easy while straddling the bike. "It was cold," she complained. "And they had a drawstring to help keep them up."

Walker got out and came around, and because he was in a better position to fix the problem, it didn't take him long to free her. "Get in."

The rain was starting to fall harder, so she didn't argue. She climbed into the passenger seat and raised the window he'd lowered, grateful that he already had the heat going, while he put her bike in the back.

He pushed his wet hair out of his face as he got behind the wheel and fastened his seat belt. "I'll dry your clothes and bring them back to you tomorrow," he said as he glanced over at her.

She lifted her leg to examine the damage to his sweats. "I wish I could say I'll do the same. But if I try to wash these, I'm afraid Aida or Claire will see them and know immediately that they aren't mine."

"I'll take care of them whenever you return them to me."

She gave him a sheepish look. "If you can't get the grease out, I'll buy you a new pair."

"I'm not worried about that. I'm just glad I came to find you right away. Who knows how long you would've been stuck in the mud and the cold."

He turned onto the road, which was clear of traffic since it was so late and storming besides.

Dropping her leg, she crossed her arms to stay warm. "Is Reese going to be okay?" she asked after several minutes with only the swish of his wipers breaking the silence.

"Yeah." That he didn't elaborate, despite the fact that his brother had shown up drunk and upset, told her he didn't care to talk about it, and Marlow could understand why. Unlike the two of them, she'd always lived a privileged life, having everything money could buy and plenty of love, too.

She'd been so out of touch with Rosemary and her boys, even though they'd been part of her daily life. As an adult, she was shocked she'd ever been that oblivious. She was paying attention now. But if Walker didn't want to open up, he probably wouldn't appreciate her probing.

They didn't speak again as he drove the rest of the way, partially because she didn't know what to say. She'd never had a relationship that was founded on sex, and she didn't really want to acknowledge that she was having one now, so she focused on what she'd overheard while rummaging through Walker's dresser, looking for something to wear. She'd known that Rudy wasn't the best husband or dad. She'd heard her parents murmuring about him now and then. But she'd never really understood that it had been as bad as Reese had just portrayed. He was always smiling and acting as though he didn't have a care in the world. Was he only playing the part of the quintessential tennis pro/playboy?

She got that impression now that she'd been able to see him a little more closely. What he'd said showed a completely different side of him—a tortured side—and it gave her a glimpse into what Walker must've suffered, too. Maybe, as the oldest, it was even harder for him. That was often the case.

"What did you tell Reese when you left?" she asked as he pulled into Seaclusion.

"I didn't tell him anything. I shoved your clothes under the bed and came out the French doors off the bedroom, like you did."

"What if he notices you're gone and starts looking for you?"

"I doubt he'll check under the bed, so he won't find your clothes. The rest he can wonder about."

She nodded. Then she said, "I'm sorry that...that it was so difficult growing up." She spoke softly and sent him a worried glance, but he continued to look straight ahead, as if he was waiting for her to get out.

"Reese will be fine. I'll be home before he even realizes I left."

Her comments hadn't been limited to Reese. But she figured Walker understood that and was simply choosing not to engage. "Okay, I'm going. Good night."

She opened the door, but before she could climb out, he grabbed her by the shirtfront and hauled her halfway across the console while he kissed her as though he might never get the chance to kiss her again. When he let go, they stared at each other for a long moment, but he didn't say anything, so she slipped out, and he turned the truck around.

When she remembered that he had her bike, she flagged him down. "You forgot—"

"The bike," he finished, realizing, and climbed out to set it on the ground for her. "Do you have my number?"

"I do." She'd had it since forever.

"Good. If you ever come over again, don't ride that damn bike," he said as he got back behind the wheel. "Call me and I'll pick you up."

If you ever come over again. He wasn't expecting anything from her. No doubt her past behavior had taught him not to count on much.

"Do you have my number?" she asked.

"No."

She noticed that he didn't ask for it, either. "Do you *want* me to come over again?"

His gaze swept over her as she stood there in his baggy sweats, getting wetter by the moment. His eyes said yes. So she was a little surprised when his mouth said, "That's up to you."

He obviously wasn't going to reach out to her. "You're indifferent?"

"Enemy sex can be some of the best sex there is. It's certainly been fun so far."

Blinking against the rain, she stepped back. She told herself he was joking and his response shouldn't have hurt her, but it did. "We're still enemies? We haven't even graduated to friends with benefits?"

"You'll be gone before we know it."

"Which means…"

"There's no need to make things more confusing," he said and drove off.

16

Claire's mind was a million miles away as they had breakfast on Monday with Eileen. Surely, Dutton wouldn't *really* come to the island. But what if he did? It was such a small place. Aida or Marlow could easily bump into him somewhere downtown.

Should she tell them in advance?

She cringed at starting that conversation. Aida would probably leave and go back to California. Telling them would only ruin their summer needlessly if Dutton didn't end up coming. And if he did, it was only for one week. Maybe there was a chance they wouldn't have to know. Seaclusion had its own private beach, so they hadn't been to any of the public beaches. Dutton didn't play tennis and was unlikely to go to the racquet club—another place they frequented. She'd just have to make sure they were never out on the streets visiting the shops and cafés at the same time he was.

Could she pull that off? See him on the side and try to determine if he was sincere? If she really wanted to reconcile with him? What if she decided she was finished with him for good? If she told Aida and Marlow that he was coming, she'd destroy her relationship with them, even though she might not get back together with him.

Bottom line, she wasn't willing to take that chance. She didn't want to lose Aida and Marlow. She was going to keep her mouth shut and hope that he changed his mind—or that if he did come, she could keep him separate from her friends.

"Claire?"

Startled, Claire looked up to see Rosemary holding a pitcher of fresh-squeezed orange juice. "Yes?"

She lifted the pitcher. "Would you like some more?"

"Um, no. Sorry." Her laugh sounded uncomfortable even to her own ears. "I was…daydreaming."

Aida and Marlow exchanged a questioning glance, which certainly did nothing to put Claire at ease. "So…what are we doing today?" she asked, wearing a big smile in an attempt to alleviate some of their suspicion.

Eileen put down her napkin. "Whatever you do, I hope you'll be back in time for dinner."

"Why?" Marlow asked. "Is there something special going on?"

"Rosemary is making meat loaf and hush puppies," Eileen replied. "It's one of her boys' favorite meals, and I've invited Walker and Reese to join us."

Aida lit up immediately. She hadn't stopped talking about Reese. But Marlow seemed a bit more tentative. Or maybe she was only curious. "Is this for my birthday?"

"No, although we'll be sure to celebrate that. I asked them to come tonight because I have something of your father's to give each of them. He tried to be such a good role model to those boys, and I think they were fond of him, too."

"They definitely were," Rosemary concurred with a grateful smile.

"I'm not going to make a big deal of it," Eileen clarified. "But I started to sort through some of Tiller's things when I couldn't sleep last night and decided that Walker and Reese should have a small token to remember him by."

"That's really thoughtful of you," Rosemary said.

"I hope it'll be meaningful to them," Eileen responded, obviously pleased with Rosemary's reaction. Sometimes Claire got the impression that their relationship was carefully choreographed and had to be in order for them to fulfill their separate roles and get along at the same time.

Marlow put down her fork. "Walker doesn't have to work?"

"He'll be off by then," Rosemary volunteered. "For the most part, he works mornings—seven to three—although he's always on call if there's an emergency or his officers can't handle some problem on their own."

"Hopefully there'll be no emergencies tonight, because he promised me he'd be here," Eileen said. "I just talked to him before breakfast."

"Being chief of police comes with a lot of responsibility," Marlow said, but Claire sensed that was some kind of smoke screen, a neutral remark to hide what she was really thinking and feeling.

"Can you be here at six?" her mother asked.

"Of course," Marlow replied. "We're going to play some tennis, then rest on the beach. We'll be around."

Her mother seemed pleased that everyone was cooperating. "Perfect," she said as if that was that, but as soon as Marlow got up to go to the bathroom, Eileen lowered her voice and leaned closer to Claire and Aida.

"I do want to give Reese and Walker a little keepsake, but tonight will be mainly for Marlow's birthday, and they both know that," she whispered. "If I waited until the actual day, she'd guess it was for her, so this was the only way to make it a surprise. Don't tell her, but try not to be late, okay?"

Aida readily agreed. "Sounds like fun. Is there anything we can bring or help with?"

Eileen waved them off. "No. You just keep her busy and distracted. Rosemary will handle dinner, and I'll handle everything that happens after."

"Will there be people other than Walker and Reese joining us?" Claire asked.

"Oh, yes. I've invited quite a few friends she knows here on the island."

"So it's a full-out party," Aida said.

"It is," Eileen confirmed. "After what we've been through the past couple of years with COVID, I think we can use one."

Claire was about to take the last bite of her spinach omelet when her phone went off. She was terrified to even glance down at it for fear it was Dutton. But it was the racquet club.

"Excuse me," she said and stepped away from the table as she hit the talk button.

"Is this Claire Fernandez?"

Claire didn't recognize the voice. It wasn't the manager of the club, who'd interviewed her. This was a woman. "Yes…"

"This is Darcy Reed at Teach Spa and Racquet Club. Phil asked me to give you a call. He'd like to have you come in and lead me through a yoga class so we can see how you'd interact with our club members."

"Yes, of course," she said, excited to have heard back so soon. If she could land this job, she'd not only have a little money coming in, she'd have an excuse to be out on her own, which could be integral to keeping Dutton's presence on the island a secret—if he ended up coming. "When would you like me to do that?"

"Tomorrow morning at…let's say, eight?"

"I'll be there."

"Great. If all goes well, we'll set up a schedule for classes."

"I appreciate that. Thank you," Claire said and let her breath go in relief as she disconnected.

Aida looked up as she returned to the table. "What is it?"

Claire didn't try to hide how she was feeling. "I have a chance of landing that job at the racquet club."

"That was the manager?" Marlow asked, having returned to the table.

"No, a woman named Darcy. I'm giving her a yoga class tomorrow. If she likes it, they're going to hire me."

"That's wonderful!" Eileen exclaimed.

"She's going to love everything about you," Marlow predicted.

"Who wouldn't?" Aida said. "You're so good with people in general and your students in particular."

Claire felt her smile widen even more. She loved being on the island. She loved Marlow and Aida, too.

She just hoped she wasn't leaving the door open for Dutton to ruin her life a second time.

Walker wished he could arrive late or simply put in an appearance and then claim he'd been called away by work. As much as he'd enjoyed having sex with Marlow and would love that to continue, he knew he was playing with fire. She'd burn him eventually, and she'd probably do it without thinking twice.

Unfortunately, he couldn't handle the evening quite as casually as he'd like to. Eileen had made a point of asking him to dinner before the party started, and he couldn't make his mother look bad by being late. He showed up freshly shaved and dressed in a golf shirt and shorts, clothes he considered a step above the beach bum tanks and cutoffs he typically donned when he was off work.

Before he knocked, he checked his phone, halfway hoping that Neal Goff, the officer actively patrolling the island right now, needed him for something. Then he could flash his phone to prove he had an issue and take off.

But everything on the island seemed to be going smoothly.

He hadn't heard from Neal, and short of an emergency, he wasn't likely to. Neal was his best officer.

His mother answered his knock. "Come on in."

The food smelled delicious. Maybe it was worth letting Marlow destroy what was left of his heart if there was a homemade meal in it, he thought wryly. No one could cook as well as his mother.

Aida and Claire greeted him next—both with a hug, so Marlow had to follow suit. As she slipped into his arms, he could feel the curves of her body underneath the thin dress and couldn't help picturing her as she'd been in his bed last night, completely nude, with her hair tumbling over his pillows.

"Glad you could make it," she murmured, avoiding eye contact as she pulled away.

He tried not to stare at her, but he'd always thought she was gorgeous, and she looked especially good in the strappy, white knee-length dress she was wearing now. "Smells great in here." He was speaking about Marlow as much as the food, but he purposely didn't make that clear.

"You know your mom. Best cook ever," Marlow said as she moved away from him and took a seat on the far side of the table, next to Reese, who was more rumpled than usual.

Reese had probably just rolled out of bed, Walker thought. Monday was his day off, and he certainly didn't allow himself much sleep on the weekends. He had a lot of catching up to do.

Eileen presided at the head of the table. "I'm so glad you could make it," she told him.

He hadn't had a choice—not really—but he thanked her for inviting him before going to the kitchen to help his mother bring out the food.

"I've got this," Rosemary said when she noticed him trailing her. "Go enjoy yourself. You get to be part of the company tonight."

"This'll only take a minute," he said and insisted she load him up.

When they returned to the dining room, Eileen gestured at one of the empty seats at the table. "Rosemary, bring in a plate for yourself. I'd like you to join us, as well."

His mother hesitated as though she wasn't entirely comfortable with that. She was used to eating with Eileen when it was just the two of them, but Walker could tell it was different when she felt she should be serving.

"I should've had you set the table for seven to begin with," Eileen added.

Rosemary acknowledged her words with a nod. "I'll grab my setting in a second. Let me pour the champagne first."

"We're having champagne?" Marlow asked.

"Yes. This is going to be a celebration of Tiller's life," Eileen explained as Rosemary went to get the bottle.

While his mother was gone, Walker got her place setting for her.

"Thank you," she said, noticing the moment she returned. She was so grateful whenever he did something nice for her that he felt guilty he didn't do more.

"No problem." He sat down as she poured. Then they all picked up their glasses for a toast.

"To Tiller," Eileen said. "He did so much for all of us. May he rest in peace, and may we remember the example he set for us and strive to be as honorable as he was."

"To Tiller," they echoed and clinked glasses.

Walker had just finished taking a sip when Eileen singled him out. "Walker, Tiller was impressed by how well you look out for your mother. I have to say I've always been impressed by it, too."

Walker hated being the center of attention, especially for something like this. "She's my mother," he said. "I *should* look out for her."

"Well, not every son does. So that makes you exceptional. I thought you might like to have Tiller's watch as a keepsake."

Walker couldn't believe it when Eileen handed him the Rolex he'd seen on Tiller's wrist since he could remember. "This is too nice of a gift," he said. He didn't know much about luxury brands, but he would guess it might be worth as much as five thousand dollars.

"I'd rather give it to you than sell it, as long as you'd be happy to own it and will think of him now and then because of it," Eileen said.

"Of course I will," he said. "But…are you sure you want me to have it?"

"I'm positive," she replied. "He has a couple of nieces, but they live in Colorado, and we've never been close to their husbands. I feel it should go to you."

"I appreciate you thinking of me, but—" Walker looked at Marlow "—I don't want to take it if…if you want it."

"No, there are plenty of other keepsakes for me," she said, but he could tell she was as surprised as he was by the gesture. Reese's eyes had gone wide, too.

"Okay, then," he said to Eileen. "Thank you." He cleared his throat. "Thank you both," he added, including Marlow.

Eileen smiled, and he could tell she was gratified when he slipped it on his wrist.

"I have something for you, too," she told Reese. "Tiller always talked about how talented you are. He loved watching you play tennis."

"I wouldn't be able to play nearly as well without him," Reese admitted.

"Which is why I'm giving you one of his racquets—and this." She handed him a ring with a large square ruby.

"Wow!" Reese exclaimed. "You're giving me his ring?"

"One of them," she clarified. "I bought this for him for

Christmas twenty-something years ago. My brother owned a jewelry store at the time and gave me a great deal on it."

Walker didn't recognize the ring. From what he could remember, Tiller had only worn his wedding ring, but it was a nice gift, and one Eileen had probably chosen because it was more or less equal in value to the watch.

"It's awesome." Reese slid it on his ring finger, but it was too big, so he moved it to his index finger.

"We'll have to get it sized," Eileen said.

Aida lifted herself up to see it better. "It looks good on you," she said, and Claire concurred.

"I'm finding it's easier to go through his things if I have somewhere to put them—someone to share them with. That makes me happy," Eileen said. "That's how I'm going to do it from now on. I'm not going to get rid of something just to get rid of it. I'm going to spread his belongings around to the people he loved."

There were tears in Marlow's eyes, which she tried to hide by taking another drink of her champagne, but Walker was so attuned to her that he definitely noticed. He hoped it was only because she missed her father, and that she wasn't upset by what her mother had done.

"Now let's eat before the food gets cold," Eileen said.

After the meal, Eileen led them down to the beach, where people had been quietly assembling for Marlow's surprise party, and he believed Marlow was genuinely shocked to find a DJ there, ready to play music, lights hanging over a large area for dancing, and tables filled with bite-size desserts and huge floral centerpieces.

"Surprise!" everyone yelled as soon as they saw her.

"You've got to be kidding me," she said to her mother.

Eileen laughed as they embraced. "Happy birthday, my love."

"Thank you!" she said. "I can't believe this! You hid it so well."

"You're too smart. I knew I had to be clever," she teased, and then the music started and Marlow was whisked away by guest after guest, all wanting to wish her a happy birthday.

Marlow danced and laughed and socialized with people she hadn't seen for years—members of the club she'd played tennis with growing up, friends of her parents, several neighbors. She'd truly been surprised by the party, and she was enjoying herself. But she found herself searching for Walker whenever she lost sight of him, which was something she'd never done before. Even when she was dancing with Reese, she couldn't stop herself from looking around, trying to catch a glimpse of Walker. She listened for his laugh, made note of the people he talked to and hoped he'd ask her to dance.

He didn't, though. He was popular in his own right—it didn't hurt that he was the chief of police—and seemed to be busy talking to someone all the time.

As the party began to wind down, she grabbed one of the shawls her mother had put out on the banister and headed down the beach just so she wouldn't have to see him paying attention to everyone but her.

She was sitting on the dock, her feet dangling in the water, when she heard the creak of footsteps and glanced up to see him carrying two beers. "Don't come talk to me now," she grumbled. "You've ignored me all night."

"You haven't lacked for attention," he said with a chuckle.

"It's my birthday party. And you haven't even asked me to dance."

"Since when have you cared what I do?" He handed her the extra beer as he sat beside her.

"I don't," she said, but that was a lie.

He took a long pull on his beer. "Do you mind about the watch?"

She'd been surprised by what her mother had done at dinner, but she didn't mind. She actually thought it was a sweet gesture and hoped it made Walker and Reese feel important. "No. She wants you to have it. So do I."

"And the ring?"

She drew the shawl closer against the breeze coming in off the ocean. "The ring doesn't mean anything to me. My father hardly ever wore it."

"But the watch does? I can give it back..."

"No, keep it. I mean it, Walker." She wasn't upset about the watch, but she didn't want to tell him what was really bothering her. It would reveal too much.

"I gave you your chance," he said with a shrug.

Leaning back on her hands, she let her breath go on a long sigh. "You're never going to forgive me, are you?"

"Forgive you for what?" he asked, looking askance at her.

"You know what."

He swallowed another mouthful of beer. "I forgive you. I just don't trust you."

In other words, he didn't think she was a good person. Her inability to change that stung. She wished she didn't care what he thought, but she did, especially after the past few days.

"Okay," she finally said. "I understand. I'll leave you alone from now on. I'll put your clothes in the hole of the gumbo-limbo tree. You can do the same with mine whenever...whenever you get the chance."

She stood up and hurried back to her party—only the closer she came, the less she felt like seeing anyone. Skirting around the lights and the revelry, she stepped into the trees, where she couldn't be seen as she made her way to the guesthouse.

17

"Fuck," Walker muttered, staring out to sea while drinking his beer. He'd just wrecked Marlow's birthday party. He'd seen her start back to where everyone was, then veer away when she thought he was no longer looking. And she hadn't come back. He didn't think she was going to. He'd hurt her, even though he'd never dreamed he had the power to do that. He'd merely been trying to protect himself.

He shook his head. He'd never been able to do anything right when it came to her...

He had her clothes in his truck. He'd been planning to give them to her tonight, after everyone left. He'd been hoping—in spite of himself—that they might spend the night together again. They certainly seemed compatible physically. But now he had to leave her clothes at the tree where they'd hidden gifts for each other as children, because she didn't plan on seeing him again.

He'd been trying to push her away, and he'd accomplished that. So why was he filled with such regret?

"Hey, bro."

Walker sat up taller as Reese strode down the dock. "Hey."

"Do you know where Marlow went?"

"No," he said, but he had a pretty good idea. "Why?"

"I thought I saw her walk this way."

"She was here for a second. Something wrong?"

Reese sat down beside him. "Not wrong. They're about to cut the cake, is all."

"It's getting late. It looks like most people have already gone home. Why didn't they do it sooner?"

"I guess her mother forgot about it."

The fact that he'd caused her to leave before the grand finale made him feel like a jerk. She'd been nice to him since she'd come home. And he certainly had no complaints about what she'd offered him physically. Each one of those encounters had been beyond incredible. But that was the thing—he wasn't used to her being that friendly, and he was afraid to rely on it.

Reese followed his gaze out to sea. "Do you think I should talk to Mom about Dad?" he asked.

Walker was reluctant to deal with their family bullshit right now. But then...he never wanted to deal with it. He didn't understand why Reese couldn't ignore it the way he did. The past was the past; there was nothing they could do to change it. He refused to acknowledge that he'd been wounded in any way and kept hobbling along. Sure, he was dragging an invisible ball and chain, but at least he kept moving. He wasn't letting his father destroy what he could have in the future.

Reese, on the other hand, couldn't quit dwelling on it. Walker was torn between trying to help his brother by being understanding and supportive and trying to keep the lid on the Pandora's box of their past. He hated to see his mother get back with his father as much as Reese did, though. Rosemary was a good woman; Rudy didn't deserve her. "How would you handle that?" he asked.

"I've talked to her once already," Reese said. "But I don't think I was adamant enough."

"Which means…what?"

"Maybe I need to be a little more insistent, get specific, remind her how terrible it used to be."

Which meant their conversation would turn into a screaming match, and Walker would have to come in and act as peacekeeper. "She'll just say he's changed now that he's sober."

"She's tried that. There's no guarantee he won't go back to the bottle."

"True, but no one's perfect. Maybe he should have the chance to change and improve."

"I'm not stopping him from doing that. Dad can change all he wants. But he's burned his bridges with us."

Walker preferred to be done with Rudy, too. But he knew their mother was lonely. "No second chances?"

"No second chances," Reese said.

Walker drained his beer. "You should let me talk to Mom."

"Why?"

Because he would be gentler, and he felt that was important. "Like you said, you've tried once already."

"I don't think I tried hard enough. We'll be doing her a favor by warning her away."

Unless their father *had* changed. But maybe, like their mother, Walker was too much of an optimist. "What if she's right? What if he's finally the man she's always wanted him to be?"

Reese got up. "It's too late."

Walker handed him his empty beer bottle to carry back to the house. "Whatever you do, just…don't say anything to her tonight. I saw her earlier, and she seemed to be enjoying herself. There's no reason to ruin that."

Reese scowled. He obviously didn't like the idea of waiting, but that came as no surprise. He wasn't known for his patience.

"I mean it," Walker said, and Reese gave him a reluctant nod before heading back to Seaclusion.

★ ★ ★

Dutton had made all the arrangements for his trip. Claire had spent most of the party texting furiously with him, trying to talk him out of coming to Florida. She told him she'd spend some time with him when she got back, that she wouldn't make up her mind about reconciling here on the island. But he kept saying he wanted to remind her how great things could be between them.

Claire had been able to extract a promise that he wouldn't make his presence known to her friends. She'd told him whatever they had would be over if he did, and she meant it. She loved Aida, and he had to respect that. He also had to respect that she needed to work through this in her own way and in her own time.

When she returned to the guesthouse after the party, Aida was with her, but Marlow must've gone back earlier because she wasn't on the beach when they cut the cake, and they hadn't seen her after, while the DJ and caterers were cleaning up and leaving.

"Are you nervous about giving that Darcy person a yoga lesson tomorrow morning?" Aida asked as they let themselves in.

"Not really," Claire replied. "I'm just going to do my best. If that's not good enough, there's nothing more I can do."

"It'll be good enough."

"I hope you're right."

Claire expected to find Marlow changing or watching TV, but she was already in bed. Once they realized that, they lowered their voices and got ready for bed themselves.

"Why would Marlow leave the party without us? Do you think she's upset?" Aida asked, jerking her head toward their friend's closed door as they met up in the hallway.

Claire considered the question. "It was probably difficult for her to celebrate her birthday without her father."

"I don't doubt that was part of it," Aida said. "But I feel

like there's more going on—and that it might have to do with Walker."

Claire had noticed the way they treated each other, too. "There's definitely something going on between them. He seemed really jealous when she was with Reese the other night."

Aida blinked in surprise. "I don't think she has any feelings for Reese. Do you?"

"No," she replied. "It's more that Walker doesn't like seeing her with anyone else, including his brother."

Aida pursed her lips as she considered Claire's response. "She'd probably feel the same if we were to show interest in him."

"Which is how I know she doesn't have any feelings for Reese," Claire said. "And you saw how hard Walker was on her during the tennis match. Even Reese was shocked."

"And then she defended him when I said something after. Although, it could also be that she was upset her mother gave away her father's watch and ring."

"I guess there's no way to know for sure, not if she won't tell us."

"The fact that she's so tight-lipped about Walker tells us more than she'd probably like," Aida joked. "It's too bad."

"What's too bad?"

"Walker's even cuter than Reese. He's more serious, but he's more mature, too."

Claire wished he could be an option for Aida. If Aida fell in love with the right man—someone who was deserving of her and would be good to her—Claire would be under less pressure when it came to Dutton. "You'd be interested in him?"

"Wouldn't you?"

Claire chuckled. She was still too stuck on Dutton to feel attracted to anyone else. She hoped, if she didn't get back with him, that would change, but she didn't dare count on it. Her heart was far more stubborn than she'd ever imagined it could be. "I think we should consider him off-limits."

Aida agreed, and they whispered good-night before going into their separate bedrooms, at which point Claire checked her phone one last time.

Dutton had sent her another text: I can't wait to see you.

While waiting until all the party guests, musicians and servers had left the house and everyone else was in bed, Walker drove around the island to make sure it was secure. He also checked in with Officer Goff, who assured him the most exciting thing that'd happened in the past several hours was the party thrown at the Madsens' beachfront property. Since Walker was responsible for the safety of everyone on the island, this came as welcome news.

It was late when he felt it was safe to go back to Seaclusion. After he parked outside the compound, he put Marlow's clothes in a bag and headed to the gumbo-limbo tree, still kicking himself for upsetting her and ruining the rest of her party.

He paused as he walked past the guesthouse, hoping there was some possibility of attracting her attention. But short of throwing a rock at the window—and he didn't know which window was hers—he couldn't think of any way to get her to come talk to him. The place was completely dark. She obviously wasn't up, anyway.

There was nothing to do but weave through the buildings and the copse of palms, southern magnolia and mimosa trees where they'd had sex for the first time and head down the beach to the "tourist tree" with the hole in the trunk.

A bank of clouds rolled across the moon almost as soon as he reached the tree. He used the flashlight on his phone so he could see well enough to stuff the sack he'd brought into the hole, but there was something in the way.

Assuming he had to clear out leaves or other detritus, he reached in. But he didn't find any leaves. There was a beach bag that held a piece of pyrite, a cheap necklace with Marlow's initial that he'd won at the state fair when he was thirteen, a wooden heart he'd carved in woodshop and a picture of them together at prom. She'd been only fourteen when they attended that dance, but Tiller had asked him to take her. Her father hated to see her miss out on the experience just because she was two years younger than everyone else, and yet he wanted her to be with someone he trusted.

Walker remembered that night clearly. She was so grateful she got to go because of him that she was much nicer than usual—until he tried to kiss her at the end of the night.

He shoved that memory away as he studied the bag. Obviously, it hadn't been here for long, which meant Marlow must've put it in the tree after she returned to the island, maybe even tonight.

Could that be right? And, if so, why did she do it? He couldn't believe she'd kept this junk to begin with—and that included the picture.

He was putting everything back in the bag when he noticed handwriting on the photograph: *Thank you for all you've done for me. I wish we could be friends.*

There was no signature, but he didn't need a signature to know who the note was from.

He sighed as he stared up at the sky. *Friends.* If only she knew what that did to him…

But he couldn't deny her, even now. So he carried her clothes to the truck, along with the trinkets she'd saved, and wrote a note to leave her instead.

When Marlow heard Claire getting ready for her appointment at the racquet club, she got up to make coffee and wish her well. She was trying not to think about Walker, but as soon as she'd opened her eyes, she'd suddenly remembered putting the beach bag full of things he'd given her in the gumbo-limbo tree where she'd told him to put her clothes, which was something she certainly hadn't meant to do. She needed to grab that stuff before he found it, and she figured it would be best to do that while Claire was gone and Aida was still sleeping.

"Wish me luck," Claire said.

"You know I do." Marlow handed her the coffee she'd poured into a travel mug and fished the key card to the Tesla out of her purse. "Here, take the car."

"I can just ride a bike," she said, sounding surprised.

"You might be late if you do, since you're not familiar with the island yet. This will be quicker. You'll be back before anyone needs to use the car today. And even if you're not, there's always the Jeep."

"Thank you! That'll make things easier."

After a quick hug, she hurried out the door and Marlow sat at the kitchen table, sipping her own coffee while waiting to see if the noise had disturbed Aida.

When she didn't hear any movement, she set her cup aside and went to her room, where she put on her bikini and threw a sweatshirt over it before gathering Walker's sweats and his T-shirt, which she'd stuffed under the bed. She figured she might as well take it all to the tree so it would be there when he returned her clothes.

The weather was already warm. As she made her way to the tree, she could tell this afternoon would be a hot one. She vowed that, once she had her clothes back, she wouldn't even *think* of Walker again. After what she'd learned about love and its betrayals as a divorce attorney, she couldn't believe she'd allowed herself to get so hung up on him.

But once she got to the tree, she didn't find her beach bag. Her clothes weren't there, either. When she reached inside, the only thing her fingers closed around was an origami bird.

Curious, she held Walker's clothes against her body while she unfolded it to find a brief line he'd written.

I'm sorry. Let me make it up to you.

Marlow nibbled on her lower lip as she read those words over and over. It was too late for this, she told herself. Some people were better off just staying away from each other, and she and Walker seemed to be a perfect example.

She wasn't going to contact him.

But she knew that was complete bullshit when she didn't stuff his sweats and T-shirt into the tree, like she'd planned. She carried them, along with his paper bird, back to the guesthouse and hid everything in her bedroom while Aida continued to sleep.

"I got the job!"

Aida leaned up on her elbows and lifted her sunglasses to see Claire rushing toward Marlow, who'd just left their spot on the sand to buy them both a margarita. Aida had talked Marlow into going to the largest public beach, where there was music, a bar and lots of people, while they waited for Claire to finish up at the club. After all, they weren't going to meet any guys on a private beach.

Aida would've been happy to hang out with Reese, but he was at work. And she'd barely seen him the past couple of days. Even at the party last night, he hadn't interacted with her very much.

She needed a distraction to keep her from obsessing over Dutton and Claire. Having someone make her feel attractive and desirable would be a plus. The divorce had left her feeling like an old sweater that'd been cast off in favor of a new one.

"I had no doubt you'd get it!" she heard Marlow say as they embraced. "I guessed when you didn't come back after an hour or so that it was going well."

Aida stood up to congratulate Claire, too. "That must've been the longest yoga class ever," she teased as she plodded through the hot sand to meet up with them. "It took all morning!"

Claire bestowed a beaming smile on her. "We had a lot to go over."

"When do you start?" Marlow asked.

"Next week. We'll offer one class a day at first. But if enough people show interest, we'll expand the schedule."

Aida slid her sunglasses higher on her nose. "How do we sign up?"

"There's a registration form at the front desk. They've added my class. And Marlow will be happy to know it doesn't start until ten."

Marlow cast a sideways glance at Aida. "Hallelujah!"

Claire shaded her eyes as she gazed up and down the crowded beach. They'd sent her a text to let her know where to find them, and she'd gone home and changed. She was wearing a black one-piece suit with a white cover-up, but she hadn't brought a hat and she wasn't wearing any sunglasses. "What made you two decide to come here?" she asked.

Marlow hitched a thumb at Aida.

"Sometimes the private beach can get lonely," Aida said.

Claire scowled. "Are you going to want to do this a lot?"

"I don't know. Why does it matter? It's fun, right?"

"It's...crowded."

"You must not want to get laid as badly as I do," Aida quipped, and a gentleman who had to be in his sixties leaned in as he passed by to say, "If you're looking for applicants, don't underestimate a man with plenty of experience."

They laughed, and so did he and his friends. "I'll keep that in mind," Aida promised, and he winked as he moved on.

"There's nothing like being totally transparent," Marlow said, still laughing as she dragged them to the bar.

They each ordered a drink, which they were given in plastic cups, before they returned to their towels and made room for Claire. Aida used her phone to show them pictures of the type of clothing she'd like to feature in her boutique, and they brainstormed how to make the space look cool with a painted brick interior and a railing that was black and ultramodern.

Aida had switched to showing them the kind of fresh flower arrangements she'd like to use in the store when she received a text from Dutton.

Your friend Jackie stopped by. You never told her we were getting divorced?

All the fun Aida had been having immediately evaporated.

"Who's Jackie?" Claire leaned back to look up at her. The text had floated across her screen while she held it in front of Claire and Marlow.

Aida could feel Marlow looking at her, too. Jackie's stopping by shouldn't have been a big deal. Aida didn't consider her a close friend. She was a catty girl she'd known in school. That was all. Most women had one or two of those in her past. "Just an old friend."

"From when you lived in North Dakota?" Claire asked. "Is she in LA these days?"

Aida shook her head. "I don't think so. Last I heard, her husband was working in the oil fields like my brothers. He was also in our class."

She texted a response to Dutton. What did she want? Why didn't she call or message me first?

He answered right away. She said she wanted to surprise you while she's in town. She had her husband and three kids with her. They've spent the past few days at Disneyland.

"Do you find her dropping by upsetting in some way?" Claire asked, watching her closely.

Aida hated that she didn't know if she could be honest with Claire. The possibility that Claire and Dutton were still talking made her feel she'd been too open in the past and needed to erect some sort of defense—and that was as upsetting as learning that the girl who'd always been the most competitive with her had just learned she'd split with Dutton and was no longer living the dream of being a doctor's wife in sunny Los Angeles. "No. Why?"

"You look as though you're upset."

"I'm not upset," she lied. "I don't care about Jackie. We haven't been in touch for years, except on social media."

"That's why you didn't tell her?" Marlow asked.

"Yeah," Aida replied, but that was another lie. She preferred Jackie not to know. Jackie was one of those people who always seemed to wish her the worst, and Aida didn't want to imagine this woman gloating over her misfortune. She already felt like a failure.

What did you tell her? she wrote to Dutton. Marlow and Claire couldn't see what she was writing since she'd pulled her phone away, but they were both watching her in concern.

That you didn't live here anymore. That we're no longer married. What was I supposed to tell her?

She felt slightly nauseous as she stared at those words. What *was* he supposed to tell her? It was the truth, wasn't it? She'd lost him, and it felt like everything else she'd had was gone, too.

Aida wished her frenemy hadn't stopped by. She wished Dutton had never cheated in the first place. She missed their big, beautiful house, their neighborhood and lifestyle. Truth be told, she missed Dutton, too—his strong arms holding her at night, his calls during the day, reminding her that she wasn't alone in the world, the way he'd laugh and then take her out to eat whenever she failed at cooking a meal. She missed the stories he'd tell about his patients, too. He could do so many good things, had helped so many people. He'd literally saved lives. And she had been proud of that—proud to be connected to him.

Marlow touched her elbow. "Let's go swimming."

"Okay." Forcing a smile as if her latest contact with her ex hadn't affected her in the least, Aida slipped her phone in her bag before turning to Claire. "Would you mind watching our stuff?"

Claire stiffened. No doubt she felt stung that she hadn't been invited to get in the water, too. It was an obvious slight—more evidence of the growing strain between them. But given the situation, Aida didn't feel capable of being more generous. She was doing all she could to hold back her tears. The only reason she'd agreed to get in the ocean was so no one would notice if she lost that battle.

18

It took forever for night to fall. Usually Marlow enjoyed the lazy days of summer, especially when she was on the island. That was one of the reasons she'd sold her condo and closed up her practice when she came to Teach even though she might return to LA—she didn't want anything drawing her back before she was ready to leave. But today it felt as though time was standing still.

"Let's go to Miami," Aida suggested as they were driving back from the public beach.

Normally, Marlow would welcome this idea, if only to show her friends what the city was like. They should see it while they were so close. But if they went there tonight, they wouldn't get back until well after Walker went to bed. Although Marlow had spent the day telling herself that, when she had the chance, she'd drop off his things, thank him for the note he'd left her and leave right away, she was already hoping he wouldn't want her to go.

While soaking up the sun this afternoon, her hat over her face, Aida and Claire beside her, and strangers laughing, talking and moving all around them, she'd been replaying some of her favorite recent memories. The expression on Walker's face as he'd stripped off her wet clothes was definitely one of them.

So was the feel of his warm, hard body moving against hers, the way he'd tasted and smelled, and how gentle he'd been the last time they were together. Knowing she was upset about her father, he'd been trying to comfort her, and the sweetness made it special.

"I'm too tired tonight," she told Aida.

"Tired?" Aida echoed. "All we've done today is lie around on the beach."

"Hanging out in the sun can make you even more tired," Claire said from the back seat, saving Marlow from having to defend her response.

"I have to fly to Atlanta to meet with my father's attorney on Saturday," she said. "My return flight lands in Miami at seven. Why don't you and Claire drop me off at the airport and spend the day in Miami? When I get back, we'll have dinner and head to South Beach to check out the clubs. It'll be more exciting on the weekend, anyway. You really have to see it in full swing."

"Okay!" they agreed.

Once they arrived back at Seaclusion, they showered and ate a late dinner at the main house. Then Aida and Claire went to the guesthouse to read or watch TV while Marlow spent a few hours with her mother.

"You don't mind that I gave your father's watch to Walker and his ring to Reese, do you?" Eileen said as she put glue on the back of a picture she was placing in the scrapbook.

Marlow looked up from the newspaper articles she'd been organizing by year. Fortunately, Rosemary wasn't around to overhear this. She'd left after dinner without saying where she was going. "Not at all. I could tell they were surprised and excited."

Her mother seemed pleased to hear that her gesture had been well received. "I considered waiting until you were married," she mused. "Then I could've given the watch, at least, to your husband. But I'm saving your father's wedding ring for that."

Marlow placed a photo of her father with the Speaker of the

House on the appropriate stack of pictures. "I'm not going to get married, Mom."

Eileen looked up in surprise. "Ever?"

"No. I've seen too many marriages fall apart."

"What about kids?"

The kids question was a difficult one. "*If* I decide to have kids, I might reconsider. But I don't want to get your hopes up, because I can't promise that will happen."

"Why not?"

"I've never met anyone who's tempted me to take the risk of going through the heartache, the fighting over assets and trying to hammer out a way to share the kids."

"You haven't found anyone because you've been too busy, too focused on your career. Maybe it's just as well you're letting your practice go. There are other things in life."

"Like trying to catch a man?"

"Like finding someone to share your life with," her mother corrected. "I think you intimidate men, or you would've found someone years ago."

Marlow scowled at her. "I don't intimidate men. I'm friendly and approachable."

"As long as you're meeting someone who doesn't want to date you. You're a wonderful person. Beautiful and smart, too. And yet you've never had a steady boyfriend."

Did she intimidate men? At her age, the fact that she'd never had a serious relationship was beginning to seem odd, even to Marlow. Several of the guys she'd dated had said she made it too hard to get close to her, that she wasn't emotionally accessible, which could be another way of saying the same thing. She'd never cared enough to take those criticisms seriously. Still, for the first time, she was beginning to wonder if she was missing out on something, after all. "There's more to life than marriage and kids."

"True, and I know times have changed," Eileen said. "It's

not the same as it was when I was your age. But I hope one day you'll know the fulfillment that comes from the type of deep and abiding love your father and I had."

Marlow smiled as her mother reached over to squeeze her hand. "Not everyone can have what you had with Dad."

"You never know," Eileen said. "It could happen for you, too—if you'll open yourself up to it."

The next morning, Rosemary hung her head as she stood on the deck and spoke into the phone. The last thing she wanted was for Eileen to overhear her conversation from inside the house. She preferred not to hear Eileen's opinion on the drama in her life, which Eileen would, no doubt, feel free to share. That was one of the downsides of accepting help. Because of the extra support the Madsens had provided while Rosemary was raising her boys, Eileen felt comfortable giving advice even on personal matters and expected that advice to be followed, just like her other commands.

As grateful as Rosemary was to Eileen—for everything, including her job—she didn't want to hear her employer's perspective right now. Eileen had been coddled and protected her whole life, first by her parents and then by her husband. She'd had a safety net beneath her since the day she was born. If anything hurt or upset her, someone would race to fix it or smooth it over. For Rosemary, it was hard to hear that she shouldn't let Rudy back into her life from someone who'd had a husband as supportive as Tiller.

"You *called* him?" she said into her phone.

"I miss him!" Rudy responded. "I wanted to talk to my son. Is that so terrible?"

She gazed out at the ocean from the lower deck, squinting at the bright sun bouncing off the water. "But I was just with you last night, and you...you didn't say anything."

"I didn't want to upset you. We had a great time last night. Didn't we?"

It *had* been wonderful. They'd wound up making love on the beach, something she'd never imagined she'd do, especially with her ex-husband and at her age. She'd been trying not to let the relationship turn physical; she was afraid it would cloud her judgment. But one thing had led to another, and it'd felt so natural she couldn't refuse.

She didn't regret giving in, though. She'd come away feeling especially close to him and more hopeful than ever, which was why it would've been nice if he'd given her a heads-up about Reese. Thanks to the call he'd placed, she'd been blindsided by an argument with their son when she went to his apartment an hour ago to make sure he was getting up for work. "I just… didn't expect you to contact him," she said. "You agreed to let me smooth the way."

"I've tried. I've waited and waited and waited, Rosemary. You and I have been talking for a long time."

It'd taken forever for her to decide to give him another chance. He'd started calling her after he split with the woman he was living with in Texas—Kelly something—and several months after that, he'd moved to Miami to be closer to Rosemary. But he'd been living in Miami for a year, and only recently had she been willing to see him. "I… I needed a little more time."

"I'm sorry. But I thought an apology might help. We all know I owe him one."

Rudy's contrition tempered her response. She'd be crushed if she were him and had a child who wouldn't associate with her, so she wasn't without empathy. "It was kind of you to try to apologize to him, but…he's not open to it yet." The mere attempt had made it more difficult for her to convince Reese that Rudy deserved a second chance. Reese had shot down everything she'd tried to say. He'd been frustrated, hurt and angry to learn that she was seriously considering a reunion with his father.

She understood how he felt. She also understood how Rudy felt. She was torn in two, which didn't make her situation any easier.

And now that she'd slept with Rudy, he was pushing even harder for a commitment.

"Yeah, I figured that out," he said. "You should've heard what he said to me."

She gripped her phone more tightly. "What'd he say?"

"He told me if I ever come near you again, he'll beat the shit out of me."

She winced. Her boys were protective; Rudy had given them reason to be. "You didn't try to call Walker, did you?"

"No. I was hoping Reese would be more receptive. That the two of you together might be able to talk Walker into…you know…letting me come around once in a while."

Rosemary heard a noise and leaned over the railing to make sure Marlow or one of her friends wasn't walking down the beach. She didn't see anyone, but she knew they could come around at any moment. It was nearly ten, about the time they usually drifted over to the main house for breakfast.

She lowered her voice. "Walker is older and less volatile. He's seen enough as a cop to understand that we all do things we regret. Maybe I'll get through to him. But, please, let *me* pave the way."

"I will. I promise. I'm sorry."

She could understand why Rudy was growing impatient. But after the time she'd spent with him in Miami last night, she was beginning to hope even more that they'd be able to bring their fractured family back together. Her unwillingness to ruin what was developing—what could be—was the whole reason she'd been putting off the conversation she needed to have with Reese and Walker.

After this morning, however, she figured she might as well

drag it all into the open and see if she couldn't soften their hearts toward their father.

"That call with Reese was—" he whistled "—rough. Believe me, I've learned my lesson."

She wasn't sure whether to apologize for Reese or not. Rudy had earned Reese's disapprobation. And yet...she still loved her ex-husband. It was hard to see him hurt, even if he deserved it. "I'll look for the right opportunity."

"Thank you. I didn't mean to push. I'm just...trying to get my life back, and the reason I'm doing that is because I want all of you in it."

"I know."

"Do you think there's a chance?"

He sounded so dejected she had to encourage him. "I do. But you have to remember that love is more malleable than trust. Once trust has been destroyed, the only way to get it back is to build it back—brick by brick."

"I've been trying to build it back!"

"It takes time."

"Okay. Thanks for...for being more willing to love me again than they are."

She still couldn't say whether that was a wise thing, only that she couldn't help it. She was finding love to be far more long-suffering than she'd ever imagined. Maybe that was because she hadn't been perfect, either. No one knew about the skeleton in her closet, but if her boys ever learned the truth, they'd hate her even more than they hated Rudy. And Rudy would hate her, too.

Should she tell them herself, so there was no risk they'd find out some other way?

She'd agonized over that question for years. The correct answer was probably yes. But what they didn't know couldn't hurt them. Her argument with Reese this morning proved he was in no state to hear what she had to tell him.

Bottom line, she couldn't bring herself to do anything that would topple either of her sons' lives, not if it could be avoided.

Marlow's text came in at eleven that night. Walker hadn't known what to expect from her—if she'd even check the tree—and the message she'd sent didn't give any indication of what she was thinking or feeling. All he received was a simple request.

Are you up? Any chance you'd come get me?

He took a few seconds to consider the question, even though he knew he wasn't going to say no. He'd decided he would sincerely try to be her friend. It wasn't her fault she'd never been interested in him. Sure, she'd been spoiled from the beginning and could've been kinder, but she'd been adored by both parents from the day she was born and had always had everything she wanted. Maybe he would've acted no better had he been in her shoes. He'd made plenty of mistakes over the years himself—like not giving up and leaving her alone. So he'd decided to let it go. As friends they might be able to reach some sort of emotional equilibrium, allowing each of them to feel good about the other.

I'm on my way.

He took the bike, but the engine was so loud that, once he reached Seaclusion, he stopped outside the fence instead of pulling into the drive.

I'm here—on the street.

The way she was smiling when she came out, as though she was excited to see him, made him smile back. Perhaps this was all she'd ever wanted—friendship. He could make it work, couldn't he? He'd simply continue to date other women, fulfill his sexual appetites elsewhere. That should make it possible, if not easy.

"So you're finally going to give me a ride?" she said when she saw the bike.

He raised his eyebrows at her saucy expression and handed her the extra helmet he'd brought, but he didn't say anything. He'd already cried uncle when he left her that note. Maybe that was why she was in such a good mood. As usual, she was getting her way.

She put on the helmet, and he helped tighten the strap under her chin. She was hanging on to a bag that probably contained his clothes, so when she climbed on behind him, only one arm circled his waist.

Once he fired up the engine and they took off, it was surprisingly chilly, thanks to the wind. On a bike, it could feel cold even when it was warm outside. He should've brought a jacket. Seaclusion was so close he hadn't thought about it. But he could tell Marlow was cold. He couldn't imagine any other reason she'd cling to him so tightly.

As soon as they reached his place, he turned off the bike and rested it on the kickstand in the driveway.

"You're a far more cautious person than you used to be," she said as she got off and removed her helmet.

He hadn't been cautious when it came to her. They'd had unprotected sex twice—something he'd never done before—and he was supremely conscious of that. He had no idea what she'd do if she got pregnant with his baby. It terrified him that he'd most likely have no say whatsoever.

"There's cautious, and then there's foolhardy," he said. "Not wearing a helmet is just foolhardy."

"We barely went two miles. It takes longer to put on the helmet than it does to make the drive," she joked.

He set both helmets on the seat. "Most car accidents happen only a mile or two from home."

She walked beside him as they started toward the stairs. "It's hard to believe you're a cop. I never dreamed you'd go into law enforcement."

"Neither did I," he admitted. "But I'm glad I did."

She handed him the bag, which contained his sweats, as he'd guessed, and also the T-shirt he'd worn to the bonfire.

"Why do you say that?"

He shrugged. "It provided structure when I needed it most. A family of sorts. A sense of purpose."

"It gave you a war to fight," she said as they started up the stairs.

"That's certainly how it felt in Miami. The drugs that go through that place... Unbelievable. But it's not that way here."

"You still like the work?"

"I do." He knew that some departments had systemic problems and corruption, but he also knew there were a lot of really good cops out there who were doing all they could to bring safety and justice to their communities. He'd been fortunate in that he'd been involved with more of the good officers than the bad, but as he got older, he found he didn't need the kind of adrenaline rush he'd been after when he was younger. He wasn't quite so restless, either. He was actually eager to settle down and start a family, and he couldn't think of a safer place to do that than Teach. "Going into law enforcement gave me a constructive place to channel my energy, and it kept me from screwing up my life."

He was tempted to take her hand as they climbed the stairs, but he refrained. He knew what would happen if he touched her. In order to make this new "friends" thing work, he'd have to keep his hands to himself.

When they reached the deck, and she saw the cake he'd

purchased in case she did call him tonight, her eyes widened. "What's this?"

He put down the sack. "Tomorrow's your birthday, isn't it? And I made you miss blowing out the candles at your party, so..."

"You bought me a cake. A *unicorn* cake."

The pink frosting, confetti and sugar-cone horn suddenly looked more ridiculous than it had in the store. "They didn't have a lot to choose from." He didn't mention that he could've gotten her a plain chocolate cake, but he somehow thought she'd like this sparkling confection better, even if it was meant for a little girl.

"I love it," she murmured. "Thank you."

"I'm not always an asshole," he joked. "Sit down. I'll open the wine."

He uncorked the bottle of merlot he'd set out along with two battery-powered flameless candles, which he'd turned on before he left so they'd be flickering when he brought her back, and poured them each a glass. "To turning thirty-five," he said, raising his in a toast. "May this be your best year yet."

She hesitated. "While I have the chance and you're willing to listen to me, can I just say... I really *am* sorry for how I behaved when we were growing up? You were always good to me."

His mind immediately went to the incident at the airport, when he'd told her he hated her. There were other times they'd argued, too, especially as they grew older and his interest became more and more sexual. "I should've taken a hint and moved on. I don't know why I didn't." He lifted his glass again, but still she hesitated. "Marlow?" he said, confused by her reaction. "Here's to being friends."

"Yeah. Here's to being friends," she echoed and finally finished the toast.

After they each took a sip of wine, he lit the three real candles he'd stuck in her cake. "Make a wish before that horn catches on fire," he said with a grin.

She closed her eyes as though she was taking what she wanted to wish for under careful consideration. Then she cast him the prettiest smile he'd ever seen and blew out the candles.

"That was too easy," he said. "I should've gotten the kind that won't go out."

She swiped some of the frosting off the top. "You don't want me to get my wish?"

His gaze fell to her mouth as she licked her finger, and his mind immediately created a picture of her naked and straddling him in the chair with the stars shining overhead and the ocean slamming into the shore down on the beach.

Clearing his throat, he forced his attention back to his wine. *Friends.* "I definitely want you to get your wish. What was it?"

"I can't tell you. Then it won't come true."

"Oh, I don't think you have to worry."

She put down her glass. "What's that supposed to mean?"

"Don't all your wishes come true?" He grinned to let her know he was joking, but he legitimately couldn't believe there was anything she didn't already have. She was rich, incredibly smart, successful, gorgeous, sexy, loved, admired. What more did a person need?

She studied him as he cut a big piece of cake and slid it in front of her. "I tried to say this before, and you didn't really want to hear it, but I really am sorry you had it harder than I did growing up."

"You weren't responsible for that."

"I know, but... I was so selfish and so clueless. I could've made your life a little easier, and I didn't. I feel bad about it."

He put down the knife. "Marlow, the last thing I want is your pity."

"It's not pity. It's—"

"It wasn't your job to look out for me," he insisted.

"It wasn't your job to look out for me, either," she said. "And yet you did. I would've drowned that day if you hadn't come out into the sea. I acted like I had it covered, but I couldn't have made it out on my own. You saved my life."

"Yeah, well, we both know why I was even aware you were out there." He'd been obsessed with her, unable to stop watching what was going on at the party for fear some other boy would touch her or kiss her—or more.

"Even though I'd been a jerk and made you feel unwelcome to join the group."

"That's all in the past," he said. "You don't have to worry about it anymore, so let's forget it and move on."

She didn't seem entirely satisfied with that answer. He got the impression that she didn't want to lose his devotion but didn't want to return it, either. "What is it?" he asked.

"Nothing." She toyed with the frosting on her cake. "So... do you see yourself settling on Teach for good?"

"I guess it'll depend on who I marry."

She seemed taken aback by his response. *"Marry?"* she repeated, looking up.

He shrugged. "Someday."

She pulled the horn of the unicorn from the cake and took a bite. "Are you dating anyone special?"

It felt awkward to talk about other women when they'd been sleeping together, and so recently, but he figured this was part of being friends. Apparently, they were going to forget the recent past, too. "I'm seeing a couple of women." He didn't add that he didn't feel much for either one. He hoped that would change.

"Do they live here on Teach?" she asked.

"One of them does."

"And the other?"

He shifted in his seat. "She lives in Miami and works as an interior designer."

"That's why you're thinking you might move?"

"I doubt there'd be enough work for her here."

She put the horn on her plate with her leftover cake. "I see."

"What about you? You dating anyone special?" He didn't want to hear about the men in her life any more than he wanted to talk about the women in his, but at least it was a natural segue from his love life—and his curiosity would be assuaged.

"No. I don't plan on getting married. I've seen too much as a divorce attorney. That's the downside of my profession, I guess."

"Life's full of unexpected turns. Maybe you'll meet the right man one day, who'll change your mind." He just hoped he wouldn't be around to see it when she did. "Here you go," he said, pulling out the gift sack he'd stashed under the table.

"You got me something?"

"Not really. You'll see."

She dug through the tissue and pulled out her father's Rolex. "You're giving it back?"

"I know how close you were with him. I figure you should have it, not me."

She blinked at him. "But my mother wants you to have it."

"We don't have to tell your mother." He was hoping she'd be glad to have it. It was her father's freaking Rolex! But she seemed dismayed.

"You'll think of him whenever you look at it," he said, still trying to gauge what she was feeling. But when tears welled up, he didn't know how to react. "Marlow?" he said, confused.

Her smile seemed forced. "It's thoughtful. Thank you—for all of this. But it's late, and you probably have to work in the morning, so I'd better let you get some sleep."

A wave of disappointment crashed through him. She wasn't happy, and yet he'd been so sure he'd done everything right with the cake, the candles and the present that should've had tremendous meaning for her. "Okay," he said because he didn't know what else to say.

He led her down to the bike, but just before he handed her

the helmet, he figured he should broach what he'd been worrying about. This evening hadn't gone as well as he'd hoped, anyway. "Will you do me one favor?"

She'd gained control of her emotions and treated him to another one of those forced smiles. "I certainly owe you a favor. What is it?"

He hated to ask, but he didn't know whether they'd ever have another opportunity like this. "I realize it's very personal, but... will you tell me when you get your period so that...so that I'll know we're in the clear?"

"I'm *not* pregnant, Walker. My period had just ended when we were together for the first time. There's no way I was ovulating. And it's not as if we... I mean... I guess we did, but..." She sighed as she combed her fingers through her long hair. "Okay. I'll let you know."

Relieved to have a commitment so he wouldn't have to wonder and worry needlessly, he said, "Thank you."

He was about to help her fasten her helmet again when he remembered that she needed something to keep her warm. "Just a sec." He jogged up to the house, went inside to grab a sweatshirt and was on his way out when something on the deck caught his eye. She'd slipped her father's Rolex over the wine bottle. He would've grabbed it for her, assuming she'd forgotten it, but it was clear that she'd left it there on purpose.

19

When Marlow had texted Walker earlier that evening, she'd been excited to see him, to put the past behind them and move forward in a more positive direction. She was grateful she'd had the opportunity to apologize and felt he'd truly forgiven her—or he wouldn't have bought her a birthday cake. He'd even tried to give her father's watch back to her.

They were truly friends now. He'd brought his bike to give her a ride. He'd provided a sweatshirt so she wouldn't be cold as they drove home. He'd behaved *perfectly*.

And yet...she was disappointed.

Was she just maudlin over her father's death? His loss hit her at odd moments. She'd be doing just fine and then something would trigger a memory and she'd realize she'd never be able to see or talk to him again. But if her sudden melancholy was strictly about her father, why did her thoughts keep circling back to what Walker had said about the women he was dating?

It also bothered her that he'd asked her to tell him when she got her period, as if that was all he needed to put an end to that brief interlude of intimacy. Granted, friends typically didn't sleep together. But they'd already had several encounters. She didn't see why they couldn't keep things physical through the summer.

The engine of his motorcycle dimmed as he drove off, and she sighed as she trudged toward the guesthouse.

"An interior designer," she mumbled and wondered what the woman looked like, what had drawn him to her and how much he liked being with her.

Instead of going inside, Marlow headed to the beach, hoping that the ocean would soothe her, as it so often had over the years. At a minimum, it would give her some solitude.

She was still wearing Walker's sweatshirt as she approached the ocean. She'd offered to give it back to him when she got off the bike, but he'd insisted she could return it another time—or even keep it.

Lifting it to her nose, she breathed in, trying to find his scent on the soft fabric. But it had been freshly laundered. She dropped it and watched the waves while thinking back through her evening with him. She'd been hoping for more, she decided. And it was probably sex.

That was why she was so out of sorts. But surely this desire and disappointment would be fleeting. After all, she'd felt nothing lasting for any other man she'd been with. She'd settle into her new friendship with Walker, and all would be right. Better. Less awkward than if they were continuing to sleep together—and without the risk of causing hard feelings between their families.

Determined to accept that as her answer, she was on her way back to the guesthouse when she smelled the scent of marijuana and began to look for the source.

She found Reese leaning up against the garage near the door that led to the apartment, smoking a joint. He was wearing only a pair of holey jeans, no shirt, no shoes. Although she wasn't attracted to him, he looked sleep-tousled and sexy. She was glad Aida wasn't around to notice.

"Hey," she said as she stepped out of the shadows and into the moonlight.

He didn't seem startled by her sudden appearance, which made her wonder if he'd seen her on the beach. Maybe he'd started down that way, spotted her and decided not to bother her. "Hey," he replied.

"Having trouble sleeping?" she asked.

"As usual."

"Does that help?"

"It relaxes me," he said and offered her a hit.

"I'm good, thanks."

"Did you have fun at Walker's?"

She froze. "What do you mean?"

He pointed at her sweatshirt. "That's his, isn't it?"

She felt foolish for forgetting that she was standing there in Walker's college sweatshirt. *Obviously*, it was his. "Yeah," she said, but didn't elaborate. As far as she was concerned, the less said, the better.

He brought the joint back to his lips, and the end glowed red as he inhaled. "Are you two seeing each other now or what?"

"We're just friends."

"Right," he said with a mirthless chuckle.

"It's true."

He hung his head as he scratched the back of his neck. "Walker could never settle for being your friend."

"Because..."

"He wants you too badly."

She frowned at him. "Not anymore."

He peered up at her from beneath the hair that'd fallen over his eyes. "I don't believe that for a second." Finished with the joint, he tossed the butt away. "The surprise is that you finally want him, too. I never saw that coming."

She opened her mouth to deny it, but he didn't give her the chance.

"I'm glad, though," he added. "Because you'd be wrong to let him go." Then he murmured a good-night and went back inside.

Claire woke up in the morning to a text from Dutton: All packed and ready to go.

As she lay in bed, staring at those words, she began to feel sick to her stomach. How was she going to keep Marlow and Aida from running into him on this small island? He was coming for a vacation. It wasn't as though he'd be willing to hide out inside the beachfront Airbnb he'd rented.

Closing her eyes, she let her breath ease out as she listened for movement in the house. She wished she could call him without waking her friends. She wanted to plead with him to wait a month, at least. Maybe by then Aida wouldn't be feeling quite so raw. After the way she'd reacted when she heard that her high school friend had spoken to Dutton and learned of the divorce, Claire knew that Aida had a long way to go. She needed more time before she could gain any perspective on the failure of her marriage. The three of them had just gotten here last week. What was Dutton thinking?

Aida would say he was thinking of himself, as usual, but Claire felt disloyal to him even letting that thought crop up.

She started to message him to say she wasn't ready for him to come—that *no one* was ready for him to come—but deleted the words. She'd tried to talk him out of it before, and nothing she'd said had made any difference.

Besides, he'd already made the arrangements. He wasn't going to change them now.

She brought up her inbox and scrolled through her email until she found the itinerary he'd forwarded to her. He was due to arrive on Saturday at four. Marlow had mentioned that she'd be getting back from meeting with her father's attorney at seven. There were three hours between his arrival and hers, and the

Miami airport was a big place. But it would be disastrous if they happened to bump into each other.

Claire could only hope that his plane wouldn't be delayed...

I'm nervous about this, she admitted.

You're not excited to see me?

She wanted to see him, to be with him, but not now. Not yet. That's not it.

There's nothing to be nervous about, Claire. We're going to have a great time.

Maybe *he'd* have a great time; she'd be a nervous wreck.

Where will you be when I get in? he asked.

No doubt he'd expect to see her right away. But she'd be shopping in Miami when his plane landed and barhopping with Marlow and Aida after that. He wasn't going to like hearing that she wouldn't be available until Sunday—that he'd spend the first night of his vacation alone—but she felt it would be better to tell him now, so he wouldn't blow up her phone with calls and texts while she was with Aida and Marlow.

Marlow wants to show us around Miami.

What does that mean?

Did she have to spell it out? She pressed a finger and thumb to her closed eyelids for a moment before responding. It means I'll be in Miami.

So...should we meet up there?

No way. I can't.

Then how long will it be until you return to the island?

He wasn't going to like this answer, either. It'll be late.

You couldn't have put her off a week until after I was gone?

Claire was so afraid her friends would catch on to the fact that she had something going on that she hadn't dared suggest a delay. She could already feel Aida pulling away from her, beginning to distrust her.

I'll only be there a week, he wrote.

She'd told him more than once that this wasn't a good time to visit. But she didn't throw that up to him. She knew it wouldn't be well received. It's just one night.

He didn't respond.

I'll say I have to go over to the club to meet with my new boss Sunday morning and come see you instead. Send me the address of the place you'll be staying. He'd told her he'd spent a lot of money on an Airbnb, but he hadn't given her the exact location. She hoped it wasn't right next door. Part of her thought that would be just like him—to care more about reestablishing their relationship than protecting her from what would happen if Marlow and Aida discovered he was on the island.

Dutton?

Again, she got no answer. He could be at the hospital, she told herself. Maybe he was heading into surgery. He was an important man with a challenging job.

But she had the sneaking suspicion he was mad at her and that wasn't a great way to start off their week together.

Rosemary was in the kitchen kneading dough for the rolls she planned to serve for dinner, along with a salad and grilled salmon, when she heard Eileen call out for her. After rinsing the flour from her hands, she hurried to see what her employer needed.

She found Eileen in the dining room, continuing to work on her scrapbook. Now that she'd started the project, she was devoting every minute she could to it—every minute she felt strong enough to be up and out of bed. She loved surrounding herself with memories of her late husband, and Rosemary could understand why.

"Yes?"

Eileen beckoned her closer. "Take a look at this picture I found when I went through Tiller's desk this morning."

Rosemary expected it to be an old photograph of him and Eileen when they were dating, or Tiller holding Marlow after she was born, or Tiller performing some aspect of his job. She wasn't prepared to see a photograph of Tiller and Reese together when Reese was only five years old.

She took it and pretended to study it. "Oh, I don't think I've ever seen this before," she lied.

"I must've taken it." Eileen smiled proudly. "Isn't it cute? Reese was such a darling little boy. Tiller loved him and Walker—but especially Reese."

"He was very generous to both boys," Rosemary heard herself say. What she didn't admit was that she *had* seen that picture before. She could clearly remember the day it was taken, because *she* was the one who'd taken it, not Eileen. She was the one who'd given it to Tiller, too. And she had a copy herself.

"That's our beach here at Seaclusion in the background, isn't it?" Eileen asked.

"Looks like it." It definitely was. Reese had wandered out while Rosemary was busy in the house. Walker was supposed to have been helping her watch him but got distracted. Once she'd realized her youngest was missing, she'd rushed out in a panic and found Tiller playing with him on the beach. Eileen had been gone that day, so Rosemary had felt free to watch them together for probably thirty minutes before Tiller put Reese on his shoulders and started to carry him back to the house. With the sun shining brightly overhead and a wide expanse of ocean behind them, they looked like an advertisement for some tropical holiday getaway.

The moment Tiller spotted her watching, he'd given her his poster-perfect smile, making the edges of his blue eyes crinkle, and she'd snapped the photograph on an old camera she'd run in and grabbed while they were in the surf together.

"I was going to put it in the scrapbook," Eileen was saying. "You and your kids have been such a big part of our lives. But now I think I'll have a few copies made first. Maybe you and Reese would both like to have one."

Rosemary definitely wanted a better copy than she already had, but she was careful not to act overly interested. "If it's not too much trouble."

"Of course it's not too much trouble. Marlow will be going to Miami on Saturday. I'll have her find somewhere we can get it done."

"There's no need to bother Marlow. I can run the errand." Rosemary hoped to get hold of the photo before anyone else saw it. Eileen might be blinded by decades of love and trust, but Rosemary worried that Marlow, who was far more astute than most people, would see what Eileen had obviously missed.

"She won't mind," Eileen insisted and set it aside.

20

After pushing herself for so long to advance her career, Marlow was enjoying the slow pace of life on the island. "I could get used to this," she said to Aida and Claire as they sat down for a very late breakfast on the top deck of the main house. They'd gotten up at nine and done yoga on the beach before showering and changing their clothes. She was wearing a gauzy white sundress with flip-flops; Aida and Claire were both wearing shorts.

Aida added some cream to her coffee. "It's heaven here. I don't know how you ever left it in the first place."

"My parents didn't really live here when I went off to college. We just spent summers on the island, and the occasional Christmas or Thanksgiving. My father was so busy with his various roles, and so was I. I never even considered living here year-round." Truth be told, she was a little envious that Walker had made it his permanent residence.

"Are you seriously considering it now?" Rosemary asked as she came out of the house with a plate of homemade snickerdoodles to offer them for dessert.

"No," Marlow replied as she helped herself to a soft, warm

cookie. Today was her actual birthday, so she was still getting well wishes and goodies. "Not really."

"Why not?" Aida asked. "You could open a boutique in town like I'm planning to do in LA."

"I don't have any interest in opening a boutique," Marlow said.

"Why not open a law practice?" Aida pressed. "Maybe business would be slow enough that you could tolerate the negativity in smaller doses."

"That's a good idea." Claire hadn't said much so far this morning. She'd wished Marlow a happy birthday, like everyone else, but she seemed mostly absorbed in her own thoughts. "As idyllic as it seems here on Teach, people get divorced everywhere."

"But we'd both be sad if you left LA," Aida said.

"If I moved here, you'd just have to come out and visit me every couple of months," Marlow told them. "Or move here, too. You could open your boutique in downtown Teach instead of LA. And Claire could work at the tennis club until she was ready to open her own yoga studio again."

"Do you think we'd be able to make a living?" Aida asked.

"Tough to say," Marlow admitted.

Finished with her meal, Aida rocked back while she also enjoyed a cookie. "Would you ever consider it, Claire?"

Claire used her fork to stir her eggs, which she'd hardly touched. "I don't know. There are plenty of tourists who might be interested in doing some yoga. But it'd definitely be a risk. And I'm not sure I can handle another business failure."

Marlow didn't hold out much hope that her friends would join her if she moved. After the year they'd had, neither of them was very big on taking risks. Of course, they didn't have the same level of security she had, thanks to her family's wealth. "It's something to think about, I guess."

Hearing the door open, they all looked up as her mother led Walker out onto the deck.

"I hope there's some cookies left, because Walker deserves a treat after moving that heavy armoire in the attic. Thanks to him, I can now get to the rest of the memorabilia I've collected over the years."

Marlow straightened in her seat. "You called Walker while he was at work?" she asked, taking immediate note of his uniform.

"He's on his break," her mother assured her.

"Still, you could've asked me to help with the armoire," Marlow said.

Eileen shrugged off her words. "It would've been too heavy for you. It took both Walker *and* Reese to budge the darn thing."

"Is Reese coming for cookies, too?" Aida asked.

"I invited him, but he had to leave for work," Eileen replied.

Marlow had a difficult time looking away from Walker. When he'd first stepped out onto the deck, his eyes had flicked her way, and his gaze had quickly run over her body, which was something he didn't do to Aida or Claire. But then he didn't look at her again. After the requisite birthday wishes, he kept his attention on her friends, who were more than eager to visit with him, while he had a few cookies.

"I'll let you ladies get on with your day," he said after about five minutes.

"You're leaving so soon?" Aida's voice was filled with disappointment. "I'm not sure if you play chess, but if you do, we need someone who can beat our birthday girl."

"*You* beat me," Marlow said, scowling at Aida.

Aida rolled her eyes. "You weren't even trying that time."

Marlow was surprised she'd noticed.

"I love chess," he said, "but—"

"But she's tough," Aida broke in. "We know that. So we'll understand if you don't want to take her on."

Obviously, Aida remembered how competitive Walker was. His eyebrows shot up at the challenge, and his gaze finally cut back to Marlow. "I can beat her."

The confidence in his voice suggested he might really be able to do it. They'd played as kids, and she hadn't always won, but that was a long time ago.

"You think so?" Marlow said.

A sexy grin curved his lips. "As long as you don't take forever to decide on each move, we might have enough time to find out."

Being the boss probably meant he could stretch his break a bit, but she didn't want to get him in trouble. "I'll get the board."

Walker knew what kind of IQ he was dealing with. He couldn't help being slightly intimidated; *he* hadn't been put forward two grades in school. But he loved chess and often played on his phone to relax after work, or with Reese, who was pretty good himself. And Marlow had let him start, which gave him the advantage.

He began with his favorite open—1. e4; she countered with the Sicilian Defense.

At first, Claire, Aida, his mother and Marlow's mother stood or sat nearby, watching them. But as the minutes ticked away, they became distracted and began to talk and move about the deck, checking back every once in a while to see who was ahead. Walker was pleased with the way he was playing. His strategy seemed to be unfolding exactly as he wanted it to. But while he deliberated over one particular move, Marlow began to slip her fingers between his on the hand he had resting next to the board.

He glanced around to see who might be watching them. He was surprised she'd touch him like that in front of the others. But no one was paying attention. Claire had spotted a turtle on the beach and drawn everyone to the banister to see it.

"Are you *trying* to distract me?" he murmured to Marlow.

She cocked her head to one side. "Maybe. Is it working?"

"Definitely." Especially since he couldn't see how this type of contact had anything to do with the friendship she claimed she wanted—the friendship they'd just started last night.

"Would you rather I stopped?" she asked.

The others were streaming back, so when he said no, it was more of a challenge to determine if she'd be willing to let them see what she was doing. He didn't think she would. He assumed this was just between them. Off the record. Nothing that came with any kind of consequences or commitments.

But she didn't remove her hand.

"Looks like you're having fun." Aida was obviously referring to their holding hands. But even then Marlow didn't withdraw.

"There's nothing like being back on the island," she said.

Forcing his mind back to chess wasn't easy. He was losing track of his strategy because there was another game going on at the same time—one he found far more interesting. He hated himself for loving Marlow, but who was he kidding? Nothing had changed.

He finally moved his bishop and watched her as she considered her next chess move. When she started to slide her queen to the far right, he knew she wasn't sincerely trying to beat him.

"Don't you dare let me win," he growled.

She gave him a sheepish look before changing to her knight, and the game waged on. It was taking longer than he'd anticipated. He was so afraid he'd make a mistake that he was the one who had to deliberate for several minutes before each move.

Luckily, he won in the end. Although it hadn't been easy, he couldn't be too proud of himself. He wasn't certain she'd tried her hardest.

"Was that your best game?" he asked skeptically as the others congratulated him for beating their champion.

"I didn't lose it on purpose," she said.

"But you didn't do your best. Why not?"

"I'll try harder next time."

He checked his watch. "I'd like there to be a next time, but I can't play anymore right now."

"Tonight, then?"

Whatever she was doing, he was falling for it again—falling for her. But she'd never acted like this, had never shown so much interest in him. Sure, they'd had sex, but this was different. This was in full view of her friends and both their mothers. That seemed to insist it was genuine. "At my place?" he said.

"Sounds good."

"Can I take you to dinner before that?" The words came out before he could stop them. Here he was, asking her out, even though he'd promised himself he never would.

Although he expected her to come up with some excuse to turn him down, she didn't. "Sure."

Claire and Aida gaped at each other. So did their mothers. But he ignored their reactions. He was afraid to trust Marlow, and yet it felt as though he was finally getting a chance at what he'd always wanted. "I'll pick you up at seven?"

"I'll be ready."

Although he knew he was pushing his luck, he lifted her chin and bent to brush his mouth lightly over hers, just to see if she'd allow it.

And she did.

Still holding her chin, he studied her in confusion after pulling away. But when she blushed and smiled, he couldn't help smiling back. "See you then."

"What was *that* all about?" a shocked Eileen demanded after Walker left.

Marlow could see Rosemary standing as still as a statue in the background, holding the last of the dishes she'd brought out for brunch. She didn't say a word, but the same shock radiated from her. Marlow didn't think Walker's mother liked her that much, not when it came to any type of romantic relationship with him. Rosemary didn't trust her to treat him right, and Marlow couldn't blame her.

Aida pulled out a chair and plopped down beside her. "Did I just see Walker *kiss* you?"

Claire sat on the other side. "If you didn't," she said to Aida, "we're somehow having the same dream."

Now that Walker was gone, Marlow regretted being so obvious. She was the one who'd started this. What had gotten into her? She could've been more discreet. There were other ways of showing interest, of letting him know that maybe she *did* want to explore the possibility of a romantic relationship with him. After all, they'd had sex without letting anyone know about it.

But Reese had caught her in Walker's sweatshirt last night. She had no doubt he'd say something to Rosemary eventually, and then Rosemary would likely mention it to her mother.

Bottom line, after the disappointment she'd felt last night, she hadn't been able to stop herself. It was that simple. He'd been so circumspect while trying to move their relationship safely into the "friend zone," and that had turned out to be a surprising letdown.

"Why are you all making such a big deal of it?" she asked, attempting to play it off. "Walker and I have been friends since I can remember."

"Friends don't kiss each other," her mother said.

Marlow waved her words away. "It was barely a peck."

"That's true," Aida agreed. "And yet it was one of the steamiest kisses I've ever seen."

"Especially the part where he gazed into your eyes afterward," Claire added, pretending to swoon.

Marlow could feel her face burning. "Stop!" she said and risked another look at his mother.

Rosemary immediately glanced away from her and carried in the dishes.

★ ★ ★

After Marlow and her friends left to go to the public beach that had all the music and vendors, Rosemary texted Walker. You know better than to get involved with Marlow.

And you know better than to get involved with Dad, came his response. I haven't had the chance to talk to you about it, but I've been meaning to remind you of what it was like when you were with him before.

Your father has changed, she wrote back, returning to that same old argument, because she hoped—and believed—it was true.

Maybe Marlow has, too.

And maybe she hasn't.

His response came back immediately. Seriously? I'm thirty-six. You're going to warn me away from getting involved with someone?

She tiptoed down the hall to double-check that Eileen was still napping, then hurried out to the deck and down the stairs to the beach, where she called her son.

Walker answered on the second ring. "Don't do it," he said before she could say anything. "I'll look out for myself—thank you very much."

"I'm just…scared for you," she admitted.

"I could say the same right back to you."

She sighed. Obviously, Reese had been talking to Walker. "Your father's been trying to get back with me for months," she said. "He's established a bit of a track record, at least. This thing with Marlow…it's brand-new. She just got here a week ago."

"Every relationship has to start somewhere."

"But you've been saying for a while you want a wife and children. I don't think Marlow's remotely interested in those things."

"It's just a date," he said.

She squeezed her forehead while moving the sand from side to side with her feet. He didn't understand. She had a strong argument for why Walker couldn't get involved with Marlow, and it went beyond what she was saying to him now. There was something he didn't know, something she needed to tell him.

She just…couldn't—not without bringing everything else crashing down.

Dinner with Walker was every bit as enjoyable as Marlow had expected. He took her to a seafood place called The Conch House, where the host sat them at a table overlooking the water. She'd never eaten at this particular restaurant and was happy to take Walker's suggestion of the conch chowder as her first course and some stone crabs for her main meal. He ordered seafood ceviche as an appetizer, which he shared with her, and gator-and-shrimp jambalaya for himself.

While they ate, he didn't bring up the past. He didn't mention their brief kiss on the deck, either, even though he had to be wondering how the others had reacted after he left. She got the impression he wanted to start over, forget about their history and simply enjoy the evening, which was easy enough for her to do. He told her stories about his job, some of which made her laugh—like the one in which he was helping to train a rookie in Miami and they went out on a robbery call. The rookie got so nervous when the guy who'd held up the liquor store began to run away that he accidentally tased Walker instead. Walker said he hit the hot concrete like a felled tree, and the crook got away.

"That must've been embarrassing," she said.

He offered her a bite of his jambalaya, which she accepted. "It was," he said. "Imagine having to tell the liquor store owner why you couldn't get the dude who'd just robbed his store."

She laughed. "Do you know if that rookie is still on the force?"

"He didn't last long. Wasn't cut out to be a cop. He also wrecked a squad car when he accidentally hit the gas instead of the brake and rammed into a cinder block wall. That spelled the end for him."

"Poor guy," she said, still chuckling.

"Yeah. I liked him, even if he did tase me," Walker said. "At least he didn't use pepper spray."

She sipped some of the wine he'd ordered for them. "Pepper spray's worse?"

"*Much* worse." He lifted his glass. "What about you? You have to have some war stories, too."

She dabbed at her mouth with her napkin. "I once represented a guy who wanted a divorce because his wife wouldn't quit overfeeding their cat."

Walker leaned forward. "Did you say *overfeeding their cat?*"

"I did. It was getting fat, and he was afraid she'd do the same thing to their unborn children."

He shook his head. "You gotta be kidding me."

"Nope. I also had a client who divorced his wife because she was sending money to some guy in another country she'd met on social media. She'd sent so much to help his fake 'ministry' she'd just about bankrupted them."

"I think that would make me mad, too," Walker said.

"Yeah. I couldn't blame that guy. But there's nothing funny about most divorces. That's why I'm considering getting out of the business."

"You've mentioned not wanting to get married." He looked hesitant to continue but did anyway. "Do you not want children, either?"

She was extremely conscious that they'd had unprotected sex—twice. She didn't think the chances of pregnancy were very high, but a possibility, however slight, was still a possibility. "I don't know," she said. "I haven't made any decisions along those lines."

Fortunately, he didn't press her. He leaned back as the waitress brought them each a piece of key lime pie. They hadn't ordered it, but Walker must've called ahead to tell the hostess it was her birthday, because there was a candle in hers.

"Happy birthday," the waitress said and gathered some of the restaurant employees to sing to her.

Walker smiled as he looked on.

When it was over, Marlow said, "Thank you. This looks delicious, but I can't eat another bite."

"You have to at least try it," he said. "Have a bite of mine and take yours home." Walker pushed his plate into the middle of the table as the waitress went to box up the other slice.

"Wow, you're right," Marlow said after she'd taken a bite. "This is the best I've ever had, and I've had a lot of key lime pie."

"They put sweetened condensed milk in it. That's what my mother said, anyway."

She mopped up the graham cracker crumbs left on the plate from her bite. "Speaking of your mother... I don't think she's too happy we're out together. She's always been kind to me—don't get me wrong—but I can tell she'd prefer I stayed away from you."

"Just ignore that."

"She's concerned about you."

"She has her own problems to worry about."

"Are you talking about the fact that she's seeing your father again?"

"I wondered how much you heard when Reese came over the other night."

"I heard the first part—while I was cowering in your bathroom."

His teeth flashed in a grin. "Bad timing."

"Had he come earlier, it would've been worse."

The way he looked at her brought back the more intimate memories of that night. "No kidding."

She picked up her glass to finish the last of her wine. "How do *you* feel about your parents getting back together?"

"I think my mom's stupid to give my dad a second chance."

She set her wineglass back down. "Maybe she thinks you're stupid for giving me one."

He put his credit card on the table for the waitress. "My mother and I don't have to agree on everything."

After dinner, when Walker brought Marlow to his house, he didn't suggest they play chess, and neither did she.

They left a trail of clothes down the hall to his bedroom. He couldn't wait to feel her naked body against his once again. Everything that'd happened since the last time they were together suddenly seemed like foreplay—it had created more and more desire, and now he was eager for the payoff.

"This certainly beats what we did last night," she said as he rolled her beneath him.

Hearing a shred of truth in her words, he raised his head. "Hey, I bought you a unicorn cake."

She grinned up at him. "I like this birthday present better."

If only he'd known… "If you wanted this, all you had to do was say so. Instead, you confused the hell out of me with that 'let's be friends' bullshit."

She laughed at his response, then sobered as she moved the hair out of his eyes. "What I want most is for you to forgive me. Can I have that, too?"

How could he deny her? She'd owned his heart since he could remember. He didn't know if they were friends or something more, and he sure as hell wasn't going to ask—all it would take to ruin everything was to scare her—but he knew for certain that the answer to her question was yes. "You're forgiven. There's no way I could hold a grudge against you right now even if I tried."

21

Marlow wished Walker could take her home on his motorcycle. She loved the thrill of riding on the back of his bike. But the engine was so loud she was afraid it might wake the others and alert them to the fact that it was nearly three in the morning.

They'd kept procrastinating the moment they had to get out of bed so she could get home. She was enjoying being with him too much to leave, even though they were just lying naked in each other's arms and talking or sleeping.

"So… I have a big day at the station today—administrative stuff," he said as they pulled up to Seaclusion. "But can I see you tomorrow?"

"I'm afraid not. I'll be out of town tomorrow."

"You're leaving the island?"

"Only for the day. I have to meet with my father's attorney in Atlanta about the estate."

"When will you get back?"

She reached for the door handle but paused before climbing out. "It'll be late. I promised Claire and Aida I'd take them to South Beach after I fly in."

"Then I'll try to free up some time today."

"Okay." She started to climb out but impulsively left her door hanging open as she turned, leaned over the console and grabbed Walker by the shirtfront—as he'd once done to her—to bring him in for another long, hungry kiss. "In case no one's ever told you before, you are so good in bed. But don't get a big head, because I *can* beat you at chess," she added and heard him chuckle as she let him go and stepped out.

She could tell that he waited until she was safely on the property before driving off, but once he was gone, she suddenly wasn't in any hurry to go inside. She doubted she'd be able to sleep even if she tried.

She'd never been in love, but she was feeling a crazy sort of drunken euphoria that had everything to do with Walker. Was this dizzying happiness simply the afterglow of great sex? Or of really liking and respecting the person she'd been with? Or both?

There was no doubt she liked Walker better than anyone else she'd dated or had sex with.

But...did her feelings go any deeper than that?

She told herself love couldn't happen that quickly. She'd only been back on the island for a week. But she supposed the length of time since they'd seen each other didn't matter. She'd known him her whole life.

A noise drew her attention, and she turned to see Aida slipping out of the door that led to the apartment over the garage. She was wearing nothing except a pair of silky pajama shorts and matching spaghetti-strap top, and her hair was mussed.

"Hey," Marlow said.

Aida jumped. "Oh, my god. You startled me."

"Imagine running into you here," Marlow said with a laugh.

It was too dark to see any red in Aida's face, but Marlow could tell she was embarrassed. "I couldn't sleep."

"So you woke up Reese?" she joked.

"I was invited over, if you must know," she said. "He texted me a few hours ago."

231

Marlow tilted her head to get a better look at Aida's expression. "And? How'd it go?"

"Let's just say he made it worth my time," she replied with a grin. "It felt great to be with a man who was that excited to have sex with me. What about you? And don't say you didn't sleep with Walker, because after that kiss on the deck—" she whistled "—I can't believe you two made it through dinner before heading back to his place."

"Dinner was incredible."

"And..."

Aida wasn't going to let her off the hook. "So was everything that happened after," Marlow admitted.

Aida's smile widened. "Wow. You're generally not one for hyperbole. For you to say that much, it *must've* been good."

"Best sex I've ever had."

"I'm not surprised. The way he looks at you almost makes *me* fall in love with him," Aida said and slipped her arm through Marlow's as they walked over to the guesthouse. "Maybe you'll be moving back to Teach, after all, huh?"

Marlow had no idea what a relationship with Walker would mean—if it would even last. She'd learned enough about romance to understand that you could never take anything for granted. What'd happened to Aida was a case in point. She'd thought Dutton loved her, that she had a solid marriage.

"I'm just going to take it one day at a time," Marlow said.

"That's probably best in the beginning."

The beginning was almost always fun. Marlow knew that, too.

It was the end that could get ugly.

Marlow slept through breakfast. It wasn't until her friends returned from the main house that she woke up. She yawned and stretched while listening to them talk about going shelling. They were speculating about which beach might be best for this—the private beach at Seaclusion, one of the public beaches or one of the smaller beaches—when Marlow climbed out of bed and shuffled down the hall to say good morning.

"How'd you sleep?" Claire asked.

Marlow shoved her hair out of her face. "Like the dead," she replied.

Aida flashed her a smile. "Me, too."

"What is it?" Claire had noticed the subtle change in Aida's tone. "What have I missed?"

"Nothing," Aida replied.

Claire clearly wasn't buying it, but she seemed determined not to react and focused on Marlow instead. "Your mother asked what time you got in last night."

Careful not to look at Aida, Marlow cleared her throat. "And what did you tell her?"

"I said I didn't know."

Marlow relaxed. "Good answer." Maybe now she wouldn't have to go into it herself.

"But she'll just ask you once you go over there," Claire said. "She and Rosemary are waiting to see you."

Of course they were. She assumed they were both uneasy after the kiss they'd witnessed on the deck. But Marlow didn't want them to make a big deal out of her and Walker seeing each other. "Which is why I'll probably text my mother to say I'm heading out to look for shells with you."

"I doubt she'll let you get away that easily," Aida said. "She'll want you to come wish her a good morning at least. And I heard her tell Rosemary to save your plate."

Marlow *was* kind of hungry. It was so nice to be home, where her mother and Rosemary took care of her. But she could always pick up something to eat in town. "Did they seem to be in a good mood?" she asked.

"For the most part," Claire answered.

Aida screwed up her mouth. "I'd say they were quiet this morning. Maybe because you weren't there."

"I don't think that was it," Marlow said. "Knowing I went out with Walker last night has probably thrown them for a loop."

Aida blinked in confusion. "Why? They both care about you *and* Walker."

Claire, who was more aware of nuance, tried to explain. "It shakes up the norm, erases the line between 'family' and 'hired help.'"

Marlow doubted her mother would ever admit to feeling "better than," but she suspected Claire was right.

"Maybe it would be different if Rosemary was new," Claire continued. "But telling someone what to do, feeling entitled to most of that person's time and energy, tends to create a hierarchy—especially after so long."

"I guess I can see that," Aida said.

"And Eileen's illness probably intensifies it," Claire added.

She had a point. Although Eileen had always been kind to Rosemary, Marlow wasn't sure she truly viewed her housekeeper as an equal. The fact that she took great pride in how she treated Rosemary, as if she deserved recognition or accolades for being such a generous employer, sort of confirmed it. Having so much money and status had imbued Eileen with more power in the relationship. Although Marlow would hate to accuse her mother of elitism, she herself had behaved similarly toward Walker when she was young, and she'd gotten at least part of that attitude from her parents.

That Claire might be right was what made Marlow so reluctant to go to the main house this morning. She knew, on some level, that her mother wouldn't approve if she were to get serious with Walker. Eileen would never expect her grandchildren—if there were any—to be Rosemary's grandchildren, too.

And, thanks to the way Marlow had treated Walker before, Rosemary wouldn't be pleased if they got together, either. She wouldn't want her son to spend his life with someone who believed she was better than he was.

"Relationships can be so complicated," Marlow said.

"You're telling us," Aida responded, joking.

Marlow managed a half smile. "I guess I'll take a few minutes to go smooth everything over."

"How do you plan to do that?" Claire asked.

Marlow started back to her room to get dressed. "By telling them last night was no big deal."

"Was it a big deal?" Claire called after her.

"No," she replied. And yet...it had certainly felt like one.

Rosemary was in the kitchen when Marlow came in—but she didn't rush out to greet her. Whatever had happened with Walker, Marlow had been out especially late. Rosemary had been listening and watching for her return but hadn't been able to stay awake past midnight.

"There you are!" she heard Eileen say to her daughter. "You slept in this morning, huh?"

Marlow: "I did, and it felt so good. I think I'm finally adjusting to being in a different time zone."

Eileen: "I'm glad you got some rest. Are you hungry?"

Marlow: "Definitely. It's such a treat to have my meals prepared. I'm so grateful to Rosemary."

Eileen: "So am I."

"Rosemary?" Eileen called. "Marlow's here."

"Coming!" Rosemary put Marlow's plate of pancakes and bacon in the microwave. When it was hot, she carried it to the dining room. "Good morning."

Marlow smiled at her. "Good morning."

Rosemary couldn't see any marks on Marlow's neck. "How are you today?"

"Better after getting some sleep," Marlow replied.

"Did you have fun last night?" Eileen asked.

Rosemary was glad Eileen had asked. She didn't dare inquire about Marlow's date with Walker, but that didn't mean she wasn't trying to catch every word. She bustled around, pouring Marlow a cup of coffee while trying not to give away the fact that she was listening so closely.

"I did," Marlow replied. "We went to The Conch House. Have you ever been there?"

Eileen had finished her breakfast but was still sitting at the table, knitting baby caps for newborns, which she donated to various hospitals in Florida. Because she'd lost so much feeling in her hands due to her disease, it wasn't easy for her to manipulate the needles, but it was something she could do when she didn't feel well enough to do much else. "Not yet. They opened after the first wave of the pandemic and had to close down again. Talk about a terrible time to start a new restaurant."

"No doubt they thought the worst was over," Marlow said. "Anyway, they have good food. We should go there sometime."

"What did you do after?" Eileen asked.

Marlow cleared her throat. "Walker showed me his house."

"And then?"

"We sat and talked on his deck."

Rosemary noticed that Marlow was looking more at the pieces of pancake she was moving around her plate than at her mother. Was it because she was hesitant to meet Eileen's gaze? Was there more to last night than she was saying?

"Do you think you'll go out with him again?" Eileen asked.

This was the million-dollar question, the one Rosemary wanted to hear the answer to, as well.

She noticed a perceptible pause before Marlow answered. "Maybe. If he asks me."

"Of course he'll ask you," Eileen said. "He's chased you for years."

Rosemary felt herself stiffen at Eileen's response. Walker was a good man. Any woman would be lucky to have him, even Eileen's overindulged "princess."

But that was defensiveness talking—the defensiveness Rosemary felt as a mother. She liked Marlow. She just didn't want her son to get involved with her.

She needed everyone to play their respective roles and remember where they belonged. Maybe then everything would be okay.

22

Walker tried to act as if it was a day like any other, but after last night, all he could think about was Marlow, especially that moment in his truck when she'd pulled him over for a final kiss.

Why the big change in her right when he'd determined that he was a fool for continuing to care so much? Was what was happening between them for real? Was it possible that they might get into a serious relationship? Was he crazy to even have that thought?

She could treat him completely different the next time they saw each other.

"Hey, Chief, are you listening?" Officer Goff asked.

Walker drew his mind back to the meeting. He and his only two officers were having their weekly briefing in his office, where they were going over the various complaints and other calls they'd received in the past seven days, as well as anything that was unresolved or they needed to prepare for in the coming days. "Of course I'm listening," he lied. "Why?"

"Because I said there were some teenagers setting off bottle rockets near the homes along the golf course last night, and you just looked at me as if you had no response."

He was glad his department didn't have bigger things to worry about at the moment. His head simply wasn't in the game. "Did you drive over there?"

"Of course."

"And?"

"The kids were gone by then, which is why I was asking if this is important enough that I should try to follow up, or if I should let it go."

"I'm on duty tonight," Walker said. "I'll cruise through the area a few times to make sure we don't have a repeat performance."

"Sounds good."

His other officer, Brody Smith, told him he'd received a complaint about a twelve-year-old who was being bullied by some other boys.

"There's not much we can do to help that situation," Walker said. "Not until the kids doing the bullying cross certain boundaries."

"That's what I told his mother," Smith said. "I felt bad—she's a single mom, and I know it's tough for her to see her child suffer—but at this point, we're only talking about some shunning and verbal taunts."

"How can we police that?" Goff agreed.

"Give me her name and address," Walker told him. "I'll swing by to have a talk with both the mom and the boy. I'll see if they feel it might do some good for me to approach the other boys with a warning."

"Will do," Smith said.

They discussed a couple of scientists who were coming to the island to study the prevalence of certain fish in Teach's waters, and Smith agreed to attend the next chamber of commerce meeting, since Walker had attended the last one and Goff had attended the one before that. Then they adjourned for lunch.

As soon as both officers walked out of his office, Walker

reached for his phone. He wanted to text Marlow to tell her he couldn't wait to see her again.

But he didn't trust last night enough to be so transparent. Every time he'd pursued her in the past, she'd rebuffed him. Revealing his eagerness would probably only chase her away.

So he shoved his phone in his pocket and walked a block to his favorite public beach, where he could purchase a hot dog from a local vendor.

Marlow grew bored searching for shells long before Claire did. Aida was ready to quit, too, so they returned to their towels and let their friend continue without them.

"Is she going to keep this up all summer?" Aida asked, watching Claire, who was diligently walking along the shoreline, her head bent as she studied the sand.

"She's pretty determined," Marlow said.

"She's *so* earthy."

"Is that a good thing or a bad thing?"

"I like it. But it's hard for me to imagine Dutton with someone like her. He's all about big boobs, high heels and long eyelashes."

Marlow could tell Aida was jealous and felt sorry for her, but she didn't want to talk about Claire in any way that could be considered disparaging. Fanning the flames of Aida's jealousy would just tear them all apart. "Dutton isn't worthy of either one of you. Why don't you tell me about Reese instead?"

"What about Reese?"

"Have you heard from him?"

"No." She adjusted the wide brim of her hat to help block the sun. "But I knew from the beginning that last night wasn't about falling in love. I'm sure he did, too."

"Will it be awkward for you to see him again? I mean, we'll be living at Seaclusion until the summer's over."

"It might be a *little* awkward. I lied when I told you he texted me." She gave Marlow a sheepish glance. "*I* texted *him*."

Marlow gaped at her.

"I was feeling so down on myself," Aida explained. "I just wanted to be with someone."

"And he said to come over or what?"

"Basically." Aida moved to avoid the sand kicked up by some kids who went running past. "So what about you? Have you heard from Walker?"

Marlow pulled her phone out of her bag to check and was disappointed when she had no texts or missed calls from him. "No."

"Maybe you should send him a message."

"And say what?"

"That you had a great time last night."

"No way. That's *such* a cliché!"

"From what you said, it's true."

Marlow had just opened her mouth to respond when Aida grabbed her wrist.

"Oh, my god, there he is."

"Reese?"

"Walker!" she replied. "Isn't that him?"

When Marlow turned, she saw Walker from the back. He stood out because he was a head taller than anyone else standing in line at Bigger Wieners, a popular hot dog stand that'd gotten a lot of press due to its name—not to mention he was wearing a uniform when everyone else was in a swimsuit. "That *is* him," she said.

Aida gave her shoulder a slight push. "Go talk to him."

"He's probably working."

"Are you kidding? He's waiting for a hot dog. I think he can talk even if he's officially on duty."

Marlow wanted to see him; she just wasn't sure what to say. Last night felt so different from the other times they'd been together. They'd entered brand-new territory, and she was slightly apprehensive about it.

"If you don't hurry, he'll leave before he knows you're here," Aida prodded.

"Okay." Marlow stood up and tied her sarong around her hips. Before she could reach him, however, a woman who looked about her age or a little younger, with long sandy-colored hair, a dark tan and a curvy figure, approached him, smiling brightly as she told him something that seemed to necessitate touching him at every opportunity.

"It's been a week since you've called," Marlow heard the woman say. "Have I done anything wrong?"

Marlow stopped abruptly. But Walker, who'd turned when the woman spoke to him, caught sight of her before he could even respond. "Um, sorry," he said, somewhat mechanically, his gaze on Marlow. "I've been busy."

The woman leaned in to make some remark Marlow couldn't hear, then laughed flirtatiously while touching his arm again.

Feeling awkward and presumptuous—foolish, too—Marlow turned around and hurried back to Aida.

"Who is *that*?" Aida asked.

"I don't know," Marlow replied.

Aida frowned. "She sure seems familiar with Walker."

"Yes, she does."

They probably would've continued to discuss what'd happened, but Aida put a quick end to it by saying, "Here he comes," and Marlow tried to force a smile for Walker's benefit.

"Hey," he said when he was close enough to speak.

Marlow conjured up a smile as she and Aida came to their feet. "Hi."

"I would've thought you'd be at Seaclusion if you wanted to lie out on a beach."

Aida shaded her eyes against the sun. "There's more action here," she said, motioning at all the fun going on around them.

"Claire wanted to do some shell hunting," Marlow added.

He nodded, swallowing a bite of his hot dog before meeting Marlow's gaze. "How's your mom today?"

Marlow tucked her hair behind her ears. "I checked in with her this morning. She's okay."

He searched her face but didn't seem to know what to say next. He attempted some more small talk and stayed long enough to finish his food, but Marlow could tell he felt uncomfortable, and so did she.

It wasn't until after he'd left and she and her friends were back at the guesthouse showering for dinner that he sent her a text referring to the incident on the beach.

I'm sorry if that was weird today. I had no idea Lisbeth would be there. Or you, either, for that matter. I was just grabbing lunch.

Marlow had a towel around her head and had yet to get dressed, but nothing else seemed as important as this. Is she one of the women you've been dating? The one you told me about, who lives here on the island?

Several minutes passed, giving her the impression that he was reluctant to respond. But eventually he wrote, Yes.

Are you going to continue to see her? Did she even have the right to ask? Probably not, but she had to know.

She paced at the end of her bed as she awaited his answer. She could hear Aida and Claire talking back and forth as they got ready and hoped they wouldn't be ready too soon. She needed this time.

Say no. Say no. Say no, she chanted silently to Walker.

That depends... came his response.

The familiar way "Lisbeth" kept touching him paraded through her mind again. On...

You.

She sent a question mark, although she could tell where this was going.

Are we just having fun for the summer? Or is there something more serious going on?

She wasn't ready to determine how she felt about him. And she certainly wasn't ready to share whatever that determination turned out to be. But the thought of him with Lisbeth made her sick to her stomach.

She sank onto her bed, and while she was stewing about her answer, she got another text from him: Marlow? Are you willing to care about me?

Marlow had never been so terrified. Caring created an obligation. Caring took things to another level and left her vulnerable. She'd never given any man the power to hurt her. She'd witnessed one ugly divorce after another. But he wasn't asking her to marry him. And when she remembered the way Lisbeth had been acting on the beach, trying to make herself so alluring, she found it upsetting enough that she knew she was no longer on safe ground where Walker was concerned whether she admitted it or not.

I already do, she wrote back.

Walker got off work at eleven. As soon as he got home, he texted Marlow to see if she was still up. She called him when she received his message but said she had her alarm set for six because she had to drive to Miami to catch a flight, so she was already in bed.

They decided to see each other on Sunday instead and hung up. But then she called him right back.

"Never mind," she said. "Come get me."

"What about your flight?" he asked.

"I can sleep on the plane."

"It only takes two hours to fly to Atlanta."

"I'll survive. I want to see you."

He felt light as air when she said that. "I'll be over in ten minutes."

Walker took a quick shower, dressed and scooped up the keys to his motorcycle.

Marlow was waiting for him outside the entrance to Seaclusion. She put on the helmet he handed her, and he helped tighten the chin strap before she climbed on behind him as though she was just as eager to see him as he was to see her.

The moment he felt her arms go around his waist, he gave the bike some gas and knew, whatever happened, he'd always consider this to be one of his happiest memories.

Walker's body was so warm and comfortable that Marlow was loath to get out of bed. Why not enjoy her time with him while she could and have him take her home in the morning a little earlier than her alarm would've gone off? She could prepare for the trip at that point, and no one would be the wiser. Fortunately, she was only going to Atlanta for the day, so she didn't need to pack anything.

"Do you need to go?" he asked as she snuggled closer.

"Not yet. I'll sleep here with you and get up at five. Want to tell me where to find the keys to your SUV? I could drive it to Seaclusion and have Aida or Claire bring it back after they wake up in the morning."

"Don't worry. I'm happy to get up with you."

She was sort of relieved he'd offered. She didn't really want her mother or his to see his truck parked in the drive so early. "What time do you have to work tomorrow?"

"Luckily, it's my day off."

"Then it sucks that I'm going to be gone."

"No kidding." He shifted to bring her even closer, and she felt him press a kiss to her temple before he nodded off again.

★ ★ ★

Getting up at five turned out to be easier said than done. When the alarm on Marlow's phone went off, she groaned and pulled the pillow over her head. It was Walker who turned off the noise.

"Want me to make you some coffee?" he mumbled, obviously still half-asleep.

"There's no time. I have to dress and get out of here right away, in case there's traffic."

"Okay." He didn't seem remotely self-conscious about his nudity—not that he had any reason to be—as he climbed out of bed, tossed her the yoga pants and T-shirt she'd left on his floor and went into the bathroom.

As the door closed, she remembered the tenderness with which he'd made love to her last night. He was the best man she'd ever known—except for her father—and sexy as hell. It was little wonder Lisbeth had approached him the way she had yesterday. Marlow was beginning to think a woman would have to be crazy not to want Walker.

"I don't hear any movement," he called out.

She chuckled as she dragged herself out of bed and slowly began to dress.

"I could've made coffee in the time it took you to put on your panties," he joked when he came out.

"I just want to go back to bed," she complained.

He lifted her chin with one finger as he slipped past her and brushed his lips against hers. "You and me both. I'm awake enough now that we could make good use of any time we had."

She caught his arm before he could move too far away from her, and they kissed again. "You're insatiable."

He grabbed her butt as he nuzzled her neck. "When it comes to you, I am."

Once he'd pulled on some sweats, he dug his keys out of the pocket of the jeans he'd thrown over a chair and, after waiting for her to finish dressing, took her hand as they walked out and hurried down the steps.

"Will you text me when you get home, so I'll know you're back safe?" he asked as he opened the passenger door of the SUV.

"Maybe I'll drop off Aida and Claire and drive over here in the Jeep."

He looked surprised. "Okay." He pulled a key off his ring. "Doesn't matter what time it is. Just let yourself in and crawl into bed with me."

She put the key in the side pocket of her yoga pants, but when she glanced up to see why he hadn't yet closed the door, she found him looking at her with an odd expression. "What is it?" she asked.

"I hope you're pregnant," he replied.

She gaped at him. "We've only been seeing each other a week!"

He shrugged. "That may be true, but I've loved you since I can remember."

23

I've loved you since I can remember.

While she was getting ready for her flight, those words sifted through Marlow's brain like sand in an hourglass that she turned over again and again. Aida and Claire chatted away on the drive to the airport, and Marlow tried to respond when necessary, but she was preoccupied with Walker's response, and that was on her mind the entire time she was waiting for her plane, too. She was *still* thinking about him and what he'd said long after she boarded and the plane took off.

Normally, such a declaration would've frightened her. She'd had other men profess their love. When it happened, it made her feel panicky and claustrophobic, as if she was getting into a situation she might not be able to comfortably extricate herself from—and that was always the beginning of the end.

But this felt like...only the beginning.

"You must be looking forward to something special," her seat-mate, a thin elderly woman, leaned over to say. "You've been absolutely beaming since you came on."

Marlow hadn't realized she'd been smiling quite that hard. "I'm just...happy today," she said with a laugh.

"How wonderful," the woman responded. "It makes *me* happy to see your beautiful smile."

"Thanks," Marlow said and hoped the feeling would last.

Despite how tired she was, she didn't nod off until there was only thirty minutes left of the flight. Then it seemed as though she was almost immediately awakened by the announcement informing her to put up her tray table and see that her seat was in the upright position.

Covering a yawn with one hand, she slid open the window shade with the other and watched the ground rushing up to meet them as they landed. She was eager to deplane, take care of business and hurry back to the airport for her return flight. She wanted to get home to Teach, and Walker, as soon as possible.

Since she hadn't needed a carry-on, Marlow walked off the plane and immediately took an Uber to Sam Lefebvre's office.

It'd been a long time since she'd visited Atlanta. This was home. Once she breathed in the warm, humid air, laden with the scent of magnolias, and her driver took her past Piedmont Park in the center of town, with its many oaks and dogwoods, she realized how much she'd missed this place. Letting the condo in Virginia go wouldn't be nearly as painful as watching her mother sell her childhood home. But it didn't make sense for Eileen to keep the extra properties, not without Tiller and his job requiring her to move between them.

If the meeting with Sam didn't take too long, she planned to go see the house today so she could say her goodbyes in case she was back in California or somewhere else when it was sold.

Her phone signaled a text. It was from her mother.

Did you arrive safely?

Yep. Almost at Sam's office. She nearly added that she was hoping to see the house, but she didn't want to trigger any more upset for her mother. Eileen was going through enough.

Call me after, Eileen wrote.

I will.

Marlow scrolled to Walker's contact record and, impulsively, sent him a message. Miss you already.

Still not sure why you had to fly to Atlanta, came his response. Most business can be handled via Zoom or Skype these days. But maybe your dad's lawyer is old school.

Yeah. This is probably a waste of energy, but the meeting shouldn't last long. And it would be nice to see the old house before my mother sells it. I'm going over there after, if I have time.

He sent a heart emoji, and she was more than a little shocked at how much pleasure that response gave her. He wasn't a man who used a lot of flowery words. He was a bottom-line kind of guy, so a simple heart went a long way.

"Damn you," she muttered. "I'm totally falling in love with you."

What if, at some point, he decided she wasn't all he'd hoped? It could be the thrill of the chase and finally getting what he'd always wanted that had set the course for their relationship so far…

"Here we are," her driver said.

She looked up from her phone to find they were at the curb in front of the steel-and-glass skyscraper that corresponded with Sam's address. She'd been here before, but only once, when her father needed to drop off some paperwork. All the other times she'd seen Sam, it had been at their house or at a social gathering. "Thank you," she mumbled and scrambled out of the car.

Sam's office had been updated and was now white and gray instead of the warmer browns and creams she remembered. His receptionist had been replaced, too. An attractive brunette, this woman appeared to be about twenty years old. "You must be Senator Madsen's daughter," she said.

"Yes, I'm Marlow."

"Nice to meet you, Marlow. I'm Jennifer, and I'm sorry about your loss. I'll let Mr. Lefebvre know you're here. Would you like coffee or water while you wait?"

"No, thanks."

Skipping coffee turned out to be a wise decision, because it would only have slowed things down. Sam walked out to greet her barely a minute later.

"Marlow, it's so good to see you," he said. "Thanks for coming."

She accepted the handshake he offered her. "Of course. I'm happy to be here."

"Why don't we go into the conference room?" He led her to a room down the hall and gestured at the large table that took up almost the entire space. "If you'll give me a second, I'll grab your father's file."

She sat down, settled her purse at her feet and interlaced her fingers.

"You look great, by the way," he said when he returned and put the file on the table in front of him. "But you always were a beautiful girl, so I didn't expect anything less."

"I appreciate that," she said. But as pleasant as he was, she was growing apprehensive. This whole thing seemed so pointless. Why was she here? Why couldn't he have told her whatever he needed to tell her over the phone?

"Your father was incredibly proud of you. And he loved you very much. I'd like to make that *crystal* clear before...before we delve into what we're about to discuss."

His words only caused more anxiety. "Why would you feel the need to say that?" she asked.

"What I have to tell you will probably be...upsetting." He seemed to be choosing his words carefully. "I hate to be the bearer of bad news, but…with your father's passing, I have no choice."

"My dad's already dead," she said. "What other bad news could there be?"

His lips compressed into a line. Then he opened his mouth to explain but immediately clamped it shut and took out a document instead. "This is your father's will."

She gave an uncomfortable laugh. "What's the problem? Has he given all his money to charity or something? As long as there's enough left to take care of my mom, we'll be fine. I can make my own way."

"It's not that. You and your mother are getting quite a bit of money, Marlow. A fortune."

Considering how Sam was behaving, she supposed that news should've come as a relief. And yet her eyes blurred with tears, making it impossible to read. "You're scaring me," she admitted, pushing the will back across the table. "Why don't you just tell me what's going on? I can read this later."

He tried to take her hand, but she pulled away. *"Tell me,"* she insisted.

He drew a deep breath before blurting, "Marlow, your father left a sizable portion of his estate to someone else."

He'd already said there'd be plenty for her and her mother. So did this explain the way he was acting? "A charity," she reiterated.

"Not a charity, no. A person."

"Who?" she managed to say in spite of the lump that was swelling in her throat.

"Reese Cantwell."

She struggled to swallow. "Reese?" she echoed, uncomprehending.

"Yes."

It took her a moment, but once she'd processed that bit of information, she weighed it for the tragedy she saw in Sam's face.

She didn't think sharing a portion of the estate with Reese was the *worst* thing that could happen. Her father had cared about him, too. "That...that's somewhat understandable," she allowed. "Dad was good to Rosemary and her boys, and they've always had much less than we have. So he...he must've left Walker something, too. Right?"

"No, Walker isn't named in the will."

"That hardly seems fair," she protested.

"It might seem more fair when you consider that..." He cleared his throat and tried again. "Marlow, your father directed me to give Reese part of the estate because he was, er, *is*—" he grimaced "—his son."

"What?"

"Reese is your half brother," he clarified.

Cold seemed to spread through her whole body, as if she had ice water in her veins. "That...that can't be true," she stuttered. "Reese has a father. *Rudy* is his father."

"No. I'm afraid that's not the case. Your father had a paternity test performed when Reese was a baby, and—" his voice dropped "—it came back positive. I have it here in the file."

He pulled out the proof—a paper filled with blurred letters and numbers as far as Marlow was concerned, so she didn't take it. She pressed a hand to her chest; it was getting harder to breathe. "But that means...that means my father was a...a liar and a...*cheater.*" The last word especially tasted bitter. Infidelity was certainly nothing she'd ever associated with her larger-than-life father, who had always campaigned for traditional family values. "He had to have been cheating on my mother and...and sleeping with our *housekeeper*! Is that what you're telling me?"

"It's a difficult situation," he said as though he didn't want to state it quite that bluntly. "I'm sorry."

He said other things, phrases meant to soothe and comfort, but Marlow's ears were ringing, making it impossible to hear most of his remarks. The parts she did pick up, she couldn't seem to grasp. She stared at the thick document on the table—*Last Will and Testament of John G. Madsen*—as tears streamed down her face and dripped off her chin. She could remember her father playing with Reese, taking a special interest in him. He'd also paid for Reese's tennis lessons and schooling, but Marlow had never imagined there was anything behind that except kindness and generosity. He'd paid for Walker to have many of the same things.

Had he been buying Rosemary's silence instead of just wanting to help?

The betrayal—staved off at first by the shock—suddenly hit her like a fist to the gut. This wasn't a dream; this was for real. Her father had put their family at risk by having sex with an employee. That meant he couldn't have cared about Eileen—or her—as much as she'd always believed.

"No," she said, rejecting it outright. "My dad would never do that. He was a good man, an honorable man." Philandering politicians were a cliché. Her father was not among the many disgraced public figures who'd ruined their reputations and careers over sex.

"He *was* a good man," Sam insisted.

She forced herself to focus on her father's attorney. "But he couldn't be a good man *and* have done this."

Sam looked helpless sitting there in his expensive suit with his narrow neck and thinning white hair carefully trimmed around the ears and collar. "Give yourself some time," he said gently. "It's a shock."

She blinked, struggling to hold back more tears. If *she* was *this* devastated, how would Eileen react? "How will I tell my mother?" she whispered, more to herself than to him. "She's been mourning his death, missing him, going on and on about how wonderful he was. I can't even imagine telling her this and ruining her most cherished memories of him. And what will it do to her relationship with Rosemary and Reese and..." She let her words dwindle away because the picture she was creating was too horrific to contemplate. What would it do to her relationships with the Cantwells—with *Walker*?

Sam formed the papers into a neat stack, probably as a way to avoid looking at her. "When your father and I were drafting these documents many years ago, it was clear to me that he expected to outlive your mother. He was always so healthy and robust. And she... Well, MS is a very difficult disease."

That was a euphemistic way of saying that her father had thought multiple sclerosis would kill Eileen before she could learn the truth, and he'd get away with what he'd done without ruining her opinion of him. "In other words, he hoped she'd never have to find out."

"I think that's safe to say, yes."

"Except...he's the one who's dead, and my mother *does* have to accept this ugly reality."

"Unfortunately."

The lie her father had lived made Marlow as angry as the infidelity. He'd always pretended to be faithful. She imagined her poor mother waiting anxiously at home for news of this meeting, barely able to get out of bed or knit for a few hours, and felt her heart sink even further. "And I have to be the one to tell her that the man she spent forty years loving and supporting wasn't worth her devotion."

He straightened his narrow shoulders. "I wouldn't go that far. As I said in the beginning, Tiller loved her—and you—very much."

"I don't doubt he said that. But his actions don't support it."

Sam didn't seem to know what to say. "I'm sorry," he repeated. "If you prefer that I tell your mother, I will. I just... I thought it might be easier coming from you."

When she sniffed, he hurried out of the room and returned with a box of tissues. As she wiped her nose and eyes, something else occurred to her, something that made her feel even worse. "Rosemary must know the true paternity of her youngest son."

"I'm sure she does."

"And she must've known all these years. Reese is twenty-two! She's remained in my mother's service the whole of that time knowing she...she has a child by my father?"

He straightened his tie as though he had no idea what to say.

"I never dreamed Rosemary was capable of that kind of...duplicity," she continued. "How long were they sleeping together? *Was it the whole time I was growing up?*"

Sam squirmed in his seat. "I didn't ask him, Marlow, and that isn't information he volunteered."

She covered her mouth. "What about Reese? And Walker? Do *they* know?"

"I can't tell you that, either. I would guess they don't."

She pressed her fingers to her closed eyelids. "But they'll both find out."

"There's no way to keep this a secret anymore," he agreed.

"Oh, my god," she said and could feel him awkwardly patting her shoulder as she buried her face in her hands and wept.

Claire had never felt so guilty. Spending the day in Miami with Aida, knowing that Dutton was on a flight to visit her—and that he planned to spend an entire week on the island—was almost excruciating. She wished she'd tried harder to stop him. She wouldn't be able to eat or sleep until he was gone.

"Isn't this sexy?" Aida pointed to a black lace teddy as they ambled around Victoria's Secret at Bayside Marketplace, an open-air mall with a marina on one side. According to what Claire had found on the internet, the marketplace was the most visited attraction in Miami. The Vizcaya Museum and Gardens, also located on Biscayne Bay, was popular, too. They'd spent nearly three hours there before coming to shop and have lunch.

"I like it," Claire said, her stomach churning after she'd forced herself to eat some of the food on her plate at the Serbian grill they'd chosen for lunch. The restaurant had fabulous reviews; she knew the food wasn't to blame.

"I think I'll try it on." Aida found her size and headed to the dressing rooms.

Claire drifted around, using the time Aida was gone to check her phone.

Dutton had sent her a message: I made my flight—I can't wait to see you.

I'll call you tomorrow, she wrote back. Please don't try to contact me before then.

She'd already made that clear; problem was, she didn't trust him to be patient.

She kept staring at her phone in case he responded. But five minutes later, she'd heard nothing.

"Any word from Marlow?"

Claire nearly dropped her phone when she heard Aida's voice. "Not yet, but I keep checking. Hope her meeting went well." She put her phone in her purse and indicated the barely there lingerie Aida had tucked under one arm. "What do you think?"

"I like it." She grinned. "I sent Reese a picture of me in it, and he said to buy it."

Claire widened her eyes. "You sent him a pic?"

She shrugged. "Might as well have some fun this summer."

At least Aida seemed preoccupied with her new love interest. Or boy toy. But Claire didn't see Reese as being ready for the kind of relationship Aida ultimately needed and was afraid this would only end in more heartache. She was tempted to warn her friend that she was heading straight toward a brick wall, but she didn't feel she was in any position to act that protective, especially when Aida would be devastated if she found out about Dutton.

24

Walker retrieved his tennis bag and checked his phone while Reese strode over to speak to a prospective client. He'd texted Marlow when he first arrived at the club to see how her meeting had gone with the lawyer, but he hadn't received an answer. Maybe she was at the house where she'd grown up—he'd spent a lot of time there as a kid, too—and didn't want to be interrupted.

He considered calling her, in case it wasn't that and she was feeling sad about her father and the impending sale of the property in Atlanta. Losing the house would be another upsetting blow, but he decided against interrupting whatever she was doing. It'd only been five hours since getting in touch. He didn't want to be too intrusive. Even if he didn't hear from her for the rest of the day, he'd see her tonight, when she came over.

"You ready for a second match?" Reese asked, acting cocky as he returned to the court. "Think you can take me?"

Walker hadn't tried his hardest the first time. Although he enjoyed sports, a win in tennis meant more to his little brother than it did to him. Reese was the "pro" on the island. The only thing Walker cared about was a good game.

"Just for that, I'm going to beat you," Walker told him.

"*If* you can," Reese retorted as he bounced the ball with his left hand. "Too bad Aida and Marlow aren't here today," he said, tossing the ball in the air for his serve.

Walker hit it back. "You want them to see me make you look bad?"

They talked smack until it came down to a tie, at which point they each became so determined to win that they quit talking. It wasn't until after Walker managed to eke out a win and they walked over to dry the sweat from their faces that Reese lowered his towel and said, "How are things between you and Marlow?"

Walker couldn't decide how to answer. He was hesitant to share too much. Their relationship seemed to be going well, but it was so new that it could easily go in the other direction. He wasn't even sure how Reese knew that *anything* was going on. "What do you mean?"

"I know she's been going over at night to see you, bro."

"Who told you?"

"No one! I've seen her. One time she was wearing your sweatshirt."

Walker wiped his face again. "We're just friends."

Reese gave him a skeptical look. "You mean sex buddies, like me and Aida?"

"You're sleeping with Aida?" Walker said.

"Dude, I tried to back off like you told me to. It's all her! She's been sending me pictures of her in sexy outfits, and—"

"She's on the rebound, Reese," he broke in. "You need to be clear that you're not in it for love before she gets hurt."

Reese sighed as he scratched his leg. "Okay, although I don't see how she could mistake it for anything other than what it is—a summer fling. But what's going on with you and Marlow, that's the real deal, right?"

"There're no guarantees," Walker said. "Maybe it'll be a summer fling, too."

★ ★ ★

Rosemary kept an anxious eye on the clock while she worked. Eileen had mentioned at lunch that Marlow had promised to call after she got out of her meeting with Samuel. But it was after two, and as far as Rosemary could tell, there'd been no word from her. What was going on?

Rosemary was afraid to find out. When it came to Reese, Tiller had never promised her anything beyond what he'd already given, which had been more than generous. He'd kept her employed, made sure she and her children always had adequate housing, and paid for private schools for Reese *and* Walker. In addition to that, he'd covered college for both boys, paid for the coaching that'd turned Reese into such a good tennis player, *and* he'd given her large Christmas and birthday bonuses, more than enough to cover food and clothing for his son. She had no reason to expect more.

But the thought that Tiller might acknowledge Reese in his will terrified her. It would ruin everything she'd spent twenty-two years protecting—the good opinion her children held of her, her relationship with Eileen, her job, and now the relationship she was *finally* establishing with Rudy, who would never forgive her if he learned Reese wasn't his.

Surely, Tiller wouldn't allow the truth to come out. It would destroy his own reputation on top of everything else. And there was no need! She'd made it clear that he'd fulfilled his obligation to both her and his son. Why reveal a secret that would devastate so many people, after all this time?

He wouldn't do that, she told herself, but there was a slim chance she could be wrong, and it was that chance that had her on edge.

When the crystal candy dish she'd just filled slipped through her fingers and shattered on the floor, the crash brought Eileen in from her bedroom. "My goodness, Rosemary! What's gotten into you lately? You're dropping things right and left."

"Sorry," she mumbled, squatting to gather the shards. "I'll get it cleaned up."

"Is there something wrong?" Eileen asked.

"No, I'm fine."

"Be careful or you'll cut yourself."

Rosemary didn't respond. She knew how to clean up glass, but Eileen had always been a worrywart. "How did Marlow's meeting go?" she asked, directing her employer's attention elsewhere and hoping to get some information, too.

Eileen looked worried. "I don't know. The meeting has to be over, but I haven't heard from her."

A sense of impending doom stole over Rosemary, causing her to stand up. "Have you tried calling her?"

"Several times," Eileen replied. "She doesn't answer."

Rosemary drew in a shaky breath. That wasn't like Marlow. Was this the culmination of her worst fears? "What about Sam?"

"I've called him, too. His receptionist tells me that Marlow left hours ago and Sam's in another meeting."

"One of them will reach out soon," Rosemary said. She supposed *that*, at least, was inevitable.

But…what would they have to say?

Marlow knew where her parents had hidden a key; it'd been in the same place since she was a child. She removed it from beneath the large ceramic frog in the planter area and let herself into the house. Since her parents had moved back and forth between their three homes frequently before the pandemic grounded them in Teach, the furnishings and everything else was intact, so it felt like coming home.

She stood inside the entryway for a moment, bracing for all the memories that assailed her—memories of the many Christmases they'd spent here, of playing with other kids in the neighborhood, doing homework in her room and having dinner together as a family, when she and her mother would listen to her father talk about his schedule, his election opponent, the national deficit or other aspects of politics that concerned him. In many ways, she'd had the perfect childhood; she knew for sure it appeared that way.

Even she'd believed it was real.

The lump in her throat that made it so difficult to swallow was even more stubborn here than at Sam's office, and it only grew bigger as she wandered through the rooms and hallways, gazing at childhood photographs of herself and all the evidence of her mother's impeccable taste and decorating ability. She paused to study the slew of pictures of her father similar to those her mother was including in the scrapbook she'd been dutifully putting together to commemorate his "exemplary" life. Eileen had quietly supported her husband and allowed him to be center stage; better yet, she'd done everything she could to help keep him there.

Marlow stopped when she spotted the black-and-white photo she'd been looking for in the gallery of pictures that lined the wall beside the stairs. There it was. A photo of Tiller teaching Reese how to fly a kite when Reese was about seven—right on the wall of their home.

Her mother had hung it under the assumption that her father was being charitable to the child of their longtime housekeeper.

Marlow felt duped, oblivious to something that seemed as though it should've been obvious to her. She felt a fair amount of jealousy, too. Her father had always wanted a boy, and with Rosemary, he'd had one.

"Wow, Dad," she murmured bitterly. "Talk about a sucker punch."

Her cell went off again. Her mother had been calling her since she left Sam's office, but she couldn't bring herself to answer. She had no idea how she was going to tell Eileen that Tiller and Rosemary had had an affair—and that Reese was Tiller's son. Then there was the news about the estate. It wouldn't be easy for

Eileen to learn that twenty percent of what should've been left to her was going to an illegitimate child Tiller had fathered with their housekeeper. That would only twist the knife in her back.

Reese would be rich. He wouldn't need to live above the garage anymore. That was the good news—if any part of this could be considered "good." He'd have the money to move, and Eileen wouldn't have to face him every day. But what would they do about Rosemary?

Marlow was glad her father hadn't left Rosemary a portion of the estate, too. That would've hurt her mother even more.

On the other hand, Rosemary still needed her job, and there was no way Eileen would keep her around.

And how would Walker react to learning that Reese was as much her brother as his?

Her cell buzzed with a text. She thought it might be from Walker. But it was Aida.

How was it at the lawyer's? Was there any real reason you had to travel all the way to Atlanta?

Marlow covered her mouth as fresh tears welled up. She sank onto the stairs and gazed at the picture of her father with Reese.

The pride in his face as he looked down at the darling little boy, who was laughing and running along with him while holding on to the kite, broke her heart. Although she'd never noticed any resemblance before, there seemed to be one now.

How had she missed the truth? How had her *mother* missed it? And how could her father have let them down so terribly?

When Marlow met her friends at the restaurant, Claire found it odd that she was wearing sunglasses. The sun was setting and long shadows were beginning to creep over the sidewalk. Claire had been anxious for Marlow to get back to Miami, if only to reassure herself that Dutton had managed to arrive at the airport without bumping into her. But those sunglasses and the way Marlow was acting—so subdued—made her uneasy. *Had* she run into Dutton? Did she know he was coming to the island?

Something had upset her. Claire knew that Aida had noticed it, too, when she asked, "What is it? What's wrong?"

Claire caught her breath, terrified to hear what might come out of Marlow's mouth, but Marlow merely offered them a wan smile. "Nothing."

Aida peered more closely at her. "How was the meeting with your father's attorney?"

"Fine," she replied.

Her answer was hardly convincing, but at least Claire was growing more certain that the way Marlow was acting had nothing to do with Dutton. "So, was there any real reason you had to fly to Atlanta?"

"No," Marlow said. "It was just...estate business."

Then why couldn't it have been handled electronically? Claire wondered but didn't ask.

"I tried texting you," Aida said. "To see how it went. But I never heard back."

"I turned off my phone," Marlow explained. "I had to be careful with my battery since I knew I'd need it to last all day."

Her words made sense; her behavior didn't. Claire studied her, trying to figure out what was going on, but a large group of people was coming up to the entrance of the restaurant, prompting them to go inside so they wouldn't be last in line.

After Aida gave the hostess their name and was told it would be another few minutes, they moved off to one side. But even in the dim lighting of the restaurant, Marlow didn't remove her sunglasses. "How was your day?" she asked.

Claire realized she was shifting the focus away from herself, but Aida either didn't notice or had decided to let it go. She told Marlow about the Vizcaya Museum and Gardens and how much they'd enjoyed the live music at the marketplace.

Marlow gestured at the bag Aida was carrying. "What'd you buy?"

"A new dress."

"That's nice," Marlow said but blanched once Aida flashed the pink Victoria's Secret bag she'd slipped inside the dress bag. "And some lingerie Reese told me I looked great in," she added.

"Please don't mention Reese tonight," Marlow said, lifting a hand in the classic stop motion.

"Don't tell me you two got into an argument," Aida said, clearly perplexed.

"No, of course not."

"Then has something happened between you and Walker?" Claire asked. She'd sensed the magnetism between them, knew their relationship was escalating even though Marlow hadn't admitted to any serious interest.

"Not really."

"Not *really*?" Claire was convinced, at this point, that whatever was going on didn't involve Dutton. She was relieved about that but still concerned for Marlow. "If...if you learned some hard news about the estate—that there's not as much money as you anticipated—I'll do whatever I can to help. Granted, I don't have that much, but if you have to sell everything and... and you need somewhere to go, you can come live with me."

Aida looked shocked that Claire had come to that conclusion based on what Marlow had said so far. "Is this about money? If it is, I feel the same. Whatever you need, we'll be there for you."

A tear slipped from beneath Marlow's sunglasses. "Thank you. That means a lot. But...it's not about money."

"What is it, then?" Aida pressed.

"I can't talk about it tonight. I... I need some time to work things out."

Claire briefly touched her arm to show her support. "Okay."

"Whatever it is, you'll get through it," Aida said.

Although Marlow nodded, she didn't seem convinced, but

the hostess approached and they fell silent while following her to a table.

"Would you rather go home than visit the clubs?" Claire asked once they had their menus.

"No." Marlow chuckled mirthlessly. "I definitely don't want to go home. I'm thinking a few drinks might help."

"Well, we can certainly make *that* happen," Aida said.

Marlow remained quiet through dinner. She hardly ate anything and never took off her sunglasses. But once they drove to South Beach, and she'd had a few shots, she seemed to forget whatever was troubling her. Claire had no doubt it would still be hanging over Marlow if she allowed herself to think about it, but she was laughing and dancing and having a great time—until she'd had *too* much to drink. Then she broke down in tears, and Aida suggested they head home.

Claire insisted on driving. She'd been so worried about Dutton coming that she hadn't been interested in drinking. He'd reached the island. She knew that from his text messages; he'd sent her a barrage so far.

I miss you.

When are you going to get back from Miami?

Why don't you just come over after you're done?

I came clear across the country to see you, and you're going to stay out drinking all night with your friends?

He was getting irate, and in a way, she couldn't blame him. She'd want a little attention, too. But he'd known before he came that she'd be putting her friends first.

She'd almost messaged to remind him that *he* was the one who was crashing *their* party. But she chose to ignore him instead.

If she answered once, he'd have her on the hook for the rest of the night, going back and forth, and she wasn't about to allow that. She was out with her girlfriends; he needed to respect that.

She didn't realize just how much pressure he was putting on her until they decided to leave. At that point, she was relieved she could quit fighting her compulsion to reassure him and make him happy. When she went to the bathroom right before they left and she had a few minutes of privacy, she was tempted to let him know she'd gotten his messages and would see him in the morning. She'd already told Aida and Marlow that she was going to the tennis club to meet with her new boss. But she knew he'd insist she come over tonight, and she wasn't ready for the intimacy he'd want and expect.

So she turned off her phone and slid it in her purse before returning to the main part of the club, where she motioned to Aida and Marlow that she was ready to go.

Once they started the long drive back to the island and it was quiet, exceptionally so after the pulsing beat of the music blaring through each club, she'd thought Marlow might open up and want to talk. Aida gave her the opportunity when she asked, once again, what was wrong. But Marlow just sniffed, wiped her eyes and shook her head—and before they'd traveled ten miles, both Aida and Marlow were asleep.

25

The moment Walker woke up, he stretched out one arm, hoping to find Marlow in his bed, but she wasn't there. Lifting his head, he squinted against the light streaming in through the French doors while searching for evidence that she'd ever come.

There was none.

What'd happened? Had she lost the key to his place? She could've knocked.

He rolled over to get his phone from where it was charging on the nightstand beside him. He hadn't received any messages from her since before she'd gone into the attorney's office…

Why wouldn't she let him know she was okay at least?

Concerned, he sat up. He didn't have to work until midnight. Brody had graveyard this weekend, but he'd asked Walker to trade with him—he had company from out of town—and Walker had been more than happy to agree, since he'd assumed it would give him the morning with Marlow.

He was tempted to call her, but it was only seven thirty. If she'd gotten in late, he didn't want to wake her. Maybe she and her friends had had too much to drink and decided to get a hotel in Miami. Or they'd partied so late she'd been too exhausted to come over once she finally got home.

He hoped it wasn't anything more serious.

He texted his mother, since Rosemary was the only person at Seaclusion who was usually up this early.

Do you know if Marlow got back last night?

No. I was so exhausted I fell asleep at 9:30. Why?

I want to know. Can you check the garage for the Jeep?

Give me a second…

He shoved a hand through his hair while he waited. If Marlow was there, he could go back to sleep. If she wasn't…

South Beach could be dangerous. He didn't want to think about what might've happened if she wasn't home, so he scrolled through the news on his phone, trying to keep from imagining the worst, until his mother got back to him.

Both cars are in the garage.

He let his breath out in relief. Okay. Thanks.

What's going on? his mother asked.

Nothing. Just checking to make sure she's safe.

Walker, I'm afraid you're getting in over your head again.

He was definitely in the deep end. But he couldn't seem to avoid taking the risk he was taking, not when it came to Marlow. So he pretended to be in perfect control. I've got it, Mom. Don't worry.

★ ★ ★

Claire kept looking over her shoulder to make sure no one she knew was coming up from behind. Last night, as she and her friends had stumbled sleepily into the guesthouse, she'd told them she planned to comb the beaches for shells after she left the racquet club this morning, and that it might take all day, and, thankfully, neither one of them had expressed any desire to go with her. That meant she had the whole day to herself, and because she'd borrowed a bike, she had transportation, too. Marlow had offered to let her take one of the cars, but she hadn't wanted anyone waiting anxiously for her return. And she'd felt that was less likely if she didn't have the Jeep or the Tesla.

The address Dutton had provided was, fortunately, on the other side of the island. It took longer to pedal there than she'd figured, but she was relieved that he wasn't closer. Aida or Marlow could still run into him somewhere. But at least they wouldn't be likely to pass him when they were pulling into or out of Seaclusion.

Claire felt an odd mix of emotions as she located the small beachfront cottage and coasted down the drive. Thanks to a plethora of tropical shrubs and trees, which had grown up along the periphery of the property, it felt secluded, and that enabled her to relax—slightly.

She got off the bike and walked it onto the lawn, where it couldn't be seen by glancing down the drive, and hurried to the entrance.

"Finally!" Dutton said, throwing open the door as soon as she knocked and scooping her into his arms.

She'd anticipated being more excited to see him. She'd been absolutely heartbroken since everything went wrong. That was why it had been so difficult to refuse his calls, and she'd ended up succumbing to his many entreaties to forgive him.

But being here, like this, didn't feel quite right, either. She wasn't convinced they'd be able to get beyond the damage he'd caused. And it felt weird to meet him here on the island. He was divorced, but the need for secrecy made her feel that what she was doing was wrong. At the very least, she was being a bad friend, and she hated that.

"I've missed you so much," he murmured into her hair.

His embrace was warm and familiar and felt a bit like coming home. For someone who'd never had the nuclear family she'd craved, it was tempting to ignore her reservations. But there was something missing—something that had been there before that was now gone.

Trying to ignore it, she told him she'd missed him, too. But as soon as the words were out of her mouth, he began to grope and kiss her with deep, hungry kisses, heavy on the tongue, and she knew she'd have to speak up or they'd wind up in bed.

"Dutton, no," she said, pulling back and moving his hands away from her breasts.

"Why not?" he asked, clearly frustrated. "I'm dying to make love to you again. And there'd be nothing wrong with that."

In her mind, there would be. He was the one who'd betrayed Aida before. Now he'd put her in a position to do it. "I'm just... not ready."

She was relieved that he didn't make a big deal out of it. "Okay," he said. "I understand. We'll take it slow."

As soon as he backed off, she felt almost weak with relief, which she considered a strange reaction. "Thank you."

"I came here so we can have some fun together," he said, re-iterating what he'd promised on the phone, even though she had no doubt he would've taken her to bed if she'd allowed it. "To get to know each other all over again—without the baggage of the past year."

She wasn't sure if he was referring to his marriage or the hurt he'd caused. She wanted to believe it was the latter, but she didn't question him to find out. It was too important that they start out on the right foot. "Sounds good. How was your flight?"

"Long and boring. But the island's gorgeous. What should we do first?"

Since she didn't want to be seen in public with Dutton, Claire was going to have a hard time suggesting activities as the days passed. But for today, she had the ocean. "We're right on the beach. Let's go swimming and explore for seashells."

"Great," he said. "But I'm starving. We should grab some breakfast first."

With Aida and Marlow sleeping, Claire thought it was probably safe to visit a restaurant. She pulled up Yelp on her phone and purposely chose a quaint-looking café on this side of the island.

It was noon, according to the digital clock on her nightstand, and yet Marlow pulled the covers up and tried, yet again, to fall into the oblivion of sleep. She would've stayed in bed indefinitely. She wanted to do whatever she could to avoid—or postpone—the reckoning ahead. She'd ignored a number of calls and texts from Eileen, but her mother was determined enough to check on her that she made her way over to the guesthouse. Marlow knew Eileen had come because she could hear Aida saying she wasn't up yet.

Walker had to be wondering what was going on with her, too. He'd also sent her a message to see if she was okay. She'd seen it when she got up to use the bathroom an hour ago, but she hadn't been able to bring herself to answer him, either. And she had no idea what she'd do if and when she ran into Rosemary. She was so hurt and angry she was afraid she couldn't trust herself to behave with any restraint.

"Marlow?" Her mother, who knocked briefly to announce her presence, opened the bedroom door.

As soon as Marlow saw her hobbling in with her cane, she squeezed her eyes shut in an attempt to stop the tears. The time had come. She had to face her mother and tell what her father had done. She couldn't put it off any longer.

"What's going on?" Eileen asked. "I've been calling and texting and..." She let her words drift off the moment she caught sight of Marlow, who scooted up against the headboard as her mother sank onto the bed beside her. "You've been crying. What is it?"

Marlow cleared her throat so she could speak. "I have bad news," she managed to say.

Eileen's expression grew stoic. "Regarding the meeting with Sam?"

"Yes."

"What is it? Are we out of money? Because I have plenty of cash on hand, and—"

"The money's still there," Marlow broke in. "Well, most of it, anyway."

Eileen stiffened. "What do you mean?"

Once again, tears slipped down Marlow's cheeks. She'd hoped to be partially recovered—at least enough to explain what'd happened as gently as possible—before she tackled this conversation. But it was still too soon. "Twenty percent is going to Reese," she clarified.

"To *Reese*?" her mother echoed. "And... Walker?"

"Nothing to Walker. Just twenty percent to Reese."

Her mother sat as still as a statue while she attempted to make sense of Marlow's words. "Why not Walker?" she asked carefully.

"Because Walker belongs to Rudy."

The blood drained from her mother's face. "What are you saying?"

She'd already guessed the truth. Marlow could tell, so she merely confirmed it. "That Reese belongs to Dad."

Eileen didn't make a sound, but one delicate hand rose to cover her mouth.

"I'm sorry," Marlow said, nearly choking on a sob.

Eileen turned to stare out the window, and Marlow couldn't even guess what she was thinking. Was she remembering certain details from the past that might confirm this? Grappling with how to accept it?

Probably both.

"Are you okay?" Marlow asked.

Her mother met her gaze. "I won't give him a damn penny. I won't let Rosemary get away with what she's done. We'll... we'll demand a paternity test."

What *she's* done. Marlow noticed that Eileen hadn't addressed Tiller's culpability. Did she think Rosemary had tricked him into her bed? Used her difficult situation to play on his sympathy? *Had* she done that? Marlow wondered. "There's already been a test, Mom. It came back positive. Sam has it in Dad's file."

This came as a more obvious blow than the news before it, or maybe her mother was simply crumbling under the pain of it all, because she gasped and slumped over, as if she was struggling to remain in an upright position.

"Mom," Marlow said, alarmed.

Eileen managed to straighten, but Marlow could see the effort that required. "Excuse me," she muttered as if she were a complete stranger, then used her cane to pull herself to her feet.

"Where are you going?" Marlow asked in surprise.

"I... I need to rest for a few minutes," she mumbled and shuffled down the hall, where she said a few polite words to Aida as though her whole world hadn't just collapsed.

Then the door shut behind her, and there was nothing but silence.

26

Rosemary stood frozen to the spot while watching for Eileen through the large front window of the living room. She had to run some errands, but she couldn't bring herself to leave until she knew all was well.

When she saw Eileen hobbling toward the house only a few minutes after she'd left, she felt a surge of relief. She'd been worried for nothing. Marlow must be fine. Otherwise, she and Eileen would've had a much longer conversation—especially if they'd just learned what Rosemary had been most afraid they'd learn.

But when Eileen came through the door, she was shaking so badly she could scarcely walk, even with a cane.

"Are you having another MS attack?" Rosemary asked, rushing forward. "Do you need help?"

"Stay away from me," Eileen bit out, eyes pinned to the hallway leading to her room as if her life depended on reaching it.

Rosemary was afraid Eileen would fall, but the vitriol in Eileen's response kept her from reaching out. "Let me help you. You're…you're hyperventilating and can hardly walk."

Eileen didn't respond. She seemed to be concentrating exclusively on making her body function. But there was no way to power through a neurological disease like MS. When she bumped into the side table, nearly knocking over a lamp, Rosemary caught her arm, but Eileen recoiled as if Rosemary had burned her. "Get away from me!"

Rosemary had never seen her like this. Was she having a stroke on top of the difficulties caused by her disease? Her chest was rising and falling so fast—as if the mere effort of walking from the guesthouse had taken all her breath. "But...something's wrong," Rosemary said. "Should I call the doctor?"

"I don't need a doctor. All I need is for you and your filthy bastard son to get off my property!"

The sting of those words made Rosemary rear back.

There it was. This wasn't an attack of MS. It was the day of reckoning she'd dreaded for more than twenty-two years. Eileen had just reacted differently than she'd expected. There were no tears, only this...violent physical response.

"Eileen, I... I never meant to hurt you," she started but didn't get the chance to say more before Eileen's foot caught on the corner of the rug between the couch and the dining table, and she fell.

Gasping in alarm, Rosemary darted forward, but coming so close sent Eileen into hysterics.

"Get away from me!" she cried and tried to club Rosemary with her cane. "Don't you *ever* touch me or come near me again! I don't want to see your face for as long as I live. And to think I've always been good to you. I... I considered you more than a housekeeper. I considered you a friend. I assumed we'd grow old together. But you've been laughing behind my back for years."

"No. That's not true. Let me explain," Rosemary said, but Eileen covered her ears.

"I don't want to hear it. *I hate you!*" she screamed. "I... I wish I was strong enough to claw your eyes from your evil head!"

"What's going on?"

Walker stood in the entryway, gaping at them both. Rosemary hadn't even heard the door. She opened her mouth to tell him to go; she didn't want him to overhear this. But he'd learned too much already.

"Get out!" Eileen cried, twisting around to face him. "Take your scheming, backstabbing whore of a mother and get off my property. And tell your brother—or *half* brother—that he needs to pack his bags, too, because he's no longer welcome here!"

Rosemary began to tremble as badly as Eileen was. She'd never heard such vile things come out of her employer's mouth. And as if matters weren't bad enough, Walker stood there, obviously horrified by what he'd heard.

"How could I have trusted you?" Eileen asked, finally breaking into sobs. "How could I have assumed you cared about me the way I cared about you? I took your boys into my home. I paid for so many things above and beyond your salary, out of the goodness of my heart. And the whole time you were sleeping with my husband?"

Walker came forward. Rosemary could tell that his first instinct was to protect her. But as Eileen's venomous words began to register, he stepped back as if he'd been slapped.

"What is she talking about?" he asked. "You never slept with Tiller. You've always been an…an honest, hardworking employee. You gave this family your best, and you were grateful for the extra help they gave you."

"I *have* given them my best!" Rosemary wished she could deny what he'd been told about Tiller. But Reese was living proof. Even if there was no record of the paternity test Tiller had requested so long ago, it would be easy enough to test Reese a second time and compare his genetics to Marlow's.

Rosemary was caught. The truth was the truth, and there was no denying it. "It's not what…what you think," she said lamely. "It wasn't a…a big clandestine affair. I was hurt and lonely and—"

"Oh, my god," Walker murmured before she could finish.

Eileen managed to pull herself off the floor by using a chair at the dining table. "No one cares about your excuses. You betrayed me. You betrayed your oldest son and your husband. You betrayed *everyone*. And you had us convinced that *Rudy* was the bad person!"

Bad person. Those words scraped through her mind, as sharp as razor wire. "*Please* let me explain," Rosemary said, feeling desperate. "I didn't try to entice him or—"

In one fell swoop, Eileen leaned forward and swept all the pictures and articles that had been organized for Tiller's scrapbook onto the floor. "I'm going to burn this stuff," she said. "I'm going to burn *all* of it and never speak his name again. And I'm going to burn everything that reminds me of you. Now get out! Reese will walk away with millions of my money. So you can clap your greedy little hands and celebrate what you've stolen from me."

Walker's arms hung helplessly at his sides. "Please tell me this isn't true," he said, his shocked voice barely audible. "Mom, this is…outrageous. Reese isn't Tiller's son. Reese is…"

His words faded when she didn't speak up to contradict what he'd heard. "This is for real?" he said. *"You did this?"*

Rosemary could no longer talk; she was crying as hard as Eileen was. "It didn't happen the way she thinks. It—"

"Get out!" Eileen yelled. "Before I burn this house down with all of us in it!"

Walker flinched. "Can I…at least help you to your bedroom?" he asked Eileen. "I don't want to leave you like this."

Clinging to the chair she'd used to get up, Eileen managed to sink into it. "No," she said and buried her face in her arms, which she'd rested on the table. "Just go away. I never want to see any of you again."

A muscle moved in Walker's cheek, and Rosemary could see his Adam's apple shift as he swallowed. "Let's get as much of your stuff as we can fit in my SUV," he said, his voice matter-of-fact. "We can't bring it all, so we'll have to come back later, but we can arrange it so that...so that Mrs. Madsen doesn't have to see either one of us."

As Rosemary moved disbelievingly down the hall to her room, she was crying so hard she was hiccuping with each indrawn breath. Eileen and Marlow hated her. Walker probably did, too.

And she couldn't blame them.

What she'd done was unforgivable.

Now Walker knew why Marlow hadn't come to his house last night or returned his texts. And he knew that she wasn't likely to. He'd been so eager for some word from her, a chance to see her, that he'd brought back the Instant Pot his mother had lent him even though he hadn't used it yet, hoping to run into her.

Instead he witnessed a scene he'd never forget.

All his life, the one person he'd been able to count on was his mother. It was difficult to believe she'd had an affair with Tiller, but once he began to search his memories, to explore the possibility, the truth became apparent.

Tiller had always taken a special interest in Reese. He'd played with him whenever he came home, taught him how to throw a ball and paid for him to participate in Little League and other sports. And he'd gone to quite a few of his tennis matches as Reese grew older. Like Eileen, and probably Marlow, too, Walker had admired Tiller for showing so much interest in a boy who didn't have a father in the house anymore. No doubt everyone had assumed Tiller was trying to be a good role model.

Sadly, those interactions no longer seemed as altruistic as they once had. Walker could even see a resemblance between Reese and Tiller he'd never noticed before. His brother's body was leaner and lankier than his own. And although they both looked a great deal like their mother, Reese had Tiller's more prominent nose.

Walker wanted to scream at his mother, too. Like Eileen, he felt angry and betrayed. But he couldn't address any of that while they were at Seaclusion, so he kept his mouth shut and grabbed as many of Rosemary's belongings as he could carry out of the house.

He had no idea where he'd take her. He supposed it would have to be his house. Where else could she go?

But he didn't want her there. Because of her, because of what she'd done, he'd lost any chance he had with Marlow.

When he went out, he had to walk past Eileen, who still had her head buried in her arms on the dining table. He was certain she could hear his movements, but she never looked up. He couldn't tell if she was crying, but it was easy to tell she was devastated.

Walker felt personally responsible—guilty by extension, even though he'd had nothing to do with whatever had gone on between Rosemary and Tiller.

After his mother came rushing out of the house with her arms full, he had her wait in his SUV instead of going back for more while he went inside himself.

"I'm sorry about what's happened," he said softly. "And I hate to leave you like this. Can I...can I help you to your bed?"

When Eileen finally raised her head, the pain in her eyes made his chest tighten. He expected her to refuse him again and start yelling like she had before—saying she hated him and his entire family and to get out. But she surprised him by nodding tiredly, and he offered her his arm.

She tried to pull herself up but didn't have the strength, even with his help, so he lifted her in his arms and carried her down the hall to her room. "I'm sorry," he said again as he put her on the bed.

She didn't say anything. She just rolled away from him.

He covered her with the throw blanket that was on the bench at the foot of the bed before stalking out of the house. As much as he longed to see Marlow, to tell her, too, how sorry he was for what his mother had done, he needed time to determine exactly what the shrapnel from this bombshell would do to his family.

Eileen was a proud woman, someone who preferred to grieve in private, especially when it came to something as scandalous and embarrassing as what they'd learned. Marlow knew that about her, because she was the same way. But at the same time, the fact that Eileen had shown so little emotion when she learned the truth worried Marlow. She tried to give her mother the space and privacy she obviously wanted, but after thirty minutes of watching the clock, she couldn't make herself hold back any longer.

After getting out of bed, she splashed some water on her red, swollen eyes, pulled her hair into a ponytail and threw on a tank top and some shorts so she could go over to the main house.

Aida was sitting on the couch when Marlow came into the living room. "Oh, boy. You don't look happy," she said.

"My mother and I are…going through a tough time right now," Marlow admitted.

"It must have something to do with the will."

"It does."

"I'm so sorry."

"I know. Just…please understand that it's nothing that…that affects you or your being here." Although, like her mother, she preferred to hide her pain, and having her friends at Seaclusion made that more difficult, she hated the thought that they might feel unwanted or unwelcome after she'd convinced them to spend the summer with her.

"It's kind of you to even consider how I might be feeling," Aida said. "But don't worry about me. Do whatever you need to do."

Marlow considered telling her about Reese. She might have, if Aida hadn't slept with him. Marlow didn't want to think that her friend's loyalties might be split between them. And she *definitely* didn't want to hear that none of this was Reese's fault. She understood that, but it didn't make what she was feeling any easier.

"I just... I need some time and space to work through what's happened. And... I have to be there for my mom."

Instead of pressing to find out what it could be, Aida respected her privacy and nodded. "No problem. I'll find Claire and spend the day shell hunting with her so you can focus on what's happening with your family and won't feel the need to entertain us."

"Thank you," Marlow said. "I appreciate it." She started to go, but Aida called her back.

"I'm here for you whenever you're ready. As you know, I've had my own problems this year. Now and then, life gets the better of all of us."

Marlow offered her as much of a smile as she could muster. What Aida had said made her feel more normal in a world that suddenly seemed completely foreign to her. What her father had done changed everything she'd believed about him and her childhood. Although she didn't want to accept this new reality, she had no choice. "Thank you."

She said goodbye and started over to the main house, keeping an eye on the door to Reese's apartment while she walked. She didn't want to bump into him, and yet that could easily happen. His truck was in the drive, so he hadn't left for work.

Briefly, she wondered how he was going to feel upon learning that the man he'd always thought was his father wasn't, but she couldn't imagine he'd be *too* unhappy. Instead of an alcoholic, he'd be able to lay claim to a wealthy and well-respected US senator. Not only that, but he'd inherit north of three million dollars, according to the estimate Sam had texted to her after she left his office.

When Marlow let herself into the main house, she found it

empty, except for her mother, who was in bed. "Where's Rosemary?" she asked as she lowered the shades to cut the glare of the sun.

"I told her to get out and never come back," Eileen said, her voice a dull monotone.

Marlow was relieved to hear that Rosemary was gone. It meant she wouldn't have to face her. "I'm so sorry, Mom. I wish... I wish there was something I could do to...to make this all go away, but..."

"I know," Eileen replied. "So do I."

Her eyes were dry, but that was almost worse than finding her in a puddle of tears. Marlow got the impression she was too devastated to even cry and hated her father for what he'd done. She'd never dreamed her feelings toward him could change quite so drastically or so quickly. That she'd believed he was the greatest man on earth only made the pain of his betrayal worse.

Her mother had believed the same.

"We'll get through it," she murmured and sat on the bed as she took Eileen's hand.

Walker rubbed his forehead as he paced in his kitchen. His mother was sitting on the sofa, holding the coffee he'd given her, but he hadn't seen her take even a sip. She cradled the mug in her lap as she stared out the front window, a vacant expression on her face.

A bright, cheery sun bounced off the ocean, mocking the somber mood inside the house. He had at least a dozen questions for her—questions he was dying to ask—but she'd said there wasn't any need to go through everything twice. So he'd called Reese and told him to get up, get dressed and come over as soon as possible. Reese had asked why, of course, but Walker had told him they'd discuss it once he arrived.

The sound of an engine finally broke the silence.

"He's here," Walker announced, although Rosemary had probably heard the same thing.

His mother didn't move as he hurried to the door and opened it before Reese could even make his way up the stairs.

"What's going on?" his brother asked once he reached the landing. "I rescheduled my first lesson, but I have to be at the club by eleven for the next one. It's Mrs. Dottinger, who buys as much of my time as she possibly can. There's no way I'm canceling on her."

He wasn't going to have to worry about money much longer. The ramifications of their mother's secret were huge. But Walker didn't announce that right away; he merely stood to one side so his brother could get past him. "Come on in."

Reese froze as soon as he saw Rosemary. "What's going on?" he asked. "Why aren't you at Seaclusion?"

When she hesitated, Walker responded for her. "She's been fired."

Disbelief registered on Reese's face. "*What?* After nearly forty years? Why?"

Walker gestured at a side chair. "You'd better take a seat for this."

Reese scowled as his gaze shifted between them. He was obviously in a hurry and reluctant to be held up for too long. But he strode over and sat down. "Okay, I'm tired of being told what to do—get up, come here, sit down. What the hell is going on?"

Walker addressed their mother. "Would you like to do the honors?"

Tears gathered in her eyes as she shook her head.

"Fine. I'll do it." Walker saw plenty of fear and uncertainty underneath his brother's bravado. But Reese was the only one in this thing who'd come out of it better off, so maybe he wouldn't take it too hard. "I wish there was an easier way to break the news, but there isn't, so…"

"How about you just get it over with?" Reese said, growing impatient.

Reese didn't have the slightest idea what was coming, but there was no good way to prepare him. "You know how...you've never really gotten along with Rudy?" Walker asked.

Reese's eyebrows slammed together. "Don't tell me you're going to remarry him," he said, shifting his attention to Rosemary. "Damn it! I knew that's what this is about."

Walker lifted a hand to let him know he'd jumped to the wrong conclusion. "Actually... I can't comment on that, but once he finds out what I'm about to tell you, I'd have to say I doubt it."

His mother dashed a hand across her cheeks but didn't correct him.

Tilting his head, Reese gave Walker a sidelong glance. "What are you talking about?"

"Rudy isn't your father," Walker said.

His brother straightened in the chair. "Of course he is! Mom was still married to him when I was born. There wasn't anyone else in her life," he said, and then, less certainly, "Was there?"

Walker drew a deep breath. "Just Tiller."

Reese jumped to his feet. "Eileen's *husband*? Are you kidding me?"

"I'm afraid not," Walker said.

Reese gaped at their mother as if she'd grown two heads. "You slept with *Tiller*?"

She didn't answer; she stared down into her coffee.

"Life can get...messy," Walker said. He didn't know what else to offer.

"Especially when you cheat," Reese retorted. "What about you?" he said to Walker. "Is Tiller your father, too?"

"No." And after what'd happened with Marlow this past week, he was infinitely grateful for that.

"How do you know you're not?" Reese demanded.

285

"Because there's no way he could be," Rosemary said, finally speaking up.

"Wow…" Reese said, exhaling a long breath. "So…it's true?"

Her silence confirmed it.

Reese focused on Walker again. "How'd you find out?"

"From what I heard Eileen say, Tiller must've left you a sizable portion of the Madsen estate," Walker replied.

Reese fell back into the chair. "Holy shit. How did this happen?"

"An explanation would be nice," Walker said, letting their mother know she had to offer them *something*.

"There were…there were a few weeks where things between Tiller and me got a little out of hand," she admitted. "That's all. We stopped seeing each other…in that way…almost immediately, but by then it was too late."

"You were pregnant," Walker filled in.

Reese brought a hand to his chest. "With me."

She squeezed her eyes closed before saying, "Yes."

"This had to have happened while you were still with Dad—er, Rudy," Reese said. "Otherwise, he'd know I wasn't his, which means everyone else would know, too. He's not the type to keep a secret like this one, especially if he feels he's the one who was wronged."

Rosemary's hand shook as she set her mug on the coffee table. "He doesn't know. And he won't be happy about it. It'll probably be the end of…of whatever we have."

"And you're sad about that?" Reese asked in surprise.

"I was hoping to make our relationship work at last," she said simply.

The honesty of that statement hit Walker hard. Her life hadn't been easy. She'd worked long hours and done whatever she could to care for him and Reese and keep their family together. "So how did it happen?" he asked. "What were you thinking?"

"Your father and I were...struggling, and I... I admired Tiller because he was such a good man."

"Apparently not *that* good," Walker said dryly.

"People make mistakes, Walker," she said, speaking more stridently. "Tiller tried to live an honorable life. I feel bad that Eileen is going to hate him—and now Marlow will, too—when he loved them both so much. Eileen's going to burn all his pictures because of me. He doesn't deserve that."

Reese seemed confused when he asked, "Are you saying that what happened was more *your* fault than Tiller's?"

She wiped her eyes. "No. I'm saying the situation got away from us both, but we regretted it almost immediately and acted to avoid the same...mistake...from happening ever again."

"Was there any love involved?" Walker asked. At least love could be sympathetic, more so than any other excuse.

"For me it was a lot of things," she admitted. "Being desired by a handsome, wealthy and powerful man raised my self-esteem. I'm not going to lie about that. It felt wonderful to have Tiller take an interest in me during that terrible time. On top of that, I cared about him and was grateful for everything he'd already done for me."

"So he took advantage of the imbalance of power between you," Walker said.

"No," she insisted. "Neither of us took advantage of the other. I think... I think the fact that Eileen wasn't feeling well, and was so often in bed, left us alone too much of the time. And it didn't help that he probably felt it would be insensitive to approach her for sex as often as he probably wanted to."

"So no love was involved," Reese said, still trying to get her to confirm where she stood on that question.

"I wouldn't say there was *no* love involved," she responded. "For a while, he believed he was falling in love with me. At least, he told me that. But he also freely admitted that he loved Eileen and Marlow, and I knew he would never leave them, even if I asked him to, which I didn't." She sighed. "I wish I could tell you more, to help you understand, but...things just got away from us. I've always loved your father, and I tried to hold our marriage together. But Rudy was so...out of control. And Tiller was there to offer me comfort and support. For a brief time, that comfort and support crossed a line that should never have been crossed. That's all."

"That's *all*?" Walker echoed.

She pinched the bridge of her nose. "If not for the pregnancy, no one would ever have had to know, and then no one would've been hurt."

"But there *was* a pregnancy," Reese said. "What I don't understand is...once you realized you were going to have me and that I was *his* baby, why didn't you at least put in your notice? Get out of Eileen's house?"

"There were too many reasons to stay."

Walker started to pace again. He had to siphon off some of the agitation that was charging through him. "Of course. What regular employer would pay for private school for both your children and do all the other things Tiller did? And Eileen supported him in his generosity, like she did everything else, without even questioning it. No wonder she feels duped."

"I've always tried to be as good to her as she is to me," Rosemary said.

"I doubt she'll interpret you sleeping with her husband as proof of that," Reese retorted.

"Why'd you keep it a secret?" Walker asked. "You had Tiller on the hook for child support. He couldn't have gotten out of it, even if he'd tried."

"I wasn't trying to get him *on the hook*," she said, showing some fight at last. "Telling the truth would've ruined Tiller's career and could've cost him his family. I didn't want to hurt anyone."

Walker shook his head, struggling to understand how this had happened and how it had remained a secret for so long. "You had to know the truth would come out eventually."

"I didn't," she insisted. "I made it clear to Tiller that he'd done enough and everyone was better off the way things were. I never dreamed he'd include Reese in his will."

"You realize Eileen and Marlow will view you as a gold digger," Walker said. "They'll assume you got pregnant on purpose to create an obligation."

"I *didn't* get pregnant on purpose. And I never used Reese to pressure Tiller for money. Everything he did, he offered."

Walker hoped Marlow would be able to believe that. He'd always thought Tiller was incredibly generous. Now he knew why.

Sinking into the recliner across the coffee table from his brother—or half brother—he dropped his head in his hands.

"So where do we go from here?" Reese asked, causing him to look up again.

"You need to move away from Seaclusion as soon as possible," Walker told him.

"But...where will I go?"

Walker sighed. "I guess you'll have to move in with me and Mom until you get your inheritance. Then you'll be able to do pretty much whatever you want."

Reese scrubbed a hand over his face, obviously overwhelmed by the news. "How much money am I getting?"

Walker shook his head. "I have no idea."

"Neither do I," Rosemary added.

"You might want to wait until everyone's asleep before returning to Seaclusion," Walker told Reese. "There's no need to risk a confrontation if you can avoid it. I have to work at midnight, but I can help you move if we do it before then."

"Marlow and her friends might still be up before midnight."

"She has to be devastated by all this, so I doubt she'll be having another bonfire," Walker said. "But if she's up and around, you'll just have to wait till later and move out on your own."

"Yeah. It won't take long."

"What about the rest of my stuff?" Rosemary asked.

Walker checked his phone. He wished he'd hear from Marlow, but he knew chances of that were slim, and, as expected, she hadn't tried to call or text him. "Can you live without it for a few days?"

"I guess," she said. "I grabbed most of the things I really need."

"Then we'll give Eileen some time to cope with her heartbreak before making an appointment to pick up the rest."

They sat in silence for a long moment before Rosemary said, "I'm sorry. To both of you."

Reese seemed to consider that statement before perking up a bit. "Well, all things considered, I can't say that *I'm* too upset."

Walker offered him the best smile he could. "I'm happy for you."

27

Aida couldn't find Claire anywhere. And she wasn't answering her phone or texts, so Aida took her tennis racquet, borrowed the Jeep and drove to the club. She hoped Reese would have an hour or two between his lessons so they could have lunch, but she didn't even get the chance to talk to him. He offered her a smile and a wave when he noticed her sitting on the benches to one side, but after waiting for what seemed like forever while he continued to coach, she wandered into the restaurant and ordered a peach margarita.

As she looked at the people around her, all of whom were talking and laughing in small groups, she felt lonelier than ever. Not only was she a recent divorcée, she was sleeping with a much younger man who wasn't interested in a serious relationship. She didn't have a career or any children. As she'd told Claire and Marlow, she'd been thinking about opening a boutique, but she wasn't sure she had the nerve. She'd never done anything like that before and was afraid to use the money she had in case her business didn't succeed. What if she wound up in an even worse situation?

With a frown, she navigated to Instagram, where she found a

DM from Jackie, the high school friend who'd just learned she was no longer happily married.

Sorry I missed you in Cali. I hope you're doing well.

She didn't know whether Jackie was being sincere or not, so she said she was fine and that she was sad they'd missed each other, even though neither was true.

Should she return to her family in North Dakota after the summer was over?

She cringed at the humiliation that would entail. She'd be the beauty queen everyone thought had made it out of their sad little town—only to return in disgrace.

Reese came into the café, but again he didn't single her out. He just nodded to acknowledge her before going into the restroom. Even if he was more interested in her, they lived on opposite sides of the country, and she didn't want to leave California—not to go home, not to go anywhere. Sex with the local tennis pro had proved exciting and fun, but it hadn't been emotionally fulfilling.

She longed for something more meaningful…

What she'd had with Dutton wasn't going to be easy to replace, she realized. Not only had she loved him, she'd admired him, she'd felt proud to be with him, she even preferred the way he made love over anyone else, including Reese, who had the body of a god. When Claire had openly admitted that she was finding it hard to get over Dutton, Aida hadn't admitted that it wasn't any easier for her. She wished she could go back in time and pinpoint the exact moment when he'd started to lose interest in her, so she could do something to save their marriage before it was too late.

But she'd spent a great many hours wishing that, and wishing didn't change anything.

After Reese went back outside, she threw fifteen dollars on

the table to pay for her drink as well as a tip, hiked her purse up on her shoulder and left—only to find him standing in the parking lot. It looked as though he was trying to get something out of his truck, but an elderly woman, tanned to a deep brown, dripping with diamonds and gold jewelry, and dressed in the type of skimpy tennis outfit normally seen on a much younger woman, had cornered him.

Before he could give Aida yet another passing acknowledgment, she shifted her gaze away from them, got in the Jeep and drove out of the lot to continue her search for Claire.

She was just turning into a beach she hadn't visited before when her phone rang, and she pulled into a parking stall so she could see who it was.

Finally! Claire was getting back to her.

"Hey, where are you?" Aida asked as soon as she answered.

"I'm at Seaclusion, sitting out on the beach."

Aida frowned at the revelers she could see through the windshield, playing in the surf, building castles in the sand or tossing around giant beach balls. The whole world seemed to be going on as if what was happening in her life held no significance. "Where have you been all day? I've been looking everywhere for you."

There was a long pause before she said, "We need to talk, Aida. Can you come back?"

Aida immediately shifted into Reverse, gripping the steering wheel tightly as her mind went directly to Dutton. This sounded ominous. Had Claire made a decision? Was she going back to him? "Is this going to be upsetting?" she asked.

There was an even longer pause before Claire replied. "Probably."

A storm was coming, the first major storm of the season. Walker cursed when he heard the news. With everything else going on, he didn't want to have to worry about this. But it was his job to help keep the island safe, so he went to work midafternoon instead of waiting for his shift to begin at midnight.

According to the National Hurricane Center, what they had coming wasn't classified as a hurricane. But that could change. Statistically, there was about a fifty-fifty chance, given that on average twelve tropical storms formed over the Atlantic every year and about half of them turned into hurricanes.

He doubted the islanders were prepared for anything major this early in the season. The city council had been disseminating the usual advice since March. He hoped everyone had been paying attention. They should've already checked their hurricane shutters and hooks and latches as well as fastened down any galvanized sheeting on the roof, trimmed the trees, especially around power lines, and stored extra food and water. There were other precautions, but Walker wanted to make sure they'd at least done the minimum.

The whole time he was busy mobilizing people on the island to do what they could, he was thinking about Marlow and how disappointed she must be in her father. Tiller had been such an advocate for integrity that Walker was equally shocked he'd broken his marriage vows. He hated that his mother had a hand in that—and yet, the more he thought about it, the more he could understand how it could've happened. After all, Rosemary had been in close proximity to Tiller for years, and she'd needed his assistance in many ways. It was natural that she'd grow to admire and appreciate him, and having a woman around who treated him as though he walked on water had to be a powerful aphrodisiac.

Walker was just entering the poorest neighborhood on the island, where he planned to do some tree trimming and roof fastening himself, if necessary, when he received a call from his brother.

"Just got off work," Reese said. "I'm heading over to Seaclusion to move out."

Walker parked alongside an empty lot where a bunch of kids

were playing kickball. "What happened to waiting until after dark?" he asked.

"There's no way to gauge when someone will be out and about. I might as well grab everything now."

Walker put the transmission in Park but left the motor running so he'd have air-conditioning. "If Eileen or Marlow happens to see you, it could get ugly."

"I doubt I'll encounter Eileen. She rarely comes outside, even on good days."

Walker waved; the kids in the lot had taken notice of him. "What about Marlow?"

"Hard to know what she'd say. She's always been nice to me in the past, but that was before she knew I was her brother."

Reese was related to Marlow—what a mind bender.

"Should I try to talk to her?" Reese asked.

"No way," Walker said. "It's too soon."

"I just want to point out that she's upset about something that happened nearly twenty-three years ago, and it doesn't really have to change anything. I mean…it's not like I'm a little boy and there are child support or custody issues. And there won't be a big scandal. Tiller's gone. I doubt the media will even care at this point. Unless we tell them, how would they find out, anyway?"

"You're walking away with a big chunk of their money, Reese. That would upset anybody."

A sigh came through the phone. "You're probably right. But it feels terrible knowing they suddenly hate me through no fault of my own."

"Hopefully, they'll get over it." But there was no guarantee they'd ever be willing to associate with Reese again—or Walker, for that matter. It was a given they'd never be willing to associate with Rosemary again.

Walker leaned forward to glance up at the sky. It was still a cloudless blue, so incongruous with the cyclone brewing over the ocean. "You know there's a storm coming, right?"

"I heard about that. But it's not expected to hit for another two days," Reese replied. "By then it could change course and miss the island entirely—or blow itself out."

"We have to be prepared regardless. Seaclusion is probably in good shape, but…will you check to see if they have plenty of food and water?"

"I thought you wanted me to keep a low profile," Reese said. "Now you want me to knock and ask Marlow if she's prepared for the storm?"

"Yeah, I guess I do," Walker said. "I'll rest a lot easier if I know they're paying attention to what's happening around them. I can't imagine they are."

"Thanks for being worried about *me*," Reese said.

"You're probably walking away from this a rich man. The least you can do for me is make sure the woman I love is going to be safe."

"Whoa," Reese said.

Walker turned off the engine but let his hand rest on the door latch. "What?"

"The woman you *love*."

"Might as well admit it," Walker said as he got out of his SUV. "I wasn't fooling anyone, anyway."

"And she was just starting to see you when this happened."

"Yeah. Things were definitely looking up."

"I'm sorry."

Walker switched his phone to speaker so he could check his text messages. Marlow still hadn't contacted him.

Had he lost her for good?

Probably. He didn't see how they could come back from something like this.

Claire had no idea when Marlow might return to the guesthouse and didn't want to run into her, so she'd asked Aida to meet her down by the beach. After all they'd been through together, she felt they needed and deserved a few minutes alone. Once she told Aida what she had to say, she'd explain the situation to Marlow, gather her stuff from the guesthouse and go.

Her phone buzzed. With a sigh, she pulled it out of her beach bag to see who was trying to reach her, in case it was Aida. But it was Dutton. Again. *Hurry back,* he'd texted and sent a picture of him grilling steaks for their dinner.

He wasn't wearing anything but a pair of swim trunks. She stared at that picture for a long time. Was she making the right decision? Would she live to regret what she was about to do? Their morning together had started out feeling so strange and wrong. She'd barely been able to let him touch her. But the more time they'd spent together, the more she'd begun to remember just how happy she'd been when she was with him and the easier it became to settle right back into their old relationship. She'd never met anyone quite so charming…

She heard Aida coming up from behind and put her phone back in her bag.

Aida didn't say hello. She wasn't smiling, either. She looked as somber as Claire felt at having to make such a terrible decision. Taking off the sarong she was wearing on her hips, she wrapped it around her shoulders before sitting in the sand.

Claire didn't know how to start. What should she say? *I'm a terrible friend? I've been lying to you—and, by the way, Dutton is on the island?*

"Well?" Aida asked at length. "I thought you wanted to talk."

"I'm working up the nerve," Claire admitted.

Aida's eyebrows furrowed. "Why don't you just come out with it? You're going back to him, aren't you?"

Once again, the fun she'd had with Dutton this morning rose in Claire's mind. After the first half hour, it'd been like old times. They'd laughed when he unwittingly came out of the restroom with toilet paper stuck to his shoe and talked about his work and her dream of opening another yoga studio. He could easily have treated her as though what he did was so much more important, but he didn't. He even told her he'd help her financially. And sliding her hand into his as they walked on the beach had been as comfortable and familiar as wrapping herself in her favorite old quilt.

Reconciling with him would be *so* easy...

But he'd been on his best behavior. She knew that. She also knew deep down that the fairy tale she was creating in her mind was too good to be true. Once he had her back, she'd wonder whenever he didn't come home on time if he was secretly meeting up with another woman. Even worse, if she let herself take what she wanted at the cost of her friendship with Aida, she'd never be able to forgive herself. That was what she'd realized as the day progressed. As much as she loved Dutton, she was making a mistake. He was missing a sensitivity gene. Between that and his general selfishness, even though those traits only came out occasionally, she couldn't trust that he could make her happy long-term.

"No," she said. "I've decided to end it, once and for all."

Aida blinked several times. "Are you serious?"

She nodded. "I know that letting him go is the best thing I could do. When he started calling me again, I...got confused and tried to fool myself, I guess."

Aida pulled the sarong tighter against the wind that was beginning to ruffle her hair. "I couldn't be more relieved," she said, closing her eyes. "But I also feel bad. Maybe I should quit thinking only of myself and tell you to go back to him if that's what you really want. He and I are over for good. If you two are better suited to each other, I should at least give you my blessing. So—" she drew a deep breath "—I won't stand in the way if...if that's what will make you happy."

That was the sweetest thing Claire had ever heard, and it showed the difference between Aida and Dutton. Aida understood what love was all about; Dutton didn't. "That's *so* nice," she said. "I love you to death."

"I love you, too," Aida responded. "I've told you this before, but you're the only good thing to come out of what I've been through this past year."

"We're both better off without him," Claire agreed. "Anyone who'd do what he's done...that's a red flag."

Aida scooted closer and put her sarong around Claire's shoulders, too, leaving her arm there as they watched the sun sink lower and lower on the horizon. But Claire knew the difficult part was still ahead. After clearing her throat, she said, "I have to tell you something else, Aida. And you're not going to like this nearly as much."

She felt Aida stiffen. "What is it?"

"Dutton's on the island."

Dropping her arm, Aida shifted so they could face each other. *"What?"*

Claire winced. "I know. I told him not to come, but he wouldn't listen to me."

Aida's mouth fell open. "When did he get here?"

Claire wished she didn't have to go into detail. But she'd decided to be completely honest, and that meant a full confession. "He arrived while we were in Miami. He's...he's rented a small beach house on the other side of the island. For a week."

"That's where you were today," Aida said, catching on. "That's why I couldn't find you."

Claire couldn't quite meet her eyes. "That's true. I wasn't shell hunting. I didn't go to the club to meet with my boss this morning, either. I'm sorry for lying to you. After all the things we've had to say about Dutton and his dishonesty, I haven't behaved any better. But—and this isn't an excuse—it took seeing him again to make me realize that I really don't want to be the kind of person he is."

Aida sat quietly for a long moment. Then she said simply, "Wow."

"I'm sorry," Claire said again. "I hope…eventually, you'll be able to forgive me."

Aida reached for her hand. "We all make mistakes, Claire. I don't hate Dutton because he made a mistake. I hate him because he doesn't care that what he did hurt me."

"*I* care," she said. "I feel terrible about it."

"I know. And that's what tells me you're a true friend." Releasing Claire's hand, she pulled her knees to her chest. "Have you told him what you've decided?"

"Not yet. He thinks I'm coming back for dinner."

She whistled. "He's going to freak out!"

"I know. I feel terrible about that, too. I created this problem right after you and I promised each other that we were done with him for good. But I tried to tell him not to come. He insisted, and he should take responsibility for that decision."

"Yet he won't."

"Another red flag," Claire said, "which I tried to ignore along with all the others." If he really cared about her, he would've listened to her when she told him not to come to the island, that she needed more time to herself. He would've understood the difficult position he was putting her in. And he would've been more respectful of the love she had for her friends. Now that she was being more honest, not just with Aida but with herself, she could see that he'd been covering up his narcissistic behavior with excuses designed to disarm her. *I have to see you. I miss you so much.* But he'd been thinking only of himself.

"He's used to getting what he wants."

Claire tucked the loose strands of hair falling from her messy bun behind her ears. "That's true. He knows how to go about it. Still, I feel bad that it took me so long to realize what I was doing. It didn't occur to me—not fully—until I returned to Seaclusion an hour ago. When I walked into the guesthouse and you and Marlow were both gone, I tried to imagine my life without you and knew that wasn't the direction I wanted to go."

"You chose us."

"I did. But I can't imagine you'll want to spend the rest of the summer with me after...after what I've done. And I can't blame you. I'll pack my things and leave as soon as I can make the arrangements." She grabbed her bag and stood up, but Aida caught her hand again.

"Wait."

Claire shifted her bag higher on her shoulder.

"Don't leave the island," Aida said. "The summer wouldn't be the same without you."

"Even after what I've done?" Claire asked.

"Of course! I'm not happy you lied to me. But neither one of us is perfect. We're not always going to get it right, but we do what we can to fix our mistakes and move on. The problem with Dutton is that he wants to blame everyone else for his mistakes."

Relief swept through Claire, as well as gratitude for Aida's willingness to forgive her. "Thank you. Dutton's missing out, because there's no one like you," she said as they embraced. "And now... I was going to tell Marlow, but maybe I should wait until—"

"There's no need to say anything to her," Aida broke in. "She's going through enough already. Let's not make matters any worse."

"You're okay with that?"

"Completely."

"Okay. Then I'll call Dutton and get that over with."

Aida grimaced. "He's not going to be happy."

Claire bit her lip. "I hope he doesn't act *too* ugly."

Aida looked worried as they started back to the guesthouse together. "I hope so, too."

28

Reese felt like a persona non grata as he parked his truck as close to the apartment over the garage as possible and got out. He'd received conflicting directions from Walker. His brother didn't want him to upset Marlow or Eileen by making his presence known, and yet he expected Reese to check that they had what they might need if the coming storm turned into a hurricane. He didn't know how he was going to do one and not the other. But he planned to pack up before he tried, so that he could make a quick exit if emotions ran too high.

He was taking the last load to his truck when he ran into Marlow. She was walking from the main house just as he was starting down the stairs outside his door with a big black garbage bag filled with shoes. He saw her first, but then she looked up and stopped dead in her tracks.

He froze at that point, too, and squinted against the sun while trying to read her expression. Was it hostile? Did it upset her to see him? They'd had fun at the bonfires, the meals they'd shared and the tennis matches. As far as he knew, they were friends. But now that they were half siblings, he wondered how that would change the way she treated him.

He was the first to start moving again. He finished going down the stairs and piled the garbage bag on top of all the other stuff he'd tossed into the back of his truck before crossing over to her.

She didn't back away from him, and she didn't tell him to get lost. But he had the impression she wasn't happy to see him.

"Hey," he said, coming to a stop several feet away.

"Hey." Although her response was muted, it didn't seem *entirely* unfriendly.

He shoved his hands in his pockets and used his foot to shoo away a mosquito that was hovering over the grass. "I'm sorry about what's happened. I know... I know it must've come as a shock. It came as a shock to me, too. And to Walker. We had no idea."

"It definitely came as a surprise." One that was, no doubt, more unwelcome to Marlow than it was to him, which was partly what made everything so awkward now.

"I don't know if you want to hear this, but my mother said it wasn't something that went on for years. She told Walker and me that things got out of hand for a few weeks, that she and Tiller both regretted what they'd done almost immediately and backed off. But by then it was too late. She was pregnant."

When Marlow blanched at his words, he knew how much it hurt her that her father had cheated on her mother—especially with *his* mother, because it made the betrayal even worse. But he thought knowing the circumstances might bring her some peace. It had to be far more painful to imagine they'd been living a secret life, cheating for years.

"How do you know what she says is true?" she asked skeptically.

Once a liar, always a liar. He understood what she meant but could only shrug. He had no way of being able to tell for sure. "I don't," he admitted. "I know you probably hate her now and might not want to hear this, either, but she seems really remorseful. I get the impression she's telling the truth."

"Okay."

He glanced toward the house. "How's your mom?"

"Not taking it well."

"I'm sorry. I feel...terrible." For them. For his mother. For Walker. For everyone except himself. The more he thought about being able to kick his difficult relationship with Rudy aside, the happier he became. It was almost as though the truth had set him free and he could now soar higher than ever before. Not being told earlier was still an issue for him. His mother had let him struggle through so many complicated feelings concerning Rudy. But it was hard to feel too bad about that when his future had grown infinitely brighter.

"So do I," she said.

Fortunately, she didn't point out that he had to be feeling pretty good about his own situation. He had far more pleasant memories of Tiller than Rudy. Although Tiller had been a busy man, he'd always been happy to see Reese and had taken great pride in his tennis ability. That made more sense now.

He reached up to scratch his neck. "Walker's worried about you."

Tears immediately began to fill her eyes, but she blinked them away. "It's going to take some time to get used to this."

"I understand. We both do. He...he wanted me to tell you about the storm that's coming."

She shoved a hand through her hair. "What storm?"

"It's a big one. They're not calling it a hurricane yet. But it could turn into one."

"How long do we have?"

"They're estimating two days."

She rolled her eyes. "Of course a storm would hit right now. That's just what we need."

"Hopefully, it'll miss the island entirely. But in case it doesn't,

Walker asked me to make sure you have enough food and water. If you don't, I could help you get anything you need."

"That's okay. We'll be fine." She gestured to his truck. "Do you have somewhere else to stay?"

He looked over his shoulder at the mound of bags peeking above the roof and sides of his vehicle. "Walker's."

"Is that where your mother is?"

"Yeah. It's a family affair," he joked, but felt embarrassed when she didn't laugh and he realized how inappropriate the comment was.

"I'm sorry you had to move out."

"No problem. It's understandable, considering the situation." He pulled his keys from his pocket, removed the key to the apartment and handed it to her. "Okay, well, I'd better go before your mother sees me. I don't want to upset her. I just came to pick up my stuff."

"Thanks for being sensitive to the situation."

He paused before he turned to go, searching her face for...he didn't know what. It wasn't every day he learned he had another sibling. He supposed he was hoping for some hint that she might still welcome a relationship with him in spite of everything. He was also searching for any kind of resemblance between them. Did they look alike in any way? Should they have figured this out sooner? "Would you like your father's ring back?" he asked. "After what's happened, maybe you'd rather have it."

He hoped she'd say no. It now held more meaning for him, so he was grateful when she said, "I'm sorry, but I can't answer that question at the moment. I'm shocked, and I'm exhausted, and I'm disgusted, and I'm...hurt," she finished. "Can we talk about it another time?"

"Of course. I'll get out of your way." He lifted his hand in an awkward wave before turning to his truck.

"Reese?"

He pivoted to face her.

"If I have to have a surprise brother, I'm glad it's someone I already care about."

He suddenly felt a whole lot better. "Thanks," he said. "I needed to hear that."

When Marlow walked into the guesthouse, she found Aida and Claire pacing in the living room, casting worried glances at each other.

"What is it?" she asked. After a long day with her mother, she was finally starting to feel better, and Reese was the reason. As hard as it had been to say what she'd said to him a moment ago, she was glad she'd done it. The relief in his eyes and the cute smile he'd given her had melted her heart.

For the first time since she'd met with Sam, she understood on an emotional level—and not just a cognitive one—that Reese wasn't to blame for any part of what she and her mother were going through. She was still thinking about what he'd said to her, too. That Walker was worried about her had cheered her up when she'd thought nothing could. It'd only been a couple of days since she'd seen him, but she suddenly craved his arms around her in spite of everything.

Or maybe because of it.

"We have a problem," Aida said.

"What kind of problem?" Marlow didn't think she could face anything else. Not now. She was eager to have a few minutes to herself so she could text Walker. She wanted to see him tonight, to get his perspective on what they'd learned. Reese had told her how shocked Walker was. He also had to be wondering if what they had was over before it really got started. When she'd left Sam's office, she'd thought for sure that was the case. She couldn't imagine letting him touch her again.

But she was beginning to think that her father's terrible secret could only ruin her happiness if she let it. Walker wasn't to blame for what his mother had done twenty-three years ago any more than Reese was. It was just a deep, dark family secret that had suddenly come to light and turned their world upside down.

Maybe there was some way to minimize the damage.

"It's *my* fault," Claire murmured.

"But she didn't mean for this to happen," Aida quickly added, surprising Marlow by being protective of Claire despite the tension that had developed between them since they'd arrived on the island.

Marlow eyed them curiously. "What are you talking about?"

"Dutton." Aida said his name on a downbeat.

"He's causing trouble again?" Marlow had thought they were finally rid of Aida's ex. The divorce was behind them. The fighting should be over. But she understood all too well that wasn't necessarily how things played out in real life.

"He's threatening to take me back to court to renegotiate my spousal support," Aida said.

Marlow scowled at her friends. *"Why?"*

"He's angry again."

Disgusted that he wouldn't give up and leave Aida alone—after all, *he* was the one who'd lied and cheated for so long—Marlow shook her head. "There's no way. If he goes that route, he stands to lose more than he stands to gain."

"He's emphatic about it," Claire insisted. "And knowing him, he won't care if it costs every penny he's got. He's the type who'll cut off his nose to spite his face if he's angry enough."

"He's already spent a couple hundred thousand in legal fees," Marlow said. "Now he wants to spend more? What's gotten into him?"

Claire, who'd been biting the cuticles around her fingernails, lowered her hand from her mouth. "I was hoping we wouldn't have to tell you, not now, when you're going through so much yourself. But..."

"But we don't have a choice anymore," Aida filled in. "Because he might not be making idle threats. He could really do something terrible before he leaves."

Marlow sank onto the couch. *"Leaves?"*

"He's on the island," Aida blurted out.

Marlow jumped up again. *"What?"*

"I'm so sorry," Claire said with a wince. "I can't believe I dragged us into this."

"What are you talking about?" Marlow asked.

Claire told her what had been going on, how he'd been texting her and calling her and wanting to see her—and that he'd rented a beach house on the island and flown in yesterday despite her many requests that he give her the summer alone.

"So you spent the day with him," Marlow said when she was finished. "And it wasn't until after you told Aida the truth that you let Dutton know you wouldn't be seeing him anymore?" Marlow said, trying to get it all straight.

Claire nodded.

"And then what happened?"

"He exploded!" Aida nudged Claire. "Show her the messages he's been sending you. Then I'll show her mine."

Marlow accepted Claire's phone. The first thing she noticed was a great many missed calls from Dutton in the space of the past couple of hours.

"I didn't want to talk to him on the phone," Claire explained. "He's so…intense and persuasive. It's easier for me to work through things when I reply by text, so I didn't pick up."

"She was trying to keep him from getting too worked up, but as you'll see, it's definitely not working," Aida chimed in.

Marlow began to read.

Dutton: What do you mean you're not coming? You said you'd be back tonight. I'm grilling steaks for dinner.

Claire: I'm sorry. But I can't. I don't want to be the kind of person who would go back to you and hurt my friend.

Dutton: So this is because of Aida? I told you that she'd turn you against me.

Claire: It's because of me, Dutton. Not Aida. I don't think our relationship will work out in the long run, and I don't want to lose Aida only to realize in a few weeks, months or years that I made a mistake.

Dutton: Don't do this. You love me and I love you. I flew across the country to be with you, and now you're not even willing to see me while I'm here?

Claire: I can't! Don't you understand? It messes with my head. Besides, I didn't want to sneak around while you were here, didn't want to lie to my friends. I tried telling you that in the beginning, when you first said you were coming.

Dutton: So don't sneak around! Tell them you're getting back with me and they can go fuck themselves if they're not happy about it. We should be able to do whatever we want.

Claire: That's just it! You want what you want no matter who ends up hurt.

Dutton: You're listening to the wrong people, and you're going to be sorry you did. Fuck you and your friends!

Claire hadn't responded to that, so Dutton had texted again a few minutes later: I'm sorry. I didn't mean that. I'm just upset. Will you come over so we can talk about this?

Again, Claire had given him no response.

Dutton: I'm trying to call you. Will you please pick up?

Claire: I'm done, Dutton. I can't be part of your life any longer.

Dutton: Claire, calm down. Take a minute to think this through. You don't mean what you just said.

Claire: I do mean it! Please let me go without all the anger and drama. It's been such a hard year, and you're part of the reason.

Dutton: Part of the reason? Who provided a place for you to live when your house burned down? Who helped deal with the insurance company and the contractors when it came to the rebuild? You have thanked me so many times for stepping up to help. Now I've made your year harder?

Claire: Everything we had was a lie, Dutton! You told me you loved me while you were going home telling Aida the same thing. And I thought you were meeting with various doctors across several states to sell them pharmaceuticals when you were gone! How can I ever trust you after that?

Dutton: Aida's no longer part of the picture. You're blowing up our relationship for no reason!

Claire: I don't want to fight anymore. Why don't we just let it go?

Dutton: You did this on purpose.

Claire: I did WHAT on purpose?

Dutton: Got me out here to break things off. This is revenge, pure and simple.

Claire: We're not even together, so how can I break up with you? And I didn't do this on purpose. I tried to talk you out of coming here, remember?

Dutton: You're going to be sorry about this. You and your stupid friends.

Claire: What's that supposed to mean?

Dutton: It's time you and the bitches you call friends get what you deserve.

Marlow caught her breath when she read that. "There's something wrong with him," she said, more convinced than ever.

"He thinks he should have whatever he wants," Aida supplied. "He doesn't understand the word *no*."

So what should they do? Marlow wondered. Was this all talk? Or did they have something to worry about?

"You don't think he'll actually do anything, do you?" Claire asked uncertainly.

Marlow had no idea. Seaclusion was so well-known on the island it would be easy enough to find. He was close, so he could certainly try to do something. And there was no guarantee they'd see it coming. Even if they did, she wasn't sure they'd be able to stop it. They didn't even have Reese on the property anymore, He'd just moved out, although Aida and Claire didn't know that yet. "I want to say no," she said, measuring the possibility in her mind as she spoke. "But I don't want to dismiss it out of hand. The news is full of angry spouses and exes who do terrible things."

Aida took Claire's phone and held hers out instead. "Now look at what he sent me."

Marlow didn't want to read any more. She knew that whatever he'd sent Aida would be worse. After all, he wasn't trying to win Aida back.

Dutton: You need to stay out of my life, or you'll live to regret it.

Aida: I'm not in your life. We're divorced.

Dutton: Then stop saying shit to Claire, trying to mess things up for us.

Aida: Anyone who gets with you is making a mistake. I have the right to warn my friend.

Dutton: If you think you're clever and this is going to turn out in your favor, you're wrong. I'll take you back to court, and this time I'll win. You'll be left without a penny.

Aida: Why can't you just respect what she's telling you? Go home and leave her alone. That's all she wants.

Dutton: That's what YOU want.

Aida: I had nothing to do with it. She made the decision on her own.

Dutton: Sure, she did. It's easy to guess what you and Marlow have been telling her about me. This isn't going to end the way you want it to, though.

Aida: If you don't stop threatening me, I'm going to call the police.

Dutton: Call them. There's nothing they can do. ☺

The smile was the most chilling part of what Dutton had

sent. Marlow remembered all the things he'd done to harass her in LA. He'd followed her around town. He'd shown up at the Starbucks where she got her morning coffee for several days in a row—was always there waiting to hold the door when she came out. He'd told her neighbors *she* was harassing *him*. He'd posted memes about attorneys on social media, like "A good attorney knows the law; a great attorney knows the judge," trying to imply that she was somehow cheating the system. It was behavior that was well beneath someone who was so educated and successful, especially a doctor. But smarter and more successful people than Dutton had broken the law.

"What do you think?" Aida asked.

Marlow sighed. "I think you should both turn off your phones. Don't give him the pleasure of having an audience with you."

"I'm afraid if he can't vent his fury, he'll only get more dangerous," Aida said ominously. "He's like that—he needs a target."

"He's not scheduled to leave the island for almost a week," Claire pointed out. "He just got here."

That meant he'd be floating around for several days, and he'd have a lot of time on his hands. To Marlow, that was a recipe for disaster. "There's a big storm coming in," she said. "Maybe he'll try to get off the island before it hits now that he knows there's no reason to stay."

"How big a storm?" Aida asked in alarm.

"It's not a hurricane," she said. "And it could easily change course or blow itself out before landfall."

It could also get a lot worse. But she didn't say so.

They had enough to worry about.

29

As Rosemary helped Reese move into the other available bedroom at Walker's house, all she could think about was Eileen yelling at Walker this morning to take his scheming, backstabbing whore of a mother and get off the property. She'd never heard Eileen use profanity before and still couldn't believe what she'd heard.

She'd spent most of her adult life working for the Madsens. She'd been dedicated and loyal, and she'd done a good job. But that didn't mean anything now. She wouldn't even be able to get a reference if she needed one. What was she going to do next?

"I ran into Marlow," Reese told her as they started up the eight steps to Walker's front door. She was carrying one black garbage bag while he hefted two.

She kept her head down instead of looking up, partially so she wouldn't trip but also because she didn't want him to glance back at her, didn't want to meet his eyes. She'd never intended to hurt anyone. Had this one mistake destroyed every good thing she'd ever done? "What did she say?" she asked dully.

"She didn't seem *too* mad. I mean… I could tell she'd been crying. And I'm guessing her mother isn't doing very well. You know how proud Eileen is and how often she touted her husband as the most wonderful man in the world. But Marlow didn't take it out on me."

The floor creaked as they reached the landing. "That was nice of her." She doubted she'd be afforded the same courtesy, though. She had a scarlet letter on her chest, even though she'd been raising two children with an alcoholic husband who wouldn't work a steady job and kept her in a state of emotional upheaval, and she'd had no one else to fall back on. What she'd done with Tiller had lasted for such a short period of time. It didn't seem fair that she was being judged exclusively on those three weeks after all her years of good behavior.

"What are you thinking about?" he asked as he held the front door for her with his foot after entering the house.

"I'm trying not to think," she replied as she strained under the weight of her burden.

He stopped in the doorway of his new room and turned back. "I'm sorry. I know this isn't easy for you."

"Does that even matter? I deserve whatever I get, right? Since I'm the one to blame?"

He didn't seem to know how to answer her. "Dad—er, Rudy—wasn't the man you needed him to be. He let you down first."

The bag in her arms was growing too heavy. She eased it onto the carpet in the hallway. "That's no excuse. There *is* no excuse. That's the problem."

He put what he'd carried in on the bed before grabbing her bag and tossing it there, too. "I'm *glad* Rudy's not my dad," he said. "I admit I wish I'd known sooner. Maybe Tiller could've been a bigger part of my life. I could've used the kind of father he was to Marlow. But I understand why you couldn't tell anyone. If I were you, I probably would've made the same decision."

She could tell he was trying to make her feel better. She was grateful that he was willing to look at the situation from her perspective. But she couldn't expect the same from Walker, who now had both of them living in his house. The news of what she'd done had ruined his chances of being with the woman he'd always wanted.

And what about Eileen? She'd *never* forgive Rosemary.

Then there was Rudy. For most of their relationship, he hadn't been able to give her what she needed, but she doubted he'd see it that way. He'd take up his old argument, insisting no regular Joe could compete with the rich, handsome US senator she admired. He'd say she kept him around to pass Reese off as his and she couldn't be trusted if she could lie about something so crucial. What had been developing between them over the past few weeks, ever since she started seeing him again, would be destroyed and the hope of a reunion would disappear along with her job and any future prospects of a job with another respectable family.

"Thanks for trying to be understanding," she told Reese.

He gave her a compassionate look. "When are you going to tell Rudy?"

Maybe *he* was glad to be rid of Rudy, but she'd been excited about starting over with him. He really seemed to have turned his life around. But she couldn't believe there'd be any hope for them after this. He'd tried to call this morning during what would've been her morning coffee break, as usual, and when she didn't answer, he'd texted her: Busy morning? Missed talking to you...

Several hours later, he'd texted again: Why haven't I heard back? Is everything okay? What's going on?

And then around dinnertime, he'd tried a third time: I'm hoping to see you tonight. You said it might be possible. Are you coming here? Where should we go?

And his last text, since it was getting late and he still hadn't heard from her: I guess you're not coming over?

"I don't know when I'll tell him," she told Reese. "I need a few days to…to cope with what's happened."

"Are you going to try to get another job?"

She didn't have any choice. The Madsens had paid her well, but most of it had been in the form of education, camps, coaching and family vacations for her boys. And because she'd been provided with room and board, she'd never made a great deal in the way of salary. What little she had now, she'd have to use to buy a car. It would require cash, since she could no longer list a job on a credit application. "Once I get my feet underneath me again."

"Will you stay here on the island?"

Opportunities on Teach would be slim. Even if they weren't, she'd be smart to get as far away from Eileen Madsen as possible, in case Eileen became vengeful and tried to destroy Rosemary's employment prospects. "Probably somewhere else."

"There are a lot of rich people in Miami. That isn't too far away. And once I receive my money, I can help you out."

"It's kind of you to offer. Thank you." She didn't know how long it would take him to get his inheritance. She'd never been involved with that type of thing, since her parents hadn't had much to pass on. But she guessed it would be a while, maybe several months. In any case, she'd have to move at least as far as Miami.

But wherever she went, she'd be going without a reference.

The house was so quiet. Eileen felt as though she'd just experienced another death. What'd happened *was* sort of like a death. It was the death of her thirty-six-year association with Rosemary Cantwell.

It was also the death of her faith in her husband.

As she wandered around the house alone, she recalled the day Rosemary had first come to interview. She'd been only nineteen, five years younger than Eileen, somewhat plain and with only a high school diploma. But she'd been eager for the position. Although she didn't have a lot of experience, and Tiller was quick to point that out, there'd been *something* about her. Eileen had liked her much better than anyone else who'd applied for the job, so she'd overridden his misgivings, and she'd always prided herself on making that decision. Rosemary had proved to be loyal, hardworking and honest.

Or so Eileen had thought. Tiller had often commented on how Rosemary had become an integral part of their lives and how hard it would be to get along without her.

Now, of course, Eileen read much more into that statement than ever before.

When she reached the dining room, she grimaced at all the pictures and articles she'd shoved to the floor. The thought of Tiller and Rosemary together made her stomach churn. She'd never dreamed anything like that could be going on behind her back. Sure, Rosemary had gotten prettier as the years went by. She'd aged well. But she'd never been a real beauty. She was, however, calm and steady—unflappable. Eileen had always admired her quiet strength in the face of adversity. She'd also trusted Rosemary, almost as much as she'd trusted Tiller. It was difficult to believe they'd been sneaking around.

Where had she been when that was going on? Sick in bed? Had he taken Rosemary into a guest bedroom? Into his office? Somewhere else?

Maybe he'd snuck up to her apartment when Rudy wasn't around…

"Hypocrite," she bit out and sank to the floor, where she tore up as many of his pictures as she had the energy to destroy. He'd always gotten so angry when news hit that yet another senator or member of congress had been having an illicit affair. *There's no integrity left in this world*, he'd complain. *If the leaders of this country don't set an example, who will?*

She laughed mirthlessly. "Great example, dear."

A noise caused her to straighten. She listened carefully, but it was just the usual settling creaks she generally paid no attention to. Normally, if Rosemary heard her up so late, she'd get out of bed, too, and come see if there was anything she could do—make a cup of tea, visit with her, draw a bath.

Tonight, Eileen was completely alone. Marlow had offered to stay with her. She'd tried to insist. But Eileen was too conscious of the friends she'd brought home with her. She didn't want Aida and Claire, or anyone else, to know the shameful truth. It was too humiliating. It proved that Tiller hadn't loved her nearly as much as she'd always believed. He'd made her into a laughingstock. She was the trusting, devoted idiot of a wife who'd been so easy to cheat on.

The fact that the two people she'd trusted most in life, other than Marlow, had betrayed her filled her with white-hot anger. Unable to resist, she struggled to her feet and went to get her phone.

After navigating to Rosemary's contact record, she scrolled back through their communication of the past few days.

Eileen: Can you pick up some strawberries while you're at the supermarket?

Rosemary: Sure. What would you like for dinner?

Eileen: Anything. I like whatever you make. But will you get the mail on your way home?

Rosemary: Already grabbed it. Be back soon.

Eileen: I should've known you'd be on it.

Rosemary had been part of her life for nearly four decades; Eileen had thought she'd known Rosemary so well. They'd become more than employer and employee. They'd become like sisters. But now she had to wonder if everything she'd ever believed about her had been an act.

How could you? I TRUSTED you, she wrote in a text message.

It was the middle of the night, so, of course, she didn't get a response. But that only made her hate Rosemary more, so much that she couldn't help adding: I hope you rot in hell.

Walker was having trouble staying awake. A general lack of sleep, combined with the emotional upheaval of the day and the physicality of repairing roofs and trimming trees for hours, had left him completely exhausted. And yet it was only midnight. His official shift was just starting.

To help him get through the long hours ahead, he was on his way to the all-night mini-mart to buy a cup of coffee when his phone lit up with an incoming call.

It was Marlow.

Surprised he was hearing from her, he pulled over immediately and answered. "Hey, is it really you?"

"Yeah."

"What's going on? How are you?"

"I'm… I don't know."

"I'm so sorry for what you're going through. I feel terrible about what's happened."

"Thanks. What are you doing tonight?"

"Working. I have graveyard."

"You sound tired."

"I am."

"Will you be okay?"

"I'm about to get a caffeine fix. That should help."

There was a slight pause before she said, "I saw Reese today."

"He told me. He called me afterward, said he was grateful you were kind to him. Thanks for that."

"What happened wasn't his fault."

It was their mother's fault, at least in part. Walker was supremely conscious of that. "Doesn't make it any easier. Is your mother going to be okay?"

"She's struggling. I've never seen her quite like this."

"It was a nasty surprise—for all of us."

"Except your mother."

Was she testing him to see how he'd react? Whether or not he'd get defensive? He had that impression. "Except my mother," he admitted.

After that there was a long silence, which he broke when he said, "Are you prepared for the storm?"

"At this point, I'm just hoping it doesn't hit the island. I can't even think about it."

"You *have* to think about it, Marlow. I don't want anything to happen to you. Tell me what you need. I'll take care of it."

"We'll be fine."

He refused to let her brush it off. "Will it upset your mother if I swing by tomorrow, so I can bring some bottled water and check the roofs and trees?"

"I don't think you should."

"Then you'll have to check for me."

She didn't make any commitments. She just said, "Walker?"

"Yes?"

"Is there any chance you can come over for a few minutes?"

"Right now?" he asked.

"Yes."

"Of course. What do you need?"

He thought he heard tears in her voice when she said, "I need *you*."

Aida and Claire had gone to bed late. They'd stopped responding to Dutton, and he'd finally given up texting them, but they were nervous about what he might do next. So was Marlow. Even if the judge who'd ruled on her request for a restraining order hadn't seen a man like Dutton as a danger to anyone, the behavior Dutton had exhibited during the divorce proceedings was classic stalking. He'd show up at odd times, follow her around and taunt her with a grin whenever their eyes met. He was persistent and intrusive and had been trying to intimidate her. That didn't mean he'd actually harm her, but he made her uneasy.

Dutton wasn't the reason she wanted to see Walker, though. With the storm coming, she didn't want to tell him Dutton was on the island—not if she didn't have to. Walker didn't need the distraction, especially tonight when he was exhausted. So she checked the windows, the way Aida and Claire had been checking before they'd finally gone to bed, to make sure Dutton wasn't lurking around the property, and when she saw Walker's headlights swing into the drive, she hurried out of the guesthouse.

He'd barely left his SUV and started toward her when she ran into his arms.

"Whoa!" He had to catch his balance, but then he held her close, just as she'd hoped he would. He even put a hand at the back of her head as he murmured, "You're going to be fine. Everything's going to be fine."

She didn't contradict him. A moment earlier, it'd felt as if her whole world had been torn apart. But now, having him there was the only thing that seemed important. As she clung to him, he kissed her temple before burying his face in her hair and breathing deeply, as if he'd needed to see her as badly as she'd needed to see him.

"Thanks for coming," she said. "I've missed you so much."

It hadn't been very long since they'd been together, but the possibility that what had happened might tear them apart was so frightening it felt like years. "I've missed you, too. And I'm sorry for what my mother did. I'd do anything I could to protect you."

"I know." She had no doubt of that. He'd proved it by risking his life to save hers when they were kids. "I've never fallen in love before," she told him. "But..."

He leaned back so he could look down into her face. "But?"

"I think I could live without almost anything—except you."

His smile made her feel warm inside, oddly happy in spite of everything. "You won't have to live without me. I'm not going anywhere."

After he'd pulled her close again, and she pressed her cheek to his chest, she could hear the steady beat of his heart and smell the wonderful scent that was so uniquely his—and somehow what'd happened with her father and Rosemary didn't matter quite as much.

That was the past. Walker was the future.

Reese hadn't expected Rudy to show up. He thought he had to be dreaming when he heard banging on the front door, followed by a familiar voice. "Hey! Walker! You home? Is your mother here?"

Reese blinked at the light streaming through the gaps around the shutters. It didn't seem early, and yet he couldn't hear his mother moving around the house. Was it possible that she was still asleep?

That was unlikely. She always got up early. So where was she?

He hoped she'd hear Rudy and take care of this. But there was no response from anywhere in the house, and Rudy kept banging. "Hello? Anyone home?"

"Mom?" Reese said.

When he didn't get an answer, he rolled out of bed and pulled on a pair of basketball shorts.

"Walker?" Rudy called, continuing to knock. "Will you please answer?"

"Coming!"

When he opened the door, Rudy stepped back and eyed him speculatively. "What are *you* doing here?" he asked.

"I got up to ask you the same thing," Reese replied and had to admit, at least to himself, that Rudy looked better than he had in years. He was showered, clean-shaven, and he no longer had that sickly yellow pallor to his skin. He'd also lost about twenty pounds.

"I'm hoping to find your mother," he said. "I haven't heard from her for more than twenty-four hours, which is unusual, so... I'm worried. Have you seen her?"

"What makes you think she'd be here?" Reese asked, stalling for time while he decided how to handle this visit.

"I already went to Seaclusion. The gardener was there and told me when he texted her to get his check, she said he'd have to get it from Eileen, that she'd moved out. Does that mean Rosemary's been fired? Or did she quit? What happened?"

Reese rubbed a hand over his face. "Give me a sec," he said and closed the door so he could look for her.

He poked his head into her bedroom first. It was empty, but her bed was neatly made. He checked the other rooms, too. She didn't seem to be anywhere in the house.

He hurried to his room to check the dresser where he'd put his keys. They were gone, which meant that she wasn't just out for a walk.

Damn it. She hadn't even asked him. And now he was going to have to deal with Rudy himself.

With a sigh, he trudged back to the front door. "She's not here," he said.

The man he'd believed, until just recently, to be his father studied him closely. "I know you don't like me. But...please. Can we set that aside for a few minutes? Something's going on with your mother. I need to make sure nothing terrible has happened to her."

"I don't know where she is. Maybe she's not interested in

seeing you anymore," he said. He knew that was mean, but he couldn't help it.

Rudy stiffened but didn't get angry. "Even if that's the case, I'd like to at least talk to her. Is that asking too much?"

"Like I said, she's not here. So I don't know what to tell you."

"You're not concerned about her?"

Reese cleared his throat. "I'm sure she's okay. She was okay last night."

"What happened between her and Eileen?"

Reese considered several responses but didn't feel comfortable revealing the truth. What his mother had done was wrong, but she'd had her own struggles, and in some ways, it would've been an easy mistake, given the various elements that were in play at the time. "I think I'll let her tell you about that."

"She's not working there anymore?"

Reese could tell he was shocked. Of course he would be. Rosemary had been with the Madsens since forever. "No."

He seemed frustrated when he couldn't get more information. "That's it? That's all you can give me?"

"I'm sure she'll show up. I'll tell her you came by." Reese started to close the door, but Rudy stopped him.

"I know you don't believe me, Reese, but I really *am* sorry for how I behaved when you were little. I can't go back and right those wrongs, but I can promise you that I'm trying harder, and...and I'd like to have the chance to build a better relationship."

Reese drew a deep breath. Tiller was dead. Rudy was all there was left. In a way, Reese was kind of sad that they wouldn't have a second chance. Rudy seemed far more earnest than he'd ever been before. "Thank you for that," he said.

Rudy's eyebrows shot up. "Are you...are you accepting my apology?"

Reese hesitated. The news that Tiller and not Rudy was his father had changed everything. He still had hard feelings about some of what Rudy had done. But the things that were the hardest to accept—that Rudy hadn't been more interested in Reese, that he hadn't loved him enough to be actively involved in his life—didn't seem to matter anymore.

"I meant what I said," Rudy insisted, obviously taking his hesitation to signify something other than it did. "I'm sorry."

Reese nodded. "It's in the past. But I think you should tell Walker what you just said to me. He's the one who deserves to hear it."

Rudy seemed taken aback. "I will."

30

Walker jolted awake at his desk. He hadn't planned on falling asleep at the station, and he had a crick in his neck to show for it, but it was probably a good thing that he hadn't tried to drive home after his shift ended earlier this morning. He'd been far too tired to get behind the wheel. He wasn't sure he wanted to return to the drama waiting for him at his place, anyway, with his mother and brother in the house.

He alternated between being angry and disgusted over what Rosemary had done. But there was compassion and forgiveness in his heart, too. He hadn't lived her life, had no idea what it'd been like for her at the time she had the affair, so he was reluctant to judge her too harshly. He just didn't want to think about her situation this morning. Why let the happiness he felt slip away while that moment with Marlow at Seaclusion last night was still so fresh in his mind?

I think I could live without almost anything—except you.

Remembering her earnest expression as she said those words made him grin. He had a future with the woman he loved and that was all he'd ever really wanted. Now if he could only convince her not to go back to California at the end of the summer.

Although…with his mother no longer working at Seaclusion, and his brother most likely moving off the island, he wouldn't have to stay here. If Marlow really wanted to go somewhere else, and he had any job prospects there, he could be flexible.

Covering a yawn, he checked the weather on his phone. As of the 5:00 a.m. update, the direction of the storm hadn't changed. Neither had the classification. He was grateful it hadn't been upgraded to a hurricane, but they would still be facing some strong winds.

He needed to finish preparing the island. But first he had to go home, have breakfast and get some more rest.

He forwarded the phone to the officer on duty and got up, but just after he'd turned off the lights and started for the exit, the door swung open, and his father walked in.

Walker hadn't seen Rudy for probably ten years. His father had tried, occasionally, to call or text him, but Walker didn't answer when he saw who it was.

"Hello, Walker."

A surge of adrenaline beat back the grogginess of a moment before. Was this where Rudy asked for his help in convincing Rosemary to give him another chance? Or did he know the truth? Had Rosemary already explained what'd happened between her and Tiller? "Hi," Walker said. "What's up?"

"I'm hoping you can tell me where your mother is."

"She's at my house," he replied. "Why?"

"Reese is at your house. She isn't. And he doesn't seem to know where she went."

Could she have gone back to Seaclusion to get her things? Walker hoped not. He'd asked her to give Eileen more time. "I worked all night, so I don't know." He glanced at his phone in case he'd received a text from her, but there was nothing.

"Will you call her?" Rudy asked. "I can't get her to pick up for me."

Rudy looked good. He seemed to be doing much better, as

their mother kept saying. But Walker wasn't convinced he should step in to help. Knowing Rudy, news of the affair would cause a nasty blowup, and Walker had had enough of Rudy's temper over the years.

"Is there something wrong with checking on her?" Rudy pressed when he didn't act.

Walker supposed there wasn't, so long as he didn't allow himself to be drawn into the coming argument. Actually, maybe he *should* be part of it. He wasn't about to let his father mistreat his mother again, even if Rudy did have a right to be upset this time.

With a sigh, Walker called up his favorites list on his phone and hit the icon for Rosemary.

She picked up on the third ring, just before he expected it to go to voice mail.

"Hey," he said when he heard her voice. "Where are you?"

"I had to run an errand."

"What kind of errand?"

"A personal one," she said.

He couldn't even guess what that meant, but it was easy to tell she wasn't going to say any more. "Dad's on the island. Did you know that?"

His announcement was met with silence. Then she said, "No."

"Can I talk to her?" Rudy asked, interrupting. "Why won't she answer my calls?"

Walker lifted a hand to acknowledge that he'd heard what Rudy said but didn't intend to pass over his phone. "Mom? Are you okay?"

He heard her release a shaky breath. "Yeah. I guess I'd better tell him and get it over with," she said. "Are you at home?"

"No. Rudy and I are at the station."

"I need to bring Reese's truck back. He doesn't usually work on Mondays, but he has a rich client who's offered to pay him double if he'll come in at noon. So tell your father to meet me at your place."

"Will do." The way his mother was acting—as if she was about to face a firing squad—made Walker protective. He planned to be there with her when she told Rudy the truth.

"Have you heard from Dutton?" Aida asked Claire while reaching for the butter.

Claire looked pensive as she shook her head. "It's been ominously quiet." She'd gotten up early and done yoga on the beach. Aida knew that was how she kept herself centered and thought it was probably a great coping tactic. But she hadn't been able to make herself do the same. She and Marlow had just crawled out of bed, so this was the first time they'd seen Claire today.

Aida glanced over at Marlow. "Do you think he's left?" Marlow wouldn't know any more than they did, of course, but she'd shepherded Aida through the entire divorce, and Aida was used to asking her opinion.

"Dutton's not the type to go away easily, not when he's *this* mad," Marlow said.

Aida opened a jar of cherry preserves for her toast. She wouldn't have known Rosemary had canned the cherries if she hadn't asked earlier, but the way Marlow stiffened at any mention of their housekeeper served as further evidence that whatever was going on with Marlow and her mother had to do with Rosemary. Aida, like Claire, was still waiting for Marlow to open up and explain exactly what was wrong, but both Rosemary and Reese seemed to have moved out. Aida had texted Reese to see if he might tell her why, but he hadn't responded.

After all the years Rosemary had worked for the Madsens, why would she quit now?

The door opened, and Marlow's mother stepped out to join them on the deck. Although Eileen had her hair done and her makeup on, as always, she appeared wan and tired. And her eyes were red and puffy. Whatever it was that Marlow was reluctant to discuss with them had hit Eileen hard, too. "I assume you slept well," Eileen said with a smile that didn't quite reach her eyes.

"We did," Aida said, but she was putting up a front, too. She'd mostly tossed and turned. Every creak, every noise made her fear Dutton had come to cause trouble. She guessed Claire hadn't slept any better. She didn't want to tell Eileen about Dutton, though. Aida hoped there'd be no reason for her to have to know.

Marlow got up, hugged her mother and helped her to the table. "What can I get you to eat?" she asked.

"I'm not hungry," Eileen replied.

Marlow scowled in concern. "You should eat *something*."

"I'll grab a bite later."

Although Marlow was obviously tempted to say more on the subject, she let it go. "You've heard about the storm that's coming, haven't you?"

Eileen seemed startled by the news. "There's a storm on the way? Not a hurricane..."

"No, not yet. And hopefully, it won't turn into one."

North Dakota had cold winters but no earthquakes or hurricanes and fewer tornadoes than most other states. Aida had no idea what to expect.

Eileen glanced around the house and yard. "Are we ready?"

"I'll go online and download a list of preparedness items and see what I can do," Marlow told her.

Marlow and her mother seemed to be taking the storm seriously, which was a concern. Maybe it'd be worse than Aida anticipated.

She checked her phone. She still hadn't heard from Dutton. But no news wasn't necessarily good news.

"Anything?" Claire murmured as Marlow and her mother continued to talk.

Aida shook her head. "Nope. What about you?"

Claire pulled out her phone. "Nothing."

"It can't be this easy, can it?" Aida whispered.

"Is something wrong?" Eileen asked.

Aida shifted her attention to Marlow's mother. "Just worried about the storm," she said. But she was far less worried about what was coming than what was already here.

Rosemary could see the fear on Rudy's face when he arrived at Walker's. It was plain that he thought she was going to break things off with him, that she'd decided it was over. The irony there was that after he learned what she had to say, *he'd* probably do the honors.

"What is it?" he asked as soon as he got out of the car. "What do you have to tell me?"

She handed Reese's keys to Walker, who'd pulled up at the same time, and beckoned Rudy to walk with her down to the beach. This was going to be difficult enough without others, especially their son, listening in.

Walker, not convinced he could trust his father, remained in the driveway, where he could keep an eye on him.

"I don't understand what's happening," Rudy said. "If you're done with me, you could've told me instead of making me worry all day and night."

A gust of wind blew Rosemary's hair into her face. She had to hold it back with one hand. "It's worse than you're thinking, Rudy."

He gave her an incredulous look. "What could be worse than that?"

"Reese is going to inherit twenty percent of Tiller's estate."

It took him a moment to absorb that before he said, "Twenty percent is probably a lot of money."

"We don't know the exact figure, but we're guessing it's significant."

"Why so much? Why Reese and not Walker?"

Rosemary braced for his reaction. She'd promised herself she wouldn't cry, but tears were filling her eyes anyway. "Because Reese is Tiller's son."

He gasped and brought one hand to his chest as if she'd shot him. "What did you say?"

"I'm sorry," she whispered.

His gaze cut to Walker, who was still watching them. Rudy opened his mouth to say something only to close it again. Then he pinched the area between his shoulder and collarbone as if it pained him. "And the boys—and Eileen and Marlow—already know this?"

Rosemary turned her face into the wind. "Yes. Marlow found out when she went to see the attorney about the estate on Saturday. Eileen learned when she got back."

"That's why you're not working there anymore. That's why you moved out."

She wiped the tears rolling down her cheeks. "It's why Reese moved out, too."

When Rudy hunched over slightly, she wondered if he was having trouble breathing. "You and Tiller had an affair. How long did it last? Was it...was it our whole marriage, or—"

"No," she said. "It was three weeks. Neither of us meant for it to happen, and we felt terrible afterward."

"If it was for such a short time, how do you know Reese isn't mine?"

She hated to dash his hopes, but there was no chance. "Tiller took a paternity test."

"And that's why he paid for so much shit."

"Yes." She bowed her head, waiting for the rage to come. The accusations. The recriminations. The blame for the destruction of their marriage.

But none of that came. He didn't even raise his voice.

"Excuse me. I, um, I'm going to need some time," he said and walked back to his car, got in and drove away.

Walker watched him go. Then he came out to meet her. "You okay?"

She couldn't talk for the lump clogging her throat, and the tears began to fall much faster. She nodded, but she could tell her son knew that wasn't the truth when he drew her in for a hug.

"We all make mistakes," he said. "I'm grateful for everything you've done for me—and for Reese."

"I'm s-s-sorry," she stuttered and felt his arms tighten reassuringly around her.

"I know."

31

Shortly after Marlow finished eating, Walker texted her to say that the National Hurricane Center, which posted a bulletin every six hours, had upgraded the tropical cyclone to a Category 1 hurricane with wind speeds between seventy-four and ninety-five miles per hour. A storm of that strength could cause some damage, but the real fear was that it could get stronger before it hit the island.

He gave her a few locations where they could pick up sandbags to help protect the guesthouse and garage—the main house was up on stilts and less likely to flood. So Marlow asked Claire and Aida to go to the library, which was the closest of those locations, and get as many bags as they could fit in the Jeep and Tesla while she stayed at Seaclusion with her mother.

Earlier, when she'd carried out the dishes they'd used for breakfast, she'd noticed that Eileen had torn up quite a few of Tiller's pictures, and as angry as Marlow was with her father, she found that almost as upsetting as everything else they were dealing with. She didn't want to do anything, or let her mother do anything, they might later regret.

"I want those burned," her mother announced when she saw

that Marlow was picking up the memorabilia. "Let's build a bon-fire. We'll take it all out and burn it while Aida and Claire are gone. We'll get rid of his shoes, clothes, everything."

Marlow remembered standing in her parents' closet just a few days ago when her mother couldn't bear to part with *any-thing* that had belonged to her father. "We shouldn't burn his clothes and shoes. There are people who could make use of those things."

"Then donate it. Get rid of it. That's all I care about. I don't want to see any of it ever again."

"I'll box these up and as many of his things as I can before Claire and Aida get back. But we need to worry about the storm first—and that might be a good thing. Maybe after more time has passed, you'll change your mind, at least about destroying his pictures."

She hobbled closer. "I won't," she insisted. "I'll never forgive him. How could he do what he did? An affair would be bad enough. But he cheated with *Rosemary*!"

One of the pictures Eileen had ruined had been taken the day Marlow was born and showed her father cradling her in his arms. That it had been destroyed made Marlow angry with her mother instead of her father. "You ripped this up?" she said, holding several of the pieces so Eileen could see what she was talking about.

"Why would you care?" her mother responded. "You should be as mad as I am."

Marlow sat on the floor, where she tried to put the picture together again. "I'm sorry you've been hurt, Mom. I'm sorry for what Dad did, but—"

"But what?" she interrupted, her voice like velvet over steel. "He didn't even have the decency to cheat with someone I could understand him getting involved with. He slept with our housekeeper!"

The way she was talking, as if Rosemary was so far beneath them she shouldn't have been appealing, bothered Marlow. Rosemary had been an integral part of their lives. She'd been good to them, despite this. And she was Walker's mother. "Please don't talk about her like that."

Her mother gripped the back of a chair to hold herself steady. "Now you're going to defend her?"

"I'm just trying to be fair."

"To her or to me?" she cried.

Marlow rubbed her temples. She could feel a headache coming on. "Mom, you loved Rosemary, too. I can't count the number of times you've said you couldn't have gotten by without her. She did so much for this family for so long."

"She took care of everything, all right—including my husband."

Struggling with an onslaught of conflicting emotions, Marlow drew a deep breath. "That's true," she said evenly. "But think of this. She could've gone public with the affair— either when it happened or once she realized Reese belonged to Dad. Think how humiliating that would've been. It would've caused a media frenzy, torn your marriage apart, broken up our family and ruined Dad's career."

"You expect me to give her credit for not making matters even worse?" Eileen shouted. "She had sex with my husband!"

Marlow knew it was probably premature to try to get her mother to look at the situation from a more understanding perspective, but she couldn't help it. Maybe it was the lawyer in her. Or maybe it was all the crap she'd seen spouses do to each other over the years. "Dad could've left you for her, but he didn't. He didn't even put her in his will. What do you make of that?"

"I make nothing of it," she snapped. "He put Reese in his will. Reese is going to walk away with three million dollars. That's bad enough."

"It's only twenty percent of the estate."

"What's wrong with you? Why are you defending them?"

"I just... I'm having a hard time suddenly hating people we've always loved. I mean...if you were Dad, wouldn't you want to leave your son something? Reese didn't do anything wrong. He's completely innocent."

Her mother's lips formed a colorless line. "You don't mind that he's getting part of your inheritance?"

"I don't want to value money over people. It's not like we're going to be destitute."

"I can't believe you're saying all this!"

"I know it's hard for you. But I want you to understand that, while Dad and Rosemary's actions aren't anything to be proud of, when you look at the situation a little more closely, you find evidence that they both did what they could to protect you. They loved you."

She shook her head. "I no longer believe that."

"*I* do," Marlow said. "It seems to me they both sincerely regretted what they did. They acted to minimize any impact it would have on you—or me, for that matter—even though having Tiller for a father would've been better for Reese. Rosemary didn't have any real hope of saving her marriage, so she didn't keep the affair a secret for her own benefit. She could've created so much more damage than she did. She could even have tried to take Dad from you."

"She never would've gotten away with that!" her mother broke in vehemently.

"Maybe not," Marlow conceded. "But as I've said, she acted to protect Dad's career as well as our family."

"Whose side are you on?" her mother asked, drawing back in horror.

Marlow dropped her head in her hands. "Yours, of course. I'm always on your side. Part of me doesn't even know why I'm pointing out these nuances to you. I'm as hurt and angry as you are. But I want to be fair. I don't want to destroy Dad's memory and Rosemary's life when she could've destroyed ours but chose not to."

"Believe me, she did as much as she felt she could get away with."

"That's not true! She moved into this house after Dad died just so you wouldn't be alone. Would she do that if she didn't care about you?"

"I paid her well, especially when you consider everything we covered over the years."

"You did. But she gave this family more than most people give a job. I can't justify her involvement with Dad, but maybe it'll help if you know more about how it happened. Reese told me the affair lasted for only three weeks, Mom. They realized very quickly that they'd made a terrible mistake and put a stop to it. If she hadn't gotten pregnant during that brief time, no one would even know it happened."

"How can you believe anything she says after what we've learned? They could've been sleeping together all along."

"I don't think that's the case," Marlow argued. "You know Dad. He was a good man. And Rosemary's always been a sincere person. She has no reason to make up a story about how the affair happened—you've already fired her."

Her mother didn't seem to know what to say. Bursting into tears, she pointed at the door. "Get out. I can't have you here right now."

Claire and Aida had filled twenty sandbags apiece and delivered them to Seaclusion. They'd also helped Marlow position them around the doors of the guesthouse and the garage. But despite using both vehicles, they hadn't been able to get as many as they needed. The bags weighed thirty pounds each. Without a truck that could handle a bigger payload, they could transport only ten at a time. So Marlow was driving the Tesla back to the library, hoping they'd still have some bags and sand, and

Claire and Aida were taking shovels over to city hall, another one of the locations Walker had given them, in case the library was out of supplies.

It'd been such a busy afternoon that Claire had all but forgotten about Dutton—until she saw a lone figure who looked extremely familiar walking along the road as they drove back to Seaclusion.

"Aida," she said, holding the steering wheel with one hand while reaching over to grab her friend's arm.

Aida looked where she pointed and gasped. "That's him!"

Dutton was wearing a ball cap, sunglasses, a windbreaker—the wind was getting stronger and stronger as the day wore on—and he had his head down, staring at the pavement in front of him. But there was no mistaking his identity.

Claire slammed on the brakes. She wanted to see why he was on this side of the island—and how confrontational he might be. That could tell her whether they had anything to worry about…

But when she pulled over in front of him, and he looked up, he didn't show any surprise. He knew exactly where he was and how close he was to where they were staying.

"What's he up to?" she murmured.

"He's trying to scare us," Aida replied.

He was doing a good job of it. His lips curved into a mocking smile, almost as if he was saying, "I don't care if you see me. I *want* you to see me. I'm right here, only a stone's throw away from where you sleep at night, and you can't make me leave."

"What are you doing?" Aida cried when Claire opened the door.

"I'm going to talk to him."

Dutton came to a stop as soon as he saw her get out. He had his hands in his pockets, but he still made Claire uneasy.

"I… I thought maybe you'd gone home," she said.

"Why would I leave the island?" he asked. "I have a whole

week's vacation, remember? There's no way I'm going to let you ruin that."

"I wasn't trying to ruin your vacation, Dutton. I admit I should've done more to stop you from coming. I'm sorry I didn't. But I... I thought we still had a chance. So I hope you're not going to—I don't know—try to punish me for not getting back with you."

"I'm not mad that you didn't get back with me," he said. "I was stupid to want you to begin with. I'm mad that you led me on. You acted as if you had fun yesterday morning. You said you were coming over for dinner."

"I *did* have fun yesterday," she said. "That's not leading you on. I made it clear that I wasn't sure about us. The fact that I wouldn't have sex with you should've told you *something*. It wasn't until you got to Teach that I realized... I realized that no matter how much I love you, I can't be with you."

He laughed without mirth. "There you go again—teasing me, Claire. You don't love me." His eyes cut to Aida, who was still in the car but had lowered her window. "You and Aida did this on purpose. You probably think it's funny that you got me to take a whole week off and squander thousands of dollars on a vacation I'd have to spend alone."

"That's not true," Claire insisted. He had everything so twisted in his mind. "It was *your* idea! I tried to tell you not to come, but you wouldn't listen to me."

"All I have to say is that you're going to live to regret what you've done."

She stepped back. "Are you threatening me?"

"He's dangerous, Claire," Aida said, raising her voice so they could hear her. "Get back in the car."

He pointed at Aida. "*You* stay out of it!"

Afraid of where this would lead, Claire tried one last time to talk some sense into him. "Dutton, please. There's a hurricane coming. Go home. I... I'll send you some money to cover the trip, if that's what you want. I can't do it now, but when I get back on my feet."

"I don't want your money," he said. "I just want you to be as miserable as I am."

She wished she could read his eyes, find some semblance of the man she thought she knew. But all she could see was herself in his mirrored sunglasses. "What's that supposed to mean?"

He didn't answer. He gave her that weird smile again, held up his hand in the shape of a gun and pretended to fire.

She caught her breath. "That's not funny."

"You might not think so, but I do," he said.

She could hear him laughing as she hurried back to the car and got behind the wheel. Wanting to put as much distance between them as possible, she drove off immediately.

But Seaclusion was only a quarter of a mile away.

Rosemary knew she should probably be out preparing their part of the island for the coming storm. Walker had slept only a few hours before leaving again. And Reese had called to say he was bagging sand for the club. She should be helping as well, but she was too caught up in her personal crisis to care about the hurricane.

She went into the bathroom and locked the door in case either of her boys came back. Then she sat on the toilet lid and opened the bag of letters she'd retrieved from under the house at Seaclusion this morning. To get them, she'd had to park down the street and sneak onto the property before anyone was awake. She'd also had to stash them under a rock along the side of the road not far away when she found out Rudy was going to meet her here the moment she returned. But she had them safely in her possession now.

Taking out the first one, her fingers encountered a folded piece of plain paper, and she began to read.

Dear Rosemary,

I'm sorry about last night. I know what we did was wrong. But there's just something about you. It's that simple. You are steady and calm and levelheaded and loyal. I know none of those things probably sound very sexy. Would you rather hear that you're gorgeous, irresistible? You are both of those things. But it's the beauty of your heart that draws me to you. You are such a fine person. Please don't quit and go elsewhere. I won't press you for...you know...again. Just stay near me.

Love,

John

She put that letter on the vanity and pulled out another. None of them were dated, so she didn't even try to read them in order.

This one had obviously been written several months after the first one.

Dear Rosemary,

Your response breaks my heart. But I know you're right and that we would only be sad about the people we hurt. I love Eileen, want what's best for her in spite of how I've behaved. And you know how much I adore my little girl. But giving you up isn't easy. Just know that if your baby is mine, or even if it's not, I'll be there for you. He or she will never want for anything.

Love,

John

As she read the other letters he'd written over a span of six or seven months, the memories they conjured up in her mind were so vivid. When she'd first started working for the Madsens, she'd had limited contact with Tiller—had dealt mostly with Eileen—but slowly, over the years, they'd not only grown to know each other, they'd developed a mutual trust and admiration. At some point, that trust and admiration had led to a hormone-fueled three weeks, during which the relationship had flared out of control, and after that they'd struggled through several long years of trying to maintain the proper boundaries. In the end, however, mostly during the last decade, their relationship had evolved into a deeper and more abiding love than ever before—one born more out of mutual respect than lust or anything else.

She hadn't expected him to include Reese in his will. But he'd kept his word about looking out for her child—both of her children, actually. She'd kept her word, too. She'd stayed by his side, even though he had a family himself. The love she'd felt for him was never the same kind of love she'd felt for Rudy. The two men were so different. What she'd felt for Tiller, at least most of the time, was based more on what her head was telling her. She respected him. She admired him. She appreciated who he was and what he did. Her love for Rudy was almost inexplicable—a raw attraction that didn't always make sense. Still, if Tiller's work hadn't required so much of his focus and attention, they might not have been able to move past the affair while remaining part of each other's lives.

After she'd finished reading his letters, she put them in the bag that had protected them for so long and leaned back. She had proof to support everything she'd said about Tiller. But that wasn't why she'd saved them. As long as she hung on to them, it felt as though she held a part of him, too. *Her* part. A part no one else had.

She wondered if turning these letters over to Eileen, Marlow or Rudy—any of the people who'd been hurt—would help them understand what'd happened. How hard they'd tried to be honorable and do the right thing for everyone involved. But it would be almost impossible to understand what their relationship had been like without more context, which meant the letters would probably just cause greater harm.

It was time, she realized—time to save Tiller's words only in her heart.

Taking the bag, she went down to the beach and lit a fire in the firepit before taking the letters out, one by one, and tossing them in.

The edges of each curled and glowed orange before turning black. Then small pieces began to flutter into the sky. It was so hard to watch his handwriting disappear, knowing he could never write her again. But, like Eileen, she had to let him go. He'd never been hers to begin with.

After there was nothing left except ash, she tilted her head back and gazed up at the wide blue sky and the tiny fragments of paper blowing in the wind. "Goodbye," she whispered.

As she trudged back to the house, she hated knowing that the letters she'd saved and treasured for so long were gone. But there was a strange peace that came with doing the right thing.

Once she went inside, she slid her phone off the counter and navigated to Eileen's contact record. Her employer's last text message stared her in the face: I hope you rot in hell.

I'm sorry to hear that, she wrote back. I wish you—and have always wished you—nothing but the best.

32

Marlow could see that Claire was worried. She sat on the sofa in the guesthouse, twisting her hands in her lap while telling Marlow everything that'd happened when she and Aida found Dutton walking on the side of the road not far from Seaclusion. "I'm sorry I got us into this mess," she said as soon as she finished the story. "I should've known better than to keep in touch with him after everything he put you both through during the divorce. You tried to warn me." She shot Aida, who was with them, a sheepish glance before returning her attention to Marlow. "Are you mad?"

After what she'd heard, Marlow could no longer remain sitting. She came to her feet and began to pace. "I *am* mad, but not at you. Dutton's not going to start harassing us. Things are difficult enough without him." And they knew why, since she'd finally been able to bring herself to explain what was going on with her mother.

"But...what can we do to stop him?" Aida asked. "You tried to get a restraining order against him before, and the judge wouldn't grant it."

"Dutton will be gone before we know it," Claire said. "We

won't have time to get a restraining order. We just have to make sure he doesn't do anything to hurt us in the next five days. Then he'll be on the other side of the country, and hopefully, once we get back to California, he'll be involved with someone else and won't feel the need to torment us."

"I wouldn't count on that," Aida said dryly. "He can hold a grudge like nobody's business."

"That tells you the kind of person he is right there," Marlow muttered.

"He had no reason to be on this side of the island when we saw him," Claire said. "He *had* to be looking for Seaclusion, trying to see where we're staying. And he made it clear he didn't care that we came across him."

"He was *glad* we did," Aida corrected. "He's trying to intimidate us."

"Everyone on the island is so busy getting prepared for the hurricane he probably feels he can do whatever he wants and no one will notice," Marlow said. "Think about it. Once the wind and the rain start up in earnest, no one will even be outside."

"What do you think he might do?" Claire asked.

"I could see him vandalizing the guesthouse or cutting up our clothes or something like that," Aida said. "During the divorce, before I moved out, he took my makeup, dumped it into the sink and smeared it around the rest of the bathroom. It was so hard to clean up. And he wrote *greedy bitch* on the mirror with my lipstick."

"He's not going to get away with that kind of behavior here," Marlow said. "We're going to be ready for him."

"How?" Claire asked.

Marlow scooped her phone off the coffee table. "Walker might have just what we need."

Aida adjusted the hoop earring that'd gotten caught in her hair. "Yeah, maybe you should tell Walker what's going on."

"I don't want to take his attention away from his job," Marlow said. "Who knows how bad this storm will get. People might need him. We can handle Dutton."

"We can?" Aida didn't sound too convinced.

"You'll see." Marlow called Walker, and he answered on the first ring.

"You ready for the storm?" he asked without preamble.

"Yeah. We've been filling sandbags all day."

"Is there anything you need me to do?"

"I could use one small favor."

"Of course. What is it?"

"Do you have a stun gun I could borrow?"

There was a slight pause. Then he said, "Did you say *stun gun*?"

"Yeah."

"Why would you need a stun gun?"

She explained what'd happened between Dutton and Claire. "I doubt he'll try to harm us," she said at the end. "He has too much to lose. But he likes to make us uncomfortable, and I wouldn't put it past him to do something malicious if he thinks he can get away with it. So we'd like to be able to defend ourselves, just in case."

"Malicious," Walker repeated, and it was easy to tell he didn't like the sound of that word. "Tell me this. On a scale of one to ten, how likely do you think it is that he'll give you any serious trouble?"

It'd been unsettling, almost creepy, to have Dutton following her around in LA. But he hadn't actually done anything he could be charged with, hadn't crossed the line far enough that she could get a restraining order. "Maybe…a five?" she guessed.

"You're saying there's a fifty-fifty chance? Should I come stay with you?"

"No," she replied. "There're people who are counting on you. Seriously, we'll be fine if I can just borrow a stun gun."

Someone said something to Walker in the background, and his voice dimmed as he responded to whoever it was. "There *is* a lot going on," he admitted when he came back on the line. "I remember one of my officers telling me he bought a stun gun off the internet for his wife when they were living in Miami. She had to work in a pretty rough neighborhood, and he wanted her to have it for self-defense. I'll see if he'll loan it to me. Then I'll swing by and teach you how to use it."

"Thank you."

"Marlow?" he said before she could hang up.

"Yes?"

"Where is this asshole staying?"

Marlow promised to get the address of the rental from Claire and text it to him.

"I'll swing by and have a little chat with him," Walker said, "let him know that there'll be hell to pay if he does anything to harm anyone. And you'll have the stun gun as insurance."

"Perfect. Thank you."

"I can't wait until this storm is over," he said.

"I bet. You sound exhausted."

"It's not just sleep I'm missing."

She smiled. "You're missing me?"

"Damn right I am."

"Let's hope it'll be over soon."

The National Hurricane Center reclassified the storm as a Category 2 hurricane first thing in the morning, but they lowered it back down to a Category 1 before it reached the island, and even then it didn't hit Teach straight on. Because it'd started to twist to the right and head farther up the coast, it delivered more of a glancing blow, but the sky was dark hours before sunset and the wind was so strong the palm tree out front was bending over like a maître d'.

Marlow and her friends traipsed across the yard in the rain to reach the main house so her mother wouldn't have to wait out the storm alone. Eileen hadn't spoken to Marlow since she'd stood up for Rosemary and taken what remained of her father's pictures to the guesthouse. She could understand why Eileen might see that as a betrayal of sorts. But she hoped her mother would eventually heal enough to understand.

For now, however, Eileen was still mad. When they filed into the house, she pretended as though she wasn't relieved to see them, as if it didn't matter whether they were there or not. But Marlow could tell it was all an act. Eileen had to be at her lowest point. She had to be worried about the storm, too. For the first time in decades, she had no hired help to look after her, and she wasn't as mobile as most people if it became necessary to evacuate.

Marlow made popcorn and put on a movie, hoping to distract everyone from the wind and the rain battering the island, but she remained conscious of the fact that this would be the perfect time to strike if Dutton wanted to cause a little mayhem. Walker and his officers were focused elsewhere, and depending on what Dutton did, he could make it difficult to determine whether he was to blame, it was someone else, or it was the hurricane. Although, if she had her guess, he'd want to do something subtle enough to create ambiguity, so he couldn't be caught, yet personal enough to let her, Aida and Claire know he'd taken his revenge.

After the third time she got up to walk through the house—she couldn't see out the windows; the storm shutters were closed and locked—Eileen finally deigned to ask her a question. Prior to that moment, her mother would only speak if someone directed a comment or question to her. "Why do you keep prowling around?"

"I'm just making sure the storm isn't causing any damage," Marlow responded. There was no reason to upset her mother by telling her about the situation with Dutton. There was nothing Eileen could do to help, anyway. As promised, Walker had provided Marlow with his officer's wife's stun gun, which was in her purse, but Dutton hadn't been at the rental cottage when Walker stopped by. Walker had told her he'd try to get over there again, but he was so caught up with the hurricane that she knew he probably wouldn't get the chance—not today. His last text indicated there was some flash flooding downtown. Trying to protect the businesses in that area was more important than stopping Aida's vengeful ex-husband from ruining their makeup, keying one of the cars or cutting up their clothes.

They watched three movies before Aida and Claire said they were tired. It was getting late, but Marlow didn't want to leave her mother alone. Most hurricanes lasted a day or two, so they had a while yet to go.

Before she could open her mouth to say she'd be staying at the main house, however, the power went out.

"There it goes," Eileen said as if she'd been expecting it, and Marlow turned on the battery-powered lantern they had on hand while Aida and Claire lit several candles.

Losing power wasn't unusual during such a big storm. Marlow got a flashlight so she could walk her friends over to the guesthouse—the stun gun in her hand—but when she carefully cracked open the door to check if the coast was clear, she noticed something odd: there were lights on in the guesthouse.

"Can the electricity go out over here but stay on in other parts of the property?" she asked her mother.

"I don't see how," her mother replied, "unless someone threw the circuit breaker on the outside panel of just this house. Why? Are the lights still working over there?"

"They are." Marlow quickly closed and locked the door. If Dutton had cut their power, she wasn't going to give him the opportunity to hurt someone. If he caused damage to their belongings or the property in general, they could deal with that in the morning.

But while they were telling her mother about Dutton, after

all, she heard two men yelling outside. One said, "What the hell do you think you're doing?"

She knew she wasn't the only one who heard snatches of that sentence above the keening wail of the wind when Aida and Claire covered their mouths as their eyes went wide.

"That doesn't sound like Dutton," Aida said.

The door reverberated as someone or something smashed into it. Then they heard more muffled voices and a curse. Silence fell—right before a male voice called her name. "Marlow, open the door!"

"Oh, my gosh!" Claire said. "That's Reese, isn't it?"

"Why would *he* be here?" Eileen asked.

Marlow had no idea, but she'd recognized Reese's voice, too. Getting the stun gun ready just in case, she told Aida to open the door.

The wind grabbed the wooden panel out of Aida's hand almost immediately and slammed it against the inside wall as the beam of Marlow's flashlight landed on a soaked Reese, who had a trickle of blood coming from a busted lip. He had Dutton in a headlock, but Dutton was flailing around, doing everything he could to get loose, so Marlow used the stun gun to subdue him.

His body locked up, sending him crashing to the floor, and Reese let him go. "Wow. Nice work," he said as he dragged a stunned and moaning Dutton inside.

"What happened? What are you doing here?" Marlow cried as Reese shoved Dutton's legs out of the way so he could close the door.

"Walker asked me to look out for you. He told you might have an unwelcome visitor tonight. And sure enough, I caught this dickhead lurking around. I waited to see what he was going to do, but when he cut the power, I decided to let him know he had company."

Trying to stop him had obviously resulted in a fight, but it appeared that Dutton had gotten the worst of it. His eye was swelling, there was a cut on his cheek and he had a bloody nose—not that she cared about Dutton's injuries.

"Are you okay?" Marlow asked Reese.

He wiped the blood from his mouth with the back of his hand. "Yeah. Dude freaked out when he realized I'd caught him. I wasn't about to let him get away, but forcing him to the house was easier said than done."

She readied her stun gun; Dutton was getting back up.

"Don't shock me again," he said, lifting a defensive hand. "I haven't done anything."

"You're trespassing," Marlow pointed out.

"So?" he said. "The police aren't going to throw me in jail for turning off someone's power."

"What else were you planning to do?" Aida asked.

"Nothing!" he insisted. "I was just trying to scare you—I swear it."

Reese gestured at a chair. "Sit your ass down where I can see you, because you're not going anywhere until Walker gets here."

"Who's Walker?" Dutton asked.

"The chief of police who *is* going to throw your ass in jail, at least for the night."

Dutton glowered at him. "And who the hell are you?"

Reese flung the wet hair out of his eyes and grinned as he jerked his head toward Marlow. "I'm her brother."

33

The wind was still blowing full force when Walker arrived. Eileen shivered against it, feeling the draft even though she sat on the sofa covered by a blanket Marlow had gotten for her.

Reese let his brother in, using his body weight to close the door, and Walker wiped the rain from his face as his eyes circled the group. Marlow had given the stun gun to Reese in case Dutton tried to force his way out of the house while she went out to restore their power, so they no longer needed the emergency lantern or candles. But the lavender scent of the candles lingered in the air, along with the musty smell of the wet earth Marlow had brought back inside with her.

Eileen noticed that Walker paused briefly when he saw her sitting next to Aida and Claire, and she wondered what he was thinking. Was he afraid he wasn't welcome in her house? Was he remembering everything she'd said the last time he was here? She'd behaved so badly she was embarrassed now.

Regardless of how his opinion of her might've changed, he nodded respectfully before shifting his attention to their unwanted guest. "So this is the asshole who won't take no for an answer."

Dutton had stopped professing his innocence. Eileen guessed he knew it wasn't going to do him any good. In the twenty minutes they'd had to wait for Walker to free himself from whatever he was doing, Dutton had grown sullen.

"What were you planning to do when you cut the power?" Walker asked him.

Dutton glared at Walker without speaking.

"You know we're in the middle of a hurricane?" Walker said. "Causing problems right now is a dangerous thing to do. It could cost a life—maybe more than one."

"I want an attorney," he said. "I'm a doctor, not some scumbag you can throw in jail for no reason."

"Well, *Doctor*," Walker said, "I don't know if a lawyer is going to do you much good. The fact that Marlow tried to get a restraining order against you in California, and now you've followed her all the way to Florida, where you've shown up on her property and cut the power in the middle of a hurricane makes for a fairly strong case that you're a threat to her well-being. I'm not sure the next judge will give you quite as much leeway because of your medical degree as the last one."

If Dutton was afraid Walker spoke the truth, he was determined not to show it. "I just want to go home."

He still seemed to think that was an option, but Walker shook his head. "Sorry. That won't be possible, not until you've taken care of your legal troubles here on Teach. But the good news is that, since you're a *doctor*, you should have the money you'll need to mount a defense." He took his handcuffs from his utility belt. "Stand up and turn around."

Dutton was wearing a windbreaker and jogging shorts—not exactly the type of clothing one would choose to wear out in a hurricane. Eileen assumed he hadn't packed anything warmer, expecting a sunny vacation without considering the possibility of a major storm. So not only was he wet, he was visibly cold. Marlow had picked up a blanket for Reese when she'd gotten

Eileen one, but she hadn't offered Dutton anything. He was shivering violently when he finally rose to his feet and turned so that Walker could cuff him.

Marlow stood up and moved toward Walker—and seemed to be carefully avoiding even a glance at Dutton. "How's the flooding in town?"

"If the storm passes soon, we'll get away with minimal damage," he replied. "I think everything's going to be okay."

"What does the National Hurricane Center say?" Eileen asked.

He looked over at her as though slightly startled she'd speak to him. "They think we've seen the worst of it."

This brought relief, a reason to celebrate. Eileen had been tense and upset for so long. First the pandemic. Then Tiller died and the nasty surprise of his affair with Rosemary was revealed in his will. And no sooner did she learn about that than the first hurricane of the season hit. Those were all things outside her control. But she hadn't improved the situation with the way she'd responded to those unfortunate events.

As she watched her daughter interact with Walker, it was easy to see that the kiss she'd witnessed between them on the deck hadn't been as casual as Marlow had made it sound. Marlow cared about him. Maybe she was even in love with him. Her body language certainly suggested it. She cared about Reese, too, of course. And Eileen couldn't expect that to change. Marlow had been raised with Rosemary's boys. Their lives, and hers and Rosemary's, were woven together so tightly it would be impossible to separate them.

She could remove herself from the friendship, love and unity they shared if she really wanted to, but would appeasing her anger and wounded pride over something that happened twenty-three years ago be worth the cost? Did she want to be completely isolated from those she loved? To stand off to one side as her daughter grew closer and closer to Walker and Reese—and maybe even Rosemary?

She let her breath go in a deep sigh. Allowing anger and bitterness to take control, especially now, with Tiller gone and their lives moving in a new direction, would not only hurt Marlow, Walker and Reese, three people who were totally innocent, it would hurt her worst of all. As much as she was tempted by her anger to let one event define Rosemary, to use what Rosemary had done with Tiller to block out all the loyalty and love Rosemary had given her through the years, life was never that simple.

Just like anyone else, Rosemary was neither all good nor all bad. And deep down, Eileen knew she was better than most.

"You're so tired," she could hear Marlow say to Walker at the door. "I'm worried about you."

"I'll be okay," he said. "We're almost through this."

"Please be careful." It didn't seem to matter that he was soaking wet. Marlow kissed him as though she was afraid she'd never see him again and came away wet herself.

Marlow's concern for Walker reminded Eileen of the love and devotion she'd always felt for Tiller. That had never faded, even after learning of his affair, she realized.

Although the pain of his betrayal was still with her, a sharp, steady ache beneath the surface, she hoped that would fade with time. But regardless of how she was feeling, she couldn't put off the choice she faced in this moment. She could square her shoulders and absorb the blow, making it easier for everyone by accepting what'd happened and forgiving Rosemary.

Or she could be far less generous—and be the one who would ultimately pay the highest price.

"You have a faraway look on your face, Mom," Marlow said, coming to kneel beside her once Walker and Reese had taken Dutton and gone. "Are you okay?"

Tears rolled down her cheeks. The next few days would set

the tone for the rest of her life. Maybe Marlow's, too. "I'm fine," she said. "I'm going to be just fine—and so are you."

Marlow slipped into the bathroom at the guesthouse while Aida and Claire were watching a movie. It was late, almost two in the morning, but time didn't seem to mean much lately. In the five days since the storm, they'd fallen into a much slower rhythm, sleeping in, playing tennis or chess, swimming in the ocean, hunting for shells or shopping and eating—with Walker or Reese or both of them, depending on who had to work.

Marlow also spent time with her mother whenever Claire and Aida went to a public beach. Eileen had finally agreed to let her box up her father's belongings. She didn't want to be part of the packing process, didn't want to so much as see the objects she most associated with Tiller. But the animosity she'd felt right after she learned about the affair seemed to be waning. Now she was just trying to heal and recover. Marlow could tell, and she could understand, since she was trying to do the same. She hoped, one day, they could both feel good about Tiller and Rosemary again.

"Marlow, you're going to miss the best part!" Aida called. "Do you want us to pause the movie?"

"No. It's fine," she called back. "I'll be there in a minute." Marlow hadn't been paying much attention to the movie to begin with. Tonight, all she'd been able to think about was the pregnancy test in her purse. She wasn't that late for her period and kept telling Walker it didn't mean anything, but the possibility was weighing on their minds more and more with each passing day, which was why he'd purchased the test.

She figured she might as well put the question to rest.

But…what if she *was* pregnant? How would she feel?

Walker had told her he wouldn't mind. But her relationship with him was so new. And a baby was a huge commitment. No matter what happened in the future, even if they remained together, it was too soon to have a child.

She eyed the digital screen as the test stick worked. If she was pregnant, the word *pregnant* would appear on the screen. And if she wasn't pregnant, the words *not pregnant* would appear instead. It couldn't get any easier than that.

But what did she most want to see?

That she wasn't fully committed to wishing against a baby was senseless. So much had changed since she'd returned home. Hardened divorce attorney Marlow Madsen, who'd so often claimed she'd never get married or have children, seemed to be open to those possibilities, after all.

Her heart pounded as the indicator quit giving her flashing dashes and the answer appeared: not pregnant.

They wouldn't be having a baby. Not now.

She told herself that was a good thing, for the best.

And yet she sighed, also feeling slightly let down as she threw the test away.

34

Rosemary sat on the beach at Walker's, watching the sunset. It was peaceful where he lived, especially when he and Reese were both at work. She'd been doing most of the cooking and cleaning, as a form of rent, since she'd moved in almost a week before. It kept her busy and made her feel as though she wasn't such a burden. But she was sensitive to the fact that her oldest son probably missed his privacy, especially because he'd started seeing Marlow again. *Thank goodness.* At least her mistake hadn't cost Walker the woman he loved, as she'd first assumed.

Marlow had been to the house a few times since the truth came out and always treated her well. Rosemary was impressed by her kindness, considering what Marlow had learned, and it made Rosemary happy that the two of them were together. She loved watching how they interacted with each other these days. But they spent more of their time at Seaclusion than they did here, even though, with Aida and Claire around, they didn't have a lot of privacy there, either.

Eager to see if she'd heard from any of the families with whom she'd interviewed the past few days, she checked her phone. She'd spent the week looking for a new job and had applied for a housekeeper position here on the island, as well as two nanny positions in Miami. The job she was most excited about hadn't been advertised, however. Reese happened to mention to his boss at the club that she was no longer with Eileen Madsen, and Mrs. McGowen—Lindsey—had called her right away to say she was looking for someone to help out at her place. Rosemary had met with her yesterday and was hoping Lindsey would soon contact her with an offer.

She hadn't received anything yet, though. It was probably too soon to expect a response, but she was getting anxious. She preferred to be working, was tired of worrying about what she was going to do in the future.

With a sigh, she got up and started back to the house to make dinner. The wind had come up and was blowing her long cotton beach dress between her legs as she moved. She bent to raise the hem above her knees to make walking easier, and when she lifted her head, she saw a familiar figure coming toward her.

It wasn't Reese or Walker; it was Rudy. She hadn't heard from him since she'd told him about Tiller, and she hadn't tried to contact him, either. She'd felt that what she'd done was too big a mistake to overcome, especially when they already had everything from the past working against them, so she was surprised to see him.

Stopping, she let him come to her. She had no idea why he was here and was almost afraid to find out. Losing him still hurt, but she was determined to accept the consequences of her long-ago mistake. As far as she was concerned, she'd gotten exactly what she deserved and didn't have the right to hope for anything more.

He didn't say a word once he reached her. He just stepped up and pulled her into his arms.

"What are you doing?" she asked as one hand came up to press her more tightly against him.

"I don't care what you've done," he said. "I don't want to go on without you."

Her arms ached to close around him, too. "You can't mean that," she said doubtfully.

"I do," he insisted. "I've spent a whole week thinking about it, just to be sure, because I don't want to make any more promises I can't keep."

She drew back to look up at him. "And what promise are you making me?"

"To be a better man, Rosey. Lord knows I've made my share of mistakes. I suppose if you can forgive me, I can forgive you."

"Even for this?" she asked. "For *Reese*?"

Lines of consternation appeared on his forehead. "How can I blame you for turning to someone else during that time?" he asked sadly. "It was probably my fault. I wasn't there for you like I should've been. I didn't do my part."

"Rudy—"

"Let's not lose the chance to find happiness together at last," he told her. "If we did… I think that would be our biggest mistake yet. What better time could there be for us to start over than now, when Eileen's out of your life? I see that as a chance to put away the old and welcome something new."

"You do?" she said, disbelieving.

"Absolutely." He gave her a crooked smile. "Will you have me? As imperfect as I am and have always been? Can you forgive me for the past?"

Forgiveness. A second chance. Nothing sounded more welcome or freeing. She knew better than to expect any forgiveness from Eileen, but if she could have Rudy's forgiveness, and Marlow's and Reese's and Walker's, maybe, one day, she'd be able to forgive herself. "Of course."

When he kissed her, she realized that what had attracted her to him in the first place was still there, regardless of everything else. She was grateful for that and all the good things he was in spite of his prior mistakes. "Thank you. Thank you for giving me exactly what I needed when I needed it most," she murmured.

He caught her chin and held her gaze as he said, "It was my turn."

Aida stretched, feeling warm and lazy under the hot sun as she lifted the wide-brimmed hat she'd used to cover her face and reached for her fruity drink with the tiny paper umbrella.

Marlow was spending some time with her mother, so Claire was the only one with her today. They'd been at their favorite public beach, lying side by side, all morning. "I love this song," she said as "Shy Away" by Twenty One Pilots came over the speakers at the bar.

"Do you really think I should open my own clothing boutique in the fall?" Aida asked as she gazed up at the clear blue sky.

"You know how I feel about it," Claire replied, her eyes closed as she continued to bask in the sun's rays. "Your dreams don't just come to you. You have to fight for them."

The thought of owning her own boutique and how hard she'd work to make it great excited her like nothing else had in a long while—since she'd given up acting. "But it could so easily go wrong."

Claire didn't seem concerned. "Then you'll pick yourself up, dust yourself off and try something else."

She made it sound so easy. "What about you?" Aida asked. "Are you going to open another yoga studio?"

"I am."

"You're not scared? Even after everything you've lost?"

"Teaching yoga is what I really love to do. I'll figure out a way."

Aida brushed some sand off her leg before settling back on her towel. "How long will it take to save the money you need?"

Claire yawned before resting an arm over her eyes. "The price of commercial real estate has come down quite a bit since the pandemic hit. I might be able to find a good location sooner rather than later."

"Are we talking months, or years?" Aida asked.

"That depends. When we were all hanging out last night, Reese offered to loan me a few thousand as seed money."

Now Aida knew what Reese and Claire had been talking about so intently when they were having a barbecue at Walker's. "That's generous of him."

"It is. He plans to buy a house here on Teach but told me he'll be keeping his job—says he can't imagine he'd enjoy doing anything else more."

"And his family's here, including Marlow now that she's decided to stay and open a law practice on the island."

"Exactly. He'll still have an income besides his inheritance, and he insisted he doesn't mind helping me. He said I could pay him back once I get up and running, a little at a time. So...it's possible I could open a studio before Christmas."

"How nice!"

"I'm sure he would help you, too, if you needed it," Claire said.

"He knows I've got the money from the divorce. All I have to do is overcome my fear of failure."

"Aida, you never know what you can do until you try." Claire leaned up to reclaim her own drink and smiled as she watched the people nearby enjoying themselves. "It's nice here, isn't it?"

"Gorgeous. As idyllic as it is in this moment, it's hard to believe we had to deal with a hurricane and a vengeful ex only ten days ago."

A handful of children nearby started to squeal and chase each other around the castle they'd just constructed out of sand.

"We got lucky," Claire said. "It was scary there for a minute. I sure hope we won't get another storm like that one."

"There may be a few more while we're here. But hopefully they, too, will pass without any major damage." There was no guarantee of that, of course. No one could predict the weather for the rest of the summer. But Aida chose to be positive. "How are you feeling about Dutton?" she asked.

"There are moments when I still miss being with him," Claire replied. "You probably have those moments, too. But I know I made the right decision. I can see so many warning signs now that I kept justifying before."

Walker had told them Dutton posted bail so he could make his flight home, but he'd have to return for a court date once he had one. "You haven't heard from him?" Aida asked.

"No. I think he's decided that we're not worth what could happen if he doesn't leave us alone."

As far as Aida was concerned, that was one good thing to come out of the past week. Another was that she'd grown even closer to Claire. Their friendship had been forged in fire from the beginning, which made her feel it would stand the test of time. "I'm glad we didn't let him tear us apart."

Claire leaned up on one elbow and grinned at her. "So am I."

Eileen had invited Rosemary over for lunch. She hadn't seen her since she'd kicked her out of the house last month, but she'd arranged this meeting when Walker had finally come to get the rest of his mother's belongings. He'd been shocked when she said she'd like Rosemary to pay her a visit, but Eileen had put a lot of thought into how to proceed, and she didn't want him to feel he had to run interference between them. He and Marlow were spending a lot of time together, and they seemed so happy. She couldn't do anything to ruin what was developing between them, least of all something she could fix by overcoming her baser instincts.

She had to admit she was nervous, though. There were moments when the hurt and betrayal she'd felt since learning of Tiller's affair still made her hate Rosemary. But there were other moments when she missed the frequency of their contact and friendship. She would often read something in the news or see something online and want to show it to Rosemary so they could discuss it, only to remember that Rosemary now worked for the McGowens. She was gone and would never be coming back—at least, it would never be the same. And that made Eileen feel a different kind of loss. She supposed they'd been together for so long it would take some time to get used to having Rosemary gone.

The doorbell rang, and her new housekeeper—a young woman named Kristen, who'd moved into Rosemary's old room—looked to her for the signal to answer the door.

"Go ahead and let her in," Eileen said and braced for those first few moments, which were guaranteed to be uncomfortable.

"Hello. Mrs. Madsen is right this way," she heard Kristen say and smiled. Kristen would never be another Rosemary, but she was sweet and, with time, they'd probably get used to each other.

Eileen, who'd refused to use a walker from the time she'd received her diagnosis, had broken down and purchased one a week ago, and she was finding it helpful. She used it to get up and move toward her former housekeeper.

"Eileen," Rosemary said with a polite dip of her head. It was easy to tell she was self-conscious, maybe even a little wary. She held a huge bouquet of flowers, which she held out. "These are for you."

They were pink and white peonies, Eileen's favorite. Leaning forward to smell them, she closed her eyes as she breathed deeply. "They're beautiful," she murmured. "How thoughtful."

"Shall I put them in water?" Rosemary asked.

Eileen was about to say Kristen could do that when she saw tears swimming in Rosemary's eyes, and her throat instantly grew so tight she couldn't speak. They stared at each other for several seconds and everything that needed to be said somehow passed between them without a word. Still, Rosemary sniffed and murmured, "I'm so sorry," and Eileen reached out to pull her into an embrace.

EPILOGUE

There was something different about the gumbo-limbo tree. It was shedding its bark, but that was normal. The locals called it a tourist tree for a reason. It was also losing some of its leaves. Although that typically happened later in the fall, it was cool for September, so that wasn't it, either.

Marlow studied it as Walker spread out the blanket they'd brought with them. She'd invited him over to Seaclusion for a picnic and had suggested they have it on the beach—but not this part of the beach. She'd imagined taking advantage of what warmth they could garner from the sun on such a chilly day, instead of blocking it out with the vegetation that grew so thick in this area.

He was the one who'd insisted they eat by "their" tree.

"What are you looking at?" he asked when he noticed her squinting.

"Something's different," she said.

"What do you mean?"

She got up. The markings she'd noticed were right above the hole where they'd stashed small gifts for each other over the years. Actually, Walker had given her far more than she'd ever given him. But those memories and this tree meant a lot to her now. She loved him so much she couldn't believe there'd ever been a time she hadn't wanted him—despite what she'd seen in other relationships, despite learning that even her parents' marriage hadn't been perfect, despite everything.

Assuming someone had defaced the tree, she marched over, already angry. But once she got close enough to really see what'd happened, she felt a smile spread across her face. Four letters, encased in a big heart, had been carved into the trunk: WC + MM.

She glanced over her shoulder as Walker came up behind her. "*You* did this?"

His hands went around her and pulled her back against his chest. "Yeah."

"I like it," she replied, reveling in the warmth of his body and the familiarity of his touch. "You used to leave me such sweet surprises here. I can't believe it took me so long to realize how rare and wonderful you really are."

"I'm just glad you think so now," he said with a chuckle. "Better late than never."

"When did you carve our initials?"

"A week or so ago. I was hoping you'd notice on your own, but when you didn't, I got tired of waiting and decided to suggest we have the picnic here."

"It's because you quit leaving me gifts that I've had no reason to come out here," she teased.

"How do you know I quit?" he asked. "Have you checked it lately?"

She twisted around to see his face. "Are you serious?"

"Of course."

"Okay." She stepped away so she could reach inside the tree, felt around and pulled out a...key? "What's this?" she asked, holding it up to him.

"It's to my house," he explained as he rested his forehead against hers. "I love you, Marlow. I always have, and I always will. I know we haven't been together that long, but... I'm hoping you'll agree to move in. I want you with me every night, and every morning, and every day..."

Marlow slipped her arms around his neck. In the past, she'd sworn she'd never put her heart at risk, never go through what she'd seen so many of her clients go through. But love had gotten the best of her, after all. "Of course I will. I want to share every moment I can with you."

He kissed her, and she tightened her arms, bringing him back for a second kiss when he lifted his head. Then she drew him down the beach toward the main house, so they could tell their mothers they'd be moving in together. Rosemary lived in a small rental house with Rudy on the other side of the island, but she and Eileen got together regularly. At the moment, they were sitting out on the deck while Eileen's new housekeeper brought them tea.

★ ★ ★ ★ ★

SUMMER ON THE ISLAND

BY BRENDA NOVAK

Reader's Guide

mira

Questions for Discussion

1. Did you have a favorite character in *Summer on the Island*? If so, who, and why?

2. Eileen's family is from a very different socioeconomic class than Rosemary's. How do you feel the author handled the divide between these two worlds? What did you think of the nuances in the relationship between the "family" and the "hired help," as the author put it?

3. Marlow's experience as a divorce lawyer has turned her off getting seriously involved in a relationship. Do you think it would be difficult to see the breakdown of so many relationships and then trust enough to love and commit? Did you find her ability to overcome this believable?

4. Marlow's fears of intimacy affect her willingness to get close to Walker. If you were Walker, would you be able to forgive her for her past behavior? Were there other factors contributing to her actions?

5. What did you think of Aida and Claire's friendship, given the way they met? Would you be able to be friends with Claire if you were Aida? With Aida if you were Claire?

6. Were you sympathetic toward Claire for remaining in contact with Dutton after everything he did? Why or why not?

7. There are a number of parallels among the different characters' story lines, including Claire's and Rosemary's—they're both considering forgiving and moving forward with men who have wronged them in the past. What did you think of how each of their stories played out? Were you more understanding of one woman's actions than the other's?

8. What did you think of the revelation brought about by Tiller's will? Did that change the way you viewed any of the characters? If so, how?

9. How did you feel about the ending with regard to Eileen and Rosemary? Do you believe they will remain friends? Why or why not?

10. If there were a movie based on *Summer on the Island*, which actors would you cast as each of the characters?

A Conversation with the Author

Where did your inspiration for this story come from?

I live in California, where Arnold Schwarzenegger was governor, and was stunned when the news came out that he'd had a child with their housekeeper. I couldn't believe that Maria had had so much contact with the boy and yet never realized—and that the housekeeper with whom he had the child had continued to work for them as if nothing had happened. I couldn't help wondering how this secret remained a secret for so long and how each of the people involved would cope with such a shocking reveal—and figure out how to move on—so I decided to examine my own version of these events within the confines of a story.

How did you decide to set this story on Teach, Florida?

I plan to write a historical series one day set during the golden age of piracy, so I've done a lot of research about pirates. Teach isn't a real island, but pirate lore is common in the area, and after visiting the Florida Keys, I could easily picture someplace like this existing.

Did you have a favorite character and why?

I really enjoyed creating Marlow and seeing her wrestle with her attraction to Walker. I also liked that she wasn't quite perfect and had some atoning to do, because the struggle she faced made the whole thing more fun.

Which story line was the most enjoyable to write?

The love story is always my favorite. I'm a huge romantic and love nothing more than happily-ever-after, so all of my books contain at least an element of that, as well as the theme that love conquers all.

Do you plot your stories ahead of time or do they unfold for you as you write them?

I don't plot my stories ahead of time. If I do, I get bored with the writing, because I already know how it will end. I let the story grow organically from the characters and the conflicts they face and love being surprised as the plot develops. This approach is also a good fit for me because then it's impossible to ruin any surprises by telegraphing what's going to happen before it does.

After writing so many novels, what's your secret to keeping your stories fresh?

Learning more and more about human behavior and psychology as I age is what I believe brings something new to every story. I see the world differently now from when I was younger and pay particular attention to the shades of gray and moral dilemmas people face. I feel like it's these dilemmas and morally gray areas that make for a richer and more intriguing read.

Who are some of your favorite authors?

I prefer stories that evoke a lot of emotion. I want to feel something when I read, so Kristin Hannah, Jennifer Weiner, Elin Hilderbrand and Nancy Thayer are some of my go-to writers.

What's your favorite place to read?

Because I have such a demanding schedule, I listen to audiobooks when I clean house or exercise, but my favorite place to read is probably on a plane. Then I don't feel quite so guilty about indulging myself when I have so many other things I have to get done.